Termination

The Boy Who Died

RICHARD T. BURKE

Books in the Decimation series

Book 1 – Decimation: The Girl Who Survived
Book 2 (this book) – Termination: The Boy Who Died
Book 3 – Annihilation: Origins and Endings

Other standalone books by Richard T. Burke:

The Rage
The Colour of the Soul
Assassin's Web

Termination:
The Boy Who Died

Richard. T. Burke

First published: March 2021

This is a work of fiction. Names, characters, places, and incidents are the products of the author's imagination or are used fictitiously. Any resemblance to actual events, locales, or persons, living or dead, is entirely coincidental.

First Printing: 2021
ISBN: 978-1916141711

www.rjne.uk

For my mother, Teddy Burke, and aunt, Erica Fifoot

Sisters both taken during this strange and terrible time

We do not need a crystal ball to predict the future. We can have the gift of foresight though by understanding how cause and effect works. Every choice and move that we make has a consequence.

Jeffrey Lehma

Decimation Recap

This book is the second in the Decimation trilogy. If you haven't read the first, **Decimation: The Girl Who Survived**, or want a reminder of the key events, a brief recap follows. Whilst this book can be read out of order, I recommend reading Decimation first.

The Orestes virus first swept across the world in 2017, infecting every living person on the planet within a matter of days. There is no vaccine, no cure. It lies dormant until a woman gives birth. Then she dies.

By 2033 nobody has survived childbirth for a generation. Pregnancy is still a death sentence. ANTIMONE LESSING is sixteen years old, paralysed from the waist down, and going into labour. The surgeons deliver her son, PAUL, by Caesarean section and Antimone flat-lines. Her body is awaiting collection by the mortuary attendants when she regains consciousness.

Nine months earlier, Antimone is a promising Paralympian, training for the 2032 Delhi Olympics. MAX PERRIN, a fellow student whose father, NIGEL PERRIN, is Chief Scientist at Ilithyia Biotechnology, challenges her to a race. They collide in the home straight and Max falls. Humiliated by his defeat, Max threatens revenge. JASON BAXTER, the adopted son of the Ilithyia Chief Executive, ROSALIND BAXTER, stands up for Antimone against Max and invites her to his sixteenth birthday party.

At the celebrations, somebody spikes the drinks, and several partygoers including Max, Jason and Antimone black out for an hour. When Antimone comes round, she sees a man fleeing through a broken window.

Six weeks later, Antimone discovers she is pregnant and realises she was raped while unconscious at Jason's party. Her family is devastated to learn the pregnancy is too far advanced for Antimone to survive a termination without activating the virus. Preliminary blood tests of the foetus reveal the rapist to be an ex-con, DANIEL FLOYD, who has recently been released from prison after serving sixteen years for the murder of his wife. When the police show Antimone the man's photograph, she recognises him as the person seen fleeing the party. Rosalind is worried about the threat of litigation and offers Antimone experimental treatments at her company's facilities.

Following Antimone's miraculous survival after the birth of her son, Paul, Rosalind recognises the teenager's unique value in the race to develop a cure for the virus. She fakes both Antimone's and the baby's deaths and transfers them to a secret laboratory. When Rosalind analyses the baby's DNA, she determines that the father is actually her adopted son, Jason. Further research reveals that Antimone is a chimera (her body contains both male and female cells resulting from the fusing of two foetuses in the womb). This new information provides the vital clue to develop an anti-viral drug and make Rosalind's company the most profitable in the world.

Rosalind confronts Jason about his role in Antimone's pregnancy. Believing Antimone to have died in childbirth, Jason protests his innocence and voices his suspicions that Max was somehow involved. Under intense questioning by Rosalind and Nigel, Max confesses that he spiked the drinks at the party with a hypnotic drug stolen from his father's office. He reveals that after raping Antimone himself, he coerced Jason into doing the same while the partygoers were under the drug's influence. The adults keep their findings secret, and Rosalind persuades Jason not to go to the police.

During a visit to his mother at the Ilithyia facility, Jason discovers Antimone is still alive and being held against her will. Knowing that Daniel Floyd is innocent of Antimone's rape, Jason tracks down and enlists the ex-con's help. Together they mount a daring rescue attempt and free Antimone, unaware that the baby, Jason's son, Paul, also survived.

After hacking into his mother's files, Jason learns the truth; Nigel Perrin and Rosalind Baxter were behind the release of the virus sixteen years earlier. Jason's biological mother worked for Rosalind and threatened to become a whistleblower to prevent a dangerous viral research programme. Nigel and Rosalind imprisoned her, then framed her husband, Daniel Floyd, for her murder. The documents also reveal Floyd to be Jason's biological father, explaining why the police found a match to Floyd's DNA when testing Antimone after the rape. Rosalind adopted Jason when his mother died in captivity after becoming one of the first victims of the Orestes virus.

Rosalind uses Antimone's baby to lure her back to the laboratory where she is recaptured. Jason and Floyd follow Antimone and are also detained but not before calling the police. Now that Rosalind has everything she needs for a cure, she plans to destroy all evidence of her past illegal activities, including Antimone, Jason and Floyd.

The police arrive just in time to prevent Rosalind from incinerating the teenagers. Nigel Perrin offers to confess in exchange for a lenient sentence, but Rosalind grabs a pen from his pocket and murders her business partner by stabbing him in the eye. As the sole remaining person with knowledge of the anti-viral research, she successfully negotiates an amnesty for her crimes in exchange for completing the development of a drug.

Seven months later, the treatment is successful, and Rosalind has evaded all charges. In revenge for his father's death, Max breaks into Rosalind's house and spikes her drink with the same powerful mind-control drug he used at the party. He orders her to commit suicide by stabbing herself in the eye with an identical pen to the one with which she murdered his father.

Friday 11th July 2036

Glasgow Olympic Stadium

The roar of the crowd reverberated through Antimone Lessing's chest.

"AN-TIM-OH-NEE! AN-TIM-OH-NEE!"

Her stomach flipped. Were they really chanting her name? As the poster girl for British athletics, this was the moment for which she and most of the people in the stadium had been waiting. The long hours of training, the soreness of tired shoulder muscles, the meticulously controlled diet; everything came down to the next few minutes and the final of the Olympic women's 1500-metres open wheelchair race. The weight of expectation hung heavy on her muscular shoulders.

Of the sixty-three entrants in the competition, only eight remained. Antimone had posted the fastest qualification time, but she knew that meant nothing. Half the field was capable of winning. All her major competitors conserved their energy in the heats and semi-final, hoping for some advantage when it mattered.

She glanced up at the giant screen. The camera panned across a packed stadium, the supporters grouped by nationality and waving brightly coloured flags. As she lowered her gaze, a different scene greeted her eyes. In reality, the crowd occupied barely a third of the vast bowl: the power of computer-generated imagery.

Almost every face wore a white cotton mask over the nose and mouth. The rest protected themselves with full plastic facemasks, complete with respirators and filters. More than three years after the cure, people were still reluctant to gather in groups without taking precautions. The general public remained paranoid about infectious diseases, aware that the deadly Orestes virus had swept across the globe and infected the entire population of the planet within days of the initial outbreak.

She let her eyes drift to the VIP section of the crowd. Somewhere up there, her three-year-old boy, Paul, and his father, Jason, were sitting. She'd never pick them out from down here, but she could imagine her son's excitement at the noise and colour of the occasion. Her thoughts turned to Jason. The situation with him was complicated and one she needed to resolve, but there would be plenty of time in the future to worry about the state of their relationship and where it was going.

A lull in the crowd noise drew Antimone's attention back to the present. Nearby, a muscle-bound athlete in the blue of Italy stepped up to the shot-put circle. The man crouched down, then exploded in a whirl of motion, heaving the black ball out beyond the twenty-five-metre line. A burst of raucous applause greeted his efforts. Antimone could almost hear her coach's stern voice inside her head, telling her to focus on the forthcoming race.

As she turned away from the field event, a shadow fell across her. A woman wearing a green, one-piece athletic outfit stood over her, blocking out the hazy afternoon sun. Emblazoned on the woman's chest was a black rectangle containing a white sickle embracing a six-sided star. She flashed a superficial smile and extended a hand. "Good luck." Her voice carried a slight Arabic accent.

The athlete from The Republic of North Africa: another of those with no disability. So far in the qualifying rounds, they had avoided each other. Today would be the first time they met in a race.

Antimone delayed just long enough to reveal her internal debate. When she finally accepted the handshake, her rival's palm felt surprisingly cool. "The same to you."

The woman turned away, revealing the competitor number on her back. Then she stopped and swivelled to face Antimone once again. "Do not judge me. You know nothing about me."

"I know you can walk." The words were out of Antimone's mouth before she had engaged her brain. Five years earlier, the Olympic Committee had abolished the T54 wheelchair events and opened up the competitions to all comers, irrespective of any disability. Their decision raised the profile of the sport but didn't prove universally popular, especially among the existing athletes.

The North African rocked backwards as if someone had slapped her. The smooth skin of her forehead creased in a scowl. "You call us Fake Olympians because we still have the use of our legs. But does it matter in a wheelchair race? Do I have any advantage over you? I think not."

"I didn't—"

The woman spoke over Antimone. "It is easy for you here in the West. Your scientists have developed a treatment for this terrible disease, but they do not share it with my people. Where I live, they do not care about women. They treat us like cattle, forcing us to have babies to increase the population. We must bear children knowing we will die when we give birth. If I was not competing in the Olympics, I too would be pregnant and facing death. This is my way of surviving. Only yesterday, my coach told me that if I do not win this afternoon, I will become a mother for my nation. You are very lucky. You had a child and survived."

Antimone's mouth opened, but no words came out. Had this woman somehow learned of her involvement in developing the cure? Her one-in-a-billion immunity to the effects of this organism? Only a handful of people, including her own family and the British Prime Minister, knew the truth. *No, she couldn't possibly know.*

"Well, have you nothing to say?" the North African athlete asked, staring down at her.

When Antimone finally forced her lips to move, all she could utter was, "I'm sorry."

The woman glared at her in silence for a second longer, then spun about and stalked back to her wheelchair. Antimone's eyes followed her opponent as she strapped herself into the machine. She flinched as a hand landed on her shoulder. She twisted around to see her coach, John Marshall.

His gaze tracked the green-suited competitor. "Has the delightful Aya Shaladi been trying to get inside your head?"

Antimone frowned at the man who had guided her preparations over the past three years. "What do you mean?"

"Let me take a guess: poor little me. If I don't win, they'll kill me... and probably a whole lot more if I'm right."

When Antimone didn't reply, he continued. "You should be honoured. She normally reserves her mind games for the competitor she considers the greatest threat. I should've warned you. She's renowned for it. If you're wondering, Miss Shaladi is in no danger of being conscripted into motherhood. Her father is a general in The Republic of North Africa's army. There's no way he would allow his little treasure to suffer the same indignities as the other women who get treated like breeding animals."

"Yes, but she—"

"What have we talked about? Visualise the race: the different stages from start to finish. Concentrate on your breathing. Conserve your energy. Don't go off too fast. This is your big chance, and you're the fastest qualifier in this final. When you hit the front, nobody comes past you. Is that clear?"

Antimone nodded.

"I asked if that's clear."

"Yes, Coach."

"Excellent. You've put in too much work to fail now because you allowed some smart-talking cow from the arse end of nowhere to mess with your head."

A bell rang. "That'll be the five-minute warning," Marshall said. "I won't wish you luck because you don't need it. You're going to smash this race."

"Yes, Coach," Antimone replied.

"Good. I'll see you after you cross the line in first place."

Her eyes followed the grey-haired, ex-army fitness instructor as he strode towards the stand. A fierce determination filled her chest. John Marshall had given up a comfortable job at the prestigious Oakington Manor private school to become her full-time trainer. She owed her presence at this final to his unwavering support and encouragement. He had placed his faith in her. *I won't let him down.*

She rotated her shoulders, trying to keep the muscles warm. Another ding of the bell drew her back to the race: three minutes to go. The other competitors were heading to the start. She tightened the strap on her helmet and flexed her fingers in the tight-fitting gloves. With a series of powerful shoves, she guided the wheelchair towards the painted number four next to the curving white line that signalled the starting point for the three-and-three-quarters lap contest.

Most of the other finalists were already in position. She inched forwards until the female official raised a hand. To her right was the green outfit of the North African. Antimone glared at the woman's back, annoyed with herself at being taken in by the mind games of her chief rival.

The announcer introduced the field. "In lane one, representing Great Britain, we have Natasha Jones from Cardiff. Natasha qualified as the fifth fastest competitor in this afternoon's final." A roar of approval echoed through the stadium.

Antimone tuned out the man's voice as he presented the French and Argentinian competitors. She closed her eyes and ran through the mental exercises her coach had drilled into her. The announcement of her own name dragged her back to reality.

"In lane four, from the town of Northstowe and also representing Great Britain, Antimone Lessing is the fastest qualifier in a time of three minutes, twenty point seven, just two-tenths of a second outside the world record."

Once again, a chant erupted from the crowd. "AN-TIM-OH-NEE! AN-TIM-OH-NEE!"

A ring of drones, each no larger than a tennis ball, settled into a tight formation around her head. They hovered in place, fixing her with the Cyclops eyes of their cameras. She raised a gloved hand in acknowledgement and fought back the irrational desire to swat away the tiny flying robots, buzzing like insects, inches from her face. She glanced up at the big screen. Should she wave towards the unpopulated parts of the stadium as well?

Before she could decide, the announcer moved onto the next competitor. "From Tripoli and representing The Republic of North Africa, in lane five we have Aya Shaladi. Aya qualified second fastest in a time of three minutes, twenty-one point one seconds."

The woman lifted her arm, but her look of cheerful confidence faded as several boos and catcalls mingled with the polite applause. Antimone stifled a grin of satisfaction. It seemed she was not alone in harbouring reservations about the relaxation of the entry requirements. The decision to allow athletes with no disability into the Olympic wheelchair events remained controversial as the Russian and Greek competitors—both of whom had full use of their legs—also discovered when they received the same reaction from the crowd.

Moments later, the announcer finished presenting the eighth finalist, an Ethiopian. A hush fell over the stadium as the race official raised the starting pistol.

"On your marks."

Antimone lowered her body and grasped the shiny hand ring. A sharp crack sent her surging into motion, her torso bobbing up and down as she accelerated to racing speed. The roar of the crowd drove her forwards, straining every sinew to emerge from the first bend clear of any bumping or barging.

As the curve ended, she tapped the compensator between strokes to straighten the wheelchair. Side-by-side, she and the North African athlete led the field. The green-suited competitor drifted to the left.

Conserve your energy. Don't go off too fast. With her coach's advice still resounding inside her head, Antimone slackened the push rate and allowed her main challenger to take the lead. The Welsh girl slipped into third, tracking the leading pair.

By the time they reached the finishing line after the first circuit, the group of three had broken away. The gap to fourth place now extended to at least five wheelchair lengths. Antimone settled into a steady rhythm, every ounce of concentration focused on maximising the output from each stroke.

At the end of the second lap, Antimone risked an upward glance at the large display screen. The distance from the leading three to the trailing pack had reached fifteen metres. Judging by the ache in her shoulders, it would be a fast time. The North African showed no signs of slackening the pace, and Antimone was consuming a lot of energy just to stay with her.

As they neared the finishing line for the last lap, Antimone's muscles burned from the build-up of lactic acid. The clang of the bell sent a fresh jolt of adrenalin surging into her bloodstream. She grimaced in pain, spurred on by the yells of encouragement from the crowd.

Despite the seething tension inside the stadium, a calmness settled over her. *This is what I've trained for. Just keep it together.* Ahead of her, the North African's technique was becoming more ragged. Antimone followed a wheel length behind, saving what little energy she had left for the sprint to the finishing line. At the start of the final bend, she allowed her wheelchair to swing wide. Agony flooded her body, but she forced her exhausted biceps to work harder. The Welsh girl tracked the manoeuvre, drawing alongside to her right. *Where the hell did she come from?*

~

The three leaders emerged into the home straight side-by-side. The audience rose to their feet, raising the sound level to a collective roar. But not everybody was watching the race. A lone camera drone drifted across the track just a few metres ahead of the leading pack, signalling the start of what was about to follow.

Moments later, the first bomb exploded.

Part One: Preparation

Thursday 12th June 2036

Infant Creche, Bani Waled, Republic of North Africa
Four weeks before the Olympic wheelchair final

"Sit still," the woman said in Arabic.

"No," the three-year-old boy replied, angling his head away.

She grabbed a tissue from the nearby box and tried to wipe the child's nose. He wriggled in her arms as she attempted to reach the twin trails of mucus dribbling down his face. She tightened her grip and pulled him closer. The boy's struggles intensified. He lashed out a foot and caught her in the stomach. Her hand immediately released his wrist, moving to the rounded bump protruding from her belly.

"Ibn kalb," she muttered under her breath. The words must have come out louder than she intended because the little girl, playing with the doll two metres away, glanced up sharply. She had just called the annoying brat the son of a dog. In truth, the identity of the boy's father was a mystery. Like all the children under her care, his mother had died in childbirth, probably moments after a multiple birth. The doctors would have given her fertility drugs to increase the number of eggs she released, then impregnated her with the sperm of a member of the ruling elite.

The woman gently rubbed the point of impact. In less than a month, she would suffer the same fate. She was already finding it hard to sleep at night. The rapidly expanding bulge in her stomach prevented her from getting comfortable. During the last inspection, the midwife had informed her she was expecting quadruplets. Not that she would ever get to see them. Within moments of severing the umbilical cord, the virus would transition to its active state. *I hope I'm no longer awake when that happens.*

The previous week, a cousin told her the Americans had developed a cure. Their women could give birth without fear of dying. It was typical of the infidel devils to keep such a discovery to themselves. No doubt it suited their purposes to reduce the number of true believers. It was her duty to help replenish her people's population, but that didn't make the burden any easier to bear. *Why do I have to die?*

Her eyes swept the room. The children played in groups of three or four. There were nineteen of them in total, twelve girls and seven boys. As well as releasing more eggs in the mother, the drugs raised the ratio of female to male foetuses. The rulers needed women to increase population numbers, but few, if any, would live past their teens.

The woman glanced at her watch. In half-an-hour, it would be time for the midday sleep. She was supposed to stay awake to supervise the children, but she would often try to grab a few minutes of rest herself. The combination of the energy-sapping heat and the steady, rhythmic whump of the ceiling fan were already making her feel sleepy. *Nobody will notice.* She closed her eyes and leant back in the wooden chair.

A tap on the knee jerked her out of her drowsiness. The boy with the snotty nose stood in front of her. He held one hand to his face. The other tugged at the black material of her robes. She swatted away his grubby fingers. He dropped the raised arm, revealing a trickle of blood originating from his left nostril and mingling with the trail of mucus.

Why can't he just leave me alone? With a groan, she reached once again for the box of tissues and tugged one free. When she returned her attention to the child, the red trail had developed into a stream. A reedy wail escaped from his lips. His open mouth revealed a rose-coloured stain on his tiny, white teeth. He balled his hands into fists and rubbed at his eyes.

The woman dragged him nearer and dabbed at the blood now gushing from his nose. Within seconds, crimson fluid saturated the tissue. She tossed it on the floor and grabbed another handful from the box.

The boy lowered his hands and grasped at his throat. His brown irises now sat amidst a labyrinth of burst veins where moments before there had been only white sclera. The boy's chest heaved as he tried to suck air into his oxygen-starved lungs. A wracking cough culminated in a spray of blood and mucus into the woman's face.

She wiped the glutinous mass away with her sleeve and levered herself upright. By the time she reached her feet, the child was convulsing on the floor. She lowered herself to one knee beside him, grunting with the effort. The boy writhed on the ground, his frantic movements creating red streaks across the discoloured white tiles.

What should she do? They hadn't trained her for anything like this. She placed a hand on his chest to still the jerking spasms that rippled through his body. With a final twitch, the child lay still. *Is he dead? That isn't possible.*

The sound of crying drew her attention away from the prostrate child. She raised her eyes to see three other children, each writhing in a pool of blood. The rest of the group backed up against the crude, childish paintings distributed along the roughly finished walls. As she watched, two more burst into a fit of coughing, hacking up gobbets of bloody phlegm.

The woman staggered to her feet, raising an arm to cover her face with her sleeve. Everywhere she looked, children were bleeding from their mouths, noses and ears. She took a step forwards as one of the closest victims stopped moving. *Is this some sort of chemical attack?* She turned in a full circle. Every single child in the room now either lay still or twitching in their bodily fluids. The mingled smells of blood and faeces assaulted her nostrils.

She stumbled to the mirror above the sink and studied her reflection: no nosebleed. The whites of the terrified eyes staring back at her remained clear. No blood emerged from her mouth or ears. *Why am I the only one not to be affected?*

When she turned around, every single child sprawled motionless on the floor. Those that faced her stared back with open, unseeing eyes.

The woman lumbered across the room as fast as her bulk would allow. When she reached the door, she fumbled with the lock and stumbled outside into the stifling midday heat.

"They're dead," she screamed. "The children are all dead."

Friday 13th June 2036

Northstowe Athletics Stadium

Four weeks before the Olympic wheelchair final

Antimone gave one last shove to propel herself across the finish line. She coasted to a halt, her breath rasping in her throat. Every muscle from her shoulders to her forearms burned from the build-up of lactic acid.

"Come on, don't forget the warm down," came a voice from behind her. The tracksuited figure of John Marshall jogged towards her, stopwatch in hand. "That was a fifty-five-second lap."

Her coach was old school. The sensors in her wheelchair rendered the archaic timepiece he used to measure her performance unnecessary, but the former soldier and PE teacher seemed to prefer the ancient mechanical technology.

A wry grin broke across his craggy features as he drew nearer. "Not bad… but still not fast enough to win a gold medal at the Olympics."

Antimone groaned. *What do I have to do to make him happy?* After a two-hour training session, it was actually a pretty good time. She considered voicing her thoughts. Instead, she bit her tongue and said, "Yes, Coach."

The sweat was already drying on her skin when her aching arms set the wheelchair into motion once again. As she coasted around the oval, her gaze wandered to a group practising high jump on the far side of the track. Somebody wearing a T-shirt and jeans was chatting to the athletes. A laugh carried across on the light breeze. The new arrival separated from the others and raised an arm in her direction. She squinted against the glare of the late afternoon sunshine, trying to identify the person. Through shaded eyes, she watched the figure head towards the finish line where her coach waited.

As she rounded the bend into the home straight, she recognised the outline of Jason Floyd. He waved once again. Antimone raised her hand long enough to return the gesture as she propelled the chair forwards. A stab of jealousy ran through her. Who had he been talking to? He found it so easy to mingle with other people whereas, for her, it was always a struggle. If only she knew what she wanted from their relationship. His good looks and effortless confidence made him popular with the fairer sex. There would be no shortage of interested girls if she ever cut him loose. Her heart sank at the thought. But could she really trust him after what had happened between them? Internally, she cursed her indecision.

She drifted to a standstill beside him.

"That looked fairly quick," he said, bending down to kiss her on the cheek.

"Yeah, but apparently not fast enough for the slave driver," she replied, rotating her shoulders to loosen the tension in her muscles. The pair turned together as John Marshall drew nearer.

"Good to see you," he said, shaking Jason's hand.

"You too, Coach," Jason replied.

"I haven't seen you down here for ages. Are you still throwing your javelin?"

"I've been to a few coaching sessions at the university, but there aren't really enough hours in the week with all the studying."

"That's a shame. You're a natural." Marshall shifted his attention back to Antimone. "That was a good workout. Are we okay for the same time tomorrow? You need to up the work rate. Another fortnight of intensive training followed by a competitive race, and I think you'll be ready. Then it's just a case of maintaining your fitness levels before the Olympics and not overdoing it."

Antimone groaned inwardly. The current workouts were painful enough as they were; the prospect of putting in more effort didn't appeal. Marshall must have spotted her expression because he grinned and said, "Remember, no pain, no gain. If you want a gold medal, you've got to work for it."

Antimone gave a grimace in return. "Yes, Coach, I'm well aware of that."

"I'll leave you two youngsters to it. See you tomorrow. 'Bye, Jason."

The pair waited until the grey-haired, former army fitness instructor was out of earshot.

"I wasn't expecting you back until later," Antimone said.

"I thought I'd catch you at the track and check out for myself how the training was going. Where's Paul?"

"Mum's looking after him at the moment."

Their son, Paul, was something of a miracle. Conceived while Jason and Antimone were both under the influence of a date-rape drug slipped into the fruit punch during a party, the three-year-old was the first child in a generation to have a living biological mother. Until he was born, every woman had died in childbirth, killed by the Orestes virus. The pathogen had infected the entire population of the planet, but only activated upon severing the umbilical cord. Antimone's unexpected survival had given the doctors the vital clue they needed to develop a cure. Pregnancy was no longer a death sentence, at least not for residents of those countries wealthy enough to pay for the treatment.

"What have you been up to?" Antimone asked.

"Oh, work, work and more work," Jason replied. "Just like you, they drive us hard." He was in the second year of a biochemistry degree at King's College in London. When it first became apparent the virus posed a serious risk to humanity's future, the British government had pumped huge sums into medical research, including grants to cover the full costs of relevant degrees. Jason was a beneficiary of this funding although now a treatment was in place, it wasn't clear for how much longer it would last.

"How long are you staying?"

"I've got lectures on Monday morning, so I'll need to leave on Sunday night."

Antimone tried to mask her disappointment. Despite her reservations about their long-term relationship, she found herself cheered by his company. Training for the Olympics was a solitary activity, and she would have enjoyed spending more time with her closest friend.

"Have you got the car?" Antimone asked.

"Yeah, your Mum sent the car to pick me up from the station and said I could borrow it to take you home."

"I just need to dump my stuff in the locker, then we can go."

Jason chewed his lip as he walked in silence alongside Antimone. When they reached the archway of the tunnel leading to the changing rooms, she stopped. "You're a bit quiet. Is something bothering you?"

Jason halted and turned towards her. He hesitated for a moment before speaking. "I wasn't going to mention it until later. I can't hide anything from you."

"Normally, I can't shut you up," she replied with a smile. "What's wrong?"

"I received an email."

"So what? Who was it from?"

"Her."

"You don't mean…?" A tremor ran through Antimone's body.

"When I got back to the house this afternoon, it was waiting in my inbox. From Rosalind Baxter, no less."

"What does that bitch want?"

"She wants to meet us."

Antimone blinked in confusion. "Let me get this straight. You're saying that evil witch wants to see you and me."

"Yes, and Paul as well."

"What on earth for?"

"Apparently, she'd like to discuss what happened—in person."

Antimone stared at Jason in disbelief, looking for some sign that he was joking. When none came and she eventually spoke, her voice started half an octave higher than usual. "I don't believe this. That woman murdered your biological mother, framed your father for her murder, killed millions of other women by releasing the virus and threatened to incinerate both of us unless she received a pardon from none other than the Prime Minister himself. And now she wants to *talk* about it?"

"I know. It's crazy, right?"

The blood pounded in Antimone's ears in time with her thudding heart. The breath rasped in her throat. For over three years, she had done her best to obliterate the memories from her mind. Now they all came crashing back.

Their eyes met until Jason could no longer meet the anger in her stare, and he looked away. When he spoke, his tone was subdued. "Don't worry, I'll delete it. I shouldn't have mentioned it."

"You weren't seriously considering saying yes, were you?" Antimone asked, her voice trembling with fury.

"Of course not. I never want to see her again. I can't even stand the sound of her name." Within weeks of escaping from his adoptive mother's hidden laboratory, he had changed his surname from Baxter back to Floyd to match that of his birth parents.

"Does she think that just because she raised you for sixteen years, it gives her any right to contact you? After everything she did?"

"I've no idea how her mind works."

Antimone's teeth ground together, trapping the inside of her cheek. The taste of blood filled her mouth. She spat on the ochre-coloured track.

"I'd rather spend an afternoon with the devil than with that murderous witch."

Friday 20th June 2036

Oakington House, Northstowe

Three weeks before the Olympic wheelchair final

Rosalind Baxter flicked a wrist to dismiss the newsfeed hovering in front of her face. The overlay faded, restoring her vision to an unobstructed view of the room. She closed her left eye, then her right, comparing the images against each other. The latter was sharper and brighter, just as the specialists had promised.

Six months ago, they had installed the latest prosthetic technology to replace the glass sphere fitted after the initial catastrophic damage to her cornea. Her brain had taken a while to adapt to the electrical signals fed directly into the visual cortex, but she had to admit the synthetic organ performed far better than the biological original. It also contained additional features such as the ability to superimpose information on her vision.

She reached out for the glass of red wine resting atop the small wooden table and took a sip. The rich flavour of the dark berries rolled across her tongue. Chateau Margaux was the closest thing to perfection on earth. At over five hundred pounds a bottle there were certainly cheaper beverages, but if money was of no consideration—and it wasn't—little else came close.

As she leant forwards to replace the glass, her right arm trembled. She grabbed one hand with the other to still the trembling in her fingers. The symptoms had first surfaced three years earlier, shortly after the attack. Not that she had explained to the medical professionals what really happened that evening.

When the paramedics had arrived to discover the pen protruding from her right eye, she told them she had slipped on a wet floor. In truth, during the long minutes before the emergency services rolled up with sirens blaring, it took every inch of willpower to prevent herself from ramming the ballpoint home. The mind-altering drug coursing through her bloodstream at the time had removed all her free will, leaving her susceptible to the implantation of suggestions.

An icon flashed in the upper corner of her field of vision, drawing her back to the present. “Expand,” she murmured, holding a finger to her earlobe. The action signalled to the implant that she was issuing it with a command.

Two circles, one red, the other green, slid to the centre of her view. Within each sat the outline of a white telephone handset. The text beneath stated *Number Unknown*.

The ability to suppress their identity suggested the caller was somebody important. Only a handful of individuals possessed the required privilege levels since it had become mandatory two years earlier for all phone users to display an identification. Her curiosity piqued, Rosalind flicked a finger to the right.

A man spoke. “Mrs Baxter?”

“Yes, who’s calling?”

“Please hold for the Prime Minister.” A click preceded a burst from a recent pop song.

Rosalind scowled and swiped to the left. “I’m not holding for anybody,” she muttered, “least of all that arsehole.”

Seconds later, the flashing icon reappeared. Once again, the message signalled an unidentified caller. Rosalind let out an exasperated huff and accepted the call with a flick of the wrist.

Before she could speak, Andrew Jacobs’ sonorous voice came down the line. “Rosalind, how are you?”

“If you’re using my first name, you must want something from me, Andrew. The last time we spoke in that incinerator room, you referred to me as Mrs Baxter.”

“Yes… well.” The Prime Minister’s tone contained an atypical nervousness. “I heard you had an operation on your damaged eye.”

“I take it you know what—or should I say who—caused the damage in the first place.”

“I did hear a rumour.”

“So, what can I do for you?” Rosalind asked, the coolness of her words suggesting whatever he wanted would be too much trouble.

“Straight down to business it is then. Our sources have reported a new strain of the virus coming out of Africa, North Africa to be exact.”

“Why are you calling to tell me that? Why would I care what happens over there?”

“As the person who created the damned thing in the first place, I thought you would consider it a significant development.”

“I still don’t see how it affects me. As I recall, you forced me to sell my company and kept ninety per cent of the proceeds.”

It was the Prime Minister’s turn to express exasperation. “Which I’m sure you’ll agree was better than the alternative of spending the rest of your life in prison. You wouldn't believe it, but I'm coming under considerable pressure to include you in the new year's honours list. If only people knew the truth."

"Just remember that your fate is intertwined with mine, Andrew. If the facts do come out, I can't see the electorate having much sympathy with the man who brokered the deal."

"I had no choice. If I had refused, thousands more women would have died, maybe the whole of the human race."

"Well, we both have to live with our decisions. Anyway, I'm still not sure what you want from me."

"I need you to reassemble a team to study this new strain. If we—"

"Let me stop you right there, Andrew. I have no interest in helping you. Why don't you contact the new owners of Ilithyia Biotechnology and ask them?"

"Ever since we cut back on the grants, they've been taking money from the Americans. There are rumours that one of the big international pharmaceutical companies is about to buy them. We might be able to delay the sale, but—"

Rosalind interrupted again. "None of that is my problem, Andrew. I have to say I think it was very short-sighted of you to reduce research funding when nobody has produced a cure."

Jacobs hesitated as he tried to make sense of her words. "I don't understand."

"Do I have to spell it out? I formulated a treatment, not a cure. The pathogen still exists in the bodies of every person on the planet. The drugs I developed address the symptoms and prevent the virus from activating its destructive phase. They most certainly do not destroy it. Until we eradicate this organism, the population will always be at risk of further mutations."

"All the more reason why you should come back to work."

Rosalind sighed. "I already told you. I'm not interested."

"And there's nothing I can do to make you change your mind?"

"No." The silence extended between them until Rosalind spoke again. "Now you mention it, there may be something that would persuade me to help you."

"And what's that?" Jacobs sounded wary at the sudden about-turn.

"Somehow, I don't think you're going to like my proposal, but my terms are non-negotiable."

"If it's about the monetary side, I'm sure we can come to an arrangement."

"It's not, but that would be a secondary precondition before I could work for you."

"If money isn't the deciding factor, what else do you want?"

Rosalind paused for a second before replying. "Have Max Perrin killed, and I'll do what you ask."

The line went quiet. When the Prime Minister spoke again, his voice came out as a whisper. "You know I can't do that."

"That's my price."

"You expect me to order the killing of a twenty-year-old boy? You can't be serious."

"Oh, come on, Andrew. I'm sure you have people who specialise in that sort of thing. In fact, I used to employ a man with the right skills myself before I fired him—in the literal sense. And of course, just to clarify, that was before you signed the pardon agreement for all previous crimes."

"Look, I know the Perrin boy blinded you in one eye, but you did murder his father right in front of him. Remember, I was there when it happened."

"He wasn't trying to blind me," Rosalind screeched. "He was trying to kill me." The terror of the moment came rushing back as she recalled the memory.

She swallowed hard before continuing. "First, he spiked my drink with a drug that removed all my self-control. He forced me to push the tip of the pen into my eye while he watched. Then, just before he left, he told me to ram it all the way in when the track ended.

"It was only his ignorance of classical music that saved me. I'm sure he had no idea that Beethoven's violin concerto in D major lasts for three-quarters of an hour. By the end, I had recovered just enough willpower to resist, but it was a close-run thing. The drug didn't dull the pain in the slightest. He wanted me to suffer. During all that time, I was fully aware and in excruciating agony."

Silence extended between them. Eventually, Andrew Jacobs spoke. "I'm sure it was awful, but I can't just order the execution of a British citizen. Rosalind, I must urge you to reconsider."

"In that case, I have nothing more to say to you," Rosalind Baxter answered, swiping left to end the call.

Sunday 22nd June 2036

Tripoli Military Headquarters, Republic of North Africa
Three weeks before the Olympic wheelchair final

Mullah Awad sat in silence, reading the printed report. The strands of his heavy beard coiled together, hiding the lower part of his face.

The scientist in the doctor's coat, Dr Naeem Kubar, licked his lips nervously as he stood before the black-robed cleric. Sitting beside the religious leader, Professor Muhammad Halfon, the director of the hospital, appeared equally uncomfortable. He fiddled with the hem of his white robes. The room was silent apart from the once per second squeal of protest as the ceiling fan laboured against the worn bearings on its perpetual cycle of rotation.

While he waited, the standing man allowed his gaze to wander. Outside the self-adjusting, tinted windows, construction cranes rose from the rubble like crooked nails. More than two decades of civil war had exacted a heavy toll on the city's buildings, many of which still exhibited gaping wounds three years after the conflict had ended.

Dr Kubar had mixed feelings about the current situation in his newly formed country. He welcomed the end of the fighting but was less enamoured by the religious fanatics who had seized control and ruled by fear and intimidation. At least the new rulers were realistic enough to understand that they required the services of doctors and scientists, especially since the Western governments still refused to supply the drugs the population so desperately needed to survive.

Many of his colleagues had fled during the war. Only the truly dedicated and those with family ties remained. The scientist had chosen not to leave, hoping that one day he would be reunited with his only daughter, who had disappeared five years earlier during a visit to the local shops. From what little information he had been able to gather, it seemed she accidentally strayed into a fierce battle between the opposing forces vying for control of this vital shipping port. Hope for her survival was waning, but he couldn't abandon the city without discovering her fate.

The cleric pushed the paper sheets away and looked up. "So, Doctor Kubar, you believe this is a new strain?"

"Yes, sir." The medic stared at the upside-down report, unable to meet the dark eyes of his interrogator, glaring at him from above the bushy facial hair like a predator studying its prey.

"I've read your words, but I want to hear your reasoning."

The scientist paused for a second as he tried to decide at what level to pitch his explanation.

"I'm waiting," said the religious man, tapping his fingers on the table.

"Of course, sir."

"And stop calling me sir. You may address me as Mullah."

Kubar took a moment to gather his thoughts. "Yes, Mullah. The symptoms in the victims match those in women who have given birth. Basically, the virus seems to have activated and destroyed all the vital organs. We are yet to perform a molecular-level analysis of the pathogen, but all the signs are that this is a mutation of the original strain."

"Why do you think it attacked these children?"

"I can't be sure of that, Mullah, but the research I have read from abroad suggests the disease is closely related to the influenza virus. The infected population is so large that mutations are inevitable. I believe this is what happened."

"What more do we know?"

"We placed the woman who was supervising the infants in isolation. She seemed unaffected, but since then she has given birth, dying shortly afterwards. Perhaps surprisingly, her four babies are fit and well, and have shown no symptoms to date."

"Is there any information on the affected age range?"

"All those who died in the original event were under five. There is currently no indication of an upper limit."

Professor Halfon cleared his throat. "If I may interrupt, Mullah. We have performed some additional tests and have established that those who have reached puberty seem unaffected. We have also proven that the Western drugs for pregnant women are ineffective in preventing the symptoms in children."

Kubar stared in surprise at his supervisor. "You didn't tell me this. How did you perform the tests? If you know who it affects, that must mean—"

"Be quiet," the mullah shouted. He waited a beat before continuing in a low, menacing voice. "I am the one asking the questions. You will restrict yourself to providing the answers or suffer the consequences."

The doctor took an involuntary half-step backwards.

When the cleric spoke again, his words carried a more conciliatory tone. "What can we do about it?"

Kubar hesitated before answering. "There's very little, really. I recommend keeping all infants in isolation. We don't possess the equipment or the expertise to develop a cure."

"We are working on obtaining the machines. They will be here soon."

"It won't make any difference," the scientist said. "Without the experts to operate them and interpret the results, they are useless."

Halfon shot an angry look at his subordinate. "Your attitude leaves a lot to be desired, Doctor. If you can't help us, we will find people who can."

The doctor's face flushed. "The Western countries have studied this disease for well over a decade. In that time, they have thrown millions—in fact billions—of dollars into medical research. All their best minds have worked on developing a treatment. Three years ago, they discovered a solution. It's not a cure, but it does prevent the virus from activating. And now a new variant of the contagion has appeared. What makes you think we can solve this problem when so many before have failed?"

The director thrust his chair back and leapt to his feet. "How dare you question our capabilities? I'm—"

"Enough!" The commanding voice of the mullah cut through the room like a knife. "If you would be so good as to leave us alone, Doctor." He gestured towards the exit.

The red-faced scientist glared at his supervisor, then stomped across the floor.

~

The mullah and the professor waited for the door to close.

"I must apologise for the behaviour of my staff, Mullah," the director said, returning to his seat.

"I like a bit of spirit," the cleric replied. "Don't go too hard on him. His report impressed me. I have learned that scientists resent being kept in the dark. He seems very competent, and we can ill afford to lose any more of the bright minds available to us."

"Even so…"

"Now, back to the matter in hand; the West will still not supply our country with this drug, Lucinase, so I want you to produce our own version."

"But…"

"You will also develop drugs to treat the new strain of the virus."

"Ah, Mullah, just the first of those will be very difficult. If I may ask, why can we not simply keep the children isolated from pregnant women?"

The mullah scowled at Halfon. "Do you expect our men to perform childcare? To cook and clean? To change nappies? This is women's work, but many have died giving birth. As we continue to grow our population, there are insufficient females for these tasks. I expect everybody in this country to do their duty, including those who are pregnant. They must contribute by caring for the infants, but until we develop a solution for the new strain, this is not possible. That is why I have commanded you to develop drugs to protect the children."

"I will do my best, Mullah."

"And I expect nothing less. It is unfortunate, but what Dr Kubar said is accurate. The machines are due to arrive in the next few days. We have been forced to deal with some unscrupulous individuals and have paid considerably more than the market value, but the equipment will not be a problem. What is more of an issue is the staff to operate them."

"I will put my top people on this project right away."

"Yes. Ensure the man who just walked out of the door is one of them. However, as the doctor said, your workers do not possess the necessary expertise."

The professor rubbed his chin. "I… I'm not sure what I can do about that."

"No, this is something which requires a different skill set. What if we could recruit the people you need?"

"How? Believe me, I have tried. The scientists with the required knowledge are only available in Europe and America, and they will not come here, no matter how much we pay them. It will take years to train our own citizens to the appropriate level."

"I am not talking about training although that is something we should do for our long term survival. No, the solution is far simpler. If the people with the skills we need won't work here voluntarily, then we must force them to come. Let me ask you this; if there was one person you could select for your team, who would it be?"

The director stared out of the window towards the signs of rebuilding amongst the ruins of the city. His gaze lingered for a few seconds before returning to the cleric. "There are many scientists in the world who could help us develop a cure, but if I had to choose one… it would be somebody who helped to develop Lucinase at Ilithyia Biotechnology."

"My thoughts exactly. What if I could offer you the former head of the company?"

"The woman?"

"Yes, Rosalind Baxter. I know we would all prefer a man, but her partner, Dr Perrin, died."

"Thank you, Mullah. That would help us greatly."

"And to make things better, what if I were to throw in the female who survived childbirth without taking any drugs?"

Sunday 22nd June 2036

The Beeches Play Area, Northstowe

Three weeks before the Olympic wheelchair final

Jason sat on the park bench and watched as Paul scrabbled over the climbing frame.

"Be careful," Antimone called.

The boisterous three-year-old ignored his mother's instructions and clambered higher. "Look at me, Daddy," he yelled excitedly.

"Very good," Jason replied.

"Come and push me on the swing," his son demanded.

Jason sighed. The opportunities for conversation were few and far between when Paul was awake. "I'll be there in a second. I just want to talk to Mummy."

Antimone stretched out a hand and took Jason's in hers. "He misses you during the week."

"Yeah, sorry to leave you with our little bundle of energy."

"Oh, don't worry about that. My parents look after him for most of the day. They love having him around. It's a good job too what with how much time I spend training."

"Did we do the right thing, keeping out of the spotlight? We can't even celebrate his birthday on the correct date."

Antimone turned and studied Jason's face. "God, yes. I get enough press attention as it is. I don't think I could take any more."

Jason laughed. "Darling of the athletics track *and* the first person in a generation to live after giving birth; your head would become so big it'd explode."

Antimone punched him playfully on the arm. "Seriously though, the media are swarming around that woman, Anna Mayfield, like flies. Barely a day goes by when there's not some new article about her and her daughter."

"I'm sure she's doing very well out of it."

"If they knew about us, we wouldn't be able to do anything like this. There'd be paparazzi hiding in the bushes and drones buzzing about, trying to capture an intimate moment."

Jason nestled closer. "Talking of intimate moments, didn't you say your parents were going out this afternoon?"

"Yes, and Paul will need his nap."

"Are you proposing to seduce me?" Jason asked, smiling.

"Perhaps," Antimone replied.

"I really miss you when I'm away at university." Slowly, Jason's smile faded. "I keep worrying that I'm going to blurt out some detail about what really happened. Sometimes, I wake up at night convinced I've let something slip, and they're coming to arrest me."

"Yeah, they certainly laid it on heavy afterwards, didn't they?"

"God knows what would happen if the full story got out. The government would fall for a start. My adoptive mother would become the most hated woman in the world."

Antimone grinned. "So, not all bad then."

"I read an article on one of those current affairs websites campaigning for her to be included in the new year's honours list."

"If only they knew the truth."

"I'm surprised Max Perrin hasn't talked to the press."

"Yeah, I wouldn't put it past him. To think our involvement in all of it started because of a stupid accident at the athletics track," Antimone said.

"That guy's definitely got a screw loose," Jason agreed. "I saw the look in his eyes after his father died. It's amazing he hasn't blabbed to somebody."

"Perhaps he did, and they've locked him up. Talking of fathers, what's yours up to?"

"He finally received the money for wrongful imprisonment. He was thinking about returning to university. I know it's a long time ago, but he has a degree from Cambridge. He told me he was planning to visit us one weekend, so you can ask him yourself."

"We certainly owe him. Without his help, I'd probably still be a prisoner in that basement lab."

The conversation lapsed into silence as they both remembered how close they had come to dying.

Jason patted Antimone on the knee. "I'm fed up with discussing the past. What about the future?"

Antimone stared straight ahead.

"Is something wrong?"

She turned to face him. "No, it's just… we're still very young. We've both got a lot on our plates at the moment. You have to finish your degree; I have to win gold at the Olympics."

Jason let out a snort of laughter. "No pressure there then."

Antimone's serious expression dissipated his attempt at humour. "I don't want you to feel you have to stay with me because…"

Jason leant in and cupped the back of her head in his hand. They kissed for several seconds. When they separated, his eyes studied every detail of her face. "I'm with you because I want to be."

The sudden appearance of an unhappy Paul broke the mood. "You said you would push me."

"Come on then, buddy," Jason replied. "Let's go to the swings."

"I want Mummy to do it."

Jason flashed a glance at Antimone. "I'm afraid she can't."

"Why not?"

"Well, it's hard for Mummy to push you when she's in a wheelchair."

"Why is she in a wheelchair?"

"Because she can't walk."

"Why can't she walk?"

"Mummy had an accident when she was younger," Antimone interjected.

"What happened?"

"A car hit me."

"Did it hurt?"

Antimone's grip tightened on the arm of her chair. "It was all very quick. I didn't see it coming, which is why you always have to check carefully before crossing the road."

"Yes, but did it hurt?"

"At first, I suppose, but then I fell asleep. Some people came and took me to a hospital. They gave me a wheelchair so I could move about."

The three-year-old's face scrunched up as he processed her response. "Couldn't the people fix you?"

"No," Antimone said. "Unfortunately not."

"I heard Grandma say they could make you better."

His parents' eyes met. Jason held Antimone's gaze for a second, then refocused his attention on his son. "Maybe one day, buddy."

"Come on, I'll try to push you," Antimone said, changing the subject. "Just as long as you don't want to go too high."

Paul scampered on ahead. Antimone followed a short distance behind, Jason's hand resting on her shoulder.

When they reached the swings, Paul was already seated and bouncing up and down in anticipation. Antimone moved to the side and pushed him gently in the back.

"Higher, higher," he yelled, forgetting all about her previously stated conditions.

"You better take over," Antimone said, backing out of the way and turning to Jason.

Soon, Paul was arcing through the air, propelled by his father and squealing in delight.

None of the young family noticed the man in the parked car taking photographs with the telephoto lens.

Tuesday 24th June 2036

Oakington House, Northstowe

17 days before the Olympic wheelchair final

Rosalind Baxter glanced blearily at her watch and then at the empty wine bottle resting atop the small wooden table beside her chair. Three-thirty in the afternoon. Already the first faint tendrils of a headache teased at the base of her skull. She leant back and allowed her eyelids to close.

The glow of the icon panel persisted in the upper corner of her right eye. She would have to mention that to her specialist. Surely, they could program the damned thing, so it turned off when her eyes were closed.

She was most of the way to dropping off when the trill of the doorbell shocked her back to full wakefulness. *Who the hell is that?* Nobody visited her other than delivery people and the occasional parcel drone, and she had ordered nothing recently.

She pushed herself out of the confines of the armchair and padded towards the front door in bare feet. The bell rang a second time.

"All right, all right, I'm coming."

She prodded the video control unit and stared blearily at the image. With a groan of annoyance, she pressed the green button and turned away without waiting to greet her visitor. Behind her, two dark-suited men slipped into the hallway, each with his right hand gripping an object beneath the cover of his jacket. They surveyed each of the rooms leading off the hall before returning to the open doorway.

"Clear, sir," one of them murmured before taking a pace to the side to allow Andrew Jacobs to enter.

"Thanks, gentlemen," the British Prime Minister replied. "Could you give us some privacy, please?"

A third man followed the leader of the country inside and took up a position at the foot of the staircase. His two colleagues stood back to back in the hallway. Jacobs trailed Rosalind into the lounge, shutting the glass-panelled door behind him. When he turned around, she had already returned to her armchair.

The Prime Minister's gaze settled on the empty wine bottle. "A little early to be sinking the booze, isn't it, Rosalind?"

"What are you doing here, Andrew? I gave you my answer over the phone, so what is there to talk about?"

"Thanks for the offer of a drink, but I'm fine."

Rosalind rolled her eyes. "You invited yourself here, so don't expect me to play the part of the gracious hostess."

Jacobs strolled to another armchair and dragged it closer until it was two metres from Rosalind's.

"Don't mind me," she said. "Just make yourself at home and organise the furniture how you like."

The Prime Minister sat and leant forwards. His hands rested on his knees. "We need to talk."

"I have nothing to say to you unless you've reconsidered your response to my terms."

"I've got people looking for Max Perrin, but he isn't living with his mother, and nobody has seen him for weeks."

"NMFP," Rosalind replied.

"I'm sorry."

"Not my—"

"Ah, yes, I get it," Jacobs interrupted. "It's not your effing problem. So, if we were to find him and come to some arrangement…"

"If by *come to some arrangement*"—Rosalind made air quotes as she spoke—"you mean ending his miserable life, then I'm all ears. But I'll need proof."

Jacobs flashed a glance towards the closed door. "This is all a bit medieval, isn't it? What do you want me to do? Bring his head on a plate?"

"That would do the trick."

"What you're asking for goes against everything I believe in."

"And yet here you are. That must mean you haven't discounted the idea."

"Look," Jacobs said, "the future of the world is at stake. If we don't get ahead of the curve on this thing, millions of children could die. Doesn't that bother you at all?"

Rosalind stared at the Prime Minister before replying. "Do you know what? Not really. I've told you I'll work on this problem if you agree to my terms."

"For God's sake, your own grandson could be affected."

"I haven't got a grandson," Rosalind snapped.

"Then why did you write an email to your son asking to meet him, his girlfriend and the child?"

"I don't believe this. You've been spying on me and reading my private messages."

An amused expression flickered over the Prime Minister's face. "You act all affronted at our surveillance activities, but you expect me to approve the execution of a twenty-year-old boy? Why won't you answer the question?"

Rosalind closed her eyes for a few seconds. When she reopened them, Jacobs' unwavering gaze remained fixed on her.

"If you must know, I just wanted to find out what he was doing. I raised him for sixteen years. It's not really that difficult to imagine I might want to keep in touch."

"As I recall, you threatened to incinerate him and the girl. That's probably not the basis for a meaningful relationship."

"I wouldn't have done it. You had me backed into a corner. Anyway, you're changing the subject. I thought you were here to discuss my proposal."

Jacobs folded his arms. "Let's say we agreed to your demands. When could you begin?"

"Have you got a sample of this new strain of the virus?"

"Not yet, but we're working on getting hold of one."

"There's not much point in me starting without it, is there? And another thing. I'll need some live test subjects."

"Jesus, Rosalind, you can't be serious."

"That's the trouble with you, Andrew. You're far too squeamish. Surely, it's all about the greater good. How can I develop a cure if I don't have any guinea pigs to trial it on? It's not like we would perform any tests before we were confident it would work."

"You really are unbelievable. What am I supposed to do? Kidnap children off the street?"

"Again, NMFP."

"You're a monster. How the hell do you sleep at night?"

"As it happens, not very well," Rosalind replied, "mostly due to the repeating nightmare about poking my own eye out. By the way, I'll also need written immunity from any future criminal charges arising from my work and a salary of fifty million pounds a year. And before you complain about the money, some footballers earn much more than that for kicking around a bag of wind."

The first hint of anger brought a flush to the Prime Minister's face.

"While we're at it," Rosalind continued, "you better have another big wad of cash to pay for the team and the equipment I'll require to support me. I reckon seven hundred million will do for starters. All the staff will want a sizeable bonus when we deliver as well. Maybe you should budget for double that figure."

Jacobs rose to his feet. "I can let myself out, Mrs Baxter."

"It's been a pleasure as ever, Prime Minister," she called after him.

Wednesday 25th June 2036

Republic of North Africa Military Headquarters, Tripoli
16 days before the Olympics wheelchair final

General Hamza Shaladi lowered himself into the chair. He would have preferred to stand, but the leader of his country had offered him a seat, so he felt obliged to accept. He was aware that his seated position emphasised the extra kilograms of fat, which seemed to have developed an affinity for his midriff.

"I need you to perform a mission for me," Mullah Awad said.

"I would be delighted to serve you however you see fit," the general replied, unconsciously sucking in his stomach.

"This particular operation is of a very sensitive nature and will take place on foreign soil. Under no circumstances must you discuss the details with anybody outside those explicitly authorised by me."

Shaladi raised his eyebrows in surprise. Over the last couple of years, his government had taken significant efforts to integrate with the international community. If the reports in the news media were to be believed, sanctions would soon be lifting. From the little he had heard so far, this possessed all the hallmarks of something from the old days.

The mullah studied the man sitting opposite him. "I know this is an unusual request. Many other nations have tried to shape and control this country, but now it is time for The Republic of North Africa to stand alone and set its own course. The Russians, the Chinese and the Americans have all flooded this region with weapons as they interfered in our affairs. This is one reason we suffered the long years of civil war. But no more. From this point onwards, our nation will become a major force on this continent and beyond."

Despite his doubts, Shaladi replied, "Of course, Mullah. You have my full commitment."

The mullah steepled his fingers. "Good, good. I knew you were a man I could trust. Failure would have a devastating effect on our relationship with the rest of the world. The success of this mission will directly impact the future of this land we have struggled so hard to bring back under control."

And it had been a struggle. Ironically, the support of the world's superpowers had been the major factor in prolonging the conflict. The supply of arms and covert intelligence to the various competing warlords meant no one faction gained an upper hand. In the end, it was the involvement of the Iranians that made the difference. After years of manipulation and subterfuge in the Middle East, they turned their attention to North Africa and found sufficient common ground for two of the main rival groups to unite.

This shift in the balance of power was enough to bring the conflict to a resolution. The major world powers, whose coffers had become depleted funding the opposing parties, uttered a huge, if temporary, sigh of relief. The price of peace was the birth of a new state. Even though the religious fundamentalists running the country made them all uneasy, none of them was inclined to intervene any further.

"Of course, all they are really interested in is making money," the mullah continued. "While worldwide fossil fuel usage is reducing, the decline in output from the Middle East means that demand is still strong. One benefit of the years of fighting on our soil is that the oil stayed in the ground and remains easily accessible. The international community are all too keen to make profits as we use the proceeds from petroleum sales to rebuild the infrastructure of this country."

"Yes, sir," Shaladi agreed, unsure where the conversation was leading.

"I have been studying your military record," the mullah said, "and it is impressive."

In truth, the general was lucky to have picked the winning side. After cutting his teeth as a young officer in the final days of Gaddafi's rule, he allied himself with a faction commanded by a former army brigadier. His tactical skill and cool head under enemy fire led to several promotions, culminating with the appointment to his current rank in the newly formed Republic of North Africa's armed forces.

"I need your skills to resolve a grave problem facing our country," the mullah continued. "This disease, which has swept the world, now offers an even greater threat."

The general nodded. He had heard rumours about a new strain of the virus, but he couldn't see how that affected him directly. The first tendrils of fear coiled in his stomach. Was his daughter, Aya, at risk? She was the sole surviving member of his family. The girl's mother had passed away years ago, giving birth to a second child who also died despite the best efforts of the midwife.

"What is the nature of this threat?" Shaladi asked, pushing the anxiety to the back of his mind. "How may I be of assistance?"

"We must grow our population, or our new country will wither and die," the mullah replied. "But now this disease has mutated and is killing our children."

The general grasped one hand in the other. "I know nothing of medical matters, Mullah," he said.

The religious leader gave a tut of irritation. "That is obvious. I have tasked our doctors with increasing the number of our citizens. This is no concern of yours."

It was hard to be unaware of what the growth in numbers entailed. The new leaders treated women like cattle, forcing them to become pregnant after pumping them full of fertility drugs. The Republic of North Africa remained on the United Nations sanctions list, and that meant no access to the newly developed Western treatments that would enable the unfortunate mothers to survive childbirth.

While the general had taken steps to protect his only child from this fate, his options were severely limited. He had considered smuggling her out of the country, but that would emphatically end his career and put a huge target on both their backs.

"The mission requires the support of your daughter," the mullah said.

In that one sentence, the general's greatest fear rose to the surface. "She has no military training," he replied automatically. "She is an athlete."

"I am well aware of that. Her role will be small, but nevertheless vital to our success. I have little time to follow athletics, but I believe she has become something of a national celebrity."

Despite having no disability, Aya had discovered a talent for wheelchair racing. Keen to improve the image of their country on the international stage, the state's rulers had approved her entry into the Olympics. She achieved the qualifying time with ease. After many years of war, The Republic of North Africa needed a hero to raise the spirits of the population. The newly created nation's hopes rested on the abilities of his only daughter.

The general swallowed hard. "Will she be in any danger?"

The mullah offered a thin smile, his lips barely visible through the dense beard. "No more so than anybody else on the team."

"Does the operation require the use of weapons?"

"That depends upon how the mission proceeds, but if all goes well, then probably no."

"Where and when will it take place?"

"You ask a lot of questions. Maybe I should brief you in full now."

"That would be useful, Mullah."

The religious leader outlined the plan.

When he had finished, the general stared at him in disbelief. "Why do we need to involve my daughter? Surely we could accomplish the same goals in a different way."

The mullah's stare hardened. "This is not for debate. If you would rather she didn't help our cause directly, she can always provide indirect support by bearing children to restore our population."

Shaladi opened his mouth to reply, but the mullah spoke again. "You must think you are very clever."

The general blinked in confusion.

The mullah continued. "Did you really believe we were unaware of the operation performed on your daughter when she was thirteen years old, General? We know all her eggs were removed and frozen. Just because she cannot conceive naturally, it does not mean the doctors cannot implant embryos."

The soldier's shoulders sagged. A lifetime of military experience had taught him to recognise tactical situations in which the overwhelming strength of the enemy made surrender the only viable option.

He rose to his feet and saluted. "My daughter and I would be happy to perform this mission on behalf of our country, Mullah."

Monday 7th July 2036

Oakington House, Northstowe
4 days before the Olympics wheelchair final

The article scrolled down automatically as Rosalind Baxter read the penultimate paragraph on the page. She had to admit this was one feature of her prosthetic eye the scientists had implemented well. It took some getting used to, but the auto-scrolling function was a definite plus point.

The latest annual report from Ilithyia Biotechnology made for interesting reading. The new management team had sought to grow the company through acquisition, but their due diligence was sadly lacking. Now, it seemed, they were paying the price for their unwise investment decisions. No wonder they were seeking external funding. If she had been at the helm, she would never have allowed the corporate finances to get into this state.

She found her mind wandering back to the Prime Minister's proposition. After three years out of the game, it would be good to rejoin the world of medical research. Maybe her terms were a little ambitious. The challenge of beating the virus for the third time held some appeal.

The principal sticking point seemed to be her demand to assassinate the Perrin boy. There had been no recent communication from the Prime Minister or his people. Perhaps she should attempt to locate a private contractor willing to undertake the task. In some ways, she regretted losing the services of her former head of security, Anders Grolby. He would have dealt with the problem with the minimum of fuss. Such a shame she had been forced to terminate his employment—and his life.

The main issue with this approach was knowing where to start. It wasn't as if one could just search the Internet for contract hitmen. After the attack, she had considered using the services of a private security consultant to provide protection. Perhaps she should revisit that idea. Even if the person was unwilling to perform the task personally, they would probably have the contacts to complete the job.

The shrill ring of the doorbell jolted her from her thoughts. She received so few visitors. Had Andrew Jacobs decided to pay her another visit? If it was him, she would drop the assassination request but instead demand the damehood he had mentioned during his last house call. It would be nice to have a day out and meet the King.

She pushed herself upright and headed towards the hallway. The video display showed a pair of men wearing dark uniforms. A third, suited figure stood behind, his body angled away from the camera. She smiled inwardly and pressed the green entry button, already mulling over in her head how she would pitch her new proposal.

As soon as the lock released, the two uniformed men stepped inside. They positioned themselves, one on either side of Rosalind. The last member of the group strolled after them in a more casual fashion and surveyed the expansive hall. He gestured with an eyebrow towards the open door. The man to his left hurriedly grabbed the handle and shoved it closed before returning to his initial position.

"This is a very nice place, Mrs Baxter," the newcomer said, his voice tinged with a slight foreign accent.

"Is the Prime Minister too busy to visit me himself these days? You can inform him that I'll only deal with him face to face and not through one of his minions."

"What is minions?" the man asked in confusion. "I do not know this word."

"Oh, for heaven's sake. Tell Andrew Jacobs I want to see him in person."

"Who is Andrew...? Ah, I understand. I think you are confusing me with somebody else. I do not work for your government."

"Then who are you?" Rosalind asked, folding her arms.

"My name is General Hamza Shaladi." He didn't introduce the other two.

Now that she had time to study the group of three up close, they all had a Mediterranean tint to their skin. "What do you want?"

"I thought we could have a little talk."

"What the hell is this about?"

"No pointless chitchat. I like that. My government has need of your specific skill set."

Rosalind scowled in annoyance. "Will you please stop talking in riddles? Why are you here?"

The general picked at some lint on his sleeve. "I represent The Republic of North Africa. My country has something of a medical emergency, and I believe you have a great deal of expertise in this particular subject area. We would like you to come and work for us."

"I have no interest in working for you or your country. I want you to leave immediately."

"Mrs Baxter, it seems you do not understand the seriousness of the situation. Did you not lead the team which developed a treatment for the Orestes virus?"

"Yes, twice in fact." Despite the unwanted intrusion and her increasing irritation, a hint of pride touched Rosalind's voice.

"And now there is another strain, which is killing the children."

"What concern of that is mine?"

The general seemed genuinely perplexed. "You do not care about saving the lives of children?"

Twin spots of red surfaced on Rosalind's cheeks as irritability turned to anger. "I've heard enough, and I have no interest in helping you. Now, get out of my house."

A hardness appeared in the general's eyes. "I wish to make one thing perfectly clear, Mrs Baxter. You will come with us, either of your own accord or by force. Which is it to be?"

"What are you saying? You're going to kidnap me?"

"I would prefer for you to join me willingly, but I cannot accept no for an answer. Of course, we will reward you for your efforts."

"I don't want your money. Do you seriously think you can abduct me from my home in broad daylight?"

The general's dark eyebrows narrowed. "Time is of the essence, Mrs Baxter. Now, you must come."

Rosalind's gaze tracked to the control panel beside the closed front door. If she could only reach the emergency button. The two uniformed men took a step closer as if reading her intentions. Her shoulders slumped in defeat. "Fine, but I want to take some things with me, like a change of clothes."

"We have everything you need," the general said.

"May at least put on some shoes?"

The man stared at her bare feet. He nodded silently at his two accomplices. They accompanied her towards the dark wood of the writing desk and the pair of low-heeled, white espadrilles lying beneath.

"Give me a bit of space, please," she said, bending down. The nearest guard took half a pace backwards. Rosalind seized the opportunity. Still in her bare feet, she burst upright like a sprinter from the blocks, making for the kitchen and the back door leading into the garden.

She had taken fewer than three paces when a muscular figure crashed into her thigh and tackled her to the ground.

"Leave me alone," she shrieked, scratching at his face with her nails.

Strong hands grasped her upper arm. The hiss of a hypodermic spray followed. Seconds later, her vision faded to black.

"Let's get her out of here," Shaladi said in his native Arabic.

The two men each draped one of Rosalind's arms over a shoulder and lifted her off the expensive carpet. They dragged her unconscious body back through the way they had entered.

The general paused at the open doorway, checking that none of the neighbours was paying any attention. Satisfied nobody had seen anything, he pulled the door shut behind him and followed the others to the waiting van.

Tuesday 8th July 2036

Republic of North Africa Embassy, London
3 days before the Olympic wheelchair final

Aya Shaladi pushed through the heavy wooden door into the oak-panelled room.

Her father stood with his back to her, staring out of the window. At the sound of her arrival, he spun around and strode towards her with a broad smile. "As-salam alaykom," he said.

Aya hugged him and returned the greeting. "What are you doing here in London, father?" she asked, still speaking in their native tongue. "I did not think you would be arriving in the UK for another day or two."

"Do I need an excuse to visit my daughter?"

"Of course not. I am always delighted to see you."

"How is the training going?"

"Very well. I achieved the fastest time of my career during practice last week. My coach is confident I will bring home a gold medal."

The general surveyed his only child. She dressed like the locals in jeans and a long-sleeved shirt. Her only deference to the dress code of her native country was the colourful headscarf covering her hair. He knew some of the more hard-line members of the ruling party objected to women who failed to follow the traditional customs. If the leaders wanted to be taken seriously on the international stage, they would have to change their views. After all, they could hardly expect his daughter to race in a burka.

Despite his own Muslim faith, he had no great love for the religious fanatics who now ruled his country. The enforcement of strict Sharia law turned his stomach at times, but he hid his misgivings and followed orders. Not for the first time, he fantasised about living here in the West, not that his government would ever willingly let him leave. In some ways, he was trapped by the success of his army career.

"Excellent, my dear. Um… there is something I need to discuss with you. It concerns the Olympics."

Aya's face tightened into a scowl. "Those bearded fools aren't going to stop me competing, are they?"

The general glanced uneasily at his daughter. "No, it's nothing like that. Our leader has entrusted me with a very important mission. I will require your help to complete it."

"I don't understand. You've never asked me before. I mean, they don't even allow women in the army."

"I know. Nevertheless, your support is vital to our success."

"What do you need me for?"

The general explained the kidnapping of Rosalind Baxter and the plan for the Olympic final. The more he told her, the darker her expression became.

"Where are they keeping this doctor?"

"They are transporting her north to meet up with us later."

"Why can't you just snatch the others in the same way?"

"The rest of the world cannot suspect our country. That is why it must appear that we have been taken as well."

"But this is my one chance to win a gold medal. How could you do this to me?"

"I'm sorry, Aya. It was not my decision. The blasts will be timed to occur after the end of the race. You can still take away a winner's medallion."

"No, I can't. You only receive those at the ceremony that happens hours afterwards."

"But you can pick it up later."

"If they give out medals at all after something like this."

"I'm sorry, Aya. There's nothing I can do about it."

"It's all the fault of those idiots who seized our country."

The general glanced nervously at the door. "Keep your voice down. This place is probably bugged."

"What are they going to do?" Aya asked with a sneer. "They can't put me to work making children like they do with the other women."

"They know about the eggs."

She glowered at her father. "Why did you tell them?"

"I didn't. They must have found out via other means. Anyway, the mullah informed me they could still implant embryos."

The self-assurance vanished from her expression. "Would they really do that?"

"Anything is possible, but if we do our job properly, they won't need to."

Aya lowered her voice. "I'm fed up with the people who rule our country and what they force the women to go through. They treat us worse than cattle. Can't we defect? If we went to the British Government and told them everything, surely they would allow us to stay."

The general paled. "Do not ever say such things. If they hear you, we are dead. They would never let us live after such a betrayal. We would spend the rest of our lives looking over our shoulders."

Aya huffed in exasperation. "It just makes me so angry. Do they really think this woman will develop a cure?"

"She has done it before," the general replied. "Even if she does not come up with a solution to the new problem, she can teach our scientists how to make the medicine so our mothers need not die when giving birth."

"What will happen to the people we kidnap?"

The general stared at his daughter in silence. When he spoke, it was in a subdued tone. "They can never be allowed to leave."

Wednesday 9th July 2036

Shipping Container, M1 Motorway near Sheffield, UK
2 days before the Olympic wheelchair final

The jolting movement gradually abated. The hiss of the air brakes penetrated the interior of the shipping container. A few seconds later, the incessant rumble of the diesel engine faded into silence.

Rosalind pushed herself upright on the mattress. The only illumination came from the narrow wedge of light infiltrating the top of the rear doors. For a moment, she considered hammering her fists against the metal sides. When she had last done that, they bound her hands and feet with thin nylon rope and gagged her. The friction burns on her wrists bore witness to how tightly they had tied the knots. The skin was still raw two days later. Perhaps that wasn't such a good idea after all.

She waited to see what would happen next. The sound of male voices speaking in a foreign language originated from somewhere down the side. She gazed towards the pile of pallets, positioned to block the interior of her prison from the gaze of outside observers. A series of metallic clanks rattled through the container. Moments later, she shielded her eyes at the sudden increase in brightness.

A slight vibration through the floor signalled that one of her captors had climbed up. The man uttered a low curse as he edged his way past the obstacles. After a few seconds, the silhouette of a man's head appeared in the bright band of sunlight streaming through the open doors. Rosalind blinked as the beam of a powerful torch swept over her.

"Everything is good, yes?" he said in heavily accented English.

"If you call being kidnapped and locked up in the back of a lorry good."

"This cannot be avoided. Here, I bring you food and drink."

The man tossed a plastic bottle of water and a cellophane-wrapped baguette onto the mattress. Rosalind grabbed them and positioned them by the side where she could find them easily when darkness returned.

"I need to pee," she said.

The man gestured towards the chemical toilet wedged in the gap between the pallets and the metal wall. "You go there. It is easier when we are not moving, no? Make sure you put it back after. You do not want it to fall over." He let out a deep, guttural laugh.

"How much longer are you going to coop me up in here?"

"What is coop?"

"Keep in a prison, like a chicken."

"First, we travel to Grainger Mooth."

"Where?"

"Grainger Mooth. It is big port."

"Oh, you mean Grangemouth. What happens after that?"

"We load this container on a ship and sail to my country. There you work to make a cure. Then we let you go."

Rosalind believed all of it except for the part about releasing her. Unless she escaped, she would probably end up spending the rest of her life in captivity. Once they reached Africa, the task would be that much harder.

"We charge the battery for one hour," the man said, "then we leave."

This vehicle had an electric motor to supplement the diesel engine. In recent years, it had become common for truck stops to include an area containing charging stations. In all likelihood, they were on a motorway or at least a major road. If she got out, she could ask another driver for help.

"Can't you leave the doors open? I just want to see some light."

"No, this is not possible. I do not think you are afraid of the dark." He laughed once more. "If you make any sound, I will use the ropes again. And this time, I will tie the knots tightly."

"I won't do anything. Please. Just a small gap."

"No," the man said. "One hour." He edged back through the narrow aisle. Moments later there was a metallic clank, and the interior plunged once more into darkness.

Oh, well. It had been worth a try.

Rosalind extended her arms ahead of her and crept towards the stack of pallets. Once there, she held out her left arm and shuffled sideways until her fingers touched the cold metal side. She reached into the gap and pulled out the portable toilet. She hadn't been lying about needing to relieve herself.

When she had finished and restored everything to its rightful place, she followed the route her captor had taken until she encountered the rear doors. There was insufficient room at the back of the container to explore further.

How the hell was she going to get out of here?

She retraced her steps and lowered herself to the mattress. The material was slightly damp and carried a faint smell of mildew. She dreaded to think where they had obtained it from, but it was more comfortable than lying on the cold, metal floor.

As she crawled towards the refreshments they had left for her, the first glimmer of an idea formed in her head. She felt around in the dark and grabbed the water bottle. After taking a long swig, she started on the baguette. It contained some type of meat, maybe beef, and a leaf of limp lettuce.

It might just work. If she failed, they would tie her up, but the longer she delayed her attempt, the fewer chances she would have. She staggered upright and approached the stack of pallets. Her fingers explored the crates and detected wooden strips running horizontally between the layers. She kicked off the cheap shoes they had bought for her to replace the ones she had left in the house and set about scaling the pile. The sharp edges cut into her feet as she rose higher. When she reached the top, the gap to the ceiling was less than half a metre.

She inched forwards. If she stretched out, she could just about reach the rear door of the container. This was it. She went over the plan one last time in her head. Taking a deep intake of breath, she pounded her fist against the metal and yelled at the top of her voice. "Help! I've been kidnapped. Get me out of here."

She continued to hammer and scream until she heard the familiar clank that signalled the door was about to open. As daylight streamed inside, she shuffled backwards.

A man's voice cursed in Arabic. From her vantage point, she sensed a slight movement as he clambered up into the container. She waited until he had moved down the side. The beam from his torch played over the mattress and inspected the corners ahead of him. He swore again as his search came up empty.

Rosalind scrambled forwards and lowered herself down. In her haste, she slipped and only just caught herself. The sudden movement drew the man's attention. She dropped to the narrow lip behind the pallets, shielding her eyes against the bright glare of the sun. A quick survey of her surroundings told her they were in a large parking area for commercial vehicles. They had parked the truck well away from any others. The closest was at least fifty metres distant, but the cab seemed to be empty.

Rosalind made the short drop to the road surface and sprinted towards the vehicle in her bare feet. "Help!" she shouted, waving her arms above her head.

A man's yell came from behind. A hand landed on her shoulder, dragging her back. She lashed out at her assailant with an elbow and connected with something soft. Shaking loose from his grip, she tried to scramble away.

She didn't see the fist coming as it slammed into her face. Once more her world was reduced to darkness.

Wednesday 9th July 2036

10 Downing Street, London

2 days before the Olympic wheelchair final

Andrew Jacobs entered the plushly-furnished cabinet room. The two people he was due to meet were already present, and both rose to their feet.

"Good morning, Prime Minister," the shorter and slimmer of the pair said. Iris Stanley wore an expensive designer jacket and matching skirt. In a world where the correction of sight defects had become routine simply by the administration of specialised drugs, the wire-framed glasses signalled her distrust of medical technology. Despite the archaic eyewear, her piercing blue eyes missed little, a characteristic that served her well in her role as the head of Britain's MI5 internal security service.

"Good to see you, Iris," Jacobs replied.

The second person fastened the middle button of his jacket as he stood and extended a meaty hand. His dark hair was thinning, and his stomach strained against the thread holding the fastening in place. When he spoke, his voice carried a cultivated public-school accent. "It's been a while, Andrew."

The two men were long-standing friends from their days at Oxford University. They had progressed in their careers at similar rates, both reaching the pinnacle of their professions at around the same time, twelve years earlier. Charles Moreland headed up MI6, the outward-facing secret intelligence service.

"Thanks for coming in, Charles," Jacobs said.

The Prime Minister sat at the head of the long oak table. His visitors took their places, one on either side of him. "Let's get down to business."

"It must be serious if you have both the internal and external arms of the security services in attendance," Moreland said, "especially since we were specifically told not to bring any aides."

Jacobs leant back in his chair. "You might say that. I'm sure you've both been briefed on the news coming out of North Africa about a new strain of the virus."

"Yes," the head of MI6 replied. "We have an informant high in the Reponan medical establishment. I guess that's the source you're alluding to." The term Repona had become commonplace when referring to the newly formed Republic of North Africa.

Jacobs nodded. "Right."

"They're in a bit of a panic. They've lost a lot of children to this new variant. I heard only this morning that one of our operatives has smuggled out a blood sample from an infected child. It's on its way over here as we speak."

"That's good news. I was going to ask about the progress on that front. Well done."

"There've been no reports of any outbreaks here," Stanley said, "at least none that I've been told about."

The Prime Minister tapped his fingers on the polished surface of the table. "Luckily, we've had no confirmed cases, but I suspect it's only a matter of time. All incoming flights from the region have been cancelled, not that there were many to start with given the sanctions. The problem is that people travelling overland or via countries not affected by the flight embargo might be carriers. We're coming to the height of the tourist season, and the timing of the Olympics up in Glasgow at the moment couldn't be worse."

"You could always cancel the games," the head of MI5 said.

"No," Jacobs replied. "That's not really an option, not when they're halfway through. Pretty much all the athletes are already over here."

"What about running the remaining events behind closed doors?"

"It's difficult enough to fill the stadia as it is. So far, we've only sold about a fifth of the tickets. The rest of the world will be watching. We want to portray a good impression. I'm not keen to follow your suggestion unless I absolutely have to."

"Changing the subject, what about offering the North Africans medical assistance?" Moreland asked.

"They've been keeping this outbreak to themselves. If we were to offer help, we'd be letting them know we have a highly placed source inside their country."

"Good point."

"The way they deliberately impregnate their women doesn't sit well with me either. Anyway, that's not the reason I've called you here this morning. I want us to get ahead of this new strain. That means starting our research efforts as soon as possible."

Stanley's brows knitted in a frown. "I don't understand. How does that affect Charles and me?"

"Who would you suggest to head up the team?"

"The woman who came up with the cure last time, I suppose," Moreland replied. "In fact, make that the previous two times."

"My thoughts exactly: Rosalind Baxter."

"I thought she had retired," Stanley said, "although I've heard rumours there might be more to her retirement than meets the eye. Despite her contribution to medical science, it seems there's a reluctance to offer her anything in the new year honours list. There must be a good reason."

"Very perceptive," Jacobs replied. "What I'm about to tell you mustn't leave this room."

When he had finished telling the story, both members of his audience sat in dumbfounded silence.

"There was nothing else I could do," the Prime Minister said. "If I had refused her terms, she would have incinerated everything, including all details of the cure, her adopted son and the girl. Without the drug she had developed, the human race was doomed."

Stanley's blue eyes locked onto Jacobs. "So, the woman who is being hailed as the saviour of mankind was in fact the instigator of the whole thing. The most prolific mass murderer in history is free to live her life in luxury, and there's nothing we can do about it."

"Not without bringing down the government and leaving us open to claims from every other country in the world. We'd become pariahs. The compensation costs alone would cripple us for years to come, never mind the sanctions we would face from the international community."

Moreland retrieved a handkerchief from his pocket and dabbed at the bead of sweat rolling down his temple. "Bloody hell. I can't believe this. Who else knows about it?"

"Only the seven or eight people who were there and a handful of civil servants who prepared the paperwork."

"Is that the reason you've called us here today?" Stanley asked. "Are you planning to reduce the number of potential witnesses?"

"What?" Jacobs replied in confusion. "You don't think I want you to..."

"We've done far worse in the past in the interests of national security."

"No. It's not that. At least, not directly."

"You better explain then," the head of MI5 said, folding her arms.

"As we discussed a second ago, of all the medical researchers at our disposal, Rosalind Baxter is our best bet to get ahead of this latest outbreak."

"Christ, Andrew," Charles Moreland interjected. "You can't seriously be telling us you trust the woman who caused all this mess in the first place to develop a cure."

"She is uniquely qualified, I suppose," Stanley added.

"You're right," Jacobs said. "She's the one person who knows the most about this virus. But unfortunately, she's set several conditions before she'll return to work."

The head of MI5 grimaced. "Oh, this keeps getting better and better. What does the woman want?"

The Prime Minister tugged at his collar. "You know I mentioned how she murdered her partner and co-founder of the company by stabbing him in the eye. Well, six months later, the victim's son, who incidentally witnessed it all, returned the compliment. He sneaked into her house, laced her drink with a drug that made her extremely suggestible, then forced her to do the same thing to herself."

Moreland paled. "You mean she poked her own eye out."

"Yes. He ordered her to wait for a while so she could experience the same agonising pain suffered by his father, then shove it all the way into her brain. Luckily for her, she recovered enough self-control to resist. The story never made it into the press. She told the doctors it was an accident, and she slipped on a wet floor."

Stanley raised an eyebrow. "It sounds to me like she got what was coming. I can guess where all this is heading; she wants revenge on the son."

"Correct," Jacobs replied.

"You're saying she won't work on developing a treatment for this new strain unless we kill the boy. How old is he?"

The Prime Minister exhaled a weary sigh. "He's twenty. There doesn't seem to be any way out of it. I tried to talk her round. I even paid the woman a visit. Now, she isn't answering my calls. She was adamant she wouldn't start work unless I met her conditions, one of which was the execution of her former partner's son."

"There were others?"

"Yes, but I can deal with those without your help."

"Let me get this straight," Moreland said. "You've called this meeting because you want us to assassinate this individual."

Jacobs nodded.

"I guess that would reduce the list of people with the knowledge to destroy this country," Stanley chipped in, drily.

Nobody spoke. After several seconds, the Prime Minister broke the silence. "There's another complication; the boy has disappeared. I've had my team and the police looking for him, but he seems to have vanished without a trace."

"And you want us to find him," Moreland said.

"Then dispose of him," Stanley interjected.

Jacobs lowered his head. When he raised his eyes, they carried a haunted look. "God help me, but yes. There is one last thing. She wants proof of his death."

The ticking of the large carriage clock sitting on the mantelpiece seemed to fill the room.

Finally, Stanley stood, then straightened her skirt. "Well, we should start by finding him. Once we've done that, we can decide how to proceed. We'll focus our search on this country, and your guys will look elsewhere, right Charles?"

The head of MI6 also rose to his feet. "I'll let you know what we turn up."

The Prime Minister stared first at one and then the other of the two secret service heads. "I'm sorry to have to make this request. But what else can I do?"

Part Two: Expatriation

Friday 11th July 2036

Glasgow Olympic Stadium
The Olympic wheelchair final

Antimone Lessing rounded the last bend, sandwiched between the other two race leaders. The gap from the leading group to the rest of the field extended to greater than twenty-five metres. With only the length of the home straight remaining, it seemed certain all three would end up on the podium; the only question was in what order. The roar of the crowd reverberated around the bowl of the stadium as they willed the finalists onwards.

A chant built up from the supporters behind the finishing line.

"AN-TIM-OH-NEE! AN-TIM-OH-NEE!"

The pain burned in Antimone's shoulders as she channelled her last reserves of strength into forcing the wheelchair forwards. Her front wheel eased half a metre ahead of the North African in the green one-piece. The Welsh girl trailed a few centimetres behind in third place. The three leaders matched each other push for push.

~

A quarter of the way down the straight, the first bomb exploded. The blast instantly vaporised the server room, cutting off all communications with the outside world. The second detonation a moment later took out the substation supplying electricity to the stadium and the surrounding area.

Other than the dull thud of the explosions, the targeted devastation did not immediately impact the spectators or contestants. It only became obvious something was wrong when the four huge display screens mounted above the stands flickered and died. The lighting beneath the roof dimmed at the same time. Unnoticed by the competitors, the cluster of tiny camera drones drifted across the track and settled gently onto the grass at the centre of the oval.

When the leaders were still forty metres short of the finish, the first of several bombs inside the stadium detonated. The explosion in an unpopulated seating area created a billowing cloud of smoke. The cheers of the crowd turned to stunned silence, then screams.

~

Antimone propelled herself forwards, aware that something unusual was happening behind her, but still intent on reaching the finishing line ahead of her two rivals. The next blast was far closer, throwing her sideways as if a giant hand had swept her off the track. Her wheelchair careened across the lanes and smashed into a prone marshal who had been knocked off his feet by the wall of turbulent air. The collision sent her into a tumble. Antimone stuck out an arm to cushion the impact. She landed on her shoulder and skidded to a halt, lying on her side and still strapped into her chair. She remained motionless for a moment as the scent of fresh grass mingled with the acrid stench of the explosion and filled her lungs.

Debris from the blast rained down all around her. A razor-sharp fragment of metal thumped into the ground less than a metre to her right. The dense, swirling clouds of smoke thickened.

Fear surged though her veins. She stuck out an arm and righted the wheelchair with a single shove. The jarring impact had disorientated her. She tried to align her sense of direction, but her gaze couldn't penetrate the choking fumes. *Oh God! My family.*

The percussive thud of another explosion sent a shockwave rolling over her from the left. A man sprinted past, his face etched in panic before he disappeared into the gloom. Shrieks of terror originated from behind. *That must be coming from the main stand.*

She spun in a tight circle and propelled herself in the direction of the cries. She had covered only a few metres when a figure dressed in green staggered through the smoke: the North African athlete.

"We must get out of here," Aya Shaladi said.

"I've got to find my family."

"They are in the VIP area, yes?"

Antimone continued to advance towards the screams, her fellow competitor jogging alongside. The drifting smoke showed no signs of clearing.

The woman placed a hand on her shoulder. "My father—he is there as well. He is a powerful man in my country. He told me that the security team has prepared a safe place for important guests in case there is any trouble. I know where they are going. I promise your family will be there. Now we have to leave. There may be more bombs."

Antimone stopped pushing and stared at the figure with the broad shoulders, wreathed in smoke. "You're sure that's where they'll go?"

"Yes. It is this way." The African athlete pointed.

Antimone hesitated, caught in an agony of indecision. There were important people here, including world leaders, and the authorities would have a plan to escort them somewhere secure in the event of a terrorist incident. This certainly qualified as such. Everything the woman said sounded plausible. She fought down the terror worming its way through her stomach and up her throat. "Okay then."

"Good. Follow me."

The North African set off at a jog, glancing back every few paces to ensure Antimone was trailing behind. She led them through the drifting smoke to the wide archway that provided the chief entry point into the stadium. Scorch marks on the walls and a patch of exposed brickwork signalled where one device had detonated.

"Down here." The woman's voice was barely audible above the screeching of the alarms. The air was clearer inside, but the corridor lay in a gloomy twilight, illuminated only by the emergency lighting. A pair of men in yellow jackets rushed past in the opposite direction, heading towards the mayhem.

The two athletes pushed through a set of swing doors. The logo of a green running man marked a fire exit to the right.

"Shouldn't we follow the sign?" Antimone asked. Her teeth chattered as the sweat from the race chilled her skin in the air-conditioned interior.

"No," the woman called over her shoulder without stopping. "This way." She trotted along the corridor to another door and held it open. As Antimone brushed past, the North African said, "You know I would have won, yes?"

Despite the desperate situation, a glimmer of a smile crossed Antimone's lips. "Yeah, right. That gold medal was mine."

"I think not. Next time I will show you who is the fastest."

Antimone shook her head in disbelief. They progressed through a further set of doors without speaking.

"Here," the woman said, pointing. She barged through the wide emergency exit and into the afternoon sunshine. Faint wisps of smoke rose from the top of the stadium into the hazy, blue sky. A solitary black van waited on the tarmac. The rear doors were open, but Antimone couldn't see into the gloomy interior.

A man with tightly cropped black hair and wearing a grey suit separated from the other two men to whom he had been talking. Both wore dark uniforms. He rushed forwards and embraced the African athlete.

"Alhamdulillaah, Aya."

"In this country they say thank God, father."

The man smiled fondly. "Of course, my dear. I'm just grateful you are unhurt."

His daughter's face remained set in a scowl. "You said they would allow the event to finish."

Antimone stared at the pair in confusion. There were only a handful of people in this area and certainly far too few to account for all the VIPs who must have been in attendance. Where was her family? Why were they talking about the race?

"Is my son here?" she asked, her voice quivering with tension.

The man released the African athlete and turned his attention to Antimone. "Hello, Miss Lessing. Please forgive my bad manners. I am General Hamza Shaladi, and of course, you already know my daughter, Aya. Your son is safe inside the van with your… friend."

Antimone wheeled herself forwards and peered into the gloomy interior. Sitting on a seat bolted to the floor, hugging the tiny figure of her three-year-old boy, was Jason. Another man, wearing the same black uniform as the other two, stood beside them. As her eyesight adjusted to the sudden reduction in brightness, she realised the man standing over her son and Jason was holding what appeared to be a pistol.

She sighed with relief. They were safe. The sensation lasted only a few seconds as Jason turned, and his gaze locked onto her. His dull, wide-eyed expression sent a shiver of apprehension through her body.

Friday 11th July 2036

Outside Glasgow Olympic Stadium
10 minutes after the start of the attack

Antimone whirled back to face the general. "What's going on here? Where is everybody else? Why did your daughter say something about finishing the race?"

The man paused before replying. "Every day in my country, women die giving birth, and yet your government will not provide us with the drugs to keep them alive. Now, a new form of this terrible disease is killing the children. We need your help to develop a cure."

Antimone stared at him, shocked into silence.

The general continued. "We know that you survived childbirth before they developed a treatment. Your boy is the first to have a mother who lived past the birth without the aid of any medicine. This man is the father of the child."

"You've got it all wrong. Anna Mayfield and her daughter came before us."

Shaladi let out a low laugh. "There is no point in lying. We already know the truth. Now, we must leave before the police get here."

"You don't seriously think I'm going anywhere with you, do you?"

A man in a black uniform stepped alongside the general. In his hand, he held a pistol. The barrel pointed at Antimone's chest.

"On the contrary. Let me be absolutely clear. All three of you are coming with us. I will show you how serious I am." He beckoned the second uniformed guard forward. "Give me your weapon."

The man handed over the firearm, handle first.

"Thank you." The general raised the gun and pointed it at the guard's head. Before the unsuspecting victim could even register surprise, the pistol emitted a loud bang.

Antimone gasped in shock and averted her gaze from the body and the rapidly expanding pool of blood surrounding it.

"Make sure he is not carrying any details of our plan," the general said to the dead man's colleague. "We do not want to give them any easy clues.

When you have done that, leave him there." He turned back to Antimone. "This man died because he did not follow orders. I instructed him to delay the detonations until after the race had finished. His actions put the lives of both you and my daughter in danger. I hope you no longer have any doubts about the seriousness of my intentions. Now, get in the van with your son and friend."

Antimone raised her eyes, taking great care to avoid looking at the dead body. Her voice came out in a hoarse whisper. "Unlike your daughter, I can't walk."

The general flicked his weapon at the remaining guard and barked a command in Arabic. The man returned his gun to a holster below his jacket and hurried to Antimone's side.

Aya Shaladi stepped to the opposite wheel. Her face was pale. "Do you need help with the straps?"

"No," Antimone snapped. Her hand moved to the bindings holding her to the wheelchair. She fumbled at the mechanism with trembling fingers but couldn't loosen them.

"Here," Aya said. "Let me." She knelt and released Antimone. "I am sorry for this."

Aya and the guard lifted Antimone out of the chair. They carried her to the back of the van and sat her on the rear shelf.

Shaladi called to the second man, who retrieved a package wrapped in clear plastic from the front seat of the vehicle. The general removed a tracksuit in the same shade of green worn by the North African athlete from the packaging. "You must be getting cold. Put this on. We do not want you to get ill."

"You," he said, pointing at Jason. "Help her to dress, then lift her up."

Jason tried to rise, but Paul buried his face in his father's chest. "I've just got to give your mum a hand." He peeled the boy away and patted the seat beside him. The frightened child sat, hunching his shoulders, his feet not quite reaching the floor.

Jason bent over under the watchful gaze of the armed man. He slipped the ends of the tracksuit bottoms over Antimone's legs and helped her pull them up over her athletic outfit. He placed his hands under her armpits and hauled her up. Once inside the van, he dragged her back towards the seat.

"No, there is a folding wheelchair," the general said, pointing with the gun. "Use that." Jason lowered Antimone to the cold, metal floor.

"Are you all right?" she whispered.

"No talking," Shaladi barked. "We must leave now."

Jason unfolded the mechanism, lifted her once more and placed her into the canvas seat. The chair had handles at the back and lacked hand rims, requiring somebody else to propel the occupant.

"Turn it sideways and apply the foot brake," the general commanded, "then sit down."

"There aren't any seatbelts," Jason said.

"Do not worry," Shaladi replied. "In our country, we must drive carefully because we do not have computers to control our cars." He turned to his daughter and muttered something in Arabic.

She glared at him for a moment, then clambered inside. As she reached the seat, she turned back. "What about her racing wheelchair?"

"Leave it. Neither of you will be in a race for a long time."

She sat on the opposite side to Jason, her face screwed up in anger. The guard took up position between them. Moments later, the rear doors slammed shut, plunging the interior into darkness.

"Don't worry, Paul," Antimone said. "Mummy's here. Just hold on to Daddy."

The clunk of more closing doors reverberated from the front of the vehicle.

"How do you think you're going to get away with this?" Antimone asked.

At first, nobody responded. Then Aya spoke. "You believe we want to do this? The leaders of our country gave us orders. If we do not follow them, they kill us. We have no choice. We do what they ask, or we die."

"Where are you taking us?"

"We are bringing you to The Republic of North Africa. There we will try to discover how you survived."

Antimone swallowed hard as she digested the answer. She had heard of the country but would struggle to point it out on a map. "I already told you, they gave me the drugs like everybody else."

"That is the story, but it is not the truth. We both know this. What I do not understand is why everyone lies, but we will find out."

Before Antimone could respond, the van set off. After the initial lurch, the movement settled into a swaying motion as they navigated the streets around the stadium. Several times over the first few minutes, the sound of blaring sirens rose, then fell away behind them. Antimone prayed somebody would stop their vehicle, but the whine of the motor and the soft rumble of the tyres became louder as the speed increased.

"Who told you about us?" Antimone asked the darkness.

When there was no reply, she repeated the question. Silence greeted her words. She chewed her bottom lip. Maybe she would get some answers when the first part of their journey ended.

Friday 11th July 2036

10 Downing Street, London

45 minutes after the start of the attack

The room buzzed with activity as members of the cabinet discussed the situation with their aides and a small army of civil servants. Andrew Jacobs ran his hands through his hair. "Can anybody tell me what's going on?"

His chief of staff, David Wagner, broke off the conversation he was having with a colleague. "Yes, Prime Minister. We know there were five bombs inside the stadium proper and one each in the server room and the electricity substation."

"Casualties?"

"We're still trying to get all the details, but there were three fatalities, including a suspected heart attack. There have also been several injuries from flying debris, but none of the surviving victims are in a serious condition. We haven't accounted for everybody yet, but the authorities on site have informed me they don't expect the number to rise significantly."

"I suppose it could've been worse."

"Definitely, Prime Minister. From the reports on the ground, it seems the bombs were placed to create maximum confusion. If they'd been inside the main stand, we'd be looking at hundreds or even thousands of fatalities. First impressions suggest the perpetrators were going for effect rather than death and destruction."

Jacobs' face clouded in puzzlement. "That doesn't make sense. Didn't you mention they targeted the server room and the electrical substation? If the goal was to send a message, why take out the means for recording the scene?"

"The teams on site are looking at all angles, but it's too soon to attribute motive at this stage."

"Were any of the athletes injured?"

"A few cuts and bruises, Prime Minister. The race leaders were close to a blast. One of our girls and a North African athlete are still unaccounted for.

It's possible they just got lost in the confusion. We're trying to track them down. I'll let you know as soon as we hear anything."

"Has anybody claimed responsibility yet?"

"So far, only the usual suspects. Most of them are small groups of lunatics without the resources to pull off something like this. From what I've heard, there haven't been any credible claims."

"What a bloody mess. Keep me informed of any progress in the investigation."

"Of course, Prime Minister."

Wagner turned away and immediately lifted a phone to his ear. The clamour of raised voices filled the high-ceilinged room. Andrew Jacobs studied the occupants as they scurried about. Instead of the usual smart attire more often seen at the centre of government, many wore casual clothes. Most displayed harried expressions as they talked into handsets or conversed with colleagues. The atmosphere was stuffy and carried a hint of body odour.

His gaze settled on a large display, which somebody had wheeled into the corner. The main part of the screen showed jerky images from inside the stadium. Three separate inset boxes displayed a variety of newsfeeds, including one from the BBC. In all of them, sombre commentators addressed the camera. The sound was either off or turned down low.

Jacobs focused on the scene from the site of the explosions. A faint, smoky haze still hung in the air. A group of paramedics in hi-vis jackets knelt beside a figure lying on the ground. The lanyard around the victim's neck identified him as a race official. His foot twitched as the man tending to him injected a colourless liquid into his arm. Everywhere, people milled about or congregated in small groups. Debris lay scattered across the track.

A slight touch on the shoulder drew Jacobs back to his surroundings. One of his personal assistants, an attractive woman in her mid-twenties, stood beside him.

"Sorry to disturb you, sir, but I have a call from the ambassador of The Republic of North Africa."

Jacobs knew the diplomat had taken up the role less than two months earlier following the thawing in relations between their respective countries, but they had never met in person. The Prime Minister scowled in irritation. "Sorry, Sally. I haven't got time for this right now."

"He's asking about their missing athlete. He claims they found a wheelchair outside the stadium alongside the dead body of one of their security team. The athlete's father is a general in their military and has also apparently disappeared."

"He seems to be better informed than I am," Jacobs snapped. "I'll take it in my office. And make sure David knows what you just told me." He whirled around and strode across the room. When he reached his well-appointed workspace, he closed the door behind him and settled himself at the polished mahogany desk. He took a deep breath and picked up the old-fashioned-looking telephone handset. Despite the antique appearance, the equipment contained state-of-the-art technology for encrypting and decrypting voice calls.

He stabbed a button on the base. "Put me through."

"Right away, sir."

A click followed moments later.

"Good afternoon, Ambassador," Jacobs said. "What can I do for you?"

"Good afternoon to you also, Prime Minister." The man spoke in a mellow baritone with barely any accent. "May I start by offering you my condolences on this terrible attack at the Olympics."

"Thank you, Ambassador. I believe you may have news concerning the atrocity."

"This is true. My security people are telling me they discovered the body of a colleague outside the stadium. He had been shot in the head."

"Ah... I'm afraid I can't provide you with any further information, Ambassador. We have several teams on site, and I assure you they are giving this crime their highest priority."

"I'm sure they are, Prime Minister. More importantly for my country, our top Olympic athlete, Aya Shaladi, and her father, General Hamza Shaladi, are also both missing."

"Yes, I heard they discovered her wheelchair beside the dead body."

"It seems you may have been misinformed, Prime Minister. The wheelchair does not belong to our athlete, but to yours."

"I'm sorry. What do you mean?"

The ambassador paused before replying. "I don't want to give you any more bad news at this difficult time, but I believe the chair belongs to the British competitor, Miss Lessing."

"Are you suggesting that whoever took your people also kidnapped our girl?"

"It is not for me to say. I do not wish to draw conclusions at this early stage, but that is how it appears."

"Thank you for bringing this to my notice, Ambassador. I'll ensure our security services act upon this information right away."

"May I ask, Prime Minister, how an attack like this could be allowed to happen? Surely it is your duty to protect the audience at such events, especially given the number of VIPs in attendance."

"You have my sincerest apologies, Ambassador. Rest assured we will put every effort into tracking the perpetrators down and bringing them to justice."

"It is just a shame you did not apply the same rigour to protecting our athletes and their families."

"Like I said, I can only apologise and promise you we'll do everything in our power to recover your countrymen."

"Thank you, Prime Minister. I will be in touch if I learn anything more. I would be grateful if you could keep me informed of any progress in your own investigation. Good day."

The line clicked before Jacobs could respond. He replaced the phone and blew out his cheeks. Then he rose and marched back to the conference room. His eyes scanned the crowd of people and settled on his chief of staff. The man was still talking on a mobile.

"David, a moment of your time."

Wagner uttered a few words into the handset and pressed a button to end the call. "Yes, Prime Minister."

"I've just held an uncomfortable conversation with the Reponan ambassador. He informed me that not only has someone in their security team been murdered, but also one of their athletes and her father, a general in their military, are unaccounted for."

"Sally told me a few minutes ago. I was just speaking to the senior police officer on site."

"Good. Perhaps you could call him back and make him aware that a British athlete is missing as well: Antimone Lessing."

"How does the ambassador know that?"

"Because, David, her wheelchair was discovered alongside the dead body. What I want to understand is why I'm hearing this information from the Reponans and not from our own people."

Wagner's cheeks flushed. "I'll get on it right away."

"And while you're at it, please track down the rest of Miss Lessing's family and check on their status."

"Of course, Prime Minister. May I ask why?"

A haunted look appeared on Jacobs' face. He stared his chief aide in the eye.

"I have a horrible feeling you may discover they're also missing."

Friday 11th July 2036

Grangemouth Docks

80 minutes after the start of the attack

After what seemed like hours but was probably less than one, the van stopped moving. The sound of doors opening came from the front of the vehicle. Moments later, the rear door swung back, flooding the interior with bright afternoon sunlight.

Antimone squinted against the glare. The figure of General Shaladi stood silhouetted before her. As her eyes accustomed to the brightness, she identified the outline of rows of shipping containers against the background of a fenced-off compound.

"I want everybody out," he said.

Aya Shaladi and the guard rose to their feet. Paul wriggled out of his father's grasp and rushed to Antimone. He flung himself on top of her and wrapped his arms around her neck. She embraced him in a tight hug and whispered soothing words in his ear.

"You." The general pointed at Jason. "Hold the boy."

Jason stood slowly and moved towards the wheelchair. As he reached out for his son, Paul clung to his mother and buried his head in her chest.

"Come on, Paul," Antimone said. "You need to go with your daddy."

Jason lifted the frightened child from his mother's lap despite the squeals of protest. "It's okay. They're just getting Mummy out," he murmured. The boy struggled for a moment before grasping his father in a tight hug.

The North African athlete and the guard lifted Antimone out of her wheelchair and lowered her to the lip at the back of the van. She sat, watching them as they passed the crude contraption down to the waiting general. Then they both jumped the short distance to the tarmac, raised her with a shoulder under each arm and repositioned her on the canvas seat.

Jason clambered down, his son still clinging to him like a limpet.

"This way," Shaladi said, striding ahead. Jason followed behind. Aya grabbed the wheelchair handles as the guard brought up the rear.

"Couldn't you have found something better, so I could at least push myself?" Antimone asked. If there was one aspect of her condition she hated more than anything else, it was when people tried to help by pushing her. She told anybody who would listen it was like being poked in the back or having somebody fiddle with your hair. On this occasion, the lack of hand grips left no alternative.

The North African athlete steered her forwards in silence.

Biting down on her irritation, Antimone took the opportunity to study her surroundings. A high metal fence enclosed the tarmacked area. Behind the barrier, several tall masts rose into the sky, draped in webs of rigging. A variety of different sized shipping containers in a range of pastel shades filled the compound. No other vehicles were visible. The sea air assaulted her senses, clogging her nostrils with the sulphurous scent of decaying seaweed.

They rounded a corner and Antimone's hopes lifted briefly at the sight of two men wearing dark-blue overalls and lounging against a large, lime-coloured unit. She opened her mouth to shout for help, but the way the pair snapped to attention at the general's arrival dashed her brief bout of optimism. They were clearly part of the team. A short conversation took place in Arabic. One of them hauled down a lever, allowing the huge doors to swing open.

"Everybody inside," the general said, pointing.

Jason stood stationary and peered into the gloomy interior. A rectangle of material occupied the furthest corner. On top lay a long, thin object. A rounded cube shape nestled on the opposite side. "You don't seriously expect us to go in there, do you?"

Shaladi withdrew the pistol from his jacket and pointed the barrel at Jason's chest. "That is exactly what I expect, and what you will do."

A muffled sound came from inside. The object moved slightly. With a jolt of recognition, Jason identified the shape as a person, tied up and lying on a mattress.

"Who the hell is that?"

Shaladi grinned. "I think it is somebody you know well. Now move or I start shooting."

Paul whimpered in fright as his father shuffled forwards.

"How long are you planning to keep us in here?" Antimone asked.

"A few hours. When we set sail, you may have more freedom if you behave."

"What about food and drink?"

The general held a brief discussion with one of his associates. The man picked up a plastic bag and emptied the contents onto the tarmac. He tossed two water bottles and a pack of sandwiches inside. They landed on the mattress, narrowly missing the bound figure.

"We'll need a toilet."

Shaladi gestured towards the cube shape. "Use that."

His daughter pushed the wheelchair forwards three paces and released the handles.

"Do not bother calling for help," the general said. "My men will be outside. If they hear any noise, they will tie you up and gag you like her. They start loading the containers on the ship in two hours. When that happens, I suggest you sit on the floor." He gestured to the man standing beside him.

The huge door started to move.

"Wait!" Antimone called. "My son is afraid of the dark. Can we at least have a torch?"

Shaladi talked briefly to his nearest subordinate. The man withdrew a cylindrical object from a pocket in his overalls and handed it over. The general threw it towards Antimone. She caught it and tested the switch, sending a beam of light carving through the gloom. "I am not a monster. I suggest you use it only when necessary. The battery will not last for ever."

The door moved again and slammed shut with a metallic clang, plunging the interior into inky blackness. Paul clung more tightly to his father. The tang of the chemicals from the toilet hung in the air, overpowering the smell of the sea. The stench of urine overlaid the mix.

"What do we do now?" Antimone asked, clicking on the torch and directing the beam towards Jason and their son.

Jason shielded his eyes. "Let's find out who else is in here with us for a start. If you hold Paul, I'll take a look." He carried the child to Antimone and lowered the boy into his mother's arms. "You cuddle Mummy," he said.

The three-year-old clambered onto her lap and buried his face in the gap between her shoulder and neck. In the meantime, Jason directed the beam towards the bound figure and inched forwards. As he drew nearer, the overpowering stink of urine became stronger, now mingling with a damp, musty smell from the mattress. Ropes secured the person's hands and feet, and a cloth tied behind the head obscured the captive's mouth.

"Who is it?" Antimone whispered.

A pair of eyes blinked in the circle of brightness.

Jason took a step back as recognition dawned. "You!"

Friday 11th July 2036

Grangemouth Docks

85 minutes after the start of the attack

Rosalind Baxter blinked in the bright light filtering into the container from outside. After her abortive attempt to escape several hours earlier, the men had left her tied up. She tried to move her head to identify the newcomers, but her bonds restricted her ability to shift position. Judging by the voices, there were at least three of them, including a young child. She struggled to pick up the exchange taking place between her captors and the new prisoners. The echoes from the metallic walls and the harsh sound of her breathing made it hard to make out the words.

The door clanged shut, once more plunging the interior into darkness. A cone of light probed the corners and settled on her face. She screwed her eyes closed and let out a groan of protest. One of the group broke away from the others and approached. The dazzling point of brightness bounced about as the figure drew nearer.

"Who is it?" came a female voice from the far side.

A sharp intake of breath. "You!"

Rosalind attempted to identify the speaker. Clearly, the person recognised her. The beam moved down her body.

"It's my mother," said the man standing over her. A stunned silence greeted his statement.

Rosalind's mind raced. The other two had to be the wheelchair girl and their child. Her heart sank. She tried to speak through the gag, but the only sound to emerge was a muffled croak.

Jason knelt on the mattress. His fingers worked on the knot behind her head. After a few seconds, the ends parted, and she spat the damp material from her mouth.

"Thanks," Rosalind rasped.

"What the hell are you doing here?" Jason asked.

"I could ask you the same thing. Obviously, I'm not here because I want to be. Those bastards kidnapped me from my home and kept me in this container. It must have been two or three days ago they took me. I assume we're at the docks. Could you untie my hands and feet too?"

"Leave her as she is for the moment," came Antimone's voice from behind Jason.

"It seems we're all in the same boat," Rosalind said, "quite literally, if we don't get out of here soon."

"And how do you propose we escape?" Antimone asked.

"I'm not sure, but whatever we do, it would be a lot easier without being trussed up like this. How did they capture you?"

"They set off bombs at the Olympic wheelchair final and grabbed us in the confusion."

"They must want you really badly to go to all that trouble," Rosalind said.

"Somehow they discovered I survived childbirth. From what they've told us, this is all about finding a cure for the virus you created."

Rosalind huffed. "I didn't create it. It evolved."

"Yeah, but it *evolved* from work at your company where you were performing recklessly dangerous research. Let alone the fact you infected Jason's biological mother, held her captive until she died and framed his father for her murder."

"She released the virus, not me. Anyway, that's all ancient history. We need to find a way out of here. Are you going to untie me?"

Antimone's voice increased in volume. "Give me one good reason why we should lift a finger to help you. The last time we met, you put us inside a medical incinerator and threatened to press the button if they didn't agree to your demands."

"I would never have done it, but I had to make them believe I would."

"What about the murder of Nigel Perrin? You killed your own partner."

"He lacked the bottle to stand up to them. He crumbled at the first threat. If he had just kept his mouth shut, he'd still be alive."

"And what about me? Did you ever plan to let me go?"

In the reflection of the torchlight, Rosalind looked away.

"I thought not. As far as I'm concerned, you can stay there and rot."

Jason shuffled sideways. "We need all the help we can get at the moment." He picked at the knots until the blue nylon cord binding his adoptive mother's wrists loosened its grip.

"Thanks," Rosalind said, flexing her fingers to restore the circulation. "Can you sort out my feet? I still can't feel anything in my hands."

Antimone huffed in disgust as Jason focused his attention on the rope around her legs.

Moments later, Rosalind sighed with relief, rubbing at the chafed skin on her ankles.

Antimone glared at Jason in the torchlight. "I don't understand why you'd want to help the woman who murdered your biological mother and damned nearly killed us as well."

"And I have no idea what he sees in you either," Rosalind snapped.

Despite being too young to follow the argument, Paul sensed the animosity between the three adults and let out a low wail. Antimone patted his back and drew him closer.

"Let's all try to stay calm. What are we dealing with?" Jason asked.

"The guy in charge—General something-or-other—told me I would be working for them to develop a new treatment," Rosalind replied, "so they must be aware I led the team."

"How much have our abductors found out about what really happened?"

"Anybody who has seen the news or can use a computer could learn about her work," Antimone said, "but they also know I was the first to survive childbirth, and that certainly isn't public knowledge."

"Why *did* you keep that quiet?" Rosalind asked.

"We didn't want all the media attention. Our lives wouldn't have been our own. And, of course, lunatics like this lot would have tried to kidnap us—oh, wait a minute, they just did."

"Well, I'd recommend we don't mention that part," Jason said. "Let's not tell them anything they don't already know. Now, has anybody got any ideas about how to get out of here?"

"We could rush them when they open the door," Antimone replied. A strong sense of déjà vu settled over her as she recalled the last occasion she had been trapped in a metal room. Back then, Rosalind Baxter had been the one making the threats.

"They'll be expecting us to try something," Jason said, "and they're armed. I think we should bide our time and attempt to catch them unawares."

Rosalind folded her arms across her chest and shivered. "Once we get to wherever they plan on taking us—North Africa from what I remember them saying—escape will be that much harder. We should take our chances now."

"Surely it's been long enough since they kidnapped us for the authorities to work out we're missing. They're bound to conduct a search."

"The more time goes by, the more difficult it will be to track us down," Antimone said. "If they haven't already located us, I wouldn't hold out much hope for a rescue. It pains me to agree with that psycho, but I think she's right. We can't rely on anybody else for help."

Jason turned away and directed the torch beam at the walls. "I'm going to see if I can find another way out."

"You're wasting your time," Rosalind said. "There's one door, and it can only be opened from the outside."

Jason ignored her statement and shuffled down the long side, running his hand over the cold metal. Antimone tracked the bobbing light as he completed a circuit. He returned to his starting point in silence.

"Well?" Rosalind asked.

Jason's eyes glinted in the torchlight. "Like you said, there's no way out and nothing we can use as an improvised weapon. We can't do anything that puts Paul at risk."

"So, what do you suggest?"

"Unfortunately, I reckon we have only one option. We wait to see what happens next."

Friday 11th July 2036

10 Downing Street, London

2 hours after the start of the attack

Iris Stanley and Charles Moreland, the heads of MI5 and MI6 respectively, sat opposite Andrew Jacobs. David Wagner, his chief of staff, occupied a chair to the side of his desk.

"What can you tell me?" the Prime Minister asked.

Stanley readjusted her glasses. "I assume we're talking about the bombing and not the…" She cast a glance towards Wagner. "… matter we discussed a few days ago. Although it's possible they might be related."

"Yes. What have you learned?"

"We know the explosives were installed in micro drones, disguised to look like the flying cameras used by the media. During the race, there were hundreds of the genuine item hovering around the stadium. They're programmed to land in a pre-defined spot if they lose contact with the controller or develop a fault. That's why nobody paid any attention to the fakes when they landed. Five of them exploded. We've recovered a small amount of debris, but so far there's not enough to determine a manufacturer or point of origin."

"Have you come up with a motive?"

The head of MI5 narrowed her eyes. "If one of those bombs had detonated above the crowd, hundreds would've died. They all went off in relatively unpopulated areas of the stadium. From that, we can infer the intention was not to cause damage or devastation. The payload also seemed designed to create a lot of smoke. Our best guess at the moment is that it was all a distraction."

"Just so they could abduct people?" Jacobs asked. "I spoke to the Reponan ambassador a few hours ago, so I know about their athlete and the general. I take it the Lessing girl is still unaccounted for."

"Yes. They're all missing. Her boyfriend and their child, who were both at the stadium, have also disappeared. Mr Wagner requested that we look into the Baxter woman. It seems she hasn't been home for several days. It's all looking like far too much of a coincidence. Five of the people involved in the events surrounding the development of the cure for the virus seem to have vanished off the face of the earth."

"I take it you haven't found Max Perrin either?"

"He crossed the Channel to Calais as a foot passenger three months ago," Moreland said. "Since that time, there've been no sightings."

"So, he's probably still in France?"

"Not necessarily. From there, he could travel pretty much wherever he wanted in mainland Europe without having to show identification. On top of that, many of their borders are porous. He could be anywhere in the world by now."

"We've tried to trace his phone," Stanley said. "The number was last used over a year ago."

"What about his mother?"

"We talked to her," Stanley replied, "but she hasn't heard a thing from him in over two years. From what I understand, there was a bit of a falling out between the pair of them."

"Any idea what that was about?"

"She wasn't exactly talkative, but it appears they had an argument about her husband's will. From what we've determined, it seems the boy received nothing. Apparently, she told him he wouldn't get a penny until he demonstrated he would use the money responsibly."

"Sounds fair enough to me." The Prime Minister rested his elbows on the polished mahogany and leant forwards. "Back to the missing people. If, as looks increasingly likely, somebody abducted them, can't we track vehicles leaving the stadium?"

"In theory, yes," the female head of MI5 replied. "What makes it a lot harder is that they took out the local electricity substation. That loss of power disabled most of the cameras in the surrounding area. As you might expect, most of the crowd were keen to get away as quickly as possible in case there were more blasts. We're processing the satellite imagery, but tracing the movements of everybody who was present will take a long time."

"So," Jacobs said, "a whole load of people associated with curing the virus have disappeared. The big question is how it ties into the Reponans. Assuming one group is behind everything, why grab the general and their athlete too?"

"All I can say at this stage, Prime Minister, is that we're still looking for answers," Stanley replied.

"What about your guys, Charles? Have they turned up anything that might indicate who's responsible?"

"Sorry, Andrew," Moreland said. "As I'm sure you're aware with any terrorist event of this magnitude, there are always groups claiming responsibility. We have to investigate all claims. So far, it seems none of them possess the capability to pull off an operation on this scale. As you would expect, several countries are revelling in our misfortune, but that doesn't necessarily make them suspects."

"Why do *you* think they were taken?"

"Given the mix of abductees, if I had to guess, I'd say somebody was trying to develop a treatment of their own," Moreland replied.

"Agreed," Stanley added. "It's the only logical conclusion."

"Well, if that's the case," Jacobs said, "we should direct our attention towards countries who don't have access to the drugs."

The head of MI6 tugged at his earlobe. "If it wasn't for the abduction of their people and the murder of their man, The Republic of North Africa would be a prime suspect. What if that was just a ploy to make us think they were the victims in all this?"

The idea bounced around the room in silence as the four people tested the suggestion in their heads.

Finally, the Prime Minister stood. "It's the most likely explanation I've heard today. I suggest you focus your attention on that angle to start with. Thanks for your time."

The two secret service leaders and his chief of staff also rose to their feet.

"I'll get on it straight away," Moreland said.

"Likewise," Stanley murmured.

Saturday 12th July 2036

North Sea, thirty miles off Newcastle
14 hours after the start of the attack

Jason sat with his arms wrapped around the chemical toilet. The other three lay on the stinking mattress, although the dark interior of their prison meant he couldn't see them. The gentle pitch and roll of the ship sent another wave of nausea sweeping through his body. His mouth filled with saliva, and he spat into the plastic bowl. The muscles in his abdomen ached from the repeated attempts to throw up, but he had long since evacuated the contents of his stomach.

A dull rumble reverberated through the metal floor. The sound had started in the early hours of the morning, shortly after loading finished. The only notice they had received of the impending activity was the clunk of the electromagnets as they landed on the metallic roof. At the first sounds, Jason turned on the torch, expecting somebody to open the door and explain what was happening.

Instead, the box in which they were imprisoned lurched upwards and swayed as a crane transferred them from the storage area and onto the cargo ship. The sudden movement caught them all unawares. Antimone's wheelchair careened from one side of the container to the other. It was only by sheer chance that she passed close enough to Jason to allow him to lunge forwards and prevent her from smashing into the wall. Fortunately, Paul was asleep on the mattress and remained unconscious until the jarring impact on the ship's deck plates woke him.

With nowhere comfortable to sit, the group were forced to share the filthy bedding. Jason had gagged at the stench of mildew and worse, but gradually, his senses adapted and filtered the foul smells from his consciousness. Three hours of restless sleep followed until the rolling motion of the waves induced the first bout of vomiting. He had spent the time since then clutching the plastic sides of the toilet.

The muffled sound of male voices distracted Jason from his misery. A metallic clang echoed through the container. Moments later, the huge door cracked open, allowing the light from an overcast sky to flood the interior, accompanied by a chill sea breeze. He glanced at the thin band of smart plastic wrapped around his wrist: seven-thirty.

Two men in blue overalls stood silhouetted in the opening. One carried a pistol, the other held a cloth rucksack. They stepped inside. The man holding the pack dropped it with a dull thud.

"Good morning," the armed man said, his voice carrying a strong Mediterranean accent. He studied Jason's position on the floor. "I hope you are not too sick." His colleague laughed. The first man frowned, then continued. "I bring you food and drink. We leave the door open for a few hours. Do not try to escape. We are a long way from land. It is too far to swim. Also, the water is cold. If you fall overboard, we cannot stop for ten miles, and you will drown."

"Where are we?" Jason asked.

"You do not need to know."

"How much longer is this journey going to take?"

"A few days."

"Can we have some more blankets? It's chilly in here."

The man pondered the question for a moment before replying. "I will ask the general. Now, you may move about outside, but do not leave this deck. If we tell you to get inside, you do this immediately. If not, you will be punished."

"What about a change of clothes? If we're going to be here for a while, we'll need something clean to wear."

"Maybe I will send my friend to the shops, yes? But it is a long swim." His colleague mimed the action of swimming.

"Is there somewhere we can wash?"

The armed man scowled. "You ask too many questions. Remember what I said."

"Right," Jason muttered.

"What's going on?" came a voice from behind him.

Jason turned to see Antimone sitting up on the mattress. "These two…" He gestured towards where the men had been standing, but they had already left. "Anyway, they said we could go out on deck. They brought some food and water."

"Can you help me into the wheelchair?"

Jason stood but quickly crouched again as a wave of dizziness swept over him. He rose again, more slowly this time, and staggered the short distance on unsteady legs. After unfolding the mechanism, he bent down, lifted Antimone and placed her on the canvas seat.

"Thanks," she murmured. "You're looking a bit pale."

"Just a bout of sea sickness. I spent half the night hugging the toilet. Did you sleep okay?"

"As well as could be expected in the circumstances."

"Should we get Paul up?"

"No," Antimone replied. "Let him rest. Did they say where we were?"

"They wouldn't tell me, but I guess we're somewhere in the North Sea."

A groan came from the mattress. Rosalind stared at the young couple with bleary eyes. Even in the dim light penetrating to the rear of the container, Jason could clearly pick out the red and purple tinge of the chafed skin around her wrists. Sensing the direction of his gaze, she rubbed self-consciously at the damaged area.

"Did I just hear you say we're allowed outside?" she asked.

"Yeah, there's also food in the bag," Jason replied.

"I'm not feeling particularly hungry."

"Join the club."

Rosalind forced herself upright and hobbled towards the open door. When she reached the opening, she stopped and gazed upwards. Jason grabbed the wheelchair handles and propelled Antimone forwards. As he drew alongside his mother, he also halted, staring in awe at the scene greeting his eyes.

Four huge sails rose to a height of fifty metres above the deck, the aerofoil shapes all angled in the same direction. The base of the masts rotated in synchrony, continuously adjusting their angle in relation to the ship to gain maximum advantage from the light wind. Two rows of containers, all the same size as the one they had spent the night in, extended along the length of the vessel.

"Wow," Jason murmured.

A child's cry came from inside the container. "You better get him," Antimone said.

Jason released the handles and turned to see Paul rubbing the sleep from his eyes. The three-year-old spotted the approach of his father and held out his arms. "Daddy."

As Jason crouched down to pick up his son, a scream rose from behind him. He whirled around. Antimone's wheelchair was moving forwards down the slope as the hull heeled over in a gust of wind. Antimone screamed again.

"Grab her," Jason yelled. Rosalind stood rooted to the spot. He abandoned Paul and sprinted after the accelerating chair. The gap was closing, but he would never make it in time. Antimone reached down in a vain attempt to slow the wheels. The black rubber slipped through her hand, stinging her palms. Ten metres to the edge and the plunge to the ocean below.

"No!" Jason howled.

Antimone heaved her body sideways. The wheelchair balanced on one wheel for a moment, then toppled over. She hit the metal plating with a resounding crash but continued to slide forwards.

Human and machine skidded across the damp deck towards the drop.

Saturday 12th July 2036

North Sea, thirty miles off Newcastle
14 hours after the start of the attack

The wheelchair tyre slammed into the raised rim at the edge of the deck, coming to an abrupt halt. Antimone's body continued its forward momentum. She slithered to a stop with her legs dangling over the side.

Jason raced up to her and dropped to all fours. He reached out an arm and hauled her back towards him. Both lay on the metal plating, inhaling the sea air through heaving lungs.

"I'm sorry," Jason murmured between breaths.

"Don't worry. It was an accident." Antimone's gaze lifted and focused on the approaching figure of Rosalind Baxter.

"I didn't really see what happened," Jason said. "I was looking after Paul when I heard you scream. It was my fault; I forgot to apply the brake."

Antimone jabbed a finger in Rosalind's direction. "She was standing right next to me. She could have grabbed the handles."

"Are you all right?"

Jason and Antimone raised their heads simultaneously. Rosalind stepped closer, her arms wrapped across her chest.

"Yes, but no thanks to you," Antimone replied.

Rosalind's brows drew together in a scowl. "It all happened so quickly."

"You didn't try to help."

"I can't run. I hurt my knee trying to escape. There was nothing I could do."

"But you wouldn't have shed a tear if I'd fallen in the ocean and drowned?"

"I never said that."

"You probably think I hate you," Antimone said, "but I don't; I pity you. You're so wrapped up in yourself, you don't care about anybody else. Your life must be so shallow. Yes, you may have loads of money, but does it make you happy? Was it worth it? Don't you feel any regret for what you did?"

Rosalind's face drained of colour apart from the two vivid, red blotches in the centre of her cheeks. "My only regret is letting you live after we worked out why you survived. You think you're special because you have this disability and race around a track in a wheelchair. What a pathetic waste of time. It's a shame the car that fractured your spine didn't finish the job."

"Well, at least we all know your true thoughts now. I told you we should have left her tied up. This psycho won't lift a finger to help either of us. Her only interest is saving her own skin."

The two women glared at each other. Jason's gaze alternated between the pair.

"Are you going to put me back in that death-trap," Antimone snapped, "or do I have to drag myself across the deck?"

"Oh, right. Sorry." Jason righted the wheelchair, taking great care to apply the brake and test its operation before returning his attention to Antimone. He knelt, placed his arms beneath her body and deposited her on the canvas seat.

"Thanks," she muttered, her eyes avoiding his mother.

Jason released the braking mechanism with his foot and pushed the wheelchair back towards their container. Antimone called out Paul's name. The brightness of the morning made it difficult to see inside the metal box, but as they drew nearer, it became clear the interior was deserted.

"Paul, are you there?" Antimone yelled. The only response was the ever-present rumble of the engines and the clink of the rigging. "Oh God, where is he? Please find him."

Jason locked the wheelchair brake in position and jogged along the length of the ship, calling their son's name.

A wave of icy terror wormed through Antimone's stomach. "Let him be okay," she whispered, repeating the words in a mantra. The faint sound of Jason's voice carried towards her on the wind. A deep sense of guilt settled over her. If she hadn't started the slanging match with the Baxter woman, they might have arrived back before Paul wandered off.

Antimone leant forwards in the chair, straining her eyes to pick out any sign of her missing son among the forest of containers piled across the deck.

"Have you lost something?" a voice asked from behind her. Antimone twisted her head. She drew a sharp intake of breath.

Rosalind stood five metres away, grasping Paul's tiny hand in her own. She offered a look of barely concealed hostility. "You really should take better care of your child. A ship can be a dangerous place, especially for small children."

"Come here, Paul," Antimone said in a strangled voice, holding out her arms.

Her son flashed a cheeky grin and shook his head.

"Let go and walk over to me," she said, forcing her tone to remain light-hearted. The muscles in her forearm contracted as she clasped the armrest to prevent her fingers from shaking.

Paul sensed the unease in his mother. He glanced up at the woman. She continued to stare straight ahead. He tried to tug his hand free, but her grip tightened.

Rosalind concentrated her gaze on Antimone's face. "You can thank me if you want."

"Thanks," Antimone said, her voice barely more than a whisper.

"I'm sorry, I didn't quite get that."

Antimone spoke louder. "I said thank you. Now, please let my son go."

"You're welcome."

Rosalind released Paul's hand, then wiped her palm on her trousers. He rushed to his mother. "Mummy," he said, clambering onto her lap.

Antimone enveloped Paul in a tight hug. She closed her eyes and inhaled the smell of his hair. After a while, he squirmed, trying to free himself from his mother's embrace.

"Thank God," said a breathless Jason as he jogged into view around the corner of the container. He swept his son up in his arms and planted a kiss on his cheek. "What happened?"

Nobody spoke until Rosalind broke the silence. "I discovered my grandson wandering about by himself, so I thought I better return him to his parents."

Jason's stare switched from one woman to the other as he struggled to navigate through the undercurrent of tension. "Um… right. Thanks."

"I'm going to stretch my legs now."

When she had moved out of sight, Jason placed Paul on the ground and rested a hand on Antimone's shoulder. She flinched at his touch.

"What was that all about?" he asked.

"I'll tell you later," she replied in a subdued voice. "Shall we see what they've left us to eat?"

"I can't say I'm feeling particularly hungry," Jason said, "but we do need to get some food inside Paul." He crouched to talk to his son. "Why don't you sit on Mummy's knee while I push you along?"

Paul needed no second invitation.

Unseen by the family of three, a figure on the bridge studied them through powerful binoculars as they covered the short distance back to the container.

Saturday 12th July 2036

North Sea, thirty-two miles off Newcastle
15 hours after the start of the attack

Jason picked the filling from the sandwich, removed the crust and handed a slice of buttered bread to his son. "Do you want this?" He lifted the sliver of meat between his fingers and offered it to Antimone.

"What?" she said. "Sorry, I was miles away."

"I asked if you wanted to eat this, although I'm not sure I could name the animal which it came from."

Antimone grimaced. "No, thanks."

Jason strolled to the entrance of the container and tossed the brown triangle outside. He turned back to her. "How about the crust?" When she declined, he popped the fragments in his mouth. As he ate, Antimone stared at the wall.

"Are you going to tell me what happened?" he asked.

"She threatened our son."

Jason frowned in confusion. "I thought she was the one who found him."

The scowl on Antimone's face deepened. "She did, but she wouldn't let go of his hand until I thanked her."

"Okay."

"She said that a ship can be a dangerous place for children."

"Well, she's right."

"She used it as a threat," Antimone yelled. She took a shaky breath and held it for a moment. When she spoke again, her voice trembled with tension. "Don't you see. She hates me. Three years ago, I stood up to her and won."

"I think you mean *we* stood up to her."

"Yes, of course. I wasn't having a go at you. She could've stopped my wheelchair from running away, but she didn't. She just watched. If we need her help to escape, we're in big trouble. And I don't trust her around Paul. She might try to use him to get back at me."

"I'm sure even somebody like her wouldn't deliberately hurt a child."

Antimone lowered her head and let out a sob. "I want to go home. I haven't got the strength for this."

Jason reached out and ran a finger down her cheek. "You're the strongest person I know. We'll come up with something. I won't allow anything to happen to you or Paul."

"You might not be able to protect us this time."

Jason leant forwards and kissed Antimone gently on the lips. She placed a hand behind his head and drew him closer.

A voice from the corner brought an abrupt end to the moment of intimacy. "I've finished my sammich. My hands are dirty."

Jason flashed a wry grin at Antimone. "We'll have to finish that another time." He pulled a handkerchief from his pocket. "Come here then, buddy. Let's get you cleaned up." Paul scrambled to his feet and approached his father with both arms extended, palms facing outwards.

Jason wiped the grease off his son's fingers. "Are you still hungry?"

Paul nodded.

Jason rummaged in the plastic bag. "There's an apple in here. Do you want that?"

"I don't like the skin."

"We don't have a knife. If I bite off the outside, will you eat the middle?"

Paul gave the question a moment's thought, then said, "Yes."

Jason worked his way around the circumference, removing the outer layer with his teeth. When he had finished, he handed what remained to Paul, who accepted it with both hands. For the next few minutes, he munched down to the core under the amused gaze of his parents.

After another wiping session, Jason suggested they go for a walk on deck. Paul asked whether he could ride on the wheelchair and scrambled onto his mother's lap when she agreed. Jason removed the brake and pushed the chair across the metallic floor of the container.

As they emerged from the shadowy interior, General Shaladi stepped into view, beaming at them. "Good morning." He ruffled Paul's hair. "How are you, young man?"

"Please don't touch my son," Antimone said, pushing the general's hand away.

The cheery look vanished abruptly from the man's face and his eyes narrowed. "That is not very friendly."

Antimone glowered at the general. "You kidnap my family, hold us prisoner in a metal box, and then you want us to be friends? You've got some funny ideas about what friendship means."

Shaladi shrugged. "These are my orders. I must do what my superiors ask. I do not wish to make your confinement any more unpleasant than necessary. Now, my men told me you nearly fell into the sea."

Antimone and Jason stared back in silence.

"A ship can be a dangerous place," Shaladi continued.

"Have you been talking to Mrs Baxter?" Antimone asked, her voice shaking with fury. "That's exactly what she said. Are you threatening us as well?"

The general raised both hands. "I have not talked to her today, and I am not making threats. I am only warning you of the dangers. We do not want to go to all the trouble of capturing you and then watch you fall over the side."

"But you have been spying on us?" Antimone said.

"Yes," Shaladi replied. "My men have been observing you. That is their job."

"It's a shame they didn't intervene and help me."

"You are right. In future, they will stay closer."

"I'd feel a whole lot safer if I had proper control over this wheelchair," Antimone said.

"I will see if it is possible to find something more suitable when we reach our destination, but for now, regretfully, I cannot do anything. However, I can improve your accommodation."

"What does that mean? Are you going to move us to a bigger metal box?" Jason asked, his voice dripping with sarcasm.

"No. I have talked to the captain, and he says he has some empty crew cabins. They are small—much smaller than the container—but more comfortable, I think. You would have a proper bed and a mattress each. Oh, and windows but unfortunately, there is no toilet inside the room. That is in the corridor. Also, my men can watch over you more easily."

"Do we have to share with Mrs Baxter?" Antimone asked.

The general's eyes crinkled in amusement. "You really dislike this woman, do you not? But no, that will not be necessary."

"In that case, we would like to accept your offer," Antimone said.

"Good. Please follow me."

The general led the way along the deck. Jason pushed the wheelchair, Paul bouncing with excitement on his mother's lap. As they walked, the low sun reflected from an object on the top floor of the rounded structure rising from the prow of the ship.

Jason shielded his eyes with his hand and stared upwards. The figure at the window continued to study them for a moment, then lowered the binoculars and turned away.

Sunday 13th July 2036

10 Downing Street, London

2 days after the attack at the Olympics

Andrew Jacobs moved behind the large mahogany desk and sank into the leather chair. "Please sit," he said, shrugging off his jacket and loosening his tie. "Sorry to have kept you waiting."

The two secret service heads who had risen as the Prime Minister entered his office followed his lead and took their seats.

"No problem," Iris Stanley replied, polishing her glasses. Charles Moreland clasped his hands in front of his stomach.

"David Wagner tells me you've made some progress in the search for our missing people," Jacobs continued. "I could do with some good news."

"It's been a mammoth job," Stanley, the head of MI5 said. "We've been working around the clock on this. As you can imagine, tracking the movements of over thirty thousand individuals was quite a task. Your suggestion to concentrate on the Reponan angle made it significantly easier.

"Once we assumed this was a kidnapping with an ultimate destination of North Africa, it narrowed down the search somewhat. The first question to answer was how the kidnappers proposed to transfer the targets over that distance. Security at our airports is so tight, they couldn't have smuggled them through that way. The only other method was to transport them by sea.

"Luckily, the skies were clear on the afternoon of the wheelchair final, so we had good satellite coverage. The resolution isn't sufficient to identify a person, but we can track traffic movements. When we searched for vehicles travelling from the stadium to a port, we came up with a handful of potential leads. After further investigation, we narrowed the results down to just one; a black van began its journey shortly after the blasts from the spot where we discovered the dead man. It led us to Grangemouth. Other than a couple of small yachts, a single vessel, a container ship, set out on the night following the attack.

"That makes sense," Jacobs said. "Grangemouth is less than an hour from Glasgow, isn't it?"

"That's right. It's a forty- or fifty-minute journey by road."

"What do we know about their destination?" the Prime Minister asked.

"The vessel is registered in Tunisia and, according to records, is heading for the port of Tunis," Moreland replied.

Jacobs leant forwards in his chair. "That fits in with your theory. Where are they now?"

"The satellite puts them roughly one hundred and fifty miles north of Spain," Stanley replied. "They're currently making way at about thirty-five knots using a combination of engines and sails. They must be working the turbines hard to achieve that speed, even with wind assistance. It's costing them a lot given the current price of fuel, so it seems they want to reach their destination in a hurry. That said, the Reponans possess some of the largest remaining oil reserves in the world, so if they are behind this, they can afford it."

"How long until they arrive?"

"If they maintain their present speed, another two or three days."

"And you say they're heading for Tunis. How far is it from there to The Republic of North Africa?"

"The two countries adjoin each other. Tunis is about two hundred and fifty miles north west of Repona. If they travel by road, it'll take them around ten hours to reach the border. We don't yet know what they plan to do with the abductees after that."

"Do we have any warships in the region?" the Prime Minister asked.

"They'll have to pass through the Straits of Gibraltar to get to North Africa. We've got a cruiser and a pair of fast patrol boats that could intercept them."

"How can we be sure our people haven't already disembarked?"

"We can't be absolutely certain," Moreland replied, "but the satellites have shown no other vessels coming close enough to offload passengers. If the analysis is correct—and I believe it is—there's a good chance they're still aboard."

"Great work," Jacobs said. "I take it you haven't mentioned to your teams any of the… ah… more sensitive details of this case?"

The two secret service leaders on the opposite side of the desk exchanged a glance. Stanley broke the silence. "Well, Prime Minister, we employ a lot of very bright individuals. Obviously, in circumstances like these, one of the initial steps is to identify the motives of the perpetrators. It's common knowledge the girl has a child, even if very few are aware she was the first to survive. It's also no secret that the Reponans are suffering under the restrictions of the trade embargo. You don't need to be a genius to work out it has something to do with this damned virus."

"But you haven't informed them of the Baxter woman's involvement?"

Stanley pinched the bridge of her nose. "You tasked us with tracking her down, so quite a few of the team know she's missing."

"For heaven's sake, make sure they don't learn about the part she played in the initial outbreak."

"Of course not, Prime Minister," Stanley replied.

"So, what are you proposing to do, Andrew?" Moreland asked.

Jacobs placed his elbows on the desk and clasped his hands together. "Step one is to summon the Reponan ambassador for a little chat. He certainly has some explaining to do. It all rather depends on his reaction. Let's see what he has to say. If he chooses not to cooperate, we'll intercept the ship and take them back by force. As for what we do after that, I don't really want to consider military action against the North Africans after the long civil war, but they need to be taught a lesson. Do we have any assets in the country?"

Moreland's eyes narrowed. "This information mustn't go any further, Andrew, but we've infiltrated the mid-levels of their government. Unfortunately, our feelers don't reach to the top. If they did, we'd probably have received prior notice of their intentions."

"The public will want to know who was responsible for the attack," Stanley said, adjusting the frame of her glasses. "The press will demand we punish the perpetrators. Given the high-profile nature of the abduction, it's likely many of the details will come out however much you may try to hush them up."

Andrew Jacobs rose to his feet. "We can worry about the news media later. Let's focus on getting our people back first."

Sunday 13th July 2036

Bay of Biscay, twenty miles west of Spain
2 days after the attack at the Olympics

Jason leant over the edge of the top bunk and looked down at Antimone. "This is an improvement on sharing a stinking mattress between the four of us."

Antimone glanced sideways at Paul and adjusted the sheet covering his small body. After the initial excitement of their new accommodation, he had crashed out and now lay asleep beside her on the narrow bed. "Keep your voice down. We don't want to wake him. Anyway, why are you so cheerful? We're still prisoners."

"We'll get out of this. I have a good feeling."

"Hmm. I'm not so sure. How do you propose we escape?"

"Ah, well, that's the problem isn't it? We have a guard in the corridor, and here we are, stuck in the middle of the sea with no land for miles."

"What about the lifeboats?"

Jason rubbed the two-day stubble on his cheek. "I've no idea how we'd go about launching one. Anyway, we might be swapping the frying pan for the fire. The ocean is a big place. We could be adrift for days. And that's always assuming we can lower one to the water without being detected."

"Surely they have emergency radios?"

"Good point. Even if we can't launch a lifeboat, we should be able to use its radio to call for help."

Antimone lifted her upper body with her elbows. "It's not the worst idea I've heard today. How would we get onboard one?"

"They must have them, but I don't remember seeing any."

"Me neither."

Jason swung his legs over the side and lowered himself to the floor. The thrumming of the deck plates seemed more pronounced in this part of the vessel. He moved to the porthole and peered through the circular window. The midday sun sparkled on the waves like thousands of diamonds.

"What can you see?" Antimone asked.

Jason shifted his head to gain a better view, squinting against the brightness. "Nothing that looks like a lifeboat."

"They must have at least one out there somewhere."

He shielded his eyes. "Hang on, there are a couple of cylinders close to the side. There's writing on them, but they're too far away to make out what it says."

"Those are probably what you're looking for. I expect you need to pull a cord or something to inflate them."

Jason turned back. "That's why they weren't overly bothered about us wandering around on deck. We wouldn't have been able to access the radio without inflating one, and no doubt they would have spotted that."

"Why does it have to be the lifeboat radio?" Antimone asked. "The main ship's radio would do just as well."

"That may be harder to reach. I can't imagine they'd be careless enough to let us walk up and start talking."

"It wouldn't hurt to find out where it is though."

Jason stared at the door. "It'll be on the bridge. That's above us. Why don't I try to get up there now?"

"There's a man in the corridor for starters."

"I'll say I need to go to the toilet. While I'm in there, you create a distraction, and I'll sneak upstairs."

"How am I going to do that?"

"You call out. When he comes in, you tell him you fell off the bunk."

Antimone glanced at the sleeping three-year-old lying beside her. "I don't want to wake Paul."

"If we don't get out of here, there will be far more to worry about than our child losing sleep."

"I suppose you're right. Can you help me down?"

Jason lifted Antimone off the thin mattress and lowered her to the metal floor. "Give it a minute or two then start banging on the door. When I hear you, I'll slip out and make my way upstairs. Try to keep the guard busy for as long as possible."

"Fine. Let's do this."

Jason pulled down on the handle and stuck his head into the corridor. A man wearing a black uniform sat on a chair, his chin resting on his chest. He jerked upright at the unexpected intrusion.

"I need to go to the toilet," Jason said.

The man gestured impatiently towards a sign two doors down from his position. "There."

Jason stepped outside the cabin and hugged the wall to get past the seated guard. As he pushed inside the small room, the overpowering floral scent of an air freshener assaulted his nostrils. In some ways it was worse than the smell it was trying to hide. He stood with his back to the metal door. The seconds extended into a minute. Breathing through his mouth, he waited impatiently for his cue. After what seemed like a lifetime, the sound of banging accompanied by the shouts of a raised female voice echoed down the corridor.

Jason pulled the handle and stuck his head in the gap between door and frame. Unseen by the guard, he watched as the man hauled himself to his feet and ambled towards the commotion. He experienced a stab of guilt at the noise of his son's crying.

Jason slipped out and jogged to the door marked with a staircase sign. He pushed through and climbed the steps, placing each foot carefully to avoid making any sound. After two flights, he arrived at a spot, which matched his starting point in every detail. Feeling like a character in an Escher print, he encountered another identical floor before reaching the top.

Here, the door contained a rectangular window. Jason crept forwards and peered through the glass. The bridge afforded a two-seventy degree view out over the sea, covering the bow and both sides of the vessel. Multiple computer screens sat atop cabinets arrayed in a semicircle around a black leather chair. Switches and indicators filled every available surface.

A man with wiry grey hair and wearing a short-sleeved white shirt occupied the captain's seat. A second figure, dressed in a brightly coloured T-shirt and khaki chino shorts, stood to his left, a pair of binoculars hanging from a strap around his neck. The close-cropped blond hair protruding from beneath the baseball cap suggested somebody much younger than his companion.

Jason's eyes scanned the console as he attempted to identify the radio among the array of instruments. He wasn't sure what he was looking for, but he assumed there had to be a microphone. Finally, he spotted what looked like an old-fashioned telephone handset attached to the front of one cabinet.

A sudden movement at the periphery of his vision drew Jason's attention. The white-shirted man leant forwards and extended a finger to press the screen mounted to the armrest. He peered closer and touched the glass a second time. He turned to his companion and said something, gesturing at the display.

The younger of the two men approached his colleague. As he did so, his gaze lifted and settled on the face peering through the window.

A shock of recognition flashed between the pair. For a moment, Jason's jaw hung open in surprise.

"Max Perrin," he muttered.

Sunday 13th July 2036

Bay of Biscay, twenty miles west of Spain
2 days after the attack at the Olympics

Jason remained rooted to the spot. The man in the white shirt leapt from the chair and grabbed the telephone handset. He jabbered into the mouthpiece in Arabic, casting frequent glances in Jason's direction. Moments later, the sound of pounding feet echoed up the staircase.

The sudden noise shook Jason from his inertia. Only two routes lay open to him: either through into the bridge or back down the stairs. Before he could decide, a pair of men in black uniforms, each holding a pistol, rounded the final bend and clattered up the last few steps. Jason raised his hands in surrender.

"What are you doing here?" one of the armed newcomers demanded, pressing the gun against his chest. "You know you must stay in your room."

"I… got lost," Jason replied. "I was going to the toilet and—"

"You are lying," the same man interrupted. He turned to his colleague and muttered a few words. The second guard stepped around Jason and pushed open the door into the bridge. There, he held a brief conversation with the ship's officer. Max Perrin stood to one side, his gaze locked on Jason.

"What's he doing here?" Jason asked, pointing at his former classmate. He found it impossible to read Max's expression.

"You, be quiet," the guard replied, jabbing him with the gun barrel.

The seconds ticked by, and still, nobody moved. Finally, the sound of more footsteps rose from below. The pair of armed men stiffened as the out of breath figure of General Shaladi came into view. A yellow, short-sleeved shirt and beige chinos had replaced the military uniform. He barked questions at the guards in Arabic. Their replies comprised monosyllabic responses.

"What is going on?" he said, turning his attention to Jason and glowering at him.

"I was just telling your men I got lost."

The general stared at him in silence for several seconds before responding. "Do you think we are stupid?"

"No, I—"

"Do not insult me further by lying. Because of your actions, you will all go back in the box."

"I'm sorry, it was a mistake."

"Yes, it was. But now you must pay the price."

Max stepped forwards and coughed. "Um… excuse me, sir, but there's something you need to see."

"I thought I instructed you to stay out of sight," the general snapped.

"How could I—?"

Shaladi cut him off with a sharply raised hand. "What is it then?"

Max took a deep breath before continuing. "The captain told me the radar shows what could be another vessel approaching rapidly from the south. The return keeps fading and reappearing, almost like the signal a whale might give—except whales don't travel at forty knots. Whatever he's picking up, it's currently about sixty nautical miles away. He thinks it may be a warship."

"Is this true?" Shaladi asked, turning to the older man. A brief conversation conducted in Arabic followed.

"Take them all and lock them in the container," the general instructed the guards. "You go too." He pointed towards Max.

"You don't seriously plan to keep me locked up with them, do you?" Max replied. "I've delivered everything I promised."

"Do not tempt me. You must stay in your cabin. My men will accompany you."

"So, it was you who sold us out," Jason said, glowering at Max.

A malicious grin spread across the face of Jason's former classmate. "I warned you not to mess with me. Now look what's happened."

"Are you saying I started this? You slipped a mind-altering drug into our drinks and raped a girl. Then, just for good measure, you forced me to rape her as well. She came within a hair's breadth of dying because of your actions, and you tell me it's my fault. You've got to be mad."

"She shouldn't have tripped me."

"It was an accident," Jason yelled. "Why would she deliberately trip you with her wheelchair? She could just as easily have injured herself."

"Wait," the general said. "You are talking about Miss Lessing?"

"Yes," Jason replied. "I bet he never told you any of his dirty little secrets, did he?"

"And the child? This is how it happened?"

"I'm the father," Jason said, "but I knew nothing about it. Antimone only became pregnant because he drugged us both with a nasty substance that removed our free will."

Shaladi glared at Max. "No, he did not tell me this."

"How much are you paying him?" Jason asked.

"I wouldn't have needed to do this if the authorities had given me what I was owed," Max shouted.

"What's that got to do with me?"

"That woman, your mother, killed my father right in front of the British Prime Minister, yet she doesn't get to spend even one day in prison. That's not to mention the millions of women across the world she..." His voice trailed off.

"What did she do?" Shaladi asked.

"Nothing," Max mumbled.

Shaladi studied Max's face, searching for answers. The boy refused to meet his gaze. After a moment, the general said, "We will continue this conversation later. Now, you go down the stairs."

Jason glared at Max for a second, then turned away. The barrel of a gun jabbed him in the back. He set off down the staircase, four pairs of feet clanking down the steps after him. When they reached the floor on which the other prisoners were being held, the armed man instructed Jason to pass through the door and followed behind. The other three members of the group continued down the stairwell.

The guard standing in the corridor sprang to attention. He brushed a droplet of sweat from his temple. His eyes flicked anxiously towards the exit. The two men conducted a brief conversation in Arabic.

"Get the woman and child," said the man with the gun, waving it at Jason.

Jason twisted the handle and entered their cabin. Antimone sat in the wheelchair. Paul clung to her, wrapping his arms around his mother's neck.

"What's going on?" she asked.

"They're moving us back to the container."

Antimone scowled. "Why?"

"They caught me outside the bridge. Guess who was there with the captain."

"I have no idea."

"Max Perrin."

Antimone's face clouded. "What the hell is he doing here?"

"It seems he sold the North Africans the information about you surviving childbirth. But there is some good news. They detected a ship heading towards us. They think it might be a warship."

"Coming to rescue us?"

"Who knows, but let's hope so."

"But that could put us in more danger. They aren't just going to let us go without a fight."

Jason shot a worried glance at Antimone. "Shit. I hadn't thought of that."

A rap on the door brought the brief conversation to an end. "We have to go," he said. "If it is one of our ships, let's pray this lot surrender." He released the brake and pushed the chair into the corridor. At the same time, his mother emerged from the cabin two doors down.

"What the hell is happening?" Rosalind asked. "Why are you moving us?"

Jason watched on in silence.

"I'm not going anywhere," she stated, jutting out her chin as she turned to the guard.

The man's hand whipped out, slapping her cheek. She staggered backwards a pace and raised a palm to the reddening skin.

"Move! Now!"

Wordlessly, she limped towards the exit sign.

When they reached the door leading into the stairwell, Jason stopped. "How do we get down there?"

"You carry her," the armed man replied, waving the gun at Jason. "I will take the wheelchair."

Paul still clung to his mother.

"I'm afraid you'll have to walk, buddy," Jason said, reaching out his arms to lift his son off Antimone's lap.

Paul uttered a squeak of denial and held on tighter.

"Come on. You need to let go."

The three-year-old reluctantly released his grip and allowed his father to pick him up. Jason deposited him on the floor, then scooped Antimone out of the wheelchair and staggered through the doorway. Paul grasped the handrail and negotiated the first step. He turned back, seeking his father's approval.

"Keep going," Jason said with a smile of encouragement.

Paul descended the next stair and once again stopped. The guard muttered something under his breath and barged past the boy's parents. He snatched the child up and, despite Paul's screams of protest, carried him under his arm down the stairs.

"Leave my son alone," Antimone yelled at the man's back.

Jason hurried down the stairwell. He apologised as Antimone's feet banged against the wall. Her body trembled with fury as they wound their way down to the next floor.

They emerged into bright afternoon sunshine. A sobbing Paul immediately rushed to his father and clung to his leg. Antimone looked daggers at the guard. The man ignored her and retraced his steps. He returned moments later carrying the folded wheelchair. He expanded the mechanism and stood back. "Come. You hurry."

Jason lowered Antimone into the chair. Paul once again clambered onto his mother's lap. The second guard followed Rosalind outside. She blinked in the brightness.

"This way," the first man said, striding ahead without a backward glance.

Jason raised a hand to shield his eyes from the sun and stared up at the huge expanse of white sails towering above them. His gaze tracked along the mast to its summit. A small black dot moved against the cloudless azure sky and drew his attention. Was it a bird? As he watched, the object dropped rapidly and hovered once again. The movements were far too jerky for it to be a living creature.

In a flash of inspiration, he realised what he was staring at. "It's a drone," he murmured.

Antimone heard and swivelled to survey the area at which he was pointing. "Where? I don't see anything."

"Just there."

A moment of silence passed as all the members of the group scanned the region of blue in the direction of his finger.

Antimone pointed in excitement. "Yes, now I see it."

Jason stood still, watching the tiny aircraft as it darted from one point to the next.

The guard poked him from behind. The action had no effect, so he smashed the gun into the base of Jason's skull.

Jason dropped to a knee, clutching the point of impact. Antimone slowly lowered her raised arm.

"Move now!" barked the armed man.

Jason rose groggily to his feet and cast one final glance towards the drone. Before he could pick it out, a shove in the back sent him staggering forwards. The other guard strode along the deck ahead of the group. Jason pushed the wheelchair after the man. When they reached the familiar yellow container, the armed guard pulled the lever and swung the door open.

A wave of warm air rolled out from the interior.

"It's too hot in there," Rosalind said.

Two guns pointed at her. "Get inside."

"We're no use to you if we die from heat exhaustion."

The man took a step forwards and placed the barrel of the weapon against her chest. "Do it."

The prisoners reluctantly entered the gloomy metal box. The sweltering, stale air rasped in their throats as they breathed it in. Within seconds, sweat broke out over their bodies.

"No noise or you will be punished," the armed man said as the square of brightness leading to the outside world reduced to a thin wedge.

Sunday 13th July 2036

10 Downing Street, London

2 days after the attack at the Olympics

"Thank you for coming in at such short notice," Andrew Jacobs said, studying the diplomat standing before him. A bushy moustache flecked with patches of white sat over his top lip. The man adjusted the knot of the striped blue and green tie, then tugged the sleeves of his dark, tailor-made suit.

"The urgency of your invitation suggested speed was of the essence," replied the Republic of North Africa ambassador with barely any foreign accent. His eyes roamed across the interior of the Prime Minister's office. He strolled to a bookcase and studied the spines of the books. "You have an interesting taste in reading, Mr Jacobs," he said, pulling one out.

"Yes. Would you like a drink? Tea or coffee?"

The man placed the book back on the shelf. "Tea would be fine, thanks."

Jacobs gestured towards a leather chair on the opposite side of the desk. "Please take a seat." He lifted the telephone handset and muttered a few words. He replaced the phone and drummed his fingers on the mahogany surface. Less than a minute later, a light tap came from the door.

"Come," Jacobs called.

An attractive woman in her early thirties entered, carrying a tray on which rested a teapot and two teacups. "Will there be anything else, sir?" she asked.

"No, thank you, Sarah," the Prime Minister responded. He turned to the North African. "Milk? Sugar?"

The ambassador watched on with an amused expression. "Neither," he replied. He waited in silence while Jacobs filled the cup. "You British are a strange people," he said. "You call me here for an urgent meeting, then spend time pouring tea. Shall we talk about the weather as well before we get down to business?"

Jacobs passed across the bone china teacup, his features tight with disapproval.

"What is this matter you wished to raise with me?" the diplomat asked.

Jacobs placed both hands on the edge of the desk, raised his head and stared the North African in the eye. "I want to discuss the terrorist atrocity at the Glasgow stadium and the abduction of several British citizens."

The ambassador pursed his lips, sipped the steaming liquid and replaced the cup in the saucer. "And what is the connection to my country?"

"We believe some of your nationals took part in the attack."

"This is a serious accusation. It is telling that you have no aides present to assist you."

Jacobs' eyes narrowed. "I thought we should keep the circle of people involved in this discussion as small as possible before it escalates out of control."

"Or you have something to hide."

"Let me be frank. There is strong evidence that your countrymen were responsible for the blasts at the Olympics, resulting in the deaths of three civilians. We also know that you kidnapped our people. They are currently being held prisoner on a containership off the coast of Portugal."

"Yes. My contacts in Tunisia have informed me that a warship of yours is harassing one of their vessels in international waters. Apparently, your ship has fired shots across the bow of the Tunisian vessel, forcing it to slow and lose valuable journey time."

"Your country has performed an act of terrorism, but I don't sense any remorse in your statements."

"Let me be blunt, Mr Prime Minister. The actions taken by my nation have been forced upon us. It is three years since you developed a treatment for this terrible virus, yet still you refuse to share it with my people. In that time, tens of thousands of our women have died. You complain about one attack in which three civilians lost their lives. This was an accident. We had no intention of causing any deaths. Many times that number die in my country every day because you will not supply us with the medicines we need."

Jacobs leant forwards. "The reason you do not receive the drugs you require is exactly because your state has performed or supported acts of terrorism in the past. That is why the international community has applied sanctions. But those were due to end soon. I don't understand why you would jeopardise the significant progress you have made in recent years by this foolish action."

The ambassador stared across the desk, the cup of tea long since forgotten. "You may regard our behaviour as foolish, but my government deems it necessary. It is probably not news to you, but a new strain of the virus has emerged. Now, it attacks both mothers and children. We cannot just sit back and allow our people to die."

"Neither can you conduct acts of terrorism and snatch the citizens of another country and expect there to be no consequences."

"My nation has suffered many *consequences* over the last two decades as the rest of the world squabbled for control of our resources. Most of my countrymen regard our petroleum reserves as a gift. I see them as a curse. Without the oilfields, we would be of no interest to anybody else. The irony is that we are only now recovering just as the value of oil diminishes."

"That still doesn't excuse your actions."

"We would prefer that we were not forced to act. Sadly, that is not so. Everything my government has done is to assist our people because others are unwilling to help us."

"In that case," Jacobs said, "you leave me little option but to instigate military action."

The ambassador chuckled. "Oh, I do not think that will happen."

The Prime Minister stared at the North African in confusion. "What on earth gives you that idea?"

"On the contrary, you will do everything in your power to provide assistance to my people." The ambassador's expression hardened. "We know how the virus originated. Your Mrs Baxter created it in a laboratory. Three years ago, you offered her a pardon, knowing she is personally to blame for the deaths of millions of women. You may think my country has a bad reputation on the international stage. Just imagine the impact such information would have on Britain's standing in the world: a British citizen responsible for creating the biggest killer the planet has ever seen and the Prime Minister complicit in covering up her involvement then allowing her to go free. I wonder how that would play in the media."

Jacobs blinked at the man sitting calmly on the other side of the desk.

"You've gone very quiet, Prime Minister. How do you say? Has a cat got your tongue?"

Jacobs shook off his inertia. "But that's ridiculous," he blustered. "I've never heard so much rubbish in my life."

"We both know it is true."

"This pathetic attempt at blackmail won't work. Nobody believes a word coming out of your country."

The ambassador flashed a wintry smile. "Let me tell you what will happen next. You will start by calling off your warship. If I hear anything in the news media about the occupants of the Tunisian vessel, I will release the information we have gathered about the origins of the pandemic to the world. Are we clear?

"Secondly, you will commence shipments of any existing treatments for the Orestes virus to the Republic of North Africa in the next week. Finally, I expect you to sign a commercially binding contract to share the results of any research into the new strain of this disease. Oh, and all sanctions against my country will cease immediately. I may have more demands in the future, but that is all for now."

Jacobs stood and glared angrily at the man sitting opposite. "Get out of my office right now."

The ambassador stood. "I recognise this has come as quite a shock to you, Mr Prime Minister. I will see myself out."

Sunday 13th July 2036

Atlantic Ocean, thirty miles west of Porto
2 days after the attack at the Olympics

The container door swung fully open. Despite the guards leaving a small gap for the past two hours, the interior had become a cauldron. A welcome gust of cooler air swept inside.

The outline of General Shaladi stepped forward, an apologetic look on his face. "I am sorry for your uncomfortable confinement. We needed to keep you out of sight while we resolved a few minor difficulties. Here, I have brought some water for you."

Antimone inhaled deeply. Every breath up to that point had felt as if she was inhaling molten syrup. She had discarded the green training top at the start of their most recent incarceration, but even so, sweat stained the fabric of her athletic vest. Her eyes took in the three other occupants. Jason and Rosalind rose wearily from their positions on the metal floor where they had moved to benefit from the meagre breeze entering from outside. Paul lay spread-eagled across the ancient mattress, his damp hair plastered against his scalp.

Antimone caught the bottle tossed towards her. Unable to move by herself, she offered it to Jason and pointed at her son. He took it from her and knelt beside the unconscious boy. A thin cry signalled his return to wakefulness. After a moment of disorientation, the three-year-old drank greedily from the plastic container.

Shaladi distributed more bottles. Despite the lukewarm temperature, nothing had ever tasted better to Antimone. She stopped drinking only when she could feel the water sloshing around inside her stomach. When everybody had satisfied their thirst, they emerged into the bright afternoon sunshine.

Antimone immediately scanned the horizon, searching for the vessel from which the drone had originated. Her gaze settled on a distant, grey smudge, hugging the boundary between sea and sky.

Shaladi followed the direction of her stare. "Please do not raise your hopes that help is coming. They are just leaving."

Ninety minutes earlier, the prisoners inside the container had detected a change in the note of the engine vibrations reverberating through the floor. An hour later, the pitch rose once more.

"Who are they?" Antimone asked.

"It is a British warship, but like I said, there will be no rescue."

"But they must have seen us."

"Yes, I think so."

"Our government wouldn't just abandon us."

Shaladi turned back to the group. "You have too much confidence in the rulers of your country. They have agreed to let us proceed."

Antimone reluctantly switched her gaze from the outline of the ship to the general. "You're lying. The British authorities would never willingly permit somebody to kidnap their citizens."

"Fine," Shaladi said. "If you do not believe me, keep watching. I promise you the warship will no longer follow us."

Antimone studied the distant grey shape in silence. She couldn't tell from this distance whether the gap between them was closing.

"Yes, it's moving away," Rosalind confirmed. Nobody questioned her conclusions.

"Why would they give up on us?" Jason asked.

"They know," Rosalind muttered in a dull voice. "It's the only explanation that makes sense."

"Very perceptive, Mrs Baxter," Shaladi replied. His expression turned cold. "I never thought I would meet the person responsible for the deaths of my wife and daughter. I should kill you now, but unfortunately my masters have ordered me to deliver you alive."

Rosalind's voice trembled with barely suppressed rage. "The Perrin boy told you, didn't he?"

Shaladi's piercing gaze homed in on her. "Not directly, but he provided enough clues for me to work it out. The vital piece of information was that the British Prime Minister saw you kill Perrin's father but agreed to let you go free. I asked myself why you would murder your partner of many years. I assume he was about to confess. Our scientists have suspected for some time that the virus was manmade. Young Perrin also mentioned millions of women dying. Mr Jacobs confirmed our suspicions."

"I'll kill the little bastard."

The general's expression darkened. "You will do no such thing. Perrin is working for me."

A vindictive glint appeared in Rosalind's eyes. "You do realise he was involved in making the girl pregnant?"

"I learned this two hours ago," the general replied.

"He raped her. There's a strong possibility his actions had something to do with her survival."

Shaladi studied her face, searching for signs of truth. He pointed at Jason. "He is the father of the child, though."

Rosalind pressed home her advantage. "Yes, but two people had sex with her. It's a potential factor in why she survived. Perrin might be the vital clue to finally developing a cure."

Antimone debated whether to chip in. She knew the scientists had ruled out the part played by Max in her pregnancy. Instead, she changed the subject. "What happens now?" she asked.

"We continue our journey to my country."

"And afterwards?"

"We shall see."

Monday 14th July 2036

10 Downing Street, London

3 days after the attack at the Olympics

The blue eyes of Iris Stanley peered through the lenses of her glasses and pinned Andrew Jacobs with her gaze. The Prime Minister seemed to be a diminished version of the man she had last seen just a day earlier. It was as if his body had shrunk in on itself.

"So, the North Africans have discovered Mrs Baxter's involvement in the creation of the virus?"

Jacobs nodded, placing a hand on either side of his face in a passable impression of Edvard Munch's painting, The Scream. "Yes, they know she released it and that I pardoned her of all crimes in exchange for the cure."

"That's not good," Charles Moreland said, loosening the middle button of his jacket. "That's not good at all."

"Have you discussed this with anybody else?" Stanley asked.

Jacobs' gaze snapped towards the MI5 head. "No, of course not. Who would I tell? How the hell am I going to persuade the cabinet to drop sanctions against the Reponans? They'll want to know why."

"Yes," Moreland said. "If Britain were to break rank, it'd also cause considerable consternation in governments across the world."

"Not to mention politicians on both sides of the House at home," Stanley added.

"How the hell did they find out?" the Prime Minister asked.

Stanley's eyes narrowed. "It seems highly unlikely Rosalind Baxter would have told them. That would be suicide. Similarly, the other two aren't stupid enough to say anything."

"Unless they were tortured or threatened," Moreland said. "I wouldn't put it past the North Africans. Remember, they've got a young child with them. That makes them very vulnerable to coercion."

"No, there must be more to it than that," Stanley replied. "How would the Reponans even know what questions to ask? I think somebody else told them."

"And I might have an idea who that could be."

Jacobs and Stanley both turned to stare at the head of MI6.

"The drone images clearly show the three missing British adults and the child," Moreland continued. "We also captured a shot of Shaladi, the Reponan General. The video failed to pick up his daughter. We spent a lot of time trying to identify the other occupants of the vessel. Some of them are members of Shaladi's security team, but there is one other person of interest. The camera didn't get a clear image, so I've had my technical experts working on cleaning up the material." He opened the folder and passed a grainy black-and-white photograph to each of the others.

The picture showed a figure wearing a light-coloured short-sleeved shirt and knee-length shorts. A baseball cap obscured the upper part of his face.

Jacobs moved the glossy paper closer. "Is this the best you can do?"

"You should've seen it before they started. We won't glean much more given the quality of the raw images. The subject was standing in shade at a distance of at least half a mile from the lens. But I think there's enough of a match to determine the person's identity with a reasonable amount of certainty."

"Really? Who is it?"

Moreland settled back in his chair. "The facial recognition algorithm puts an eighty percent probability on our mystery man being none other than Max Perrin."

"Perrin?" the Prime Minister asked, his eyebrows lifting in surprise.

"That makes sense," Stanley said. "It would explain why we couldn't track him down. He knows all the history. From what you told us, the Baxter woman murdered his father. That would provide him with all the motive he needed to tell the Reponans."

"Yes, there's no love lost between him and the other two either," Jacobs said. "His actions resulted in her getting pregnant. What's he doing on the ship though?"

"Maybe they're paying him."

"Well, if it is who we think, I feel less bad about considering Mrs Baxter's demands to liquidate him. Where are they now?"

"They've passed through the Strait of Gibraltar and are north of Morocco as we speak," Moreland replied.

Jacobs switched his gaze from the head of MI6 to his counterpart in MI5 and back again. "What do I do next?"

A moment of silence followed the question. Finally, Stanley leant forwards and inhaled deeply. "It will all come out in the end, whatever you do. My recommendation would be to control the narrative by informing the world before they find out for themselves."

The Prime Minister turned pale, and his mouth opened like a stranded fish. "You mean confess to all of it."

Moreland nodded. "I agree with Iris. It'll be bad now, but a whole lot worse if you try to keep it quiet. In this case, honesty is the best policy."

"But..."

"Look, Andrew," Moreland said. "If you just go along with the Reponans' demands, you'll have to answer some impossible questions. People will want to know why you're stopping sanctions. I doubt you could push something like that through without considerable support from Parliament. And how are you going to obtain that unless you reveal some part of the truth? If you confess to the global press what really happened, the Reponans will no longer have a hold over you."

"But that would be the end of my career. Hell, the entire country will be ruined. We'll become outcasts among the international community. Half the world hates us already. We'd be providing all the evidence to convert the other half."

"I'm afraid there are no easy options," Stanley said. "Of course, you could just destroy all the evidence."

Jacobs looked up hopefully. "What do you mean?"

"I'm not suggesting this for one moment, but ships sink without trace all the time. Without any witnesses to what happened back then, it would be their word against ours."

The Prime Minister covered his face with his hands. "I need some time to think about this."

Tuesday 15th July 2036

The Mediterranean, thirty miles north of Tunis
4 days after the attack at the Olympics

The orange orb of the sun kissed the horizon. The corona blazed in a sky transitioning from blue to grey, sending a cascade of sparkles across the shimmering ocean. Jason shielded his eyes as he craned his neck to peer through the porthole at the distant low-lying land off the starboard side of the ship. The first twinkle of streetlights appeared, glittering like fireflies.

"We must be getting close," he said.

Antimone acknowledged his statement with a grunt. Their imprisonment seemed to have lasted forever. At least the general had spared them from the cauldron inside the metal container and allowed them to return to the cabin. Now boredom was the main enemy. Keeping a boisterous three-year-old entertained had sapped her energy. With few resources to hand, she and Jason had resorted to making up stories for their son. As she concluded Paul's latest request for a tale involving a monkey, a dog and a magic rabbit, she was ready to scream.

"And so they lived happily ever after."

"No, they didn't," Paul said. "The monkey had a baby and—"

"Why don't you come and look out of the window?" Jason asked, flashing a glance of sympathy at Antimone.

Paul bounded over to his father. Jason lifted the boy so he could peer through the circular glass frame and pointed. "Over there. Can you see the land?"

Paul nodded. "When are we going home, Daddy?"

"Well… it'll be a few days yet."

"Are the nasty men coming to live with us?"

"No, of course not."

"I want to go back to our house."

"I know, but we can't at the moment."

"Why?"

"Because we're stuck on a ship."

"But why?"

Jason glanced towards Antimone, searching for an answer. She shrugged in response. "This is all a big adventure, isn't it?" he said. "You hadn't been on a boat trip before this one, but you have now."

"I still want to go home."

"We will… soon."

"Put me down." The three-year-old wriggled in his father's grasp until Jason lowered him to the ground.

Paul clambered onto the bottom bunk. "I want another story," he announced.

Antimone groaned. "Why don't you try to sleep?"

"I'm not tired."

"It's after your bedtime. Maybe if you lie down and close your eyes, you'll start to feel sleepy."

The past few days had played havoc with Paul's sleeping patterns, not helped by the lack of exercise during their confinement in the tiny cabin.

Jason moved away from the porthole and approached his son. "Let's take your shoes off and get you under the sheets." Antimone watched as Paul placed his head on the lumpy pillow. At least the bed-linen was clean compared to the stinking mattress in the container.

Jason perched himself alongside Paul and gently stroked his hair. After several minutes, the three-year-old's breathing settled into a regular pattern. Taking care not to disturb the sleeping child, Jason rose gingerly and crept over to Antimone. There, he crouched beside her.

"How are you holding up?" he whispered.

Antimone took a deep breath, then exhaled slowly through her mouth. "I'm terrified about what'll happen to us."

"We'll find a way out of this."

Antimone studied Jason's features. "Nobody's coming to rescue us, are they?"

He hesitated before replying. He met her gaze for a moment, then looked away. "No, I don't suppose they are."

"When we saw that drone, I thought we'd finally be freed."

"Yeah. But then Max Perrin opened his big mouth and gave them the ammunition to blackmail our government. He obviously hadn't previously mentioned that Rosalind Baxter created the virus with his father. Why do you think that was?"

Antimone bit her bottom lip in concentration. "It's probably not something he wanted to broadcast. He realised he could earn some money by selling us out. The North Africans would already have known about Baxter's involvement in developing the drug, Lucinase. It's common knowledge, and that's why they grabbed her. But if he mentioned the part she played in the creation of the virus, he'd also be incriminating his own father. Whatever the reason, it's out in the open now."

"Still, if he hadn't said anything, we'd be on our way home instead of heading towards Africa."

Two days earlier, as the general had promised, the warship gradually fell back before disappearing over the horizon. Even when they passed through the Strait of Gibraltar, within ten miles of the British base located there, no military forces approached the ship.

"I can't believe he sold us out," Antimone said.

"There's something seriously wrong with that guy," Jason replied. "He still feels justified for everything he did because you tripped him. But I suppose he didn't exactly have a good role model for a parent."

"I could say the same about you, but you turned out okay."

"That's the weird thing. My mother—my adoptive mother—spent all her time working, but she never treated me badly. I find it hard to reconcile what we discovered about the crimes she committed with her behaviour towards me. She was always just my mum."

A grim expression settled on Antimone's features. "Don't forget, the murderous bitch threatened to kill us both. She told us she wouldn't have gone through with it, but I saw the look in her eyes. She practically admitted that she had no intention of letting me go. If there's an opportunity to escape, she's on her own. And if that bastard, Max Perrin, gets in the way, God help him."

Wednesday 16th July 2036

The port of Tunis

5 days after the attack at the Olympics

The clank of metal on the roof of the container dragged Antimone from the drowsy half-sleep in which she had been lingering for the past couple of hours.

"Something's happening," she said, reaching over the sleeping form of her son to shake Jason by the shoulder.

In the pitch dark, he groaned and propped himself up on an elbow. The four prisoners lay sideways across the ancient mattress. Rosalind Baxter occupied one end and the family of three, the other. Both groups were eager to avoid any contact. After much begging and cajoling, the general had permitted the occupants to take the sheets from the cabin with them. They were a poor fit, having been designed for the narrow bunk beds, but the thin covering was infinitely better than lying directly on the suspiciously stained bedding.

Even though it was night-time, the interior was still uncomfortably warm. Shaladi had promised that on this occasion their confinement would be a short one, lasting only as long as it took to unload the container. Once again, he had warned them against making any noise.

Suddenly, the floor tilted. Antimone squealed in fright at the unexpected lurch sideways. For a moment, she had the sensation of being on a giant swing until the motion smoothed out. Moments later, a loud thud reverberated through the interior. Paul stirred briefly, letting out a whimper of protest before his breathing settled back into a steady pattern.

"We must be down," Jason whispered.

"What's going on?" came a bleary voice from his right.

"As far as I can tell, we're on dry land," Jason replied. They were the first words he had spoken to his mother since the guards had returned them to the metal box.

"What time is it?"

Jason peered at the faintly glowing digits of the watch band on his wrist. "It's just after three in the morning."

"Wake me if anything else happens."

Jason sat fully upright, straining his ears to detect sounds of movement from outside.

"What is it?" Antimone asked.

"Nothing. I guess we wait until they come and get us."

"Let's hope they arrive before the sun comes up. I imagine it'll be like a furnace in here, especially with no ventilation."

Jason lay down again. A waft of something unpleasant permeated through the thin sheet. He turned sideways and reached out an arm, touching Antimone on the shoulder. She took his hand in hers and kissed it gently. Despite their dire circumstances, both drifted into an uneasy sleep.

A clang from outside woke all the adults simultaneously. The metal door swung open, and the bright beam of a torch swept over the occupants.

"I know it is the middle of the night, but everybody must come out now," called General Shaladi, clapping his hands.

With a groan, Jason levered himself off the mattress. A glance at his wrist told him another hour and a half had passed. He shuffled over to the collapsed wheelchair and reassembled it into working order. Paul lay in the same spot, asleep despite the disturbance taking place around him. Jason left his son where he was, bent over Antimone and lifted her in his arms. After depositing her in the chair, he returned to Paul and hoisted the three-year-old off the sheet. The sleeping child moaned without waking up. Placing him in his mother's lap, Jason wheeled the pair out into the Tunisian night.

The location reminded him of the shipping yard in Grangemouth. Huge, multi-coloured containers lay stacked across a fenced compound. One major difference was the chirping of cicadas, which provided a constant background noise. Jason inhaled the warm, dusty air. The odours of raw fish and jasmine competed for dominance as he filled his lungs.

The general paced impatiently beside his three men. His daughter, Aya, and a smug-looking Max Perrin stood apart, several yards away.

"You two and the child get into that car," Shaladi said, pointing to the nearest of two large, black vehicles with tinted, one-way windows. One guard pulled on the handle and swung the sliding door back. Inside, two rows of seats faced each other. A glass partition separated the passenger area from the driver.

The general beckoned Rosalind forwards. "You too."

"It's not autonomous then," Jason asked, gesturing at the man waiting patiently behind the steering wheel.

"Not everywhere in the world is quite as technologically advanced as your country," Shaladi replied. "Here, we still do things the old-fashioned way."

"I see you don't have a child seat either."

"And?" the general said.

Jason peeled Paul from his mother, eliciting another cry of protest, and fastened the seatbelt around his tiny body. He returned to Antimone and placed her next to their son by the furthest window.

Jason turned back to Shaladi. "What shall I do with the wheelchair?"

"Leave it. My men will take it with us."

Jason stepped further inside and settled into the one remaining space on the forward-facing row. Rosalind sat on the opposite side.

Shaladi spoke to the closest guard and pointed to the occupied car. As the man climbed into the vehicle, the general beckoned Max Perrin closer. A low conversation ensued, Perrin's face growing darker by the second.

Perrin took a pace backwards. "No, that wasn't the deal," he yelled.

Shaladi tilted his head towards the guard to his left. Seconds later, a pistol pointed at Perrin's chest.

Jason watched in fascination as his former classmate jabbed a finger at Shaladi.

"I'm not coming with you. I want the rest of the money paid into my account like you promised."

"Get in the car," the general growled.

"No."

Shaladi took the gun from his man and smashed the base of the grip into Perrin's face. Blood immediately welled from an inch-long gash in his cheek. Perrin dropped to one knee. The general muttered a command to his men. One of them jogged to the boot of the second vehicle, delved inside and withdrew a length of nylon rope.

He returned as Perrin pushed himself upright. The other guard yanked Perrin's hands behind his back while his colleague bound his wrists.

"I'll get you for this," Perrin yelled, the spittle flying from his mouth.

Shaladi took a pace forwards and slammed his fist into the defenceless man's stomach. He followed it up with a vicious punch to the side of the head. Perrin collapsed, the breath wheezing in his chest.

The general gestured towards the man with the rope. Moments later, Perrin found both his hands and feet trussed. Shaladi poked a booted foot into the abdomen of the prostrate figure. "I do not want to hear any noise during the journey. Am I clear?"

When there was no response, he swung his boot again, harder this time. "Is that clear?"

Perrin choked out a "Yes".

"Good. If there is shouting, you will suffer much pain, and then I will see to it that you are incapable of making further sounds."

The general gestured towards his men who lifted their new prisoner, one at each end, and slung him into the boot. He strolled to the first car and peered inside.

"I apologise for the unpleasantness. Mr Perrin will be joining us in Tripoli. Unfortunately, it is a long journey. I will see you when we arrive. Have a good trip."

The door slid shut with a metallic clunk.

As Jason turned forwards, he met his mother's gaze. A malevolent grin formed slowly on her face.

Part Three: Investigation

Wednesday 16th July 2036

Cabinet Room, 10 Downing Street, London
5 days after the attack at the Olympics

Andrew Jacobs rose to his feet and waited for the hubbub of conversation to die down.

"Good morning, everybody. Thank you for coming in."

"It must be important if we aren't allowed to bring any aides," said the Home Secretary, a smartly dressed man in his early forties. At most cabinet meetings, a circle of men and women sat at the periphery of the room, ready if required to assist the political leaders of their departments.

"I don't seem to have received an agenda," added the Chancellor of the Exchequer. She was a thin, black woman in her late fifties. Her fingers fiddled with the string of pearls around her neck.

Heads shook, and a variety of whispered exchanges took place.

"When you hear what I have to say," Jacobs said, "you'll understand why no aides are present and why we haven't published an agenda. I want to start by telling you all that I plan to resign."

A deathly hush settled over the room.

"What I'm about to tell you will be difficult for you to take in, and there will certainly be dark times ahead. It is just under two decades since the deadly Orestes virus first emerged. Until recently, no woman had survived childbirth for a very long time. Three years ago, I learned that this terrible disease did not evolve naturally; it escaped from a British laboratory."

Consternation erupted around the table. Voices rose as the members of the cabinet tried to make themselves heard. Andrew Jacobs watched on helplessly as the volume increased.

"Please," the Prime Minister shouted, raising his hands. "Let me finish what I have to say, and then I will answer your questions."

Gradually, the sound level reduced.

"Who was responsible?" called out the Secretary of State for Health. Anger blazed on the face of the grey-haired man sitting to Jacobs' left.

"The virus originated at Ilithyia Biotechnology, a company run at the time by Rosalind Baxter and Nigel Perrin. The events surrounding the release are not entirely clear, but from what I have learned subsequently, it was an accident. We can't be sure, but it seems there was no deliberate intent to infect the population. That doesn't alter the fact that the company's actions were highly irresponsible in both failing to follow adequate safety precautions in the first place and not informing the authorities afterwards.

"Just over three years ago, by sheer chance, a woman survived childbirth at Ilithyia's facility in Northstowe. Her survival provided a vital clue in the development of a drug to treat this awful disease. In fact, the owners of the company believed this event was so significant they told the mother's family she and her child had died. They held her prisoner in a secret underground laboratory and studied her biological makeup. We only uncovered the facts sometime later when Mrs Baxter's adopted son, who was a friend of the kidnapped mother, alerted the authorities. As it turns out, he was also the father of the child, but that's another story.

"I found myself in an impossible situation. The same organisation responsible for creating the virus had developed a cure. In doing so, several of their employees committed a range of serious crimes, including kidnap and murder. Mrs Baxter threatened to destroy all their research and findings. She had also imprisoned three innocent people—the mother and father of the child and the child's grandfather—and planned to execute them unless I accepted her terms.

"The price for providing the treatment and sparing the captives was a full, legally binding pardon. As part of the deal, she agreed to complete development of the drug—the same Lucinase now routinely prescribed to all pregnant mothers—then sell the business and hand over ninety percent of the proceeds to childcare charities. By this stage, Nigel Perrin was already dead, murdered by Mrs Baxter in front of my eyes because he was about to cave in. They had been careful to ensure nobody else at the company knew any details about the drug's composition. I had no option but to accept the agreement."

Stunned silence greeted the Prime Minister's statement.

The Secretary of State for Health was the first to speak. "That bloody woman stood in this very room and briefed us on her company's progress. I remember thinking at the time she was arrogant and full of herself, but I never took her for a murderer."

"You were more than happy to continue funding her," the Chancellor of the Exchequer snapped in reply. "I recall trying to convince you to transfer the funds to international research efforts. If my memory serves, you were also one of those pushing for her to receive a damehood in the new year's honours list."

"Excuse me, Prime Minister," said a rake-thin man in his mid-fifties. Gregory Charlton had held the role of Defence Secretary for the past decade.

"Clearly, you didn't see fit to inform us three years ago. So, what has changed now?"

Jacobs rubbed his eyes. An overwhelming tiredness settled over him. "The Republic of North Africa has discovered what happened."

Once again, the room broke out in an uproar. Several minutes passed before the sound reduced to a level where Jacobs could be heard.

"Somehow they found out that Mrs Baxter created the virus," he said, speaking above the babble of voices. "They're threatening to tell the rest of the world unless we agree to their demands. I might add that they have kidnapped at least four of our nationals, including Mrs Baxter, the child and the child's parents I mentioned earlier."

"Is this anything to do with the attack at the Olympics?" Charlton asked.

"Yes. Antimone Lessing was, in fact, the first to survive childbirth."

"The wheelchair girl?"

"We agreed to keep secret her natural immunity from the virus and her role in developing the cure. We thought it might make her a target. Despite our best efforts, it turns out we were right. We have determined the incident at the stadium was actually a kidnapping. They also snatched her child and her partner, the father of the boy, at the same time. They abducted Mrs Baxter separately."

"So, the taking of their own people was all a smokescreen? Sneaky bastards. I can hazard a guess, but what are their demands?"

"As you might expect, an end to sanctions, drugs for the virus and access to any future research. As you are probably aware, a new strain has recently emerged in North Africa. Now it's attacking their children. We think they took Mrs Baxter to develop their own treatment."

"This is outrageous. We can't just let them kidnap British citizens when they feel like it."

"I suppose you called us here because you plan to call their bluff," said the Secretary of State for Health. "Do we have any idea where they're holding our nationals?"

"Yes, I won't allow us to be blackmailed by a rogue state. At the moment, we believe they're transporting our people from Tunis to the Republic of North Africa by road," Jacobs replied. "We don't know their ultimate destination, but it's likely to be somewhere around Tripoli."

"The bigger question is what we tell the rest of the world," said the Chancellor of the Exchequer. "The reparations will bankrupt this country."

"But this crime was committed by a private company," the Secretary of State for Health replied. "They can't hold the government responsible."

"I'm not sure the international community will see it that way," Jacobs said in a resigned voice. "No doubt they'll argue that once we had a cure, we should have provided the drugs to anybody who needed them."

"Didn't we do that?"

"Well, yes, apart from the obvious exceptions, which is presumably why the Reponans took matters into their own hands. And Ilithyia Biotechnology still charged everybody. They made billions from the sales of Lucinase. The taxes more than funded our own purchase of the drug."

"Let's just hand her over to the International Court of Justice. We may not be able to prosecute her, but that won't stop anybody else having a go."

Jacobs sat and watched the discussions unfold around him. After several minutes of intense debate, the Defence Secretary stood and banged the table for attention.

"Excuse me, everybody. There's something I'd like to say to you all. Andrew Jacobs has led this country and this party for over a decade. At the start of this meeting, he announced his intention to resign. If everything he has told us is true—and I have no reason to doubt him—then he faced an impossible decision: allowing a murderer to go free or standing by as three innocent people died along with countless pregnant women. It's not a choice I'd have wanted to make myself.

"Now is a time for strong leadership. I recommend that we ask him to continue as Prime Minister, at least until this crisis is resolved."

Most heads around the room nodded together with voices of assent.

Jacobs rose once again, his gaze lingering on each person at the table in turn. His eyes took on a steely sheen. "I'm humbled by your support and will put all my efforts into addressing our problems. Thank you."

Wednesday 16th July 2036

Tripoli Infectious Diseases Hospital, Republic of North Africa
5 days after the attack at the Olympics

Jason leant forwards in his seat as the first of the black vehicles rolled past the raised barrier and through the entrance to the underground car park. Its twin followed a few feet behind.

"Does that mean we've arrived?" Antimone asked the guard sitting opposite.

The man ignored her question. He turned away and gazed through the tinted glass.

The car slowed to a stop at a second security point where two men, each carrying a locally manufactured variant of the ancient AK-47 automatic rifle, stepped forwards. The driver wound down the front window and held a brief conversation in Arabic. After a few seconds, the rear window also lowered. A wall of warm air rolled over the occupants as an armed guard peered inside, studying each of the passengers carefully. Satisfied by what he saw, he stood back and waved the vehicle on.

Several turns later, the engine fell silent. With a groan, the man behind the wheel eased himself out of his seat and strolled stiffly to the side of the car. He grabbed the handle and slid open the door. The pleasant coolness of the interior dissipated immediately to be replaced by an oppressive heat accompanied by the smell of exhaust fumes.

"Out! Now!"

They were the first words he had spoken over the entire journey. Antimone leant over to unstrap Paul. Her son's head lolled to the side. He opened one bleary eye, emitted a brief cry of protest, then closed his eyes again.

The guard got out, followed by Rosalind. Jason picked up the sleeping child and shuffled across the seat. He stepped out onto the concrete and winced at the harsh glare of the fluorescent lighting. The second car drew up alongside. The engine rattled to a halt. Moments later, a suited General Shaladi, his daughter and a pair of armed men emerged.

"Good, we are here," Shaladi announced. He muttered a few words in Arabic to the nearest guard, who moved to the rear of the first vehicle and returned carrying the folded wheelchair.

Paul continued to sleep, his head resting on his father's shoulder. Jason's gaze wandered over to the six adults. "Could someone look after my son while I get Antimone out?"

Nobody stepped forwards. The general gestured to one of his men.

"I'll hold him," Rosalind said before the man could move, holding out her arms.

Jason hesitated for a moment before handing over the sleeping child. A thread of drool landed on Rosalind's shirt as Paul's head lolled against her shoulder. Rosalind glanced down at the damp spot with a look of distaste.

Jason pretended he hadn't noticed and turned his attention to the folded wheelchair. A few seconds later, he clicked the frame into place.

"Is anybody going to get me out of here?" Antimone called from inside the car.

"I'm coming," Jason replied, pushing the chair around to the far side of the vehicle. He slid back the door and lifted her out, then deposited her into the seat.

"Thanks," she murmured.

For a moment, he contemplated making a run for it, but reality soon returned; he could hardly leave Paul behind. In any case, they wouldn't get ten paces before the guards intervened. In a minor act of defiance, he left the door open as he wheeled her towards the waiting group.

Antimone clenched her fists when she spotted who was holding her son. "Give him to me," she snapped.

"You're welcome," Rosalind replied, her face an expressionless mask, "but you could say please."

Antimone accepted the sleeping child. She opened her mouth to hurl an insult back when a commotion a few feet away drew her attention. Two guards dropped a bruised and battered Max Perrin onto the concrete beside them.

General Shaladi stepped up to the prostrate form and prodded a boot into his ribs. "Now, are you going to behave, or do I need to keep you restrained?"

Max muttered an inaudible response.

The general jabbed him again with his toecap. "I'm sorry, I didn't quite hear that."

"I said yes," Max replied in a louder voice.

"Excellent. In that case, we can untie you." Shaladi flicked a finger towards the bound figure and watched while his men unravelled the knots.

Max rose shakily to his feet, wincing as he rubbed his wrists.

"From now on you will do exactly as I say. Understood?"

Max nodded.

The general glowered at him for a second longer, then turned back to the rest of the group. "Right. Let's get you inside. Follow me." He led them towards a set of swing doors labelled with Arabic script. "Wait here," he commanded.

Moments later, two men in white hazmat suits emerged. One carried a clipboard while the other held an instrument that looked like a futuristic pistol in his hands.

"Roll up the sleeve on your left arm," Shaladi said.

Tired after the long journey, the prisoners did as instructed without complaint. The first figure moved from person to person, starting with the North Africans. As he approached each subject, he held the device against the exposed skin and pressed the trigger, generating a sharp click. A few seconds later, he peered at the small display on the top of the instrument and read out the reading, which his colleague noted down on the sheet of paper. The general confirmed each person's name as they passed around the group.

When it came to Jason's turn, the man pressed the object against his arm. A sharp sting accompanied the clicking sound. "What's this for?" he asked, wincing.

"We must check that you do not have the new virus," Shaladi said.

"And do I?"

"No," the general replied, moving on to Antimone. Paul was the last. He cried for a moment but soon returned to a state of drowsiness in the stifling heat.

Shaladi moved to the front and addressed the group. "You will be pleased to learn that you are all clear."

"What would have happened if we weren't?" Jason asked.

The general's brow lowered in annoyance. "We would be forced to keep you in isolation. Now, please follow these men."

The two white-suited figures pushed through the swing doors and led the way down a brightly lit corridor with no doorways on either side. The prisoners followed, trailed by Shaladi and the three guards. Both drivers stayed with their vehicles.

The air became cooler the further inside they progressed. At the same time, the acrid odour of disinfectant grew stronger. The passageway ended at a set of double doors, each with a small, inset, rectangular window.

Shaladi moved to the front and pressed a button mounted on the wall. A buzzing noise sounded from within. Several seconds passed before a face peered through the glass. Moments later, a clunk signalled the operation of the lock, and a thin man in a white doctor's coat stepped out. The most noticeable feature about him was his jet-black hair. Antimone wondered whether it was dyed or a wig.

"Welcome, welcome," he said, holding the door open. "Do come in."

The general entered, and the white-coated man followed the group, allowing the doors to swing closed behind him. Moments later, the lock shot home with a loud clunk.

Jason inhaled the scent of antiseptic and fresh paint. They stood inside a square area with doors set in each of the four sides. The walls and ceiling were painted white. A reception desk, currently unmanned, sat in the centre of the room.

The door on the left opened, and five armed men wearing dark uniforms emerged. They held their weapons ready but with the barrels pointing down, warily eyeing the newcomers. The man in the lab coat shuffled from foot to foot in excitement, studying each of the new arrivals in turn. His every movement was short and abrupt, like a robin pecking for worms. "Allow me to introduce myself. I am Professor Halfon, the director of this facility. You must be General Shaladi. And this is your lovely daughter, Aya, I assume. I am pleased to meet you."

Halfon pumped the general's hand and then Aya's.

The professor turned his attention to Rosalind. "Mrs Baxter, we have much to discuss."

Rosalind folded her arms and stared stony-faced at the director.

Next, he focused on Max. His genial mood lost some of its shine as he studied the bruised cheekbones and dried blood around the nose. "Mr Perrin, I once attended a lecture given by your father. I was sad to learn of his passing."

"His murderer is standing right there," Max replied with a grimace, pointing at Rosalind.

Halfon ignored the comment and spoke to Antimone. "Miss Lessing, if what I have heard is correct, you are a remarkable woman. I am fascinated to discover how you survived. And this must be your son, Paul."

Once again, a wall of silence met his greeting.

"And finally, the father of the child, Mr Baxter."

"Actually, it's Floyd," Jason replied.

The professor stared at him in confusion. "I do not understand."

"My name is Jason Floyd."

"But I—"

"I changed my surname back to my father's after…"

"Oh, I see," Halfon said. "Well, welcome, all. You must be tired and hungry after your journey. Please follow me, and we will find something for you to eat."

As he turned, Rosalind placed a hand on his shoulder. Halfon spun around.

"What's going on here?" she asked. "You kidnap us and transport us halfway across the world, then greet us like a long-lost uncle. You can't seriously expect us to help you?"

The genial expression vanished from the professor's face in an instant. "Let me be absolutely clear, Mrs Baxter. You will assist us with whatever we ask for, or your life will become very unpleasant. My sources tell me you were responsible for the terrible disease that is afflicting this planet. There are many people in this country who have lost loved ones and would dearly like to spend several minutes alone with you. But you are of no use to me dead. In here, you are safe, but out there... Well, let's just say, I don't think you would survive for long."

"You can't force me to work for you."

Halfon marched to the reception desk and picked up a black, cylindrical object. He returned and stood opposite the former head of Ilithyia Biotechnology. He glared back at her with narrowed eyes. "We will see."

He jabbed the end of the cylinder into her shoulder and pressed the button on the side. A sharp crack echoed through the room. Rosalind immediately dropped to the floor where she flopped about, writhing in agony. The rest of the group watched on in horrified silence.

"We may not be as advanced in treating diseases as you Westerners," Halfon said, raising his voice above the gasps of the prostrate woman, "but we have learned many ways to inflict pain." He barked a command in Arabic, and two of his men grabbed an arm each and dragged a semi-conscious Rosalind Baxter through the doorway at the back of the reception area.

The commotion woke Paul, who began to cry. Antimone tried to shush him, but that only made matters worse. Soon, he was bawling at full pitch.

General Shaladi winced at the high-pitched noise. "Well, if you have everything you need, Aya and I will be leaving."

Halfon gestured to the armed men standing behind him. The barrels of their automatic rifles lifted to point at the general and his daughter.

"I'm sorry," the professor said, "but I regret that won't be possible. I am under strict instructions to keep you here with the other prisoners. Now, please place any weapons you may be carrying on the ground."

Shaladi opened his mouth in shock, but no words emerged. After a few seconds, he regained his composure. "What are you talking about? I have always been loyal to this regime. Who gave these orders?"

"They came from Mullah Awad himself. The rest of the world believes that you were abducted at the Olympics. If you were to appear in public, they would know this to be a lie."

"I could stay out of sight. I have completed this mission exactly as ordered, at considerable risk to both myself and my daughter. And this is how I am rewarded? I demand to speak to the mullah."

"Unfortunately, he is otherwise engaged. I am sure he will find time to talk to you in the coming days, but for now you must put down your weapons."

"Or what? You will shoot me?"

Shaladi's soldiers looked to him for guidance. He gave a slight shake of the head.

Halfon sighed. "There has been enough unpleasantness already. Let me point out to you that they"—he gestured towards the British contingent—"are of great importance to the future of our country. You, on the other hand, have no such value. If you do not surrender immediately, I will order my men to open fire."

The general stared belligerently at the director for a moment, then slowly withdrew the pistol from his jacket and placed it on the ground. "All right, but do not think this ends here. I shall complain to the highest level of our government about my treatment." He uttered a brief command. Moments later, the members of his team placed their weapons on the floor.

Jason glanced sideways at Max Perrin. Their eyes met briefly. A smirk flashed across Perrin's face, then disappeared just as quickly.

Halfon nodded to the nearest guard, who scooped up the assortment of guns and knives and carried them through the door from which he had emerged moments earlier. The remaining men kept their weapons trained on the prisoners.

The professor waited for his man to return. "Given the circumstances, I think perhaps we should escort you to your accommodations directly. Please follow me."

He strode towards the doorway through which Rosalind had been dragged and down a featureless, white corridor. The smell of fresh paint and disinfectant became stronger. He stopped at a door with a reinforced glass window, presented a card to the wall-mounted reader and pressed a button on the keypad beneath. The electronically operated bolt slid back with a metallic clunk. Halfon ushered Shaladi and his daughter inside.

"Each room contains a bathroom. My men will return shortly with refreshments."

Shaladi turned and glared at the professor but said nothing. Seconds later, Halfon touched the control panel again, and the lock clicked into the closed position.

Halfon repeated the procedure at the next doorway. "Miss Lessing, Mr…" He hesitated.

"Floyd," Jason interjected.

"Yes, of course. The pair of you and your child in here, please."

Jason pushed the wheelchair holding Antimone and Paul inside. Three single beds extended from the wall with just enough gap between for a person to walk. A folded beige blanket and a white towel sat at the foot of each bed. The décor matched everything else in the facility, comprising white walls and ceiling. Judging by the odour of fresh paint, the decoration work had only recently finished.

"I'm getting a strong sense of déjà vu," Antimone muttered as the door slid shut, followed almost immediately by the thud of the lock.

Thursday 17th July 2036

Tripoli Infectious Diseases Hospital, Republic of North Africa
6 days after the attack at the Olympics

Rosalind Baxter opened her eyes and found herself lying fully clothed on top of the sheets of a single bed. Her feet rested on a folded blanket and a towel. For a moment, she tried to remember how she had arrived there. As her brain ground into gear, the memories returned: the black cylinder, the jab to the shoulder and the sudden, all-consuming agony. She sat upright and gingerly probed the area of contact. She undid the topmost buttons of her shirt and pulled back the material to study the twin purple bruises on her left side, just below the clavicle.

With a wince of pain, she refastened her blouse and inspected her surroundings. She was in a room, approximately five metres square. Every surface was white, the uniformity broken only by a large clock with an analogue dial hanging on the wall. There were no windows other than a rectangular clear panel set in the closed door in the corner. On the opposite side was a second, partially open door. A single, unshielded bulb hung from the ceiling. On top of the small bedside cabinet to her left rested a plastic tray containing a covered plate and a glass of water.

As she sat gathering her wits, she noticed a green flashing light in her right eye at the periphery of her vision. After a moment's confusion when she thought the source originated from inside the room, she realised it was a status signal from her prosthetic implant.

She touched her ear and murmured, "Expand."

A message box appeared at the centre of her view. *Battery Low.*

"That's all I need."

The damned thing needs recharging. It wasn't something she had worried about before. She vaguely recalled the doctors telling her after the operation that her false eye contained a rechargeable cell. They had reassured her that the batteries would recharge overnight while she slept, as long as she kept the specially designed pillow containing the inductive charger plugged into the mains. She remembered asking what would happen if the battery ever went flat, but right now she couldn't recall the answer. No doubt she would find out soon enough.

She swung her legs onto the floor. Somebody had placed her shoes beside the bed. She slipped her feet inside and pushed herself upright. The sudden increase in pressure sent a stabbing pain through her knee. Her fall the previous night must have exacerbated the injury she sustained while trying to escape from the truck. Resting a hand on the mattress for support, she stumbled towards the open door into a narrow, tiled bathroom. The room adopted the ubiquitous white colour scheme of the facility, with a shower stall at one end, a toilet at the other and a sink in the middle.

She relieved herself, then splashed the lukewarm offering from the cold tap onto her face. The metal hoop beside the basin was empty. She navigated her way back, blinking to clear the water from her eyes. When she re-entered the main room, a figure was standing in the doorway to the outside corridor.

"Good morning, Mrs Baxter," Professor Halfon said. "I trust you slept well."

Rosalind grabbed the towel off the bed and dried herself. "No thanks to you. Don't you know it's bad manners to enter a lady's bedroom without knocking first."

The director acknowledged her statement with a tilt of the head. "I should point out there are cameras in every room within this facility. There is no such thing as privacy here. But I must apologise for the unpleasantness last night. I hope we can get over that and work together productively. Now, I see you have not eaten the food we brought you. Would you care to join me for breakfast to discuss my proposed itinerary?"

"You can talk about your itinerary all you want, but I still have no intention of working for you."

"At least allow me to show you around our facilities. Perhaps you will reconsider."

Despite her misgivings, Rosalind was eager to learn what the professor had in store for her. "Fine, I'll take a look, but before we start, I'd like to wash properly and change my clothes. I feel as if I've been wearing this stuff forever."

Halfon pointed at the bedside cabinet. "You will find something to wear in there together with basic toiletries. I will return in twenty minutes." The man turned away, allowing the door to close behind him.

Rosalind knelt and examined the items. She pulled out a clear plastic pouch containing soap, toothbrush and a small tube—toothpaste, she assumed. She deposited the pack on the bed. The folded clothes beneath comprised plain, white underwear and a cheap, blue dress. She inspected the room, trying to spot the cameras but couldn't identify anything beyond the smooth walls.

She removed her shirt, then wrapped the towel around herself before removing the remainder of her clothing. The linoleum felt cool on her feet as she padded into the bathroom. She brushed her teeth at the sink, then turned on the shower. A spluttering stream of lukewarm water emerged from the nozzle. She adjusted the controls, but the temperature remained the same. With a glance behind and keeping her back to the rest of the room, she stepped beneath the flow. The bar of soap barely produced a lather, but it still came as a relief to rinse away the grime of the last few days.

When she had finished, she dried herself. She returned to the bedroom with the towel fastened above her chest and slid the loose-fitting, blue dress over her head before allowing it to drop. She manoeuvred the bra into place beneath the coarse material and slipped into the panties.

There was no comb in the plastic pouch, so she ran her fingers through her damp hair. No sooner had she finished than a clunk emanated from the door and it swung open. Either the timing was a coincidence or they really were watching everything she did.

"Please follow me," Halfon said. "I will see that your clothes are washed and returned to you."

Rosalind followed him down a corridor. A series of equally spaced doors lined both walls, each inset with a glass panel. They emerged through a doorway at the end into an area containing four plastic tables, each with three chairs arranged per long side. Jason, the girl and their son sat at one table. General Shaladi, his daughter and their team took up another while Max Perrin occupied the third on his own. All the prisoners wore cheap Western clothes, dresses like her own for the women, and loose-fitting shirts and trousers for the men. A pair of armed guards watched over them.

The eyes of all the occupants tracked the new arrivals as they entered, but nobody offered a greeting. The professor gestured towards a steel cabinet on the opposite side of the room. On top sat plates containing an assortment of different foods, including a range of breads and fruits. A basket of plastic cutlery lay beside the food.

"Help yourself," Halfon said.

Rosalind grabbed a piece of fruit loaf, an apple and a banana. She followed him to the one vacant table and lowered herself into the chair on the opposite side.

Halfon placed his elbows on the table's surface and leant forwards. "When we have finished here, I will introduce you to our team and show you the equipment. We have spared no expense."

Rosalind uttered a non-committal grunt as she tucked into her meal.

"We have a Genesys four thousand gene sequencing machine."

“I hope you aren’t trying to impress me. That technology is at least five years old.” Secretly, she was surprised they had got hold of such sophisticated equipment. But she wasn’t about to reveal her true thoughts.

The professor seemed taken aback at her apparent lack of enthusiasm. “The Americans won’t sell us the latest machines, but it is still good enough, is it not?”

Rosalind shrugged her shoulders. “Those things need a lot of maintenance. I assume you’ve assembled a team of technicians to keep it running.”

“Yes, of course,” Halfon replied, but his thoughtful expression told a different story. He watched in silence as Rosalind consumed her meal. “Shall we go?” he asked as she placed the last piece of bread in her mouth.

“Is there no coffee?”

The professor tutted. He pushed back his chair, strolled to the steel cabinet and returned seconds later with a cup of steaming black liquid.

“What about milk?”

Halfon let out a huff of exasperation. “We only have goat’s milk. I do not think you will like this.”

“Don’t worry. I’ll drink it as it is.”

The director drummed his fingers on the table as Rosalind sipped the hot beverage. “I’ve had better.”

“You should be grateful. Most of my countrymen do not have the opportunity to consume such luxuries.”

Rosalind grimaced as she put the half-full cup down. “Aren’t they the lucky ones?” she muttered. “All right, show me what you’ve got.” She rose slowly, wincing as she flexed her bruised knee.

Halfon led her to the doorway opposite the one through which they had entered, their progress tracked by every other eye in the room. He held a card to the reader. The lock released with a clunk, and he pushed through the door.

A large open space greeted them. Half a dozen large floor-standing machines occupied the periphery, each surrounded by workstations. Shelves holding an assortment of glassware and chemicals behind padlocked transparent doors split the room up into sections. Computers dotted the work surfaces. On the right, glass panels provided three sides of a square, enclosing an area at least twice the size of Rosalind’s bedroom. Through the windows, Rosalind could see workbenches on which a variety of equipment rested. There was no way in or out other than through the door in the outside wall.

Between ten and fifteen scientists, not one female among them, congregated in small groups. All wore white lab coats and seemed focused on their work, barely glancing up at the visitors. Four armed guards patrolled the workspace.

"Doctor Kubar," Halfon called.

A scientist on the far side of the room rose from behind his computer screen and hurried to greet the professor. The man was short, standing only two inches taller than Rosalind.

"This is Rosalind Baxter," the director announced. "She is the former head of Ilithyia Biotechnology."

Kubar extended a hand. "Pleased to meet you." His palm was clammy as Rosalind accepted the shake.

"Doctor Kubar is one of our foremost scientists. Perhaps he could introduce you to the team and show you our equipment. Meanwhile, I have other matters to attend to. You will be interested to see the demonstration I have planned for you later this afternoon."

The doctor waited until his superior was out of earshot before speaking again. "We are very honoured to have you working with us on this project. However, I must admit I am surprised that somebody with your background would be prepared to come to The Republic of North Africa. This is my country, but there are many problems here, and it would not suit everybody."

Rosalind stared at the man. His words seemed genuine. She hesitated for a moment, unsure how to respond. Maybe this was some kind of test. She chose not to reveal her situation. "It was an offer I couldn't refuse," she said, maintaining a deadpan face.

"I see," Kubar said. "Unfortunately, we always must pay much money to get what we need." His tone brightened. "Let me show you our machines."

Rosalind scrunched her eyes closed, distracted by the flashing green light at the edge of her vision.

"Is something wrong?" Kubar asked.

Rosalind blinked twice. "It's nothing. Professor Halfon already mentioned the Genesys four thousand. What else have you got?"

The doctor guided her to the nearest machine. An overweight man in his early fifties was peering at the display. As they drew nearer, he pressed a button on the front panel. "Allow me to introduce my colleague, Dr Brandt," Kubar said.

The scientist turned to the new arrivals. His eyes widened in surprise. "Mrs Baxter?"

"So, you two already know each other?"

"Have we met?" Rosalind asked.

Brandt shook hands. "I have attended many conferences in Europe. I watched your presentation on viral mutation rates five years ago in Berlin: very interesting. Please call me Gerhard."

"Gerhard Brandt, that name rings a bell. I remember reading something in the press—"

Brandt's face flushed red. "Yes, that was some time ago. Unfortunately, the regulators decided my methods crossed ethical boundaries. I may have cut a few corners, but I still believe the risks were worth it. Anyway, you won't find such restrictions in place here. And thanks to the scientific authorities in Europe, my opportunities to work elsewhere are somewhat limited."

Rosalind recalled the scandal. Brandt had been caught performing unauthorised experiments on human subjects and had been struck off the medical register. It seemed he was here of his own volition. "What are you working on?"

"I'm developing an uncoating inhibitor using this Labtech molecular synthesiser. It holds promise, but initial patient trials have shown up some severe allergic reactions."

"I assume there was no reaction during animal tests?"

Brandt stared at Rosalind for a second before replying. "We went straight to human testing."

"I see." In the highly regulated medical industry of the West, that kind of approach would be unthinkable. Rosalind glanced towards Kubar and detected an almost imperceptible shake of the head.

"Thank you, Dr Brandt," Kubar said. "We will talk more later."

They strolled to the next machine, which was unattended. Kubar cleared his throat. "You will find that the methods used here are... somewhat different to what you are familiar with. I hope this will not stop you working with us."

Rosalind shrugged. "I don't really have much choice." Seeing his confusion, she decided to reveal her true situation. "They took me from my home. I didn't choose to come here."

The doctor stared at her in surprise. "I had no idea. I can only apologise."

"It's not your fault. You didn't abduct me."

Kubar lowered his voice. "If I may offer one piece of advice to you, make yourself useful and do not go up against my superiors. Those who oppose the regime have a tendency to disappear."

Thursday 17th July 2036

Tripoli Infectious Diseases Hospital, Republic of North Africa
6 days after the attack at the Olympics

Professor Halfon drummed his fingers on the top of the desk as he waited in his office. He stopped for a moment and wiped his hands on his trousers. It wasn't every day Mullah Awad himself chose to make a surprise visit. The last time had been three years ago during the opening of this refurbished section of the hospital when the cleric turned up unannounced. That had been a stressful event, and today would likely be no different. The man was notoriously intolerant of any failings in his subordinates. At least on this occasion, the religious leader had provided an hour's notice.

A message box popped up on the screen; the mullah's entourage had just left the airport. Halfon jumped up and left to greet the ruler of his country. He reached the reception area to discover his head of security waiting with a team of five armed men.

"Why are they carrying guns?" Halfon yelled.

"I'm sorry, sir. I thought—"

"You didn't think. That's the problem. Why am I surrounded by incompetent morons? You should know the mullah's people are the only ones permitted to carry weapons of any type in his presence. Get them out of my sight immediately. And make sure the rest of your team does the same."

The chastened head of security barked out a command. His men rushed away and returned moments later unarmed.

Halfon's heart thudded in his chest after the close call. After several failed assassination attempts, Mullah Awad was rightly paranoid about his personal safety. The director dared not imagine what would have happened if the leader of the country had arrived to discover a weapon-carrying reception committee. "Now, where is the convoy?" he asked.

"The mullah's cars have passed through the entry gates and will be here shortly."

"Well, let's not keep him waiting."

Halfon placed his card against the reader and pushed the door open. He stepped into the uncomfortable heat of the underground car park. Moments later, the roar of an approaching engine echoed through the concrete space. A grey van screeched to a halt by the entrance. As soon as it stopped moving, eight heavily armed men surged through the rear doors and took up position, weapons at the ready.

A black sedan drove up at a far more sedate pace and braked gently to a stop. A second dark-coloured van followed, stopping behind the car. Another group of weapon-toting troops emerged from the rearmost vehicle to take up station.

Nothing happened for a few seconds until an armed man raised his wrist and spoke into a device that looked like a large wristwatch. The driver of the limousine got out and rushed to the passenger door. Moments later, Mullah Awad eased himself out of the plush, air-conditioned interior.

Halfon stepped forwards and bowed his head. “Welcome, Mullah. I am honoured that you have chosen to visit my humble facility.”

The bearded man in the black robes flicked a hand in dismissal. “Enough with the trivialities. I want to know how the research is going.”

“Our… ah… guests only arrived yesterday. Our new recruit started work this morning, familiarising herself with the equipment.”

“Her first task is to provide the information we need to manufacture Lucinase.”

Halfon frowned in surprise. “But I thought—”

“The British have not yet agreed to our demand to supply us with the drug. I do not want to depend on foreign sources in the future, so we must obtain the instructions to make it ourselves.”

“I understand, Mullah.”

“Make sure she gives us everything we need to start production. I hear you used excessive force to reprimand her.”

Halfon cursed inwardly. *How did he find out about that?* “She resisted initially, but now she is cooperating fully with my people.”

The mullah narrowed his eyes. “I did not take the risks to capture this woman so you could risk her life before she has completed her work.”

“Of course not, Mullah. It will not happen again.”

“It better not. Show her to me. I want to meet her.”

“Please follow me.”

Halfon led the group into the facility. Half the mullah’s men walked ahead of him; the rest followed behind. They emerged into the laboratory area and followed the professor towards the workstation where Dr Kubar sat alongside Rosalind Baxter. All conversation stopped immediately as heads whipped around to identify the visitors. Halfon breathed a sigh of relief that the members of the security team guarding the room appeared to be unarmed.

The North African doctor jumped to his feet at the sight of the new arrivals. Rosalind was slower to react, rising slowly with a wince of pain.

"This is one of my senior researchers, Dr Kubar."

"Yes, yes. We have already met," the mullah replied. "So, this is Mrs Baxter."

Judging by the way the woman glanced sharply at the cleric, she must have recognised the mention of her name.

She extended a hand. "Hello, I'm Rosalind Baxter," she said. When the bearded man failed to reciprocate her gesture, she slowly lowered her raised arm.

Halfon turned to Kubar. "You may leave us now." The doctor needed no second invitation as he bowed briefly at the mullah and went to talk to one of the other scientists.

The cleric in the black robe spoke in Arabic again. He stared at a spot between the professor and his prisoner, avoiding eye contact with both.

"Our leader, Mullah Awad, welcomes you to our country," Halfon translated. "He trusts that you have all the equipment you require to develop a cure."

"Pleased to meet you," Rosalind replied. "Some of the machines are a little dated, but the main issue is people to operate them."

Halfon began to translate, but the mullah cut him off. "Just because I choose not to address her in English, it does not mean I cannot understand her words. Tell her she must work with what we have."

Halfon addressed Rosalind. "The mullah understands your concerns and will do everything in his power to provide you with the equipment and personnel to perform the required tasks."

The bearded leader turned to Halfon and glowered at him. "That is not what I said."

The professor bowed again. "I have found she responds better to politeness rather than threats."

"I have a question," Rosalind began. "Will your boss allow me to leave if I deliver a cure?"

The mullah let out a grunt of derision. "The only thing I will release her to is a prison cell, followed shortly afterwards by a long length of rope with a noose at the end. But tell her what you like."

Halfon nodded. "He will be happy to return you to your home if you can develop suitable drugs."

"Good. I appreciate knowing where I stand. I will do my best to do what you ask."

Halfon's lips twitched in a self-satisfied smirk. "Excellent." He turned to the mullah and switched back to Arabic. "If there is nothing else for Mrs

Baxter, General Shaladi requested a conversation with you. As per your instructions, we are holding him here with his daughter and his men."

"We cannot allow him to leave. It is a shame because other than allowing the drone to approach the ship, he performed his mission almost without fault. Take me to him."

Halfon sent a guard ahead to inform the prisoner of his important visitor. He guided the mullah's entourage back the way they had come, leaving Rosalind in the laboratory. They entered the dining area just as the dishevelled general and his daughter emerged from their room.

Shaladi smoothed down his unruly hair and flashed a salute. "It is a pleasure to meet you again, sir."

"Congratulations on a well-executed operation," the mullah replied. "I regret having to confine you in this facility after your excellent work, but we must keep you here for a few days longer until matters settle down."

"Aya and I can stay out of sight at our home. Nobody would see us."

The mullah glared at the general. "That will not be possible. You will obey my orders."

Shaladi flushed. "I apologise."

The mullah's stern expression softened. "We cannot afford to take any chance that you could be seen. Once we have a cure, the rest of the world will beg us to give it to them. Maybe then we can allow you to leave."

The general's frame sagged in a subconscious sign of defeat. "Of course, I am happy to follow your instructions, Mullah."

The bearded cleric turned to Halfon. "That reminds me. We cannot permit any of the workers here to have outside contact for the same reason. We do not know who they might tell about what we are doing. If your work is successful, none of the foreigners can ever be allowed to leave. We do not want the rest of the world to steal our hard-earned secrets."

"Very good, Mullah."

"I expect to see results within three weeks."

"Three weeks?" Despite the exalted rank of his visitor, Halfon failed to hide the incredulity from his voice. "But that's—"

The mullah cut him off with a raised hand. "I have given you what you requested. Now, I trust you to make it happen. My staff will be in regular contact to monitor progress."

The mullah turned away and headed to the exit, surrounded by his men. As Professor Halfon followed behind, one thought hammered at the centre of his brain.

A cure within three weeks? That's totally impossible.

Thursday 17th July 2036

Tripoli Infectious Diseases Hospital, Republic of North Africa

21 days until the deadline

Rosalind stared at the computer screen. Dr Kubar was explaining the direction of his previous research, but her thoughts were elsewhere. She kept thinking over the conversation with the mullah. When she asked whether he would release her if she successfully delivered a cure, his immediate reaction had been in direct contrast to Halfon's translation. Was there any chance they would let her go?

The arrival of Professor Halfon dragged her back to the present.

"I hope you have everything you need," he said.

"There are some expensive machines here but—"

"Excellent," Halfon said, interrupting Rosalind. "I mentioned a demonstration earlier. We are ready to start if you would like to follow me."

Halfon led Rosalind and Kubar towards the window separating the central area from the rest of the laboratory. He tapped on the glass.

"Whatever it is you're about to show me," Rosalind said, "I doubt I'll be impressed."

Halfon ignored her statement. His gaze remained fixed on the empty chamber.

The door to the enclosed room swung open, and a man dressed in a white hazmat suit came in. He held the hand of a barefoot boy wearing shorts and a colourful T-shirt. The child, who couldn't have been more than five years old, looked around in bewilderment.

"Good," Halfon said. "Now observe carefully."

Rosalind dragged her gaze away from the pair who had entered the confined space and switched her attention to Professor Halfon. "What is this? What's going on?"

Halfon continued to stare straight ahead. "I told you to watch."

She ignored the constant distraction of the green icon blinking at the periphery of her vision and turned back to the enclosed room. The scientist in the white hazmat suit released the boy's hand. The child's disinterested eyes flitted across the observers regarding them through the glass. He jammed his thumb in his mouth and settled onto the floor. The man retraced his steps and pushed through the door. Moments later, he returned, this time accompanied by a woman wearing a black, full-length dress together with a matching headscarf.

The woman's pale features peered out from beneath the head covering, taking in the onlookers. She seemed as bewildered as the child as she shuffled forwards. Her right hand grasped the man's elbow for support. Her left rested on the bulge protruding from the dark material. Clearly, she was heavily pregnant.

The man gently prised her grip loose and retreated towards the sole exit. The woman took a step after him. She stopped as the door swung shut behind him with a metallic clunk. For a moment, she stood still, then she shuffled around to scrutinise her audience. Her gaze settled on the boy as she noticed him for the first time.

A low moan escaped from her mouth. She backed away until she butted up against the locked door. A tear ran down her cheek. She covered her face with her hands and sank down on her haunches. After a while, she used the sleeve of her dress to dry her tears and stared at the child in weary resignation.

The boy sensed her distress and clambered to his feet. He took a tentative step towards her. He asked her something, and she snapped a reply back at him. Wearing an expression of bewilderment, he retreated to the opposite side of the room.

Rosalind repeated her initial question. "What the hell is this?"

Halfon replied without looking at her. "She is eight months pregnant. Now, just keep watching."

The boy once again sat on the floor and put his thumb in his mouth. Every so often, he lifted his gaze towards the woman. She stared back at him in silence.

Rosalind became aware that all conversation in the laboratory had ceased. She glanced behind her. All the scientists and guards had stopped what they were doing. Every eye in the place stayed locked on the scene in front of her. She returned her focus to the child.

What was Halfon trying to prove?

The first trickle of blood appeared at the boy's right nostril. He ran his hand over his nose, smearing a crimson streak across his skin. He let out a choking cry. The trickle developed into a flood. Moments later, he was convulsing on the floor.

Rosalind could no longer watch. She turned away. To her left, Kubar stood with a troubled frown on his forehead. She twisted to her right, and her gaze locked onto Halfon. His lips parted slightly as he stared straight ahead.

"Why did you do that?" Rosalind asked. Her voice crackled with tension.

Halfon tore his gaze from the occupants of the enclosed room. "I wanted you to see first-hand what we are up against."

"You could have just told me."

"I believe actions speak louder than words. It surprises me that you are squeamish at the death of a single street urchin."

"It was totally unnecessary."

"That may be so, but I want to make one thing perfectly clear to you, Mrs Baxter. In three weeks, I shall repeat this experiment. On that occasion, the child in the room will be your grandson. Unless you wish to see him die, you must develop a treatment. I also expect you to provide us with the details to enable this country to manufacture Lucinase."

"I already told you I'd help you but three weeks? That's just not feasible. Anyway, he's not my grandson." She turned to Dr Kubar. "Tell him. You know as well as I do that he's asking for the impossible."

Halfon continued before the doctor could reply. "Then I will let you explain that to the boy's parents. I wish you luck." A cold expression settled on Halfon's face. "Now, are you ready to get to work?"

Rosalind studied the professor for a moment before replying. "I'll do what I can, but it's still a ridiculously tight deadline."

"In that case, I suggest you start right away. I will provide you with whatever you need if it is in my power to do so. As you have just witnessed, you will not be constrained by conventional medical ethics. If it costs a few lives to develop a cure, the sacrifice will be well worth it. You may use as many test subjects as you require."

"And if I do deliver, you'll release me like you promised?"

The professor shot her a haughty smile. "Of course. When the work is complete, we will discuss how to get you home. Now, I have other matters to attend to. Dr Kubar will assist you with anything you may need."

Rosalind stared at the departing director's back as he strode across the laboratory. When she returned her focus to the enclosed room, the pregnant woman was no longer present. The rasp of a zip carried through the glass as two men in white hazmat suits zipped up a small body bag and lifted it through the door on a stretcher.

Thursday 17th July 2036

Tripoli Infectious Diseases Hospital, Republic of North Africa
21 days until the deadline

Antimone stared across the table at her son. Jason was trying to persuade him to eat the mixture of tomato and couscous on the plate before him. They were the only prisoners in the dining area. A bored-looking armed guard stood silently on the other side of the room.

"I don't like this," Paul said. "I want chicken nuggets." His face was still blotchy from the tears of the last few hours.

The scientists had performed a battery of tests over the course of the morning, including the drawing of numerous blood samples. Despite vociferous protests, the men in white coats had poked and prodded all the members of the young family. Now, the mere sight of a needle was enough to send the three-year-old screaming and sobbing into his parents' arms.

Jason puffed out his cheeks and caught Antimone's eye. "Unfortunately, they don't have that here. You need to eat, or you'll never grow into a big, strong boy."

"But it tastes horrible."

"What about some bread?" Antimone asked. "You like that, right?"

Jason rose from his chair, walked over to the array of food and returned carrying a thin, circular loaf with a hole through the middle. He tore off a piece and handed it to Paul. "Here, what about this?"

The three-year-old studied the unfamiliar offering for a moment, then shook his head. "No."

"At least try a little." Jason lifted the bread to his son's mouth. "Come on. Open the gates and let the train in."

The food touched Paul's lips, but he stubbornly kept them sealed.

"Well, it's up to you, but don't complain if you're hungry later."

Antimone closed her eyes for a second. At home, it was her mother who performed most of the childcare duties. In some ways, Antimone's relationship with her son was more that of a big sister rather than a parent. When it came to feeding Paul, the boy's grandmother was the one who could persuade him to eat when others failed. Antimone wondered what her parents were doing at that moment. No doubt they would be worried sick.

Her reflections were cut short when a side door opened and a man wearing a white robe emerged pushing a trolley. He moved to the steel cabinet and began transferring the leftover food to the cart.

"Let's take the bread with us," Antimone said, her thoughts turning to their current situation. "I'll look after it."

"Good idea," Jason replied, placing the remaining segment of the loaf on her lap.

The man collected the plates from their table without a word or any sign of acknowledgement. He piled them on top of those he had already stacked and left the way he had come.

"Service with a smile," Jason said.

"What now?" Antimone asked.

"More tests, I suppose."

Paul yawned.

"It's time for your afternoon nap," Antimone said. "Why don't you have a lie down?" In the moments between the sessions with the scientists, the guards had allowed them free access to their room and the dining area.

"Not tired. I want Granny Helen." This was the name they had given Antimone's mother.

Jason picked him up. "Unfortunately, you can't see her at the moment."

"I want my toys."

"Why don't we do some colouring?" Half an hour earlier, a woman had brought a pad of paper and a variety of coloured pencils.

"No." Paul wriggled in his father's arms. "Put me down."

Jason shot a glance at Antimone. "I really think—"

His thought went unspoken as the door from the laboratory opened. Professor Halfon stepped into the room. An armed guard stood two paces behind the director.

Jason released his son. Sensing the sudden tension, the three-year-old clambered onto his mother's lap.

"I trust everything is good," the professor said.

Antimone scowled at him. "If you call treating us like lab rats—"

"Let me assure you," Halfon interrupted, "things could be a lot worse. You have suffered a small amount of discomfort. Many of my countrymen would kill to eat the food you are given. You should consider yourselves lucky."

"Have you finished taking samples?" Antimone asked.

"For now," the professor replied.

"Good. So, you can release us then?"

Halfon let out a humourless laugh. "Unfortunately, not. In three weeks, we will see whether we have what we need. In the meantime, you will remain our guests."

Jason let out a derisive chuckle. "Guests? You mean prisoners."

"If you prefer, perhaps we should move you all to the cells, but believe me, they are far less comfortable than here."

A shiver ran through Antimone's body. "Wait. What happens in three weeks?" she asked.

"We conduct the final tests. Your son will play a major part."

Antimone felt her scalp tighten, and the blood drained from her face. "What the hell do you mean?"

The professor hesitated a moment before replying. "Mrs Baxter will tell you later."

A surge of rage flooded Antimone's veins. "What does that murderer want with Paul?" she yelled.

"You keep her away from him," Jason growled.

The guard stepped forwards and jammed the barrel of his weapon into Jason's chest.

Halfon raised a calming hand. "You misunderstand, Mr Floyd. All I said was that your mother—Mrs Baxter—will explain my statement to you."

Jason stared hard at the professor. "That woman is not my mother, and I swear, if either of you hurts our son in any way, I'll kill you both."

Halfon's eyes narrowed. "You are in no position to make threats. Please remember that if you do not cooperate, life could become very uncomfortable for you. Now, I have much to attend to."

Halfon beckoned to the guard. The pair departed, but the atmosphere of trepidation they had created stayed in the room.

Thursday 17th July 2036

Tripoli Infectious Diseases Hospital, Republic of North Africa
21 days until the deadline

Rosalind Baxter glanced up at the dial of the wall clock. It was just after seven in the evening. All the other workers apart from Dr Kubar and a solitary guard had departed at least half an hour earlier. The armed man paced back and forth with a bored expression on his face.

The doctor, who had spent the past few hours talking her through the current state of their research, glanced at his watch. "It has been a long day. Perhaps we should stop and start again tomorrow, yes?"

Rosalind yawned. "It looks like we're the only ones left, and I must admit I could do with a rest." The flashing rate of the green warning indicator had increased, and her headache was getting worse.

"What do you think of our work?"

She turned and studied the scientist. "Do you want an honest answer?"

Kubar met her gaze. "If we are to be colleagues, honesty is best."

Rosalind hesitated before replying. "Well, you asked for it. The team is woefully inexperienced to understand the problem, let alone to produce an effective treatment within three weeks. The facilities are actually pretty decent. I can see you've spent a lot of money to pull together the right equipment. You have some promising ideas, but that's all they are. Unfortunately, there is no chance of meeting the goals set by Professor Halfon."

Kubar lowered his eyes. "Thank you for telling me your true thoughts. What can we do?"

Rosalind sighed. "Short of bringing in better qualified people, nothing. Even if you kidnap them like you kidnapped me, and they all agree to work for you, the timescales are simply unrealistic. Don't you realise the rest of the world has been trying and failing to solve a similar problem for the past two decades? And I'm talking about well-funded, well-trained teams, not a bunch of mavericks who've only come here because nobody else will employ them."

"So, you believe we will fail."

"Look, if you get really lucky, you might develop something to a level suitable for widespread use in five to ten years."

"Maybe we do not need to apply the same level of safety testing as in the West. But in any case, you had some luck, did you not? I understand the girl was in your hospital when she gave birth."

Rosalind folded her arms. "Yes, it was certainly a stroke of good fortune when she fell into our hands. Although on balance, I would have preferred it if we'd never met."

"You cannot mean that. Thousands of women—perhaps not in this country but elsewhere—survived because you studied her biology."

"You may be right. But in some ways, it felt like cheating. She handed us the answer on a plate. I'd rather have found a solution without her."

"I do not understand why you say this. It is not a game. But now you can tell us how to make Lucinase, the drug you developed at Ilithyia, no?"

"My colleague, Dr Perrin, was responsible for most of that, but I know enough to put you on the right path."

Kubar rubbed his hands together. "Good. This is progress for us."

"That's if I choose to give you the information. And it won't help the boy, will it?"

Kubar's upbeat tone turned more sombre. "No, I am sorry for this. It is not my decision. But you must tell me what you know, or they will punish both of us. We will start this tomorrow."

Several seconds of silence passed between the pair.

"So, why are you working here?" Rosalind asked. "You seem different to the others."

The doctor's eyes flicked towards the guard, who seemed disinterested in the conversation. He moved his head closer and spoke in a hushed voice. "I cannot leave. They watch me closely."

"But presumably you chose to stay during the fighting."

"My daughter: it is five years now. She went to the shops but did not return. I think somebody took her. Maybe she is still alive."

"That's a long time."

Kubar's shoulders sagged. "Yes, I know, but she is my only child. I cannot give up hope."

The germ of an idea formed in Rosalind's head. Was it worth the risk? What could be worse than her current predicament? "If you help us escape," she said in a whisper, "we could take you with us. I still have a lot of contacts. I'm sure I could find you work in Britain."

The colour drained from Kubar's face. He cast several surreptitious glances around the room. His accent became stronger as he replied in a hushed voice. "Like I say, they watch me. If I try to leave, they kill me no matter how important the research I do here."

"You don't have to decide now. Let me know when you make up your mind."

Kubar turned away and spoke louder. "Come with me. I will take you to eat."

Rosalind trailed behind as he led the way towards the dining area. He presented his card and stepped back to allow her to pass. They proceeded down the corridor to the next security door.

The doctor once again waved his badge at the reader. "I will leave you here."

Rosalind took a pace through the doorway, then turned around. "Think about what I said."

Kubar stared at her in silence as the door swung closed.

Two men guarded the room. Jason and the girl in the wheelchair were the only detainees present. They sat at a table but didn't seem to be eating. Their eyes tracked her as she limped across to the steel counter and loaded her tray up with food. The child was nowhere in sight.

Rosalind took a seat two tables away and glanced at the young couple. "Everything okay?"

Jason rose, strode towards her and sank into the chair opposite. Antimone manoeuvred herself beside him. Both glared at Rosalind with stony expressions.

Jason folded his arms and leant forwards. "What are you planning to do to our son?"

Rosalind's petulant gaze switched from one to the other. "I don't know what you're talking about. Where is he, anyway?"

"He's asleep in our room at the moment, but they—you—have something planned. That arsehole, Halfon, told us you would explain."

"I honestly have no idea what you mean."

"He said they would perform some big test in three weeks. What's that about?"

Damn! Why did Halfon wait for me to tell them? "All I can say is it's nothing to do with me," Rosalind replied.

Jason slammed a clenched fist down on the table. "What the hell is going on?"

The guards, who had been leaning against the wall on the other side of the room, both advanced a pace and raised their weapons.

Rosalind lifted her eyes to the ceiling and took in a deep breath. She would have to reveal what she knew. She lowered her head and met Jason's gaze. "All right, I'll tell you what they told me. But you won't like it."

"I swear, if I have to ask again..."

Rosalind's jaw muscles tensed. "You should already know I don't respond well to threats. And you need me on your side, now more than ever.

You asked for it, so here it is. Professor Halfon gave me a first-hand demonstration of the effects of the mutated virus. He placed a pregnant woman and a young boy in the same room."

Antimone held her hands to her cheeks. "What happened?"

"What the hell do you think?" Rosalind snapped. "The child died."

Antimone let out a sob. "Why would they do that?"

Rosalind cleared her throat. *Here goes*. "Halfon told me he would repeat the experiment in three weeks—this time using your son as the subject."

The young couple stared back at her. The silence extended to several seconds.

"But why?" Jason croaked eventually.

"He expects me to develop a cure."

"But that's a ridiculously short—"

Rosalind cut in. "I said exactly the same thing."

"Why didn't Halfon tell us about this test himself?"

"I'm not sure, but if I had to guess, I imagine he's trying to apply pressure to make me cooperate."

Antimone leant forwards. Her face had taken on a similar shade to the white walls. "What are the chances of developing something in that timescale?"

Rosalind hesitated before replying. "I promise you I'll do my best."

"That's not what I asked. Just answer the question."

Rosalind looked away. After a moment, she turned back to meet the accusatory stares. She spoke in a hushed voice. "The probability of producing a drug to counteract the symptoms in that timeframe, with the facilities and staff they have here, is somewhere between zero and a very small number."

Friday 18th July 2036

Tripoli Infectious Diseases Hospital, Republic of North Africa
20 days until the deadline

"It's nice to be wearing my own things," Rosalind said as she followed Dr Kubar into the laboratory. Somebody had returned her clothes to her room the previous afternoon, washed and folded, although they had been unsuccessful in removing the stain from the knee where she had fallen during her escape attempt.

The doctor seemed distracted as he led the way. She glanced around her. Most of the other stations were already occupied. "Good morning," she said. Several heads swung in her direction, but nobody acknowledged her greeting. "Friendly lot, aren't they? Is something wrong?"

Kubar gave a non-committal grunt. He headed to an unoccupied desk. He dragged across a second chair from an adjacent workstation and sat, gesturing towards the spare seat. "This morning, I want you to tell me everything about the drug, Lucinase, you created at Ilithyia. Please explain how you discovered the formula and how you synthesise it."

Rosalind lowered herself beside him. "As with many serious problems, the solution was actually quite simple and was largely down to luck. The girl was pregnant and survived childbirth. Of course, we studied her carefully to understand the reasons behind her survival. It turns out she's a chimaera."

Kubar scribbled the information in a notebook, then continued his questions. "You say a chimaera?"

"Yes. Unknown to the girl's mother, it seems she was pregnant with twins, one male, the other, female. At an early stage of the pregnancy, the two foetuses fused together. The single remaining foetus contained cells from both."

"So, her body contains DNA from two separate individuals?"

"Correct. We took extensive biopsy samples. At first, I thought the technicians had mixed up two different patients. It turned out they hadn't. As you know, although males are carriers of the Orestes virus, they don't exhibit symptoms."

"Until now."

"Well, yes. That may be the case today, but it wasn't then. We realised that the reason she survived was because the male cells somehow prevented the organism from triggering its lytic phase."

"Fascinating," Kubar said.

"That was the vital clue we were missing. Effectively, Lucinase masks the pheromones emitted during childbirth. Provided the mother starts taking the drug at least a week before going into labour, the virus remains dormant when she gives birth."

"Did you discover anything special about the father or the child?"

"No. We performed extensive tests. I take it you know how she became pregnant?"

Kubar gave a slight nod of the head. "Yes, I heard from one of the other scientists. It is a shocking story."

"The Perrin boy raped her while she was under the influence of a mind-altering drug, but he wore protection. He instructed my adopted son, who he also drugged, to have sex with her, then told them both to forget what had happened. She didn't realise she was pregnant until it was too late to have an abortion. As far as we could tell, there was nothing significant or unusual about the child."

Kubar scribbled in the notebook, then looked up. "Even so, we have taken samples from all involved."

"That's sensible after going to so much trouble to kidnap them." Her lips twisted in a malicious smile. "And don't forget Perrin. I'd especially like to take a biopsy from his retina, preferably while he's still conscious."

"Why do you say this?"

Rosalind studied the North African doctor. *What should I tell him?* "This is artificial." She pointed to her right eye. "And Perrin caused it."

Kubar blinked in surprise. "I did not know. What happened?"

"It's a long story. Maybe another time."

Kubar hesitated a second before continuing with his questions. "Let us talk about the production of Lucinase."

Rosalind exhaled slowly, relieved to be on firmer ground. She explained the main steps in the manufacture of the drug. Kubar entered the details in his notebook as she spoke. When she next glanced up at the wall clock, over two hours had passed.

"I need caffeine," she said. "I don't suppose you could find me a coffee."

Kubar rose from his chair. "Wait here. I will return soon."

Rosalind watched him cross towards the door. As her gaze swept across the room, the eyes of all the other occupants seemed to focus on her. The hum of background conversation ceased. She glanced uneasily at the nearest guard. He glowered at her, his finger tapping the stock of his automatic rifle.

She sensed movement to her left and spun around. A man in a white lab coat approached her. His Mediterranean complexion identified him as a local. She put his age at somewhere between forty and fifty. He stopped a pace away.

"Can I help you?" Rosalind asked.

The man regarded her silently for a moment before speaking. "You did this."

"I'm sorry. I don't understand."

He uttered a low curse in Arabic. Then he lunged at her. Light glinted off the scalpel he wielded in his hand like a dagger. She barely registered the narrow blade as it sank into her biceps. The assailant drew back the weapon for another strike and rapidly stabbed twice more in the same place. She raised her forearm to block a blow aimed at her neck.

Rosalind was dimly aware of shouts from the other side of the room. Blood bloomed on the material of her blouse around the sites of the stab wounds, but as yet there was no pain. The man readied himself to fling his body at her again. Before he could move, a pair of armed guards wrestled him to the ground. The assailant continued to struggle until the butt of a rifle slammed into his skull. All the fight went out of him. He lay curled in the foetal position, sobbing and mumbling in Arabic.

Rosalind blinked in confusion. She rose to her feet and stared at the crimson stain expanding at the top of her sleeve. As the adrenaline dissipated from her bloodstream, the lacerations began to throb. The pain built to a crescendo of agony. She bent over, clutching the site of the injuries. Nobody moved to help her.

A barked command came from the far side of the room. She raised her head and spotted Dr Kubar approaching at a run. The crowd of onlookers parted to allow him through. In his hand, he carried a white plastic box marked with a green cross. He placed it on the ground and rummaged inside. He withdrew a pair of scissors.

Rosalind backed away.

"I must cut the cloth so I can treat the injury," Kubar said, panting from his recent exertion.

Rosalind uttered a groan.

The doctor moved slowly as the blades neared her arm. "Please stay still."

The thin material parted, exposing three closely spaced, centimetre-long slits in the skin. Blood seeped out of the wounds and dripped onto the floor.

Kubar once again poked around in the medical kit and grabbed a gauze pad. He ripped away the covering and slapped it over the wound. "You will need stitches," he said, "but this will stop the bleeding for now. Here, hold it in place."

"But why?" Rosalind stammered.

Her eyes strayed to the screen of a nearby workstation. A video played with the sound turned off. The pictures showed an angry crowd surging towards a closed, wrought-iron gate. Armed men stood behind the barrier, facing the mob. A stone flew through the air, landing harmlessly on the ground. A man held a burning Union Jack aloft before dropping it on the floor as fire consumed the thin material. The mass of bodies backed away, forming a circle around the flames. Arabic writing scrolled along the bottom of the picture.

The newsfeed swapped to another location with a similarly incited crowd. Moments later, the video shifted again to an almost identical scene. The montage of enraged crowds gave way to a different setting, this one immediately recognisable to Rosalind. With a gasp of shock, she identified the outline of her home in Northstowe. Tall flames leapt from the upstairs windows, licking at the roofline. The screen reverted to a young male news presenter.

She turned to Kubar. "What's going on?"

"Is it true?"

"Is what true?"

The doctor studied her for a moment before replying. "Your Prime Minister has announced to the world that you and your company were responsible for the creation of the virus. Many people are very angry. Crowds demonstrate at British embassies. In your country, they burned down your house."

The breath caught in Rosalind's throat. Her dark secret was out. "It was an accident. We never meant to…"

"So, it was your company that created this disease?"

The shock of the attack combined with the blinking green light in her right eye was giving her a piercing headache to add to the pain of her injuries. "It all happened a long time ago. A patient escaped from a quarantine area. She was carrying an experimental virus that mutated. It certainly wasn't deliberate. I have devoted my life since to developing a cure."

"But the pathogen originated from Ilithyia Biotechnology?"

"Isn't that what I just said?" Rosalind snapped.

Kubar remained silent as he wrapped a bandage around her upper arm.

The screen changed to a shot of Rosalind accepting an award at a medical conference. Moments later, a picture appeared of Antimone Lessing crossing the finishing line in a racing wheelchair, hands aloft in a victory salute.

"What are they saying about her?" she asked.

"They say she is the first to survive, not the other woman. There is also much anger that she hid her involvement from the world."

A shot of Antimone's parents being escorted by police into a waiting car filled the screen. An angry mob jostled the couple and their escorts.

"Everybody here has seen these pictures," Kubar said. "We must be careful nobody else attacks you."

Rosalind's eyes darted around the groups of scientists. A battery of stony glares greeted her gaze.

The doctor studied her with an unreadable expression. "Come with me, and I will see to your injuries properly."

Friday 18th July 2036

Tripoli Infectious Diseases Hospital, Republic of North Africa
20 days until the deadline

Dr Kubar knocked on the door of Professor Halfon's office. Should he reveal Rosalind Baxter's offer to his supervisor? She had made the proposal over twenty-four hours ago, so if they knew what she had said, his window of opportunity was diminishing rapidly. The news about her role in the origins of the virus had cemented his decision.

"Come in," came a voice from inside. Kubar turned the handle and stepped into the well-appointed room. The dark wood of the desk contrasted with the white walls. A large, framed photograph showed Halfon standing in front of his staff and welcoming Mullah Awad at the opening of the new research wing of the hospital.

Halfon sat in the leather-backed chair and pointed to the basic wooden seat opposite. He placed his elbows on the polished surface and leant forward. "I take it everything is going well. The woman is back at work, right?"

"That is correct, sir. Her wounds were superficial. Did you know about her involvement in creating—?"

"Of course."

"But, would it not have been advisable to inform me?"

Halfon steepled his fingers. "What difference would it have made?"

"She is responsible for the deaths of millions of women. The rest of the science team does not want to work with her. Many have lost loved ones to the disease she created."

"Surely her background also makes her best qualified to develop a cure."

"I suppose so."

"Before we discuss this further, there is another matter we must talk about. As you know, our leader visited yesterday. He is concerned about our research getting into the hands of the Westerners. Many of our workers come from the West and have friends or family there. We cannot risk them stealing our work."

"Yes. I—"

Halfon glowered at his subordinate. "Do not interrupt me until I finish speaking."

"Of course, sir."

"As I was saying, the mullah is worried about losing our intellectual property. We have taken many risks and spent much money to bring this team together. We must prevent anybody from stealing our findings. For that reason, from now on, all people working on this project will remain on site. We cannot permit them to communicate with the outside world. I want all portable devices confiscated. All forms of communication in this building will be carefully controlled and monitored. Nobody who works here can be allowed to leave."

"This will not be good for morale, sir."

"I am not stupid. I know it will be difficult. That brings me to another matter. I have decided to step back and allow you to lead the scientific activities."

Kubar's mind spun. The pieces fell into place immediately inside his head. He had worked with Halfon too long to be taken in by his machinations. The professor needed a fall guy in case they failed to attain their goal. No doubt, he would be more than happy to grab the glory if they succeeded. Unfortunately, there was no option but to accept.

"I would be honoured to take on this responsibility, sir."

"Excellent. You may tell your staff this confinement is a temporary measure if you wish."

Kubar swallowed hard. "Yes, of course, sir." The change would have little impact on him; he already spent most of his time on site, and he had no immediate family other than his missing daughter. The others, however, would not be happy. It was all very well paying them a good salary, but at some point, they would want the opportunity to spend the money. This would only add to their discontent about working with the woman who had created the virus.

"I will make the announcement tomorrow," Halfon said. "Do you have any questions about this?"

Kubar hesitated. He had been about to reveal Rosalind Baxter's offer of work in the West in exchange for helping her to escape. The more he considered it, the more convinced he became the conversation had gone unheard. Surely, Halfon would not have given him this new responsibility if he suspected him of plotting to abscond. Assuming that to be true, it would do no harm to have a backup plan in the likely event they failed to deliver a solution within the three-week deadline.

"Come on," Halfon said, "I am a busy man."

"Sorry, sir," Kubar replied. "I was just thinking about your instructions. You realise it will be very difficult to achieve a cure in three weeks?"

"I am aware this is a big challenge, but I have every faith in you, and so does Mullah Awad. Failure is not an option. Do not let us down."

"I will do what I can. May I ask a question? Where will the workers sleep if they are to remain on site?"

"Good point. Are there no spare rooms?"

"There are a few free ones, sir, but we're using at least five to hold the prisoners. There is much space on the next floor down, but it is in severe need of refurbishment. The facilities there are in a much poorer state of repair. We need to accommodate twenty or twenty-five people."

"They can share," Halfon said.

"We will still be short."

Halfon's eyes narrowed in thought. "In that case, move the prisoners to the lower level. That will free up another five rooms, no?"

Kubar did a quick calculation in his head. "If we put two scientists to a room and transfer the captives to the next floor, we should have sufficient space."

"Good. That is settled." Halfon drummed his fingers on the desktop. "Now, there are some other matters you wished to discuss with me?"

"Um... I just wondered if there was any news of my missing daughter. You remember I asked you about this a few weeks ago."

The professor huffed. "I am very busy, but when I get some time, I will chase them for a response. If that is all, I have much work to do. Please see yourself out."

Kubar rose from his seat. As he crossed to the door, he questioned whether he really wanted to receive the information he had requested. Until he heard otherwise, a sliver of hope remained that his daughter was still alive.

Saturday 19th July 2036

Prime Minister's Office, 10 Downing Street, London
19 days until the deadline

Andrew Jacobs sank into the high-backed leather chair. He pressed the intercom button. "Send them in, please."

His secretary gave a brief acknowledgement. Moments later, the secret service leaders entered his office.

"Take a seat," he said, waving a hand at the two chairs on the opposite side of the desk.

"Good afternoon, Prime Minister," Iris Stanley said. She removed her wire-framed glasses, pulled out the front of her blouse and polished the lenses. Despite the current crisis, the head of the British inward facing security agency seemed totally unfazed.

Charles Moreland took out a handkerchief and dabbed at the trail of perspiration at his temple. He lowered himself into the second visitor's chair. "How are things, Andrew?"

Jacobs drummed his fingers on the polished wood. "They could certainly be better. Pretty much every leader in the world has been on the phone demanding to know why we didn't inform them sooner of the true cause of the virus. Funnily enough, one of the few people who hasn't asked to speak to me is the head of the Reponan government. Ever since I made my statement, they've been noticeably silent."

The Prime Minister paused for a second and regarded each of the two secret service heads in turn. "Do you think I did the right thing when I revealed the source of this virus?"

Moreland nodded. "I don't see that you had any option. We couldn't carry on allowing the Reponans to dictate their demands to us. It's better the announcement came from you than from them."

"You were in an impossible position," Stanley added. "It was going to be bad whatever action you took."

"Thanks. I keep wondering if we handled things correctly. If I'd acted sooner, we could've rescued our people from that ship. I don't suppose we can do much about it now. Give me an update on the foreign situation, Charles."

The head of MI6 replaced the handkerchief in his pocket and fixed his gaze on the Prime Minister. "As you might expect, there's been a huge amount of anti-British sentiment around the world. Crowds have been demonstrating outside almost all our embassies. We've been forced to shut down some of them. Demonstrators broke into the compound in Baghdad. Luckily, we had already evacuated the staff. The building is well fortified, so the only damage is some broken windows. We have marines on site. They used a sonic cannon to disperse the trespassers. I can assure you anybody who experiences that won't be keen on a second dose. Our guys are under instructions to open fire with conventional weapons if the protesters get inside."

"Let's hope it doesn't come to that. We don't need any more bad publicity. I take it all sensitive material has been taken care of?"

"Of course, Prime Minister. Most intelligence is quantum encrypted as soon as it's received, so there's little danger of it falling into the wrong hands from that route."

"What about the terrorist groups?"

"As you might imagine, we've seen signs of increased activity. The current threat level is at critical. I'm afraid for the foreseeable future, we can expect our people and assets, especially those on foreign soil, to be targets. Perhaps unsurprisingly, the Reponans still deny they had anything to do with the attack at the Olympics and for the kidnapping of our citizens. We released the drone footage showing the captives on the deck of the ship."

"Humph," Jacobs grunted. "I saw that. The cheeky bastards claimed it was a fake and put out their own shots, replacing Shaladi's face with mine. I assume nobody believes their denials."

"Opinion seems to be split along normal lines. Countries we traditionally count as allies have acknowledged their belief that the original pictures are genuine. The usual suspects have sided with the North Africans. There appears to be one thing they all agree on, however; everybody wants to extradite Rosalind Baxter and try her for her crimes."

"They're welcome to her as far as I'm concerned. Talking of that bloody woman, do you have any more information on the location of our people?"

"Even though our warship backed off," Moreland replied, "we continued to track the container vessel using satellite surveillance. They docked in Tunis as expected. From there, we tracked two vehicles as they travelled to Tripoli. It seems the group is being held at the Infectious Diseases Facility, but it's a huge site, so we don't know their exact whereabouts."

"Could we send in a team to retrieve them?" Jacobs asked.

"There's a large military presence in the city, and they're sure to be well guarded. The chances of a successful operation are very slim, in my opinion. If we knew exactly where they were being held, the odds would be far higher."

"So, we just let them keep our people?"

"We can't do much else for now, Prime Minister. I suggest we relocate at least one of our cruisers to the Mediterranean and put a rescue team onboard so that if an opportunity does arise, we're ready to go."

"That's a good idea, Charles. I'll talk to the admiralty and get them to do as you propose. Do you have any update on the new strain of virus?"

"There've been several outbreaks in The Republic of North Africa and a few cases in Tunisia, but for the moment, it hasn't expanded outside that region. Travel restrictions seem to be slowing the spread, but it's only a matter of time before it gets here."

"The infected blood sample arrived a few days ago," Stanley said. "We've got a team at Porton Down working on it. That said, if this strain is anything like the original, it'll take a lot of effort to develop a cure."

Jacobs rubbed his face with his hands. "I want our top people on this. There's no higher priority."

"Understood."

"What about the home front, Iris?" the Prime Minister asked.

"A very similar story to abroad," the head of MI5 replied. "There've been mass demonstrations in every major city. As you might expect, Northstowe has been particularly badly affected. A mob stormed the Ilithyia facility and caused a lot of damage. The company has filed for administration, not that I suspect there will be many takers in their current position. Rosalind Baxter's home was destroyed in an arson attack."

"So, not all bad news then," Jacobs said, remaining deadpan.

Stanley suppressed a smirk. "I suppose not." Almost immediately, she rearranged her features into a serious, thoughtful expression. "We also had to relocate the Lessings. Some online newsfeeds are suggesting their daughter should've revealed that she was the first to survive. A crowd gathered outside their house, and things got a little ugly."

"That girl doesn't owe anybody anything," Jacobs replied. "I'm surprised she agreed to keep quiet after what she went through. And now she and her family are caught up in this new mess."

"I understand your concerns," Stanley said, "but until we have more information about where they're being held, there's not much more we can do."

"I want you to put all your efforts into determining their location. If there's any chance of rescuing them, I'll take it. She doesn't deserve any of this."

Saturday 19th July 2036

Tripoli Infectious Diseases Hospital, Republic of North Africa
19 days until the deadline

Antimone sat in her wheelchair, enjoying a rare moment of peace while Paul took his afternoon nap. Jason lay on the adjacent bed with his eyes closed and his hands behind his head. This incarceration should have been an opportunity for the couple to spend precious time with their son, but they were finding it increasingly hard to provide the enthusiasm and energy required to keep him entertained.

For Antimone, the hardest part of being held in captivity was the lack of exercise. After the intensive training and the high of the Olympic final, the enforced inaction was sapping her spirits. She could sense her fitness draining away with each passing day, leaving her feeling weaker and diminished. At home, her mother took on most of the childcare duties, allowing Antimone to concentrate on her athletic career. The time spent with her son had been a rewarding distraction. Now, the monotony was driving her mad. Worse still, it made her feel like a bad parent.

A knock at the door drew Antimone from her morose thoughts. Jason sat up. *Not more tests.* Moments later, Dr Kubar entered. He held a green canvas sack in his hand.

"I hope I am not disturbing you," the doctor said. "I must talk to you both."

Antimone shrugged. "Don't let me stop you. There's not exactly a whole lot going on here."

"I know this is difficult for you. I will see if I can find some toys for your boy. Here are some books for you. I studied them when I was learning your language. They are not recent. We do not have access to modern western literature here."

Antimone picked one up and inspected the cover: Harry Potter and the Chamber of Secrets. The smell of the old paper reminded her of her childhood. She grunted her thanks. She had read the books several times as a child and seen all the films but didn't want to come across as ungrateful.

An uneasy silence developed. Eventually, Kubar drew a deep breath and spoke again. "I am afraid I have some bad news." Seeing Antimone's expression, he quickly pushed on. "It is nothing to do with our work, at least not directly. Professor Halfon has decided that all the scientists must remain on site at all times."

"Are they prisoners as well, now?" Antimone asked.

"Ah… no. But they need to live here."

"So, you're saying they're not allowed to leave, but they aren't prisoners. I'll take your word for it. That's all very interesting, but why are you telling us?"

"We require this room."

Jason swung his legs off the bed. "So, you're moving us?"

Kubar glanced away for a second. "Yes. Unfortunately, your new accommodation is—how to say this?—not so good. Also, you must move your things now."

Antimone glared at him. "Can't you see our son is sleeping? If we move him, he'll wake up."

"I am sorry, but I have no choice. Place your things in here." He handed a bag to Jason.

Jason studied the doctor for a second, then muttered, "Whatever." He moved to the bedside cabinet and transferred the few items within to the green sack. Meanwhile, Kubar removed the blankets from the bed, put them in another bag, then proceeded to the bathroom. Moments later, he returned. "I think that is everything. Let us go."

Antimone reached across and placed a hand on her son's shoulder. "Paul, you need to wake up." The three-year-old gave a whimper of protest and jammed his thumb in his mouth. She gently shook him. "Come on, we have to leave."

Jason leant over, lifted the boy and deposited him in his mother's lap. Paul opened a bleary eye and cried.

Antimone tried to comfort him, but the crying continued. "Somebody will have to push me," she snapped. "I can't turn the wheels on this piece of crap by myself while I'm holding my son. That reminds me; General Shaladi promised to get me a better model."

"I will see if I can find something more suitable," Kubar replied.

Jason handed his bag to Kubar and guided the wheelchair down the corridor behind the doctor. At each set of locked doors, Kubar presented his key card. They turned a corner and came to a lift. To the right, a staircase sign hung over another sealed door.

Once again, the doctor applied his pass to the control box, and the two metal panels parted. Jason pushed Antimone's wheelchair into the cramped interior while Kubar peered at the Arabic writing beside the buttons. The doctor selected the second button from the bottom. The floor sank down before juddering to a halt moments later. It seemed they had dropped just a single level. By now, Paul's cries had diminished to sniffles of discontent as he jammed his head beneath his mother's chin.

The panels parted to reveal a grey concrete wall, partially coated with peeling, discoloured, white paint. The air was warmer and carried a faint, unpleasant, musty smell. Kubar pushed the wheelchair down another corridor and used his key card to pass through a set of swing doors. The odour of cigarette smoke immediately stung Antimone's nostrils.

To the left was a glass-fronted office occupied by three armed men. On the right was a large open area, lit by a flickering fluorescent strip light. Ten equispaced beds extended in a row along the far wall, the metal frames streaked with rust. Thin, cream-coloured curtains stained with speckles of something dark and unpleasant-looking surrounded each bed. The state of the décor matched what they had seen upon exiting the elevator. In the middle of the room sat a long wooden table with benches on either side.

Three men perched at the far end. All held lit cigarettes between their fingers. Antimone recognised them as members of Shaladi's team. They were playing cards and glanced up briefly at the new arrivals before resuming their game.

"What the hell is this?" Antimone asked, glaring at Kubar. "You're not telling me we have to sleep next to them, are you?"

"I apologise for the poor conditions, but there is no space. We stopped using this part of the hospital ten or fifteen years ago. Now we must put it to use again."

"Why are they smoking?" Jason asked. "It's a criminal offence back home."

Kubar tilted his head apologetically. "Standards are different in my country. Here it is common. I cannot stop them."

"You can't seriously expect us to live like this," Antimone said. "We have a three-year-old child."

Kubar's face hardened. "I know it is not perfect, but it is all I can offer unless you would prefer a prison cell. Believe me, that is much worse."

"I want to talk to the man who runs this place."

"It was Professor Halfon who instructed me to put you here. He will not change his mind. Perhaps you forget you are a prisoner."

"Don't worry," Antimone replied, sarcasm dripping from every word. "That's one thing I won't be forgetting in a hurry. So, who else will be sleeping in this… this hovel?"

"All the prisoners will stay here."

"What? Rosalind Baxter and Max Perrin too?"

"Yes, together with the general, his daughter and their men."

"Oh, fantastic. You're putting us next to a bunch of murderers and kidnappers. How do you know they won't try to hurt us in some way?"

"Do not worry. Somebody will always watch them carefully."

"What about toilets and washing?"

"There are bathrooms there." Kubar pointed at two adjacent doorways on the far side of the room. "You must ask the guards before you enter."

"And do they have facilities for disabled people?"

"Of course. Remember, this was once a hospital ward. Now, I have much to do."

"Don't forget you promised to find me a better wheelchair."

Kubar deposited the green sacks on the endmost bed, then headed towards the exit. Halfway there, he turned. "I will see what I can do."

Antimone waited until the doctor passed through the secured door. *Let's check out how bad it really is.* "I'm going to take a look at the bathroom," she announced. She lifted Paul and handed him to his father. Her son's fists made a half-hearted attempt to retain a grip on his mother's training top, but the material slipped through his fingers. Jason accepted his sleepy son, hugging him close to his chest.

"I'll be back in a minute," Antimone said.

She manoeuvred the wheelchair across the cracked tiles in a zig-zag, bending down awkwardly on each side to push one wheel at a time.

"Do you need any help?" Jason asked from behind her.

"I can manage," she snapped.

The three guards in the office ceased their conversation as she approached the twin doorways at the opposite end of the large room. The nearest man stood and strolled nonchalantly towards her. He raised his cigarette to his mouth, inhaled deeply, then blew the acrid smoke at the ceiling.

"I want to use the bathroom," Antimone said, pointing.

The guard stared at her stony-faced for a moment, then turned silently to rejoin his colleagues.

I guess that's a yes. She guided the wheelchair towards the door with the female symbol and shoved it open. The room contained a porcelain toilet with a cracked plastic seat accompanied by a rusty bar to assist disabled users, a washbasin without a plug and a showerhead over a slatted metal grid. A white chair with rust-streaked legs lay on its side beside the shower.

She twisted the lock. It rotated freely, but the mechanism stubbornly refused to engage. *Okay, so no privacy then.* Her eyes scanned the room, searching for hidden cameras, but she failed to spot anything suspicious among the mildew-stained walls and ceiling. Her skin crawled at the thought the men in the office might be watching her, but there was no option if she wanted to relieve herself.

She steered herself towards the toilet. As she drew nearer, a stomach-churning sewage smell rose from the dark recesses of the grate beneath the shower. Gagging from the stench, she leant forwards to peer into the porcelain bowl and was relieved to find clear water at the bottom despite the limescale stains. The bar lowered with a squeal of protest, and she used her powerful arms to shift herself across to the seat.

When she had finished, she shifted back to the wheelchair and moved to the sink. She turned the tap. For several seconds, nothing happened. Eventually, a meagre stream of rust-stained water spluttered from the spout. She rinsed her hands, drying them on her tracksuit bottoms.

She emerged through the door to discover Jason waiting for her, watched over by one of the armed guards. The breath hitched in her throat. "Where's Paul?"

"Don't worry. He's on the bed, asleep. So, how is it?"

"It's a shit hole," Antimone replied. "Literally."

Saturday 19th July 2036

Tripoli Infectious Diseases Hospital, Republic of North Africa
19 days until the deadline

"I'm sorry, my dear, but you must be patient," General Shaladi said, addressing his daughter in Arabic. "Hopefully, it won't be for long."

"It's totally unacceptable," Aya replied in the same language. "We did everything they asked, and they treat us like this. Do you even think they'll let us go when this is over?"

The general turned sideways on the bench and studied his only child for a moment, then looked away. "I don't know. Professor Halfon told me we can't be seen in public, at least not until they have a cure. From what I've overheard, the scientists are not optimistic about meeting the deadline."

"So, they may never release us. How do they expect us to live in these conditions?"

"Unfortunately, we can do nothing about it."

"This has ruined everything. Just a few days ago I was in an Olympics final with hopes of a gold medal. Now, it looks like I'll never race again."

The general stared angrily at his daughter. "There's more at stake than your precious wheelchair racing career. If we hadn't done what they asked, they would've killed us. Be thankful we're both still alive."

Aya folded her arms. "It's just not right. And he's creeping me out." She angled her head towards Max Perrin. "He keeps staring at me." Her father directed his gaze to observe the fair-haired Westerner.

It seemed the focus of their attention had not gone unnoticed. A few metres away, Max eased himself off his bed, strolled to the wooden table and sat opposite the pair. "Well, here we are, all together. If it wasn't certain before, there's little doubt now; you're both prisoners here as much as we are. I have to say, I'm not happy about the situation, but it makes me feel better to have you stuck in the same hole as the rest of us after you broke our little agreement."

Shaladi's men stopped playing their card game as they watched to see what would happen next. Rosalind Baxter had not yet returned from her day at the laboratory. Jason was taking a shower. Antimone, who had been helping Paul to draw a picture, glanced across from her position by the second bed from the left.

Shaladi glowered at the man sitting opposite. "You did not inform me of your involvement with the girl," he said, his voice low and menacing. "And I feel no need to honour agreements with people who lie to me, especially if they are rapists."

"I didn't lie. You never asked. Anyway, she was desperate to sleep with me."

"I find that hard to believe," the general replied. "But we can ask her if you want."

"Perhaps I could spend the night with your daughter. She looks like she could do with the attentions of a real man."

"I would not go to your bed if you were the last person alive," Aya said, her eyes blazing with fury.

Max let out a bark of humourless laughter. "Maybe I'll sneak in beside you tonight and cuddle up. I bet this is hard for you, Princess, isn't it? One minute you're the darling of the athletics track and a celebrity in this armpit of a country, the next you're just a lowly prisoner along with the rest of us."

"You will not speak to my daughter like this," Shaladi snarled. He rose and leant forwards across the table. His men also stood.

"And what are you going to do about it?" Max asked with a sneer, mirroring the general's stance.

Before Max could react, Shaladi shot out his left hand and grasped him around the collar. Shaladi's right fist slammed into the younger man's jaw. Two further blows followed in quick succession. Shaladi straightened his arm and tossed his victim backwards. Max toppled over the bench, sprawling on the floor with a thud. One of Shaladi's security team exchanged a comment with his colleague. All three laughed.

Shouts erupted from the glass office. Shaladi moved swiftly for a man of his size as he rounded the end of the table. Max scrabbled like a crab to escape his enraged attacker. He staggered to his feet and backed towards the approaching men.

"Did you see what he did to me?" he screamed at the nearest guard, pointing a shaking finger at Shaladi. The man's rifle butt smashed into Max's face. He crumpled to the floor and rolled half-conscious onto his side.

The aim of the guards' rifles transferred to Shaladi's chest. The general raised his hands slowly. A rapid-fire conversation in Arabic between Shaladi and the armed men followed. The man who had struck Max lowered his weapon and spoke into the device strapped to his wrist.

Seconds passed as both sides stared at each other in silence. The clunk of the lift doors and the sound of rapidly approaching footsteps drew all the eyes in the room. Professor Halfon marched through the doorway and surveyed the scene. He stormed up to the general, his features contorted in anger. Shaladi and Halfon exchanged several words in Arabic. The professor barked an instruction at the man with the wrist communicator. He lowered his mouth to the device and spoke in a hushed voice.

Max pushed himself to a sitting position and spat a bloody gobbet of saliva on the floor. "He hit me."

"Be quiet," Halfon bellowed. "Miss Lessing," he added in a calmer tone. "Please join us. You may leave your boy where he is."

Antimone murmured a few words to her son and manoeuvred herself awkwardly the few feet to the rest of the group. "What's going on?"

Halfon raised a finger to silence her. A guard crossed to the male bathroom and barged in without knocking. Moments later. Jason emerged with a towel around his waist. He stood beside Antimone, water dripping on the surrounding floor.

"Wait there," Halfon barked, "and no talking."

Jason shot Antimone a questioning look. She responded with a shrug of the shoulders.

The general glared at Max. The rasp of Max's breath in his throat was the only sound to break the silence. His fists clenched and unclenched periodically. One minute turned into two. Eventually, the muffled clunk of the lift doors parting reached their ears. Seconds later, Rosalind Baxter entered the room, accompanied by Dr Kubar. She stared at the others in confusion.

"Good. We are all here," Halfon said. "Let me start by apologising for the lower quality of your accommodation. Unfortunately, this is necessary due to lack of space."

His voice took on a frostier tone. "Now, I want to make this absolutely clear. I will not tolerate any insubordination. If you misbehave, we have prison cells, which are far more uncomfortable than this. Any further incidents like the one that happened here this evening will result in all of you being transferred there… or worse. Mr Perrin, you will sample the delights of a cell tonight."

"But I didn't do anything," Max said, the words distorted by his swollen mouth. "He hit me."

"Enough!" Halfon yelled. The guard raised his rifle butt again.

"Okay," Max muttered, shuffling backwards.

"The work we are doing here is extremely important. Having prisoners on site is a distraction I do not need. In future, you will do as you are told without question or complaint. Am I making myself clear?" Halfon stared belligerently at each of the captives. "Good. Food will be here shortly."

~

Professor Halfon beckoned to Dr Kubar, turned and moved out of earshot of the others. When the doctor joined him, he spoke to his subordinate in Arabic, his voice just above a whisper. "This incident has made me think. The Westerners are needed for the medical research and might be useful as hostages. Shaladi and his daughter may also still have their uses. The general's men, however, are simply a potential risk. While I escort Perrin to the cells, talk to our security people. I do not want them here any longer."

"So, you're freeing them?"

Halfon tutted. "Of course not."

"You wish to transfer them somewhere else?"

"In a manner of speaking. They know too much. If they are kept with other prisoners outside this facility, they will discuss what they have seen."

Kubar turned pale as he comprehended the professor's intentions. "You intend to have them killed?"

Halfon's eyes narrowed. It seemed his subordinate might not yet be ready for the additional burden of leadership after all. "That is not your concern. Never mind. I will arrange it myself. We will talk later." His gaze followed Kubar as he passed through the doorway leading to the elevator. When the doctor had disappeared from sight, Halfon returned to the group. He uttered a series of curt instructions to one guard and beckoned to another to join him.

"You will come with us now," he said to Max. "We will see how you like the facilities in our basement. This way."

Halfon turned and strode towards the same door through which Kubar had just passed. He didn't look back. Max limped behind, shoved forwards by the armed man. The professor used his key card to summon the lift.

"I can help you," Max said as he drew alongside.

Halfon whipped around and looked the injured prisoner up and down. "How could you possibly help me?"

A shrewd expression crept onto Max's face. He leant closer and spoke in a low voice. "I could spy on them for you, let you know if they're planning an escape."

"I have guards to watch them. What makes you think I need you?"

"They won't discuss their plans in front of your men, will they?"

"Yet you expect them to do so when you are present?" Halfon asked.

"I could still eavesdrop on them. It's worth a try, isn't it?"

"Even if they escaped this facility, they would never get out of this country."

"But it would be better to stop any attempt before it happens, wouldn't it?"

"Hmm." Halfon tapped his teeth with a fingernail.

Max studied the professor hopefully. "I saw the girl take a knife. I bet your guards didn't notice that."

Halfon lifted an eyebrow in surprise. "Which girl?"

"The one in the wheelchair," Max replied hurriedly.

"And what sort of knife?"

"Ah… just a normal cutlery knife."

Halfon's eyes bored into Max. "The kitchen workers are under strict instructions that the prisoners should not be given metal knives or forks. How did she get this item?"

Max swallowed hard and looked away. "Um… I don't know."

The professor maintained his glare. "Really?"

"Look, I'm sorry I lied," Max gabbled. "I'm not like them. I'll do whatever you ask."

Halfon allowed himself a moment of smugness. *The boy might have his uses after all.* "Oh, I believe you will. But what do you wish for in return?"

"I understand that you have no intention of releasing us. For the moment, all I'm after is preferential treatment. I really don't want to spend the night in the cells. In time, I could perform other tasks for you. Surely it would be useful to have a Westerner working for you. I'd be happy to act as a spy for your government if you were to pay me."

Halfon stood silently for a moment, his eyes narrowed in thought. "Very well. I like people who are motivated. Tonight, you may return to your old room. Tomorrow, we will bring you back here. You can tell them you enjoyed our hospitality in the basement. But I expect results. I want you to inform me immediately if they have any plans to escape. And if you lie to me again, you will be severely punished."

Max nodded enthusiastically. "You won't regret this. I'll let you know if I hear anything at all."

Sunday 20th July 2036

Tripoli Infectious Diseases Hospital, Republic of North Africa
18 days until the deadline

The clatter of crockery woke Jason. He eased an eye open and glanced to his right. Paul lay in the adjacent bed and Antimone one further over against the wall. Both were still asleep. A thin curtain divided their set of three beds from the rest, although the stained material provided no privacy from the gaze of the guards in the glass-fronted office. A man wearing a white jacket over dark robes was transferring food from a trolley to the end of the wooden table.

Jason's eyes felt gritty as he rubbed his cheeks. The fluorescent light had remained on all night, and the persistent buzzing and flickering had kept him awake. To make matters worse, in the early hours of the morning, a group of men had entered the room and dragged Shaladi's team from their beds. After a loud argument that lasted for several minutes, the guards and their prisoners departed, leaving General Shaladi and his daughter behind. The army officer continued to pace backwards and forwards until threats of violence from the armed watchers drove him back to his bed. Thankfully, Paul slept through it all.

Sheets rustled to his right. Antimone propped herself up on an elbow, her hair tousled. Judging by the dark crescents beneath her eyes, the disturbances during the night had affected her sleep as much as his.

"Do you need any help getting into your wheelchair?" Jason asked.

Antimone glanced to her left at their son. "Yeah, if you wouldn't mind," she replied.

Jason swung his legs onto the floor and hesitated for a moment before standing. They both still wore the clothes they had been wearing the previous day. Neither was comfortable stripping to their underwear in the shared accommodation, particularly under the watchful gaze of the guards. "That was some night. I barely slept a wink. What do you think happened to Shaladi's men?"

"Who knows?" Antimone replied. "Perhaps he'll tell us later."

"They will probably execute them," came a gruff voice from behind the curtain. "It is what I would do. I am surprised they did not also take me."

Antimone and Jason exchanged a glance. It seemed the general had been listening to their conversation.

"Um, right," Jason said. His eyes locked onto Antimone's. "Thanks." He laced his shoes and crept past the end of the bed in which his sleeping son lay. He lifted Antimone, then deposited her on the scuffed, black seat of the wheelchair. "Shall I push you?"

He half expected a sharp retort. Instead, she shrugged. "If you don't mind."

"Do you need anything?"

"Yeah. Can you get my toothbrush? It's in there."

Jason retrieved a toiletry bag and towel from the battered bedside cabinet and handed it to Antimone, then went back to grab his own. He pushed the wheelchair across the cracked tiles towards the twin doorways. One of the two guards on duty stepped out of the office, his weapon aimed casually at Jason's chest. A cigarette dangled from the corner of his mouth.

"We want to use the bathrooms," Jason said, pointing.

The guard nodded and returned to the smoke-filled room. Jason guided the wheelchair towards the entrance to the ladies.

Antimone twisted around. "I can take it from here." She leant to the side, alternating between each wheel, and steered herself in a zig-zag through the doorway.

When he emerged a few minutes later, the sound of running water continued from the adjacent room. General Shaladi and his daughter sat beside each other at one end of the table. The dishevelled form of Rosalind Baxter still lay in bed. She raised her head and studied him with bleary eyes. Paul showed no signs of stirring. Jason chose to let his son continue sleeping.

He replaced the sponge bag and towel in the bedside cabinet, then returned to the stack of food and loaded up his plate. He was about to lower himself onto the bench furthest from the Shaladis when the general spoke in a low voice.

"We must talk."

Jason turned, wondering whether the comment had been addressed to him.

Shaladi gestured towards the seat to his right. "Please sit."

Jason moved along and sat beside the general.

"You know they will never let us go," Shaladi said without turning his head. "Do not look at me and keep your voice low."

Jason popped a fig into his mouth but didn't reply.

"So, we must escape," the general continued. "I have men loyal to me if we get out of here. And I need your help for that."

"How will you contact your people?" Jason whispered.

"This is the first problem."

"And how do I know I can trust you? I mean, you're the reason we ended up in here. What's to stop you abandoning us once we're out?"

"I give you my word. We will take you as far as the border. After that, you are on your own."

"What do you want me to do?" Jason asked, turning to stare at the general.

"They must not see us talking."

"Right," Jason said, facing forwards. "Sorry."

"We have to combine forces. First, we need a plan."

"Don't you have any ideas?"

Shaladi gave a brief shake of the head. "No. Not yet."

"Okay. This offer of yours; who does it extend to?"

"I do not understand."

"If we do as you suggest, who comes with us?"

"Just you and the girl and of course, your son."

"What about Mrs Baxter?"

Shaladi's jaw clenched. A vein pulsed at his temple. "This woman is responsible for the deaths of my wife and millions of other women. Did she not also kill your real mother? She can stay here and rot."

Jason inhaled deeply and stretched his neck muscles. "Fair enough."

"And the Perrin boy, I will not work with him."

"You'll have no complaints from me on that front."

The sound of approaching footsteps came from the door leading to the lift. It opened to reveal the figure of Max Perrin, accompanied by a guard.

"Talk of the devil," Jason muttered.

As Perrin drew nearer, the vivid purple bruising around his left eye became apparent. The scent of body odour wafted over the table. He grinned as he studied the diners. "Are you glad to see me?"

"I thought you'd be spending more time in the cells," Jason said.

"I missed your sparkling company so much, I begged them to let me come back." He grabbed a plate, filled it with fruit and bread and plonked himself down beside Aya. She immediately shifted along the bench away from him.

"Aren't you pleased to see me, Princess?" he said, talking through a mouthful of food.

She glowered at him silently.

Max continued to eat as the others studiously ignored him. After a while, he placed his hands on the table. "So," he whispered, leaning forwards conspiratorially, "if you three are suddenly friends, you must be up to something. What are we doing to escape?"

Nobody replied.

“Come on,” he tried again, “we should make a plan... unless you already have some ideas. Hey, there are only two guards over there. If we could get close enough, we should be able to overpower them and take their weapons. The lifts are just over there. What do you think?”

A wall of silence greeted his question.

“We need to create a distraction. Maybe one of us could go up to them and ask to borrow a cigarette. Or perhaps we could simulate a fight.”

“That is a great idea,” Shaladi growled. “Then I could hit you again.”

“Look, we’re all in the same boat. We’ll never get out of here unless we work together. Think about it. Let’s have another chat later and pool our ideas.”

General Shaladi rose and marched towards the bathrooms. “I don’t think so,” he said over his shoulder. “I have better things to do.”

Sunday 20th July 2036

Tripoli Infectious Diseases Hospital, Republic of North Africa
18 days until the deadline

Antimone lay facing Jason as they shared the narrow mattress. A loud snoring sound came from behind the curtain separating their group of three beds from the rest. Another day of stultifying boredom had passed. Her right hand grasped Jason's left. Paul occupied the adjacent bed, his head barely visible where it poked out above the threadbare sheets. His chest rose and fell in a regular rhythm as he slept beside them. Despite somebody turning off the fluorescent strip lights, both adults were finding it hard to sleep. The only source of illumination was the glass-fronted office where the two guards smoked their ever-present cigarettes.

"I'm scared," Antimone whispered. "What are we going to do?"

Jason stared up at the ceiling. "What can we do?" he replied. "She said she would try her best to develop a cure."

"I don't trust her. Anyway, she also admitted the likelihood of developing anything in the time available was practically zero. Somehow, we have to find a way out of here."

"Do you think we should join forces with Shaladi? I mean, he's no better than her, but at least he's got people on the outside."

Antimone turned sideways. Her eyes glinted in the near darkness. "We need to come up with something. If he can help us to get out of here, we shouldn't turn him down. We can't just sit around and wait for that woman to save our son."

"What chance do we have? We're locked in a room with armed guards watching our every move, day and night. Even if we managed to escape from this building, we're in a hostile country."

Antimone raised herself on an elbow. "So, what are you suggesting? We should just give up and hope for a miracle?"

"That's not what I'm saying at all, but what other options do we have?"

She sank back onto the pillow. "Do you really think they'd go through with it? Threatening Paul won't make her work any faster, will it? That bitch doesn't care about our son. I don't know what I'd do if something happened to him."

Jason sighed. "For the moment, she's all we've got. She told us she'll do everything possible, and I believe her. They'll use whatever they can to put pressure on her. They killed a child just to prove a point. That shows how ruthless they are and how little they care about human life. We can't assume they won't follow up on their threat. Maybe we should do what Perrin suggested; try to overpower the guards and take their guns off them."

Antimone squeezed his hand. "It's too dangerous. We could be shot. Even if we did grab their guns, how would we get past the locks? They'd see us coming. Remember, there are cameras everywhere. Somebody would definitely notice, and they're all heavily armed."

"Do you have any better ideas?"

"No, not at the moment."

The pair lapsed into silence, each lost in their own thoughts. Suddenly, Jason twisted towards Antimone. "They keep us locked up in here day and night. There's nothing in this room to help us escape. But what if I got into the laboratory?"

"I don't follow," Antimone whispered.

"There must be computers in there. If I could get access to one, we might be able to send a message to somebody back home and tell them where we are."

"Who would you contact?"

"Anybody. Who cares? The first step is to find a way in there."

"Okay, but you've got the same problem as before. How are you going to sneak past the armed men and the locked doors?"

"I've worked in a lab. Perhaps they'd let me help my moth—I mean Mrs Baxter."

Antimone was thankful the darkness hid her expression of doubt. The last person she wanted to involve was the woman who three years ago had threatened both their lives. She hesitated before replying. "It may be worth a try."

"They have to agree to it first."

"They're bound to keep a close eye on you. You'll need to be careful. You don't want to end up in the cells like Perrin."

"At least it'll feel as if we're doing something rather than waiting for the axe to fall. Anyway, I'm going to get some sleep."

Jason rolled off the narrow mattress, bent over and kissed Antimone. "I love you," he said, returning to his own bed.

"You too," she replied.

Both adults lay on their single beds, wide awake and staring at the ceiling.

Monday 21st July 2036

Tripoli Infectious Diseases Hospital, Republic of North Africa
17 days until the deadline

The sound of clanking plates woke Rosalind Baxter. As her eyes blinked open, the vision in her right eye remained dark. Still half asleep, she raised her hand and rubbed at the eyelid. Eventually, realisation dawned. *Damn. The rechargeable battery has finally lost all its charge.*

She cursed under her breath. She had been putting off bringing it up with Dr Kubar in the hope the implant would keep working for a while longer. Now, she would have to ask him about finding a charger. If they wanted her to work at peak effectiveness, they would have to find a way to recharge the battery.

She swung her legs off the bed and winced as she placed her weight on her right knee. Maybe she should request the services of a physiotherapist at the same time. She limped to the bathroom and returned a few minutes later refreshed by the shower despite the gut-wrenching sewage smell emanating from the drain.

Jason ate alone at the wooden table. She walked straight to the food trolley without acknowledging him. She loaded her tray and sat at the opposite end.

Jason rose from where he was sitting and joined her. "Good morning to you, too," he said.

Rosalind looked up. "Eating by yourself today? Where's the love of your life?"

Jason scowled. "She's sorting out Paul. I offered to help, but she insisted on doing it by herself even though she can't—"

"You realise they could probably cure her now, don't you? From what I've heard, the operation is fairly routine these days. It sounds to me like she wants to stay in a wheelchair."

"She said she'd consider it when she stops racing. Anyway, it's her decision."

Rosalind made a non-committal grunt and continued to eat. Jason's eyes bored into her. Eventually, she raised her head and met his gaze. "Look, I told you I'll do what I can to develop a vaccine for your son, but the chances of producing anything in three weeks are infinitesimally small. Sorry to be so blunt, but you need to be prepared."

Jason leant forwards. "I want to help."

Rosalind lowered the fruit in her hand. "Really? How?"

"I'm in my second year at university, and I know my way around a laboratory. I could act as your assistant, like a lab technician or something."

"Well, thanks for your kind offer but—"

"Surely you could use somebody to assist with data entry and stuff. And I certainly have a vested interest."

Rosalind leant forwards and stared at Jason. "I really don't want someone I need to nursemaid."

"Come on. When I was growing up, you were always keen for me to join you in the business. Let me show you what I can do."

"That was before you betrayed my trust by siding with the girl."

Jason folded his arms. "Remember that you kidnapped her and told me she was dead. You forced me into a choice between the pair of you, and she'd done nothing wrong. If I hadn't intervened—"

"We'd all be living comfortably at home and not in this bloody prison," Rosalind interrupted.

"Look, let's not rake over old ground. We're all in this mess together. I genuinely want to help."

Rosalind eyed Jason with a calculating stare. In the past, she had hoped one day he would join her at Ilithyia Biotechnology. As a child, he had shown promise for a career in science and surprised her on several occasions with his intelligent questions. Both his biological parents had worked in the medical field, so perhaps it ran in his genes. She would need somebody to monitor the test results, and as he had explained, he didn't lack motivation. *Hell, why not?*

"Fine. I'll ask Dr Kubar if you can be my assistant. Now, will you please allow me to eat the rest of my meal in peace?"

Jason grinned as he rose from the table. "You won't regret this."

Rosalind continued to chew in silence. She had just emptied her plate when the doctor arrived. "It is good you are up early," he said, standing over her. "We have much work to do today."

"Give me a second to drink my coffee. Why don't you join me?"

"Um, okay," Kubar replied, taking the seat opposite.

"Actually, there were a couple of things I wanted to ask you."

"Go on."

"You know I have an artificial eye. It has a rechargeable battery, but now it's run out of juice. Can you find me a charger?"

Kubar leant forwards to study her implant. "I cannot tell. This is not something we have in my country."

"From my understanding, it uses inductive charging. They use the same technology for phones and electric toothbrushes. At home, I have one built into my pillow."

"I am certain I cannot obtain this here."

Rosalind gave an exasperated sigh. "I just told you they build the same thing into all sorts of everyday devices. Perhaps you could buy a wireless phone charger. I'm sure that would do the job."

"I will see if I can get this for you."

"Thank you. If you want me to work at my best, I need the use of both eyes." Rosalind drained the cup, wincing at the bitter taste, and replaced it on the table. "There was another thing. My son asked whether he could assist me."

"Your son?"

"Yes, Jason. He's studying Biochemistry at university. It would be useful to have somebody to enter data while we focus on the important stuff. And he also wants to save his boy."

"Okay," Kubar said. "If you think he can help, I will ask Professor Halfon."

"Good. And the other matter we talked about?"

Kubar threw a glance at the guards sitting in the glass-fronted office on the other side of the room. "I do not want to discuss that here. Now, if you are ready, shall we start work?"

Rosalind rose to her feet and followed him to the locked door. He waved his badge at the reader, and the lock clunked.

"If you don't mind me saying, it doesn't seem very high tech to open doors with a card," Rosalind said.

Kubar turned to her. "Oh, it is not just that. Somebody is watching all the time." He gestured towards a small black circle in the ceiling. "It will not operate unless an operator in the control room gives approval. It is like when you buy petrol."

"Petrol?"

"Ah, of course. I forget. All cars in the west use electricity now. Here, we still burn oil. When you pick up the handle, a person must approve before fuel flows."

"Yeah, I vaguely remember those disappearing a few years ago when everybody swapped to electric. So, you're saying you can't open the door without somebody operating the lock remotely."

“Yes, that is true for most,” Kubar replied. “I heard a colleague say Professor Halfon does not need this. His card operates the locks immediately. He does not like to wait.”

“Hmm. I get the impression he’s not a patient man.” Rosalind put down the empty cup. “Shall we go?”

Monday 21st July 2036

Tripoli Infectious Diseases Hospital, Republic of North Africa
17 days until the deadline

Dr Kubar lowered himself into the uncomfortable wooden chair.

Professor Halfon regarded him from the other side of the heavy wooden desk. "So, tell me, how is the research going?" he asked.

"She has given us much information about the manufacture of Lucinase. I have passed it on to the chemists."

Halfon grunted. "I know this already. I expect production to start in the next few weeks. What of the work on developing a cure for this new strain?"

"We have been reviewing the previous research from the team."

"*Your* team," Halfon interjected. "Go on."

"Yes, of course, my team. We have not yet discussed her ideas."

"I am sure I need not remind you that time is short."

"No, sir. I am well aware of the deadline. This is why I wanted to talk to you. I have some requests to help speed up our work. Did you know the Baxter woman has an artificial eye?"

Halfon let out a scoff. "Yes, this is the reason she hates another of our guests."

"She told me Max Perrin was involved, but she did not tell me what happened."

"He broke into her house and gave her a drug that removed her free will, the same one he used to rape the girl. Then he ordered her to push a pen into her own eye."

Kubar gasped. "Why did he do this?"

Halfon leant forwards. "She killed the boy's father in front of him using an identical pen she snatched from his pocket. Perrin senior was about to give the formula for Lucinase to the British authorities before she had negotiated an amnesty for their past crimes. You wouldn't think she was capable of such violence to look at her. Anyway, why do you bring this up?"

Kubar hesitated for a moment as he processed the professor's words. There was far more to the woman than he had ever imagined. Still, she had offered him a possible route of escape. After what he had heard, could he trust her? He took a deep breath before continuing. "Her implant contains a rechargeable battery, which is now empty. She needs a charger to replenish the charge and make it function again."

"She has another eye. Isn't that enough?"

"Perhaps, but she tells me she requires the use of both eyes if she is to work at peak efficiency."

Halfon studied his subordinate carefully. "And you are sure this is not a trick?"

"I don't think so, sir."

"Where would we get such a thing?"

"It is unlikely the manufacturer would sell us this item, and in addition, it would take too long to import. She has informed me that the technology is the same as that used to charge mobile phones. This we can buy at the local market."

Halfon nodded slowly. "All right, but I hold you personally responsible if there are any problems. Was there anything else?"

"Yes. She has also requested that we allow her adopted son to work with her."

"You surprise me. Did she not threaten to kill him along with the girl? At least that is what Mr Perrin told us."

"I was not aware of that, sir."

Halfon tapped the table with his fingernails. "Well, if she is asking for his help, it seems they must have put it behind them. Go on."

"He is studying Biochemistry at university. He has the skills to perform the role of a lab assistant. We can always use more staff."

Halfon glared at his subordinate. "You lead the science team. The decision is yours. He is your responsibility. Is that all?"

"Have you had the time to check up on—?"

"Enough!" The professor leant forwards with both palms on the desk. A deep scowl clouded his features. "I told you before, I am still waiting for a reply about your daughter. When I receive an answer, you will be the first to hear."

Kubar stood. "Thank you, sir. I will get back to work."

Thursday 24th July 2036

Tripoli Infectious Diseases Hospital, Republic of North Africa
14 days until the deadline

"There, that should do the business," Jason said, pointing to the device on the desk. This was his third day working with the science team. So far, he had helped one scientist to monitor an experiment, but the others seemed suspicious of the relationship between him and his adoptive mother and declined his offers of help.

"What?" Rosalind Baxter replied. She was deeply engrossed in an article from a virology journal.

"The charger for your eye."

Earlier that day, Dr Kubar had brought a couple of different charging devices. Jason had skimmed through the pidgin English of the manuals and connected the larger of the two. Operation of the units seemed simple enough.

Rosalind studied the black plastic slab lying on the surface of the desk with a wire trailing to the mains socket. "Are you sure this will work?"

"There's only one way to find out. I assume your implant uses the same frequencies to charge as mobile phones. If it works, I can look at ways of charging while you do other things."

"Let's give it a go. What shall I do?"

"We need to get the pad as close to your eye as possible. Rest the right side of your head on there."

Rosalind followed his instructions. "Like this?"

"Yeah. Is anything happening?"

She waited a moment before responding. "Nothing yet."

"It might take a minute or two."

Rosalind held the same position. "No, nothing's... hang on. I just saw a flicker, but it was very faint. I can't quite make out... There's some text. It says it's booting."

"Excellent," Jason said. "I was wondering whether you had become desensitised to the signals."

"What do you mean?"

"The human brain is always making and breaking connections. You remember the experiments they did in the nineteenth century when they got people to wear glasses fitted with special lenses which inverted the images reaching each eye. At first, the subjects couldn't see properly, but after a few days, they adapted and saw things correctly even though the light hitting their retinas was the opposite way to normal."

Rosalind grimaced. "Yes, Jason. I have read a thing or two about science in my time. Afterwards, when they took off the glasses at the end of the experiment, everything was upside down again for a while until the patients' eyesight automatically adjusted back."

Jason grinned sheepishly. "So, you already know the story. I was worried your brain might have forgotten how to process the signals."

"Well, the good news is that the startup messages are visible. And they're the right way up. It's about to reach a hundred percent. Yes! I can see again."

"So, everything looks all right?"

"There are various message boxes popping up. There's a warning that the charge is low. Hardly surprising, I suppose. Let me just clear that." She swept a hand in front of her face as if waving away an insect. "The next one is asking if I want to connect to a Wi-Fi network."

Jason grasped Rosalind's arm in excitement. "You never mentioned you could link to wireless networks." He lowered his voice to a whisper. "Maybe we could use your eye to contact somebody back home and ask for help."

"It never occurred to me until now. Let me check which ones are available." She held a finger to her earlobe and muttered a few words.

"Sorry, I didn't get that."

Rosalind released her ear. "I wasn't talking to you. It lets the implant know I'm giving it a command. I've no idea how it works. Anyway, there are two signals: TIDH one and TIDH two. Damn! Both are password protected."

Jason's shoulders sagged in disappointment. He was about to ask another question when he sensed a presence behind him. He whirled around as Professor Halfon strode towards them.

Rosalind hadn't detected the director's approach. "Perhaps we could—"

Jason dug his fingernails into Rosalind's arm.

"Ouch! Why did you—?"

"Hello, Professor," Jason said in a loud voice. Rosalind jerked upright.

"Did you not sleep properly last night, Mrs Baxter?" Halfon asked as he stared down suspiciously at the two prisoners. "I hope it is not because of your new accommodations."

"I don't know how you expect us to work at peak efficiency when you're detaining us in these appalling conditions," Rosalind replied, "but as it happens, I slept fine."

"We were charging her eye," Jason added.

"Ah yes, Doctor Kubar mentioned this to me. But how do you intend to perform research with your head on the table?"

"I won't," Rosalind said, her tone frosty. "We're just proving the charger works. Now that we know it does, we'll set up something more practical. Is there anything else we can help you with?"

"What progress are you making? Are you any closer to a cure?"

Rosalind stared at Halfon. "We've been here about a week. I'm not a miracle worker. I retired three years ago, so it'll take a while for me to catch up with the latest research papers."

"Just remember that in two weeks, your grandson will be the test subject. His life depends upon your efforts."

"I'm well aware of that," Rosalind snapped, "and as I've told you several times already, that's a ridiculously short amount of time to solve this problem."

"Be that as it may, the deadline remains the same. I am sure we will talk soon."

Halfon turned away and headed across the room.

"The damned thing's packed in again," Rosalind said.

Jason waited until the professor was out of earshot. "I take it you still believe the timescales are unrealistic."

"What do you think? Of course they are. I told you the chances of developing a cure in a three-week timeframe were almost non-existent, and we're already one-week in."

Jason stared at his mother. "In that case, we'd better start planning our escape. And the fact you can link your eye to Wi-Fi networks may help us. Now what we need is a password."

Friday 25th July 2036

Tripoli Infectious Diseases Hospital, Republic of North Africa
13 days until the deadline

Jason slipped the T-shirt over Paul's head as Dr Kubar entered the room. Antimone rearranged her son's fine hair. A few yards away, Rosalind Baxter sat at the dining table, a look of thunder on her face. The doctor's arrival came as a welcome relief to the tension in the room.

"Did you sleep well?" Kubar asked.

Rosalind fixed the doctor with an icy stare. She gestured towards the black slab of plastic on her bed. "They wouldn't fetch an extension lead for the charger, so I'm still blind in one eye."

"I apologise. Tonight will be different. I will speak to the guards. Are you ready to start work?"

"I'm good to go," Jason replied.

"Excellent. I have some ideas I want to discuss with you," Kubar said.

"Can't wait," Rosalind muttered.

Jason bent to kiss Antimone on the cheek. "I'm off to the lab now." He patted his son on the head. "See you later, buddy. Look after Mummy."

Antimone stared up at him listlessly. She wasn't coping well with the boredom of their confinement.

"I'm sorry," he said. He lowered his voice. "I'll try to get hold of the Wi-Fi password."

"Good luck," she murmured.

He shot her a guilty sideways glance as he walked away.

The threesome made their way to the lift where Kubar presented his access card. The doors opened, and they stepped inside. Jason watched as the doctor selected the centremost of five buttons. "What's on the bottom level?"

"It is the basement where the cells are. You do not want to go there."

"Is that where they're keeping Max Perrin?"

Kubar glanced at Jason but didn't reply.

"I was just curious," Jason said.

They emerged from the lift and followed the corridor through the dining area. The low hum of conversation quietened as Kubar led them past the tables where groups of scientists sat eating their breakfast. Several pairs of distrustful eyes tracked their progress. After passing through a final set of locked doors, they entered the laboratory.

Nobody acknowledged their arrival as they approached a pair of workstations.

"So, what was this idea of yours?" Rosalind asked.

"Oh, it is probably stupid," Kubar replied, "but we know the lytic phase of the virus is triggered by pheromones emitted by pregnant women. I wonder if we can stop these molecules binding to the receptors on the target cell's outer membrane. Without a trigger, the cell won't lyse."

"I was reading an article on the subject only yesterday. In principle, something like that might work."

"I think I understand what you're saying," Jason said. "If we block all the cell receptor sites with a compound that doesn't react with the virus, it would never receive the signal that makes it activate."

"Correct," Rosalind agreed. "The big problem is finding a substance that won't prevent normal operation of the cell causing it to die and that isn't toxic to the patient in some other way. It's an approach we spent a lot of time on at Ilithyia."

Kubar's eyes lit up with excitement. "Good. Tell me more about this work."

"Before we do any of that," Rosalind replied, "I'm going to charge my implant." She moved across to the desk she had been using the previous day, flicked on the mains switch and rested her head sideways on the charger pad.

"Mrs Baxter," the doctor said, "your grandson's life depends on this research. Can you not do this tonight?"

"Well, if the guards had brought the extension lead last night as I requested, I wouldn't need to do it now, would I?"

Kubar shot a glance at Jason.

"All right," Jason replied, "I can't really contribute much to the medical side. But I can probably improvise something that would enable you to work and charge your eye at the same time."

"How long would that take?" Kubar asked.

"Half an hour at most."

"Surely you can wait for thirty minutes, Mrs Baxter."

Rosalind raised her head. She alternated her gaze between Jason and the doctor. Finally, she let out a sigh of exasperation. "If this doesn't work, I'm going to lie here until my eye is fully charged."

"Good. What do you need, Mr Floyd?"

Jason reeled off a list of items. Kubar left to pass on the request.

Jason cleared his throat. He turned to his mother but didn't speak.

"Is something on your mind?" she asked.

"Ah… I was just wondering."

"Go on then. Spit it out."

Jason stared at the surface of the desk. "That email you sent: the one where you wanted to see us. What was that all about?"

Rosalind glared at him. "Why does that matter now?"

Jason raised his head slowly. "Three years ago, you trapped us in an incinerator and threatened to turn it on. Then a few weeks back, you proposed we meet up as if nothing unusual had happened. Isn't that a bit strange?"

Rosalind looked away. After a few seconds, she returned his gaze. "I don't know. I'd probably had too much to drink."

"Is that really it?"

Rosalind hesitated for a moment. "Okay, I'll admit I missed having another person in the house. I never had any close friends, at least not in recent history, and it was hard having nobody to talk to. All my life, I've struggled to achieve something, to prove I'm the best. Then, at last, it happened. It was like swimming underwater, being pulled along by a strong current. I surfaced only to find I was all alone, miles from land."

"So, you felt sorry for yourself?"

"No… well, maybe a little. If I'm being totally honest, I regret the way I behaved towards you. You might not believe it, but I'd become quite fond of you. I allowed my anger to get the better of me, and now… I wish things had turned out differently between us."

"Why did you bring Antimone and Paul into it? Why didn't you ask to see me alone?"

"I'm not sure. I guess I wanted to apologise to her as well."

Jason frowned. "Seriously? You never liked her, even before everything."

Rosalind stared at him for a moment. "If you really want to know, I thought you could do better."

"Is that why you made no attempt to stop her wheelchair when we were on the boat?"

"No, of course not. I told you I couldn't move properly because of my knee, and that's the truth."

"Anyway, we're an item now, Mum."

Rosalind blinked at the unexpected term of address. "Yes, I realise that."

"So, why ask to see all of us together?"

"I thought there was more chance of you coming if I invited the three of you."

Jason mulled over his mother's words. He still didn't fully trust her, but they bore the ring of truth. He stared at her for a moment before speaking. "Fine. If we ever get out of here, we'll come as a family and visit you—but only if you save Paul."

Rosalind ran her fingers through her hair. "I've already told you, the likelihood of developing a cure in the available time is miniscule. We have a far better chance of surviving by escaping from this hole—and at the moment, our only hope of doing that depends upon me connecting to the Wi-Fi and getting a message out."

"A day or two back, General Shaladi suggested we join forces. He has people on the outside who are still loyal to him. He wants us to work together."

"And you trust that bastard?"

"Not entirely, no, but he gave me his word that if we help him, he'll get us out of here."

"Who would he take with him?"

Best not to tell her what Shaladi had said. "You, Antimone, Paul and me. And of course, his daughter."

"So, not Perrin?"

"No."

"Good." Rosalind's eyes narrowed in thought. "Maybe Shaladi knows the Wi-Fi password. The other option is Kubar. I've told him I'll try to find him a job in Europe if he helps us escape. I reckon he'd do it except that he doesn't want to leave until he finds out what happened to his daughter. She went missing a few years ago, and he hasn't heard from her since."

"Does he know about the wireless function of your implant?"

"No, I haven't told him about that. I'm not sure I trust him enough yet."

"Surely he would have the Wi-Fi password."

"You'd think so," Rosalind agreed, "but I can't ask him without telling him what my eye can do."

"I suggest we keep it that way for the moment."

"Agreed. Here he comes now."

Kubar strolled towards them. "Here are the items you asked for, Mr Floyd."

"Thanks."

"Mrs Baxter, while Jason works on the charger, perhaps you can tell me more about your previous work."

Rosalind and the doctor moved to the adjacent workstation. Soon, they were deep in discussion. Kubar scribbled in a notebook, stopping occasionally to ask a question, as the former CEO of Ilithyia Biotechnology described the research her company had undertaken.

Jason laid out the parts. He picked up the baseball cap, tore off a length of duct tape and used it to attach the charging pad to the right side. It took several attempts to get the plastic slab to hang in the right position. When he was satisfied, he strengthened the join with more strips. He placed the contraption on his head and adjusted the strap at the back of the hat until it was a tight fit. The design wouldn't win any awards for style, but hopefully, it would perform its function.

He detached the mains cable and carried the assembly to where Rosalind and Kubar sat. "Are you ready to give it a try?"

Rosalind couldn't hide her dismay as she took in the arrangement. "You don't seriously expect me to wear that?"

"I know it doesn't look great, but it should mean you can work and charge your eye at the same time. If you put the charger under your pillow tonight as well, you probably won't need it tomorrow."

Rosalind reluctantly accepted the equipment. "If either of you two laughs, I'm taking it off immediately."

Jason stifled his amusement and helped her to tighten the strap. Next, he plugged in the power cable and flicked the switch. "Is anything happening?"

Rosalind stared straight ahead for a moment. "Yes, there was a flicker. It's booting."

Jason flashed a glance at Kubar. Somehow, they needed the wireless password. The doctor was their best chance, but would he help or turn them in?

Friday 25th July 2036

Tripoli Infectious Diseases Hospital, Republic of North Africa
13 days until the deadline

Jason glanced at his watch band: 19:05. A surge of guilt hit him. During his long day in the laboratory, Antimone had been looking after Paul by herself.

Dr Kubar rubbed the back of his neck. "So, you do not want to sleep with the charger beneath your pillow?" he asked.

Rosalind continued to stare at the screen. "No," she replied absentmindedly.

"But I thought you wanted to charge it fully."

She tore her gaze away from the computer display and turned to the doctor. "If I wear this ridiculous contraption again tomorrow—no offence, Jason—it should reach at least seventy percent."

"None taken," Jason said. "I told you it wouldn't win any fashion prizes."

"Hmm," Rosalind grunted. Her focus had already returned to the three-dimensional molecular model that spun as she waved her fingers in front of the monitor. She continued to study the image for a few seconds longer, then sat back. "It's worth a try," she said. "Do you have any way to make this?" she asked, directing her question at Kubar. "We should perform some cell culture trials when we've done a few more simulations."

"Doctor Brandt has used the molecular synthesiser a few times to manufacture various compounds."

"I don't think I'm his favourite person," Rosalind said. "Then again, none of them seem to like me."

"You can hardly blame them. Everybody has lost loved ones to this virus, and you created it. On top of this, they all hold you responsible for Professor Halfon's demand that they do not leave the building."

"But that's nothing to—"

"I know, but it does not stop them making you a—how do you say?—escape goat.

Jason stifled a snort of laughter. "I think you mean a scapegoat."

Kubar smiled apologetically. "Ah yes, please forgive my poor English."

Rosalind remained unamused. "Have you considered my offer?"

Kubar's smile dropped instantly. He glanced anxiously at the bored-looking guard, leaning with his back against the wall on the other side of the room. He lowered his voice to a whisper. "As I have told you before, I cannot leave until I know the fate of my daughter."

"And what are you doing about that?"

"I have asked Professor Halfon."

She raised an eyebrow.

Kubar stared at her for a moment. "He promised me he will check the database. I will ask him again."

"Well, here's your chance." Rosalind's gaze shifted to an approaching figure.

The doctor twisted in his seat, then hurriedly turned back.

"What is this?" Halfon asked, pointing at the screen.

"You're not one for small talk, are you?" Rosalind said, scowling at the director. "It's an idea we've been discussing this afternoon, but we're not ready to take it further yet."

Halfon's eyes narrowed before he spoke. "There is no shortage of test subjects. Please remember there is a tight deadline."

"We haven't forgotten that, but it's still at a preliminary stage. It'll be a few days before we contemplate any form of testing. We'll run it through a suite of simulations first. If you want me to work for you, we'll do things my way."

"Very well, but Mullah Awad is not a patient man. Now, is there anything you need for this to go quicker?"

"Not really," Rosalind replied. "A team of real experts would help, but nothing that you can provide right now."

"In that case, I will leave you to your research."

~

"Excuse me, sir," Kubar called as he jogged after Halfon.

The professor stopped and turned to his subordinate. "What is it?"

The doctor lowered his head in deference. "If I may speak in private for a moment," he said.

They moved a few paces away from Rosalind and Jason.

Halfon glared at Kubar. "If this is about your daughter again, I told you I would look into this matter. However, I am a very busy man. Your only concern right now is to find a cure for this disease. Unless we deliver a treatment, I cannot guarantee any of us will leave this building. Do you understand?"

Kubar bobbed his head in acquiescence. "Yes, of course."

"Good. If there are any *technical* matters for which you need my help, please do not hesitate to contact me. If there is nothing else, you should get back to work."

"Right away, sir."

"By the way, I assume that ridiculous contraption the infidel woman is wearing is for her eye."

"Yes. It is an improvised charger."

"Well, as long as it doesn't stop her working."

"On the contrary. Unless the battery is charged, she cannot see properly."

"If we ever solve the virus problem, perhaps we should study the technology inside her head. It might provide our people with something we can use ourselves."

"That is a good idea, sir."

"Right, I have much to do."

Halfon marched towards the exit without acknowledging the two Westerners.

After he had passed through the security door, Rosalind asked, "What did he say? I bet he hasn't done anything, has he?"

Kubar picked at a fingernail. "He told me he is looking into it."

"Just like he does every time you ask. You have to accept he can't be bothered."

Kubar's jaw took on a stubborn tilt. "I cannot leave until I discover my daughter's fate. As a mother yourself, you must understand this."

Rosalind locked eyes with Jason. Nobody spoke for a few seconds. Eventually, she broke the silence. "Don't you think we've done enough for tonight?"

Kubar glanced at his watch. "I have nowhere else to go, but I am feeling hungry."

"Let's call it a night then. We'll look at this with a fresh perspective tomorrow. I need a rest."

"I will take you back to your quarters," Kubar said, standing.

Rosalind removed the headset and placed it on the desk. "It's a relief to get that thing off."

"What's the charge level?" Jason asked.

Rosalind's features took on an absent expression as she studied the image being transmitted directly into her brain. "It's saying thirty-six percent. That should keep me going for at least a week."

"You're welcome," Jason said drily.

Rosalind scowled at him. "I already thanked you earlier. But if it makes you feel better, thanks again."

Kubar's gaze switched from one to the other. "Come. Let us find some food." He gestured towards the doorway.

Jason led the way, trailed by Rosalind and the North African doctor. They followed the corridor to the eating area. Once again, the conversation hushed as they entered.

"Murderer," a voice whispered.

Rosalind whipped around. Several of the seated scientists glared at her with hatred in their eyes.

"Just ignore them," Kubar muttered, lengthening his stride. They reached the next sealed door without further incident. Moments later, the group of three stepped into the elevator.

"That was uncomfortable," Jason said, glancing at Rosalind. She stared straight ahead without acknowledging his comment.

The doors slid apart. Kubar led them down the corridor and into the area holding the other prisoners. "Here we are," he announced brightly. "Enjoy your meal. I will see you tomorrow morning. I hope you dream of a solution to our problem."

Rosalind grimaced. She waited silently until the doctor was out of sight.

"I can't wait to get out of here," she said.

Friday 25th July 2036

Tripoli Infectious Diseases Hospital, Republic of North Africa
13 days until the deadline

When they arrived back at the communal area, Paul was sitting on Antimone's lap, his arms wrapped around his mother's neck. Jason lowered his upper body to envelope mother and son in a tight embrace. Meanwhile, Rosalind grabbed a plate and filled it with food from the dishes laid out on the trolley.

"What's your day been like?" Jason asked. "I see you've got a new wheelchair."

"Boring as hell," Antimone replied, "but this one is a vast improvement. At long last, I can steer myself around without having to lean down to those tiny wheels. I've been spending some time with Aya Shaladi too. She's not so bad when you get to know her."

"Really? I thought you hated her guts."

"She was telling me what it's like for women here. The men treat them as second-class citizens. It's like something out of the dark ages. If she'd refused to help her father in their mission, the authorities would've had both of them killed."

"That doesn't excuse what they did to us," Jason said, grimacing.

"Maybe not. She's been helping me keep Paul entertained as well. She was driving him around in my old wheelchair. He told me afterwards he wanted to be in a wheelchair when he grew up."

Jason stifled a laugh. "That's kids for you."

"He even asked me whether she could be his mummy too."

"Christ."

"Anyway, what about your day?" Antimone asked. "Are they getting any closer to developing something to keep Paul safe?"

"Well, all the other scientists seem to hate us, and Professor Halfon is itching to test every random compound we consider on a live subject before we've even simulated the effects, but apart from that, it's been great. Seriously though, I think we're making good progress."

"Enough to come up with a cure in the next two weeks?"

Jason lowered his voice. "Probably not. My mother keeps saying the timescales are impossible."

Antimone glanced around. Max sat alone at the far end of the adjacent table. Rosalind occupied a spot on the opposite side, maximising the distance between herself and the main target of her hatred. General Shaladi and his daughter were helping themselves to food.

"That just confirms what we suspected all along; we've got to escape," Antimone whispered. "Have you made any progress on a plan?"

"Not so far," Jason replied.

"Well, we better come up with something unless you fancy trying to overpower those three." She nodded towards the guards sitting in the smoke-filled office a few yards away. The armed men seemed more intent on playing cards than guarding their prisoners.

"My mother's eye is charged again. If we got hold of the Wi-Fi password, she could use the in-built wireless link to connect to the outside world and get a message out."

"And how are we going to find that out?"

"As I see it, there are two people who might have it. One is Doctor Kubar. The other is sitting right there." Jason's gaze flicked towards the general and his daughter. "Do you think we can trust him?"

"Like I said, they had to follow orders, or they would've been killed."

"He didn't have to execute his own man though, did he? Judging by what he told us a few days ago, he wants to get out as much as we do. Even if we escape from this building, we'll need his help to reach the border."

Antimone studied Jason's face. "I think we should ask him."

"Okay, but we have to play this carefully. We mustn't tell him why we want the code."

As Shaladi turned with a full plate in his hand, Jason spoke in a low voice. "General, would you like to join us?"

The general shrugged and sat opposite Jason and Antimone. He leant forwards and rested his elbows on the table. "Do you have a plan?" he whispered.

Jason moved his head closer to Shaladi's. "Maybe. Do you know the Wi-Fi password?"

A glint of excitement sparkled in the general's eyes. "Why? Did you find a phone?"

"No, but we may have a way to link to the Internet."

"Oh." Shaladi's body seemed to deflate. "I am sorry, but I do not have this information. If you do discover the password, I must send a message to my people so they can help us once we are out."

"What are you talking about?" Aya Shaladi asked, sitting beside her father.

“Our friends have found a way to communicate with the outside world, but they need the Wi-Fi password.”

Jason exchanged a glance with Antimone at the mention of the term *friend.*

“Could you ask one of the scientists?” Aya said. “They may know it. They must realise they are also prisoners.”

“Why don’t you just announce it to the guards?” came Rosalind Baxter’s petulant voice from behind them. “Try to keep your voices down. And by the way, you need my help to do this.”

A guilty silence fell over the group. Antimone glanced towards the glass window of the office. Their minders were engrossed in a card game and seemed oblivious to the conversation taking place on the other side of the room. Her gaze swung to the figure of Max Perrin. He was staring in their direction. As their eyes met, he looked away.

“Actually,” Jason said, his voice now a whisper, “there may still be a way you can help us. Do you have access to any of your government databases?”

The general gave a low laugh. “There are many different systems. What do you require?”

“Is there one to track down a missing person?”

“Yes, but a lot of people in this country disappear with no trace. If the government has knowledge of a citizen, then I can check their status. At least, I could before this. I do not know if I still have permission. Why do you ask?”

“I may be able to get the Wi-Fi password in exchange for finding out what happened to a specific person.”

“So, you want me to tell you how to access this site?” Shaladi asked. He rubbed the back of his neck. “And how well can you read Arabic?”

“Not at all,” Jason replied

“That is a problem. How will you understand the words?”

“Um… I don’t know.”

“If they find out that I gave you this information, it is not like in the West. There will be no trial. They will kill me.”

Antimone sighed. “I hate to break this to you, but isn’t there a good chance they might do that anyway? You already told us they probably executed your men.”

Once again, silence descended, broken only by the muffled laughter of the guards in the nearby office. The general sat with his head lowered.

Finally, he raised his eyes and stared at Jason. “You may be right. I will give you my decision in the morning.”

Saturday 26th July 2036

Tripoli Infectious Diseases Hospital, Republic of North Africa
12 days until the deadline

The next morning, Jason was reading the Harry Potter paperback when General Shaladi settled down on the bench beside him. Antimone was washing Paul in the bathroom.

"I have given your proposal much thought," the general said. "You need four pieces of information to access the website containing details of our citizens: the site address, a username, a password and a military service number. Before I give this to you, I must understand how you will use it."

Jason took his time placing the book on the table as he thought. What should he reveal? Could he really trust the general? "Okay," he said, drawing out the last syllable. "Somebody is worried about a family member. If we discover what happened to her, he may give us what we want."

"You mean Doctor Kubar?"

Jason felt the blood rush to his face. *So much for not revealing anything.* "Yeah," he murmured.

Shaladi's lips curved into a smirk. "I thought so. If you find the information for his daughter, he will help us? If the authorities are holding her, it is unlikely he will risk her safety. This is how they work. They make threats to keep the people in order."

"I don't know."

"It is true. You better hope she is not alive."

Jason turned sideways towards the general.

"Do not look at me," Shaladi hissed. "If I was a gambling man," he continued in a conciliatory tone, "I would bet that she is dead. Many women have died in this country. You will need the doctor's help to access the database—unless you have learned to speak Arabic overnight."

"So, you'll give me the information?" Jason said. A prod on the thigh provided the response.

"Take it," Shaladi whispered. "Put it in your pocket. Do not let the guards see."

Jason's fingers closed around a scrap of paper. His gaze flicked towards the two men in the glass-fronted office. They sat with half-open eyes, staring at a screen. Neither seemed to be paying any attention to their prisoners. He slipped the note into the pocket of his jeans. "Thanks," he replied.

"It is extremely dangerous for me to give you this information. As I told you yesterday, if they discover what I have done, they will execute me immediately. Only use the database if you are confident you can do so without being discovered."

"How are we going to escape from here with all these guards?"

Shaladi tapped the table with a fingernail. "I do not know yet, but we will not get far unless we have outside help. And remember, I can only take you to the border. You must find your own way home from there. Now, do not let them see us talking, so please sit somewhere else."

Jason opened his mouth to object. Why should he be the one to move? But maybe this wasn't the time for an argument. He picked up the book and shuffled down the bench away from the general. He opened the pages but found he could no longer concentrate on the words. Moments later, Antimone and Paul returned from the bathroom.

"Shaladi has given me his login details," he whispered as he leant over to lift his son off Antimone's lap.

"Good luck," she replied. "Be careful."

He tried to entertain his son with made-up stories, but his mind kept wandering much to Paul's annoyance. It was another forty minutes before Kubar arrived.

Jason lowered his face to kiss Antimone and patted Paul on the head. "Sorry, but Daddy's got to go to work."

"Please," the doctor said. "Come with me." Unlike the previous day, his features were set in a sombre expression.

"Is something wrong?" Jason asked.

Kubar didn't reply. He watched Rosalind as she put on her shoes. "I'm ready," she announced. "I thought we were going to have an early start."

The doctor ignored her statement and marched towards the door. Jason and Rosalind exchanged a glance as they hurried to keep up. They entered the lift and rode up a floor in silence. They passed through the dining area, once again running the gauntlet of cold stares from the few scientists who were still eating. Kubar led them down the corridors and into the laboratory. The group of three crossed the room to the workstations they had occupied the previous day.

Rosalind settled into a chair. Her eyes surveyed the work surface, looking for the cap and improvised charger. "Where's it gone?" she asked, glancing up sharply. "I left it here."

Kubar pointed at the small, circular bin beside the desk. "It is in there."

"What? You've thrown it away?" Rosalind asked in astonishment.

"Yes," the doctor replied, "but it is of no use to you now."

She leant forwards and reached inside to retrieve the contents. A piece of tape still attached the charging pad to the hat, but the black slab now comprised two parts, each with a jagged edge where it had snapped in half. A thin strand of wire connected the halves. Somebody had also hacked off the power cable.

"Who did this?" Rosalind asked, glowering at the doctor.

Kubar shrugged. "I do not know."

"There's some writing on the front of the cap," Jason said in a low voice.

Rosalind rotated the material in her hand and read the single word: *Murderer*. Her face drained of colour except for the bright-red circles forming on each cheek. An uncomfortable stillness settled on the room. Rosalind raised her head. All conversation ceased around them. Her eyes darted from one group of scientists to another as she tried to identify the culprit. The onlookers, who had been watching the exchange with keen interest, looked away under the fierce coldness of her gaze.

She turned her focus to Kubar. "Are you going to do something about this?" she asked, her voice trembling with barely suppressed fury.

The doctor cleared his throat. "Unfortunately, we do not know who is responsible."

"And you still expect me to work with these people?" A speck of saliva flew from her mouth as she spat out the last word.

"I agree this is unacceptable," Kubar said. "I will arrange for somebody to buy the parts so we can make a replacement."

"That's hardly the point though, is it? How can I trust my colleagues when this sort of immature behaviour takes place as soon as my back is turned?"

"It will not happen again."

"This whole exercise is futile. You pull together—or in cases like mine, kidnap—a team of misfits and mavericks who have never worked with each other before, then you prevent them from leaving the site or communicating with the outside world. Yet somehow, in a few weeks, you expect them to deliver the solution to a hugely complex problem. Frankly, it's ludicrous."

Kubar drew in a deep breath. He seemed about to say something when the direction of his gaze shifted.

Jason turned. "It looks like we've got company," he murmured.

Professor Halfon strode towards them purposefully. He stopped a pace away and surveyed the group of three. "Good morning," he said. "I trust everything is fine."

"Yeah," Rosalind replied, her voice dripping in sarcasm. "Just fantastic." She opened her fingers and allowed the broken contraption to drop into the bin.

If the director detected the simmering tension, he chose to ignore it. He cleared his throat. "There is something I want to show you. Please come with me."

Rosalind rose to her feet with exaggerated slowness. "What is it?"

"You will see."

Jason, Rosalind and Kubar trailed after the professor as he led them towards the enclosure in the centre of the room and peered through the clear panels.

Jason's pulse quickened. His mother had told him about the previous experiment they forced her to watch. With a surge of relief, he realised the area was empty. "What are you going to do?"

Halfon didn't reply. Instead, he tapped on the glass. The door at the end of the enclosed space opened. A man in a white protective suit entered, pushing a hospital trolley. A naked three- or four-year-old boy lay on top, his ribs prominent against the skin of his chest. Straps extended over his thin body, preventing him from moving. The child's eyes gazed listlessly at his surroundings.

Rosalind turned sideways and grasped Halfon's forearm. "What is this?"

The professor lowered his gaze to her hand. After a second, she took the hint and released her grip. Halfon focused his attention back on the boy. He nodded to the suited attendant and spoke without turning his head. "The child is conscious but has been sedated. The doctor in there is about to inject him with the compound you designed yesterday."

Rosalind's mouth opened in shock. "What? That was just an idea. We haven't even run any simulations yet. You have to stop this."

Halfon's eyes stayed locked on the restrained boy. "There are many test subjects but little time. Doctor Brandt programmed the molecular synthesiser last night."

"What effect will it have?" Jason asked, staring intently at Rosalind.

"I have no idea," she replied. "Anything could happen."

The white-suited figure picked up a syringe gun from the table at the side of the room and fitted a small vial of clear liquid.

Jason hammered his fists on the glass. "Hey! Leave him alone."

Rosalind joined in, slamming both palms against the window.

Halfon held up a hand and dragged his attention away from the trolley "Enough!"

A rifle barrel jabbed into the centre of Jason's back. A second guard pointed his weapon at Rosalind.

"If you cannot watch in silence," Halfon said, "I will have you bound and gagged."

The Westerners fell silent, although both still rested their hands on the glass. The man inside the room placed the syringe against the boy's upper arm and depressed the trigger. A low whimper emerged from the child's throat. Outside, the observers held their breath, waiting to see what would happen next. The suited doctor picked up a torch and directed the beam at the site of the injection. He leant over the boy and peered through his facemask.

Seconds passed in silence. Halfon withdrew a mobile device from the inner pocket of his jacket, tapped a few icons and stared at the screen. "Excellent. All his vital signs are stable. There is no immediate adverse reaction. We will observe him for twenty-four hours before performing further tests. Now, I suggest you get back to work."

Jason released the breath he had been holding and turned to Rosalind. "We can't allow that to happen again," he whispered.

Saturday 26th July 2036

Tripoli Infectious Diseases Hospital, Republic of North Africa
12 days until the deadline

The group returned to their workstations. Rosalind stared at the display for several seconds, then turned to Dr Kubar. "Did you know he was planning to do that?" she asked, her voice trembling with fury.

"No, he did not tell me," the doctor replied. "He must have looked at our work last night."

"This is totally unacceptable. Is he going to test every compound we come up with on a live subject before we've even had time to model it or test it in cell cultures?"

Kubar sighed. "I will talk to Professor Halfon."

"And what about Brandt? Aren't you in charge of him now? Doesn't he work for you?"

"Yes, but if the professor tells him to do something, he must obey. Everybody is under much pressure to deliver a solution."

"So, what happens next? Do they intend to expose that boy to a pregnant woman?"

"I do not know, but I think so."

"But that's ridiculous. The chances of it working are miniscule. The child will die needlessly."

"I am sorry, but there is little I can do."

The breath rasped in Rosalind's throat, and her pulse raced. "I'm going to delete the work from the machine at the end of every day."

"That would not be wise," Kubar said. "The professor will punish us if we do not deliver."

Rosalind slapped the surface of the desk. "How am I supposed to perform at my best under these conditions?"

Kubar shot an anxious glance towards the guards. "Please. You must remain calm."

Rosalind's eyes stared at the screen but took nothing in.

Several seconds passed until Jason broke the silence. "Have you given any more thought to helping us get out of here?" he asked, turning to the doctor.

Kubar looked away for a moment, then turned back. "I told you," he replied in a low voice, "I cannot leave until I learn about my daughter."

"What if we could access the database and find out?"

Kubar's gaze locked onto Jason. "How can you do this?"

Jason lowered his head. "I've got a username and password," he whispered.

"Where did this information come from?"

"I'll tell you when you agree to help us."

"It will not work," Kubar said. "The guards have taken all the mobile phones, and they monitor all the workstations."

"We may have a way around that too, but we don't have the Wi-Fi password. Do you know what it is?"

Kubar's eyes widened in surprise. "You have a phone?"

Rosalind's hand touched Jason's thigh. He met her gaze as she gave an almost imperceptible shake of the head.

"Something like that," he replied. "All we need is the password for the wireless network."

Kubar went still. He remained silent for several seconds. When he spoke, his voice was subdued. "I am not sure I want to find out."

Jason frowned in puzzlement. "Why not?"

"For now, there is hope. If I discover she is dead, then it is gone."

"But isn't it better to know one way or the other?"

"Perhaps." Kubar hung his head for a moment, then seemed to come to a decision. He looked up. "You are right. I will tell you the Wi-Fi password. In return, you will find out about my daughter. But we must be careful. They are always watching."

"Will they be able to detect a connection?"

"If they are looking, perhaps. I am not an expert in such matters. You should disconnect when you are not using the link."

"Can they tell what sites we've logged into?"

"Maybe. I do not know."

"Could you write the password down?"

Kubar's eyes flashed to the nearest guard. Satisfied the man was paying them no special attention, he grabbed a pen and scribbled a series of letters and digits on a piece of paper. "I cannot be sure it still works," he said.

Rosalind's face took on a blank expression. She touched her earlobe and muttered a few words. Moments later, she smiled. "It does work."

Kubar stared at her in surprise. "But… ah, of course, your eye."

"There's one other small problem," Jason said. "I assume the website is in Arabic, and my mother doesn't speak the language."

"Actually, I may have a solution for that," Rosalind said. "After the doctors installed my implant, they wanted to test it was working correctly, so they linked it wirelessly to a computer display to check out the quality of the image. I'm assuming we can do the same. That way you'd be able to see the same as me, and Doctor Kubar could tell me what to type in."

"You mean casting," Jason said. "These computers look fairly up to date. That should work." He tapped some keys on the virtual keyboard floating in front of the screen. "If you find the right menu option, you should be able to connect now."

A blank expression returned to Rosalind's face. The background hum of the machines filled the silence. Eventually, she turned to Jason. "There, I think I've set it up correctly."

A circular image of Jason's features appeared on the display. The contents jerked about as she changed the point of her focus.

"Now all we have to do is pull up a browser," she added. A rectangular window overlaid the central third of the picture.

"Can you show a keyboard, preferably with Arabic characters?" Kubar asked.

While Rosalind concentrated on responding to his request, Jason glanced surreptitiously around the room, then retrieved the scrap of paper from his pocket. He placed it on the work surface. After a few seconds, an array of keys materialised at the bottom of the screen.

"So, your secret helper is General Shaladi," Kubar said, studying the Arabic words.

"How did you—?" Jason started. Then realisation dawned. "Ah, of course: the username. Yeah, he told us he'd help us to escape."

As they watched the display, a series of characters appeared in the address bar. Moments later, a form popped up with three empty text boxes. Kubar showed the letters he wanted in each field.

"Come on," Jason said. "This is taking too long."

"That is the last one," Kubar replied. "Now click the button."

A list containing three results in Arabic script appeared on the page. The doctor leant forwards. He pointed to the middle entry. "This is my daughter."

The image changed once again. None of the characters meant anything to the two Westerners. Jason turned his attention to Kubar, watching as the doctor's gaze tracked down the rows of text.

"What does it say?" Jason asked.

Kubar did not respond at first. Then he leant back in his chair, his expression devoid of emotion. "You can turn it off now."

The image from Rosalind's eye disappeared from the screen. "I've disconnected from the wireless network," she said. "Is your daughter still alive?"

Kubar sat motionless, staring straight ahead. Rosalind shot a glance at Jason. He shrugged. Finally, the doctor turned his head slowly towards them.

"She died five years ago."

Saturday 26th July 2036

Tripoli Infectious Diseases Hospital, Republic of North Africa
12 days until the deadline

Max Perrin walked one pace ahead of his escort, standing to the side whenever they reached a locked door to allow the armed man to present his identity card to the reader. His mind raced. A week had gone by since striking the deal with Professor Halfon. What could he tell the administrator about the other prisoners? In truth, he had little to report, but if he didn't provide anything, he knew he would soon find himself sleeping in the cells.

When they arrived at the final set of doors before the professor's office, the lock refused to operate. The guard raised both hands in a petulant gesture as he glared up at the camera lens.

Perrin's gaze strayed to the holstered pistol on the guard's hip. The man subconsciously detected the focus of his prisoner's attention and moved his fingers down to the strap. After presenting the identification a second time, the mechanism operated with a loud clunk. The guard shoved Perrin down the carpeted corridor ahead of him, muttering curses under his breath.

"Easy, tiger," Perrin said, glancing backwards. "I think your boss will be interested in what I have to say."

His reward was another push in the back. They stopped at a door decorated with a large sign in Arabic script. His escort knocked once. A voice called out from inside, and the armed man turned the handle before ushering Perrin forwards.

"Please take a seat," Halfon said, gesturing towards an uncomfortable looking wooden chair. He uttered a brisk command to the guard, who departed without another word. "Can I get you anything? Tea? Water?"

"No, I'm fine," Perrin replied.

"I trust your accommodation is acceptable."

"Yeah, it's okay." Every evening, somebody came to collect Max from the communal prisoner area under the pretence of taking him to the cells. In fact, he spent the night in the relative comfort of his old room before they returned him to the other detainees in the morning.

"It is a week since we last talked. The deal was that you agreed to spy on the others for me. In exchange, I gave you certain privileges. There is still plenty of space in the basement. I hope you bring some news."

Perrin nodded.

Halfon placed his hands on the wooden surface of the desk. "So, tell me, are they planning anything?"

"Well… they're careful about discussing things in front of me, but something's definitely going on."

"What do you mean?"

Perrin leant forwards. "General Shaladi and his daughter kidnapped the rest of them, yet now everyone's acting like best buddies."

Halfon glowered at his prisoner. "Explain."

"Um… okay. Last night, the general sat beside Floyd while they ate. The girl joined them. I've never really seen them together before yesterday. They talked for a few minutes."

"What did they talk about?"

"Right, well the thing is, I didn't catch very much. They don't seem to trust me. I heard them mention the word *friends*."

"Hmph," Halfon said with a sneer. "This is hardly proof of a conspiracy. Maybe they have agreed to forget their differences."

"No, I'm sure it's not that. They were definitely planning something. They also mentioned the other scientists."

"Do you expect me to be impressed by this? I should throw you in the cells. That may concentrate your mind."

"Actually, there's more." Perrin lowered his voice. "The English group seems very friendly with that doctor."

"Kubar?"

"Yeah, that's him."

Halfon crossed his arms, his face set in a thoughtful expression. "This is perhaps not surprising. They work together. Did you hear what they were discussing?"

"Not really, at least nothing interesting beyond the usual everyday stuff."

"So, all you have brought me is your suspicions with no real evidence to back it up. I have heard enough. It is time for you to—"

"Look, I've done what you asked. I'll see if I can get closer to them. As soon as I hear anything at all, I'll tell you about it."

Halfon splayed his fingers, took a breath and held it for a moment. "All right. I will give you one last chance. I believe you are still motivated. Do not let me down."

Saturday 26th July 2036

Tripoli Infectious Diseases Hospital, Republic of North Africa
12 days until the deadline

Rosalind glanced towards Dr Kubar. He had barely spoken a word since learning of his daughter's death that morning. Both Jason and Rosalind tried to engage him as they explored possible approaches using the powerful molecular modelling software. Despite her initial reservations, Rosalind had to admit the tools at her disposal exceeded the capabilities of those at Ilithyia Biotechnology, the company she had once owned.

"Let's set this simulation going," she said, pointing to the screen. They had reviewed several compounds over the day, but the most promising candidate remained the same one Halfon had given to the boy earlier that morning. Even with the latest quantum algorithms, the program predicted the job would take at least seven hours to run. "What do you think?"

Kubar didn't reply. He stared sightlessly at the three-dimensional image.

"Doctor Kubar?"

The doctor's eyes regained focus. He turned to Rosalind. "I am sorry. Please repeat your question."

"It doesn't matter," Rosalind said. "You've not really been paying attention all afternoon." Her tone softened. "Not that I blame you in the circumstances. It must be a big shock."

Kubar took a deep breath and exhaled slowly. "I always feared she might not be alive. It is still hard for me to hear it confirmed." He lapsed once again into silence.

Jason cleared his throat. "I know this is a difficult time, but now that you've found out what happened to her, will you help us get out of here?"

The doctor's face tightened in anger. "I have lost a daughter, and all you care about is escaping."

"I have a child as well," Jason replied. "Unless we escape, he'll probably die too."

Kubar's angry expression morphed into one of remorse. "I am sorry. You are correct. The work they are doing here is wrong. I have—how do you say?—turned an unseeing eye for too long."

"Blind," Jason said.

"Yes, a blind eye," Kubar continued. "So many people have died. So many terrible things have happened, it starts to become normal. Now, they use children like test animals." He twisted to Rosalind. "You told me you will try to find a job for me in the West. Is this true?"

Rosalind looked away. She forced herself to turn back and meet the doctor's questioning expression. She spoke in a subdued voice. "I'll do what I can, but you saw the television pictures. I'm not exactly the world's most popular person at the moment."

Kubar stared up at the ceiling, then focused his gaze on Jason. "I will help you escape, but you must take as many of the children with you as possible. You tell me your son will die if he stays here; the same is true for them."

"That sounds like a fair deal," Jason agreed. "How do you plan to get us out?"

"Let me think about it," Kubar replied. "We will discuss this tomorrow."

"I propose we finish for the day," Rosalind said. "If we start the simulation now, it'll be done by morning. Will you please persuade Halfon to hold off testing on the boy?"

The doctor gave a resigned sigh. "You know what the professor is like. He will not listen to me, but I will try."

Rosalind reached out a finger and started the analysis. "At least there's nothing new today for that bastard to trial on one of those kids."

Kubar stood and led the two Westerners towards the exit under the watchful eyes of the guards. As before, a sudden hush in the conversation greeted their entry into the dining area. The doctor hurried past the seated scientists, ignoring the hostile glances cast in their direction. Moments later, he deposited his charges in the living quarters a floor down.

"I'm sorry once again for… you know," Jason said to Kubar. He glanced towards the general, whose gaze lasered in on him.

"Thank you. I will see you in the morning."

~

Dr Kubar turned around and retraced his steps, his mind a mass of conflicting emotions. He had agreed to help the Westerners escape, but was that the right decision? He had little left to live for following confirmation of his daughter's death. His own life counted for little in the grand scheme of things, but was he prepared to gamble everything on the chance of a new start in the West?

Maybe he should stay and continue to lead the efforts to develop a cure. Using children to test possible treatments turned his stomach, but if they were successful, how many more lives would be saved? What would his daughter want him to do?

Dr Kubar found himself outside Professor Halfon's door with no recollection of how he had arrived there. He wiped his damp palms on the white lab coat and knocked.

"Udkhul," came a shout from within. *Come in.*

Halfon looked up from his desk as the doctor entered. "Ah, Doctor Kubar. This is fortuitous. I wanted to speak to you. Please take a seat."

Kubar lowered himself into the wooden chair and found himself looking upwards slightly at his superior.

"There is good news," Halfon said, leaning forwards. "I checked on the status of your daughter this afternoon. She is alive and well, living in Alzintan, a town a few miles outside Tripoli. I contacted the local military commander, and he has agreed to bring her here in a few weeks."

"But..." Kubar stopped. He desperately wanted the professor's words to be true. But he had seen the entry with his own eyes. "Are you sure?" Every square inch of his face felt numb.

"Yes, of course. I checked it myself."

"She was born in two thousand and six."

Halfon tutted impatiently. "I know this. I spoke to the commander just a few hours ago. Your daughter is definitely alive. A group of rebels were holding her prisoner. The army discovered her during a raid last week. Unfortunately, it is not possible for you to see her until you finish your work here. I am sure you are very excited, but we must deliver on time. We cannot afford to lose even one day. It will be a double celebration when we come up with a cure."

The blood rushed in Kubar's ears. Could it be true? Had he examined the wrong entry earlier that morning? No, he had confirmed the date of birth... unless there was another woman with the same name and an identical birthday. But there had been only three entries, and the other two were considerably older than his daughter.

"You don't seem pleased." Halfon's words intruded on his thoughts.

"I am just surprised. I didn't expect after all this time..."

"You should be grateful. Now you can be reunited with your daughter."

"Could I speak to her on the phone?"

"Do you think it would be fair if we had one rule for you and another for everybody else?"

"Well—"

"I share your frustration, but I cannot make an exception. When you finish this work, you will be able to talk to her for as long as you like. Now, was there some other matter you wished to discuss with me?"

Kubar scratched his head as he tried to place his thoughts in order. "Actually, there was another thing. The boy who you gave the drug—"

Halfon drummed his fingers on the desk. "You need not worry. He has shown no adverse reaction."

"Yes, but we never even modelled the behaviour of this substance. Anything could have happened."

"But it didn't, did it? You should have more faith in your own work."

"I have faith in the scientific process. That means we run simulations, we test on cell cultures, we perform animal tests and only then do we consider conducting human trials."

Halfon banged the table with the palm of his hand. "You have not been listening. There is a deadline. If we do not deliver on time… well, I dare not think of the consequences. I gave a personal assurance to Mullah Awad that we would prepare a treatment within three weeks, and I intend to keep that promise. More than a week has already passed. You have been freed from the restrictions of conventional medical ethics so we can meet this commitment. This was a difficult decision, but we must sacrifice the lives of the few to benefit the many. Do you understand?"

"I…"

Halfon rose from his seat and leant over the desk, glaring down at the man sitting opposite. "I asked if you understood."

"Yes, Professor."

"Excellent. We will study the child's blood count over the coming days. In one week, the subject will be placed in a room with a heavily pregnant woman. I expect your full cooperation in analysing the results. Now, if there is nothing else, I have much work to do."

Kubar stood and nodded his head. Without another word, he turned and let himself out. He walked a few paces down the corridor, leant against the wall and exhaled a deep breath. If there had been any doubts before entering the professor's office, there were none now.

Whatever the consequences, his mind was made up.

Saturday 2nd August 2036

Tripoli Infectious Diseases Hospital, Republic of North Africa
5 days until the deadline

Jason raised his eyes from where he sat alongside his mother and the general, picking listlessly at the food on his plate. Another week had passed, and the research efforts had still brought them no closer to developing a treatment for the virus. Nor had the doctor come up with any proposals for how to get past the armed guards and break out of the facility. In five days, Paul would become a test subject. Luckily, his son was blissfully unaware of the looming deadline as Antimone dressed him by the bed.

Max Perrin occupied a spot at the opposite end of the table. Like every other morning, a guard had escorted him to the communal area to eat breakfast with the other prisoners. The rest of the detainees reserved any discussions about escape plans for times when he wasn't present. Max had attempted to engage them in conversation on the topic, but the other members of the group mostly ignored him.

The clunk of the electronic lock echoed through the room holding the prisoners. The door leading to the elevators opened, and Dr Kubar crossed to the wooden table. "Are you not ready?" he asked, folding his arms.

"I'll just be a second," Jason replied, cramming a piece of bread into his mouth.

Rosalind made no attempt to hurry as she sipped tea from a clear glass.

Kubar's gaze lowered to a piece of paper on the table. "What is this?"

"It's one of Paul's masterpieces."

The doctor picked up the drawing and studied the crude interlocking circles drawn with different coloured pencils.

"What's so interesting about it?" Jason asked.

"It reminds me a little of the compound we are working on. But come. We must go. Professor Halfon will start the test on the boy in fifteen minutes," Kubar said, putting down the picture and glancing at his wrist.

Rosalind glanced up sharply. "What test?"

"It is as we feared. He will put a pregnant woman in the same room."

"I thought you were going to talk to him out of that."

A flush crept into Kubar's cheeks. "I tried, but unfortunately, the professor chose not to listen to my advice."

Rosalind slammed the almost empty glass down on the table. "This is ridiculous. I'll tell him myself."

"I would not do that."

"We'll see." She rose and stormed towards the exit.

Kubar's eyebrows rose. "Your mother is a difficult woman," he said, addressing Jason.

"Yeah, but on this occasion, she's right."

"Still, it is not a good idea to confront the people with power."

"That's just the way she is."

"Come. Let us go before the guards decide there is a problem."

Jason followed a pace behind as Kubar approached the locked door.

"What does he hope to achieve?" Rosalind asked as they drew alongside, her face a thunderous mask of anger.

"He is under much pressure," Kubar replied. "He has made a promise to our leader, and now he must deliver, or there will be serious consequences." The lock clunked as he raised his card.

"Well, he's a fool if he thinks this problem can be solved by trialling random compounds on live subjects."

"But if what I have heard is correct, did you not perform human trials at Ilithyia?"

A vein throbbed at Rosalind's temple. "That was totally different. We researched everything thoroughly before we went to that stage, and we never tested on children."

The rest of the short journey passed in silence.

"Shall we have a look at the latest simulation results?" Jason asked as they neared the workstation.

"What's the point?" Rosalind replied. "It seems Halfon is intent on testing anything we develop on a live subject."

Ignoring Rosalind's negative attitude, Jason sat in the chair and studied the screen. "Well, it ran to completion." He scrolled through several graphs. "But there's no discernible effect on the simulated virus activation rate from what I can see."

"Just like all the others then," Rosalind said, leaning over Jason's shoulder.

"What if we modified this area?" Kubar asked, pointing at a part of the molecular structure. "That might alter the absorption factor."

Despite her initial reluctance, Rosalind drew up a chair of her own and peered at the three-dimensional image. An intense debate between the British scientist and the North African doctor ensued. On average, Jason understood about every other word.

As they argued, other researchers congregated around the glass-encased room in the centre of the laboratory. Halfon's voice rose above the hubbub. "Are the cameras recording? What about the telemetry links?"

Rosalind sprang up from her seat and marched towards the professor. Kubar tried to grab her arm, but she shook off his grip.

She placed a hand on the professor's shoulder and spun him around. "This is a total waste of time. I can tell you now, this won't work. You'll be killing a child for nothing."

Halfon took a step back, his eyes blazing with fury. "How dare you touch me? Are you forgetting that you are a prisoner here?"

The blood drained from Rosalind's face and pooled in two bright red spots in the centre of her cheeks. "How could I possibly forget? You treat us as slaves without even a day off. Now, you're about to expose a four-year-old boy to a trigger that will cause his certain death. For God's sake, we've run the simulation. We already know this compound won't protect him."

Halfon spoke in a low, menacing voice. "This test will happen whether you like it or not. There is no time for the cautious approach to medical research you follow in the West. We must be bold and push the boundaries."

"You can't—"

"ENOUGH!" bellowed Halfon. His hand reached into the pocket of his white coat. It emerged holding a black cylinder. He jabbed the tip against Rosalind's shoulder and depressed the button with his thumb. She cried out and dropped to the floor, writhing in agony. But the professor wasn't finished. He leant over her and delivered another jolt of electricity to her midriff. An inhuman scream tore from her throat.

Halfon barked a command in Arabic. Two guards stepped forwards. They hesitated for a moment as if unsure whether the agonised thrashing of the prostrate woman was somehow contagious, then each grabbed hold of one of Rosalind's arms. They dragged her still-convulsing body upright and hauled her across the floor.

Halfon turned to the small crowd of scientists, brandishing the stun baton. "Does anybody else have any objections?" Silence greeted his question. "Good. Shall we continue?"

A low murmur rose from the group as most of the eyes in the room, including Jason's, followed the two men and their incapacitated prisoner. Somebody grabbed him by the arm.

"Do not do anything stupid," Kubar hissed in his ear.

Jason nodded, and the doctor released his grip. A movement behind the glass panels snapped his attention back to the enclosed space. A trolley emerged through the doors at the far end, pushed by a man in a white protective suit. Held down by straps, the same boy they had seen a week earlier gazed blearily at the onlookers.

The suited medic applied the wheel locks and retreated the way he had come. Moments later, he returned, pulling a woman by the arm. She wore a headscarf and a black dress, which reached the floor and protruded around her belly. A deathly hush descended on the spectators as the man dragged the reluctant mother-to-be closer. She spotted the trolley holding the test subject and tried to pull back. The man's grip tightened. She cried out in pain, but still, he moved forwards, stopping only when they stood a yard away from the foot of the metal frame.

The woman stared at the young child, the whites of her eyes reflecting the bright overhead lighting. She muttered something under her breath.

Nothing happened for several seconds. The murmur of conversation rose from the group of spectators. Then a thin trail of blood flowed from the boy's left nostril, rolling across his cheek onto the white sheet. He tried to raise a hand to brush it off, but the straps prevented any movement. Similar streams emerged from his ears. A tremor ran through his body, and his eyes rolled up in his head.

Jason could no longer watch. The pointless death sickened him to the core of his being. He turned away and meandered back to the workstation. There, he dropped into the chair and buried his face in his hands. In a few days, his son, Paul, would be strapped to the trolley: another innocent sacrificed to the goals of the ruthless men running this country. A rushing sound whooshed in his ears. His throat tightened up. He tried to inhale, but it felt like he was breathing through a straw.

A gentle hand brushed his shoulder. Jason recoiled at the touch.

"Your mother was right," Kubar said as he dropped into the adjacent seat. "She predicted the drug would not work."

"That bastard doesn't care about that though, does he?"

"No."

Both men sat in silence, each lost in their own thoughts. Finally, Jason spoke. "We have to get out of here. Have you had any ideas?"

Kubar flashed an anxious glance at the nearest guard, who stood ten yards away, leaning against the wall. "Actually, yes."

"Well?"

"A lightbulb in my room failed yesterday, and it reminded me. Two or three months ago, we had a power cut. When that happened, all the lights turned off, the electronic doors opened, and I heard Professor Halfon complain that the cameras no longer worked either. There is a backup generator, but it only provides electricity to the isolation areas. It is not powerful enough for the entire building."

"So, how does that help us?"

"When the power fails, it will go dark for a moment before the emergency lighting comes on. Perhaps we can overpower the guards and take their weapons."

Jason turned to Kubar. "That might just work. But how do we turn the supply off?"

"Yes," the doctor said. "That is a problem. There are probably fuses somewhere, but I do not know where they are. I think they are in another part of this hospital. Unfortunately, they will not allow me to leave this section."

Jason's eyes narrowed in thought. "General Shaladi has people on the outside who are prepared to help him. They might be able to cause a power cut."

Kubar leant forwards. "This is good. How do we contact them?"

"That could be an issue. The one person with the means to get a message out of here is currently in the cells, recovering from an electric shock."

Saturday 2nd August 2036

Tripoli Infectious Diseases Hospital, Republic of North Africa
5 days until the deadline

For the rest of the day, Jason and Kubar worked with the molecular modelling software. Much of what the doctor proposed was beyond Jason's grasp, even if he had been able to concentrate fully. As it was, his mind kept wandering to plans for escape. Key to everything was getting a message to the outside world.

"There, that might work," Kubar said as he jabbed a finger at the save icon.

Jason forced himself to focus on the screen. "What? Oh, yeah. Have you set up another simulation?"

"Yes. The circles on your son's drawing gave me a new idea to try. This one will take nine hours because the compound is more complex."

"How do we stop Professor Halfon from manufacturing it and testing it on some other poor child while we aren't here?"

"When the software is running, he cannot access the model without stopping the job."

Jason glanced towards the nearest guard. "Good. I've been thinking about how we could send a message to Shaladi's people."

"Go on."

"Tonight, I'll ask him for their contact details. Tomorrow, I'll give them to you."

"I do not understand. I have no phone. How will this work?"

"You tell the professor that you need my mother's help with some technical questions. Assuming he agrees, you visit her in the cells and pass her a note. Then she uses the wireless interface in her eye to send the message. If he releases her beforehand, I can ask her myself."

Kubar ran a hand through his hair. "I fear she may have pushed Professor Halfon too far this time. Perhaps I will talk to him again tonight and tell him I need her support to continue this work."

"Why don't you go and see him now? It's a little early to stop, but while the simulation's running, there's not much else we can do."

The doctor hesitated for a moment. "Yes. That is a good idea."

~

Professor Halfon glared at Dr Kubar from the other side of the desk. He desperately wanted to grab the scientist by the neck and crush his windpipe. Despite the hammering of his heart, he forced himself to breathe slowly and maintain an outwardly calm demeanour. "If you cannot control your staff, I must reconsider whether you deserve this position of responsibility."

Kubar shifted uncomfortably on the wooden chair. "I understand, Professor. She is a difficult woman, but her expertise is vital to our success."

"That may be so, but her behaviour cannot go unpunished. I will not tolerate insubordination in my people."

"I agree. But hasn't she already suffered considerable pain?" Kubar's gaze tracked to the slight bulge in the pocket of Halfon's jacket. "What further punishment do you propose? It cannot be anything that prevents her from working."

Halfon steepled his fingers and glowered at his subordinate through narrowed eyes. "You definitely need her help?"

"Yes. She is not easy to work with, but she is an expert in her field. Is that not why you kidnapped her?"

Halfon tamped down his rage. Unfortunately, the doctor made sense. He released a deep sigh. "Very well. She can stay with you during the day, but she will spend the night in the cells. If she delivers what we need, I may allow her to return to the others."

"That is generous of you, Professor. I will make sure nothing like this ever happens again."

Halfon leant forwards and lowered his voice to a growl. "Let me tell you something, which I trust you will keep to yourself. When we develop a treatment that works, she will be punished for her crimes. She has caused many thousands of deaths. Our people will demand justice."

"I know."

Halfon sat back. "What about her son?"

Kubar stared at the director in confusion. "I do not understand your question."

The professor tapped the desk impatiently. "Mr Floyd. Is he proving useful? I have not seen him performing any technician's work."

"He is inexperienced, but he has a good brain. He shows much promise."

"Despite their past, I think the woman is still fond of him. Maybe we can use that to our advantage."

"What do you mean?" Kubar asked.

"He may provide leverage."

"But..."

"I hope you are not becoming too attached to the prisoners. They are here for one purpose and one purpose alone: to help us develop a cure. Once we have accomplished that, we have no further uses for them."

"Of course, sir," Kubar replied.

"So, how is the research progressing?"

"We are running a simulation tonight. We should know by tomorrow morning whether it is worth pursuing further."

"Shall I get Dr Brandt to work on synthesising it?"

"I suggest we wait until we see the results."

"Very well. Just remember that time is short. We cannot afford to fail or we will all suffer the consequences."

"Thank you, Professor."

"There is one more thing. We must think about preparing the child."

Kubar's face blanched. "You mean Paul Lessing?"

Halfon leant closer to study his subordinate's reaction. "Yes. Who else?"

"So, you really intend to perform a test on the boy?"

"Is that going to be a problem?"

Kubar looked down at his shoes, then raised his eyes to meet those of the professor. "No, of course not. I just thought perhaps—"

The blood pounded in Halfon's veins. Why did this man always query his decisions? He slammed a fist down on the desk, causing the doctor to recoil at the sudden impact. "This is something that is already decided. You will not question my orders. Ever."

"Yes, sir. Sorry."

"Good. Take the child to the isolation area now. On second thoughts, I will do it myself. You need to get back to work."

Kubar rose. "Right away. Thank you for your time."

Halfon's gaze followed the scientist as he crossed the room to the door. He waited a few seconds, then raised his hand in front of the computer screen and selected a name from the contact list. The face of his head of security filled the display.

"Good evening, sir. How may I help you?"

"I am concerned about Doctor Kubar. I want you to monitor him. He is getting far too close to the prisoners. Also, I am not sure your idea to inform him that his daughter is still alive is working. He seems… unsettled. I expected him to be much more enthusiastic."

"Of course, Professor. I will tell my men to watch him closely."

Saturday 2nd August 2036

Tripoli Infectious Diseases Hospital, Republic of North Africa
5 days until the deadline

Antimone lifted the plastic fork to her son's mouth. "Please, Paul. Eat this for Mummy."

The three-year-old angled his head away, his lips tightly sealed.

She raised her eyes in exasperation. With nothing to occupy her except childcare duties, she felt her mind and body atrophying. "I've really had enough of this. Can you try?"

Jason, who had returned from the laboratory earlier than usual, lifted his son off Antimone's wheelchair and placed him on his lap. "Come on, buddy. This is yummy. Let's drive the car into the garage. Beep! Beep!"

Paul giggled and allowed the food to pass through what had moments earlier been an impenetrable barrier.

Antimone picked at the contents of her own plate.

"What's wrong?" Jason asked, his face etched with concern. "I mean apart from the obvious."

"This is driving me nuts," she replied. "Every day is the same. I love being with Paul, but it's just so boring. My brain is turning to mush."

Jason leant forwards and lowered his voice. "We'll find a way to escape. I promise."

Antimone shot a glance towards the general and his daughter, sitting at the other end of the table. "Do you really trust those two?"

"I don't see we have much of a choice. We all need to work together." Jason lifted another forkful of food to his son's mouth. By now, the novelty had worn off, and Paul pushed his father's hand away.

Antimone gave a wry smile. "Not so easy after all, is it?"

Jason continued his half-hearted attempts to force nutrition past Paul's lips while he spoke. "We need Shaladi's people to knock out the power. To do that, my mother—I mean Baxter—has to get a message out to them, and she can't do that while she's stuck in the cells. Dr Kubar said he'd tell Halfon the research couldn't progress without her, but who knows whether that bastard will listen."

"Speak of the devil. Here he comes now," Antimone said, staring at the entrance.

Jason's head swivelled. "What the hell does he want?" he murmured.

Professor Halfon strode towards them, trailed by a pair of armed guards. He stopped a pace away. "Good evening."

Neither Jason nor Antimone responded.

"I hope the food is to your liking. "This"—he pointed to a piece of dough on Antimone's plate—"is Zummeeta. You should dip it in the sauce."

"I'm not hungry."

"Very well. I am not here to engage in—how do you say?—chitchat. I must take your son."

Antimone's blood froze in her veins. "What do you mean?"

"Are my words not clear? He will come with me."

"No way," Jason said, pushing the bench back as he stood. "He stays with us." He clutched Paul tightly to his chest.

Halfon's eyes narrowed. "I think you misunderstand your situation, Mr Floyd." He beckoned the armed guard closer. The man raised his weapon. "You are in no position to make demands."

"Is this for the test?" Antimone asked. The roaring sound in her ears made her voice seem distant. "There are still five days to go."

"If you behave, you may visit him. If there is any trouble, you will not see him again."

A shiver ran through Antimone's body. "Tell me what you're going to do to him."

"Miss Lessing, I am losing patience. If I wanted to, I could just take him with no discussion. My men are armed. There is nothing you can do to stop me. I would prefer to do this without causing the boy distress, but understand that I will use whatever means are necessary."

Antimone could barely breathe. A prickly sensation ran across her scalp and down her neck. She trembled uncontrollably. Her lips moved, but no words came out.

Halfon glared at Jason. "Now, I must insist that you hand the child to me, or I will have no alternative but to use force."

Jason met the professor's stare for a moment, then kissed Paul on the forehead and placed him on the ground. "This man is going to take you to meet some new friends," he whispered. "You be good." He turned to Halfon and spoke in a low voice. "I swear, if any harm comes to him..."

Halfon's brows drew together in a frown. "Be very careful what you say next." He reached down, grasped the three-year-old's tiny hand and walked towards the exit.

Paul tried to pull away, casting an uncertain backward glance. Despite the terror clawing at Antimone's insides, she forced a smile and gave him a reassuring wave. “Have fun,” she said. Her son held her gaze for a second, then continued to walk alongside the professor.

As Halfon and the boy passed through the door, she slumped onto the table, deep sobs wracking her body.

Sunday 3rd August 2036

Tripoli Infectious Diseases Hospital, Republic of North Africa
4 days until the deadline

Antimone propelled herself after the tall scientist in the white coat, her heart pounding in her chest. Black spots danced in front of her eyes after a sleepless night. The professor had tasked the man with escorting her to visit her son.

"What's your name again?" she asked. He had told her a few minutes earlier, but in the excitement at being allowed to see Paul, it had already slipped her mind.

"Doctor Fernando," the man replied. He was in his early forties with tight-cropped, short hair and expressive brown eyes.

"Is he all right? Did he eat any breakfast? Did he sleep well?" She knew she was babbling but couldn't stop herself.

"I am sorry. I do not know." The doctor's voice carried a slight Spanish accent. "My expertise is cell cultures. I do not look after the children."

"So, you're a scientist?"

"Si."

"And you think it's okay to murder young kids and kidnap people?"

The doctor cleared his throat. Just when Antimone thought he wouldn't reply, he spoke. "I have made some mistakes in the past which I do not wish to talk about. They will not let me work in my own country. The other European countries and America are the same. Here, they allow me to do what I love, and they also pay me well. I do not agree with some things they do, but if I want to stay, I must follow orders."

"So, you just turn a blind eye to kidnap and murder and get on with your job?"

This time, Fernando remained silent. They followed the corridor until they came to a sealed double door. The doctor fumbled in his pocket for the key card. "One moment," he mumbled, staring up at the black circle of the camera lens.

The light turned green, and the deadbolts slid back with a metallic clunk. Fernando pushed through the swing doors. Antimone raised her arms just in time to prevent the edges from banging into her.

They entered an open-plan laboratory area. An array of large, complicated-looking machines occupied the floor space. A group of scientists in lab coats stared at them in silence as they passed. Fernando didn't acknowledge his colleagues. He led Antimone to another set of doors and repeated the procedure to pass through.

"Here we are," he announced.

The room was five metres square with white walls. Directly opposite, a row of yellow hazmat suits hung from a metal rail. Two separate sliding doors, each containing a rectangular glass window, took up most of the left wall. Mounted between them at chest height was a large green button. A sign in Arabic occupied the space above the button.

"What's that?" Antimone asked, pointing at the twin mechanisms.

"Those are airlocks," Fernando replied. "This side is the entrance. The right is the exit. Before we can go through, we must wear protective clothing."

Antimone pointed to the rack. "I assume you mean one of those? How am I supposed to put that on?"

The doctor picked up a hazmat suit and glanced down at her. "We need some help." He stepped towards a small speaker grill set into the wall beside the left door, pressed the pushbutton and spoke in a low voice. Several seconds passed, then a hissing sound emerged from the right side. Moments later, a figure covered in yellow plastic stepped out, dripping water. A harsh chemical smell permeated the room.

Antimone coughed at the acrid scent. Fernando and the newcomer exchanged a few words. Peering through the curved glass of his faceplate, she identified the suited person as a middle-aged man with receding, black hair. She had never seen him before. The Spaniard unzipped the front, and between them, the two men manipulated her body into the hazmat suit. She experienced a moment of claustrophobia as the zip closed, sealing her inside.

"I will leave you with Doctor Gregg," Fernando said, his voice muffled by the thin material. "The airlock is not wide enough for the wheelchair. There is another one on the other side. My colleague will take you through."

The suited figure grunted as he lifted Antimone in his arms, then carried her to the leftmost door. Fernando prodded the green button. The man shuffled into the enclosed space sideways. Antimone's legs scraped against the wall. A rattling noise filled the small chamber, and her ears popped with the sudden change in air pressure.

The sound stopped abruptly, and the panel ahead slid open. Gregg staggered out into a brightly lit foyer area. A wheelchair sat to one side, and he lowered Antimone into the seat. She turned her attention to her surroundings.

A huge expanse of glass lined the entire right wall of the long corridor. The rectangular outlines of doors broke the smooth surface. Behind the floor to ceiling window, white partitions divided the space into separate rooms. A green button mounted beside each door apparently controlled access. She peered past her reflection into the first room and saw the interior contained a pair of empty beds. There was no other source of entry or exit.

"Is this where they're keeping Paul?" Antimone asked.

"It's this way," Gregg replied, striding ahead. He spoke with an American accent. When they reached the next glass-walled chamber, a woman wearing a black robe stared at them from where she perched on the edge of the bed. Her hands rested on top of her stomach. She was either obese or heavily pregnant. Antimone guessed the latter based on what Jason had told her.

The doctor passed another empty room, then stopped. Antimone rolled up behind him. Three young boys sat on the floor with their backs to the window. They chattered to each other happily as they played with a variety of cheap plastic toys. None of the children had noticed the adults yet. Antimone's heart lurched as her gaze settled on the child in the centre of the group with the palest skin: Paul.

She leant forwards, placing her palms on the glass. Tears streamed from her eyes and rolled down her cheeks. She raised a hand to brush them away but came up against the thin plastic of the hazmat suit. She choked a little as she inhaled. The sound must have carried inside the room because the boy on the left turned. He stared open-mouthed at the strange-looking people on the other side of the window.

Paul was the last to turn. His gaze settled on the wheelchair and tracked up to the features behind the transparent headgear. Their eyes met. He scrambled to his feet and rushed to the glass, screaming, "Mummy!" at the top of his voice.

Without a second thought, Antimone spun the wheels of her chair and slammed her palm against the green button. The door swung open towards her. Paul raced through the gap and flung himself into his mother's arms. He grasped her around the neck and nestled his head beneath her chin.

Antimone pulled her son's tiny body into her chest and lowered her face to kiss his hair, but instead, her lips came up against the smooth surface of the polycarbonate facemask. "Paul," she murmured in a strangled voice.

"Be careful," an alarmed Dr Gregg said, stepping forwards. "You must not break the seal."

Gregg's words of warning penetrated to Antimone's unconscious but had the opposite effect to what he intended. Maternal instincts took over. She could no longer remain separated from her child. Her fingers lifted and grasped the pull tab of the zip. She yanked downwards. The rasp of the zipper sounded incredibly loud in her ears.

The doctor lunged to stop her, but the years of athletic training had given her tremendous upper body strength. She shoved him away and pulled the seams apart. Seconds later, she had thrown the hood back over her head and released one arm.

As she embraced her son tightly, tears dripped from her chin and mingled with his.

Sunday 3rd August 2036

Tripoli Infectious Diseases Hospital, Republic of North Africa
4 days until the deadline

Jason sat at the table as he waited for Dr Kubar to arrive. He pushed the food around his plate. His appetite had deserted him. Neither he nor Antimone had slept at all during the previous night. She had departed ten minutes earlier with the Spanish doctor. Despite their protests, Dr Fernando was adamant only one parent at a time could visit their son.

General Shaladi approached the bench with a half-filled plate and sat on the same side, a metre away to Jason's left. Jason had explained Kubar's proposal to him the previous night. Shaladi's mouth barely moved as he spoke. "Do not look at me. Just listen. Now take this."

Jason glanced down. Something white lay on the wooden seat. He stretched out an arm and closed his fingers around a tightly folded piece of paper.

"Put it in your pocket," Shaladi commanded. "It contains a web address and some English text. You must comment on the first article using the words exactly as written. The website is in Arabic and appears to be for a company selling deep sea fishing trips. The top line is a code to tell my people it is from me and that nobody is forcing me to write the message. This is why you cannot make a mistake when you enter it on the page. Do you understand?"

Jason continued to stare straight ahead, but he tilted his head downwards.

"Good. My men check all comments. They delete everything so nothing appears on the site. If they wish to send information back to me, they comment on the second article. If you want to reply to them, you must do so on the same page and include the phrase *fishing boat*. This is important. Do you have any questions? Cover your mouth so they cannot see you talking."

Jason leant forwards, resting his chin on his right hand to conceal his lips from the guards in the office. "Won't they be expecting you to write in Arabic?" he asked in a low voice.

"Yes, this is true, but they will understand as long as the correct phrases are present."

"Right, I think I've got all that."

"Good luck."

Jason rose and deposited his plate at the end of the table, then strolled back to his bed. He removed his shoes and lay down with his hands behind his head. The entire plan depended upon his mother being able to access the website. It would be hard to explain to her the instructions for using the site unless they could spend a few minutes together in private. He grasped the tightly folded paper in his clenched fist. Despite the setbacks, they were finally taking action to get out of this place.

~

The door at the end of the room opened. Jason shoved the note into the pocket of his trousers as Dr Kubar entered. He swung his legs onto the floor and tied his laces.

"How's my son?" Jason asked, looking up as Kubar drew nearer.

"He is well," the doctor replied. "I am sorry they have taken him from you."

"Yeah. If they hurt him in any way… What's happening about my mother?"

"I spoke to Professor Halfon yesterday. I told him she was vital to our research. He agreed to let her work with us during the day, but she will return to the cells at night."

Jason breathed a sigh of relief. *That would certainly make things easier.* He caught the eye of the general who was still sitting at the table and nodded.

"Shall we go?" Kubar asked.

Jason followed him across the room. When they arrived at the lifts, the green numbers on the control panel indicated that the car was one level up. Moments later, the doors parted to reveal Max Perrin, accompanied by a guard. Jason stepped back to allow the two men to pass. Neither Westerner acknowledged the other.

Jason and Kubar rode up in silence. When they emerged into the corridor, Jason turned to the doctor. "They told us he was spending the night in the cells."

Kubar stared at him in confusion. "I am sorry. Who?"

"Max Perrin. The lift started on the floor above. If he was in the basement, he should've been going up not down."

"He sleeps up there," Kubar replied. "I thought you knew that. Is there a problem?"

"No," Jason said. "It's nothing. Never mind." Perrin was definitely up to something. This served only to confirm his deep mistrust of his former classmate.

The doctor led him to the workstation, then strolled over to the nearest guard. A brief conversation ensued. He returned moments later. "They will bring Mrs Baxter up."

Kubar sank down on the seat beside Jason and studied the display. "The simulation is complete." He waved a hand in front of the screen and peered at the tables of results.

Jason tried to interpret the data, but much of it was beyond him. He waited for the doctor to reach the end.

"Hmm," Kubar murmured.

"What does that mean? Is it good news or bad?"

"We should wait until Mrs Baxter arrives, or I will have to explain twice. Ah, here she is."

A guard pushed the dishevelled form of Rosalind Baxter forwards. From her appearance, it seemed she hadn't slept much the night before. She flopped into a chair, saying nothing.

"Are you okay?" Jason asked.

She turned her head sideways and glared at him. "Do I look okay to you?"

"Um… not particularly, no."

She rubbed her shoulder. "Well, that's not surprising. If you thought conditions were primitive in that shared room, it's palatial by comparison. The cells are crawling with rats and insects. I barely slept a wink with all the scratching and squeaking. Something big even ran over my leg in the night."

Jason shuddered. "That sounds bad."

"You have no idea." Rosalind rotated her chair. "Anyway, what's going on here?"

Kubar pointed at the screen. "I started with the molecule we worked on a few days ago."

"The one Halfon gave to that poor kid?"

"Yes. I modified it here and here." He jabbed a finger at the display. "The simulations show that it may be effective."

"No doubt that bastard will inject another child with it before we've run any more tests."

"I hope not. We should trial it on a cell culture."

"Let me have a look."

Kubar rolled his chair back.

Rosalind moved closer to the screen. She brought up the molecular model, then used her fingers to manipulate the images and examined them from several directions. Finally, she studied the simulation report. "Yes, this all looks very promising, but before you get too excited, there's a long way to go. However, I agree it's worth taking further."

"Doctor Fernando is our expert on cell cultures. Doctor Brandt can synthesise the compound. I will ask them both to start now. If there are no problems, we should be able to begin testing in one or two days."

Kubar pushed back his chair and strolled towards a tall man with close-cropped hair. Soon, they were deep in conversation.

"Is the battery in your eye still charged?" Jason whispered.

Rosalind's expression went blank for a second. "Just over thirty percent. Remember to ask Kubar for the bits to build another charger. Why are you asking?"

Jason flashed a glance at the guard, then turned back to his mother. "Shaladi is planning to get us out of here. We need you to send a message to his people."

Jason explained how the secret messaging system worked and the general's plan.

"What happens when the power goes down?" Rosalind asked.

"All the doors open, and we overpower the guards. He reckons only six or seven of them work at night. After nine o'clock, most of them will be off duty."

"I'll be in the cells by then. You aren't thinking of leaving me behind, are you?"

Jason met her gaze. "No, of course not. You have my word, we'll get you out of there. That reminds me, Kubar only agreed to help if we promise to rescue the other kids as well."

Rosalind massaged her temples. "Talk about trying to make this as difficult as possible. How many of them are there?"

"I'll have to ask him when he gets back, but I don't think they keep more than a few on site at any one time."

"When do I need to send the message?"

Jason's eyes surveyed the room. Nobody was paying them any attention. "How about now?" he said. He dug his fingers into his pocket, retrieved the folded piece of paper and, with another surreptitious glance at the nearest guard, pushed it across the surface of the desk.

Rosalind unfolded the note. She studied it for a moment. "I look forward to meeting you beneath the blue sky on your fishing boat; that hardly sounds like a comment you'd leave on a website, does it?"

"What does it matter? You have to get the first part exactly right," Jason said.

"I know that," Rosalind snapped. "Fetch me one of those equipment manuals from the shelf over there."

"Why? What do you need it for?"

Rosalind raised an eyebrow. "You still can't help questioning every request I make, can you?"

"Apparently not."

"I'm going to use it to hide the note in case anybody comes."

"Oh, I see." Jason strolled across to the row of books and selected one at random. The guard's eyes tracked him all the way back to the desk. He allowed the manual to fall open and pretended to study the contents. Then he passed it to his mother.

After a few seconds, the armed man lost interest and looked away. Rosalind placed the note between the pages and stared at the dense writing. Jason read over her shoulder. He scanned the second line written on the paper.

Tripoli IDH. Cut power at night. Urgent. Confirm date and time.

"What's happening?" he asked.

"Be quiet. I'm trying to concentrate." Rosalind shook her head. "Damn, there's an error message."

"Did you type it in correctly?"

"Just checking. I'll try again."

More seconds ticked by. "I'm in."

Jason exhaled the breath he had been holding. "Thank God for that."

"There are photographs of people with fish they've caught."

"That sounds about right."

"I'm clicking the link. Everything's in Arabic. There are photos of boats. There's a button at the bottom of the page. That must be for the comments… Yes, a text box has opened."

A frown of concentration formed on Rosalind's forehead. A bead of perspiration rolled down her temple.

"The first line's done."

"Have you checked it?"

"For Christ's sake, will you let me do this without nagging me every few seconds?"

Jason bit his tongue. He jiggled a leg in nervous anticipation.

"That's it. Everything looks good. There are two buttons. I assume one must be okay and the other cancel. The button on the right is highlighted."

"Perhaps we should wait for Dr Kubar."

"I'm going to click it. The box has disappeared."

"Make sure you disconnect from the network."

"Hang on. I've done that, too." Rosalind closed the manual with the note still between the pages. "What now?"

"We give it an hour or two and see whether they've replied."

Sunday 3rd August 2036

Tripoli Infectious Diseases Hospital, Republic of North Africa
4 days until the deadline

"Shit! She did what?" Jason asked.

Dr Kubar sighed. Moments earlier, he had returned from a brief meeting with the head of security. "When she saw your son, she pulled off the hazmat suit to embrace him."

"That's just typical," Rosalind said.

Jason ignored the acerbic comment. "So, now both Paul and Antimone are infected with the virus?"

"Yes, I am afraid so," Kubar replied. "It is very infectious."

"Damn it."

The doctor raised an eyebrow. "It seems you are surrounded by impetuous women."

"Yeah, tell me about it." Jason sank into a morose silence. This would only complicate the escape.

The morning had passed in a state of nervous tension. An air of purpose filled the scientists as they set about the tasks required to test the new compound. Jason had overheard two of them discussing what they would do when they were allowed to leave. Of the science team, only Dr Kubar seemed withdrawn.

When the doctor departed to attend a staff meeting, Jason and Rosalind found themselves alone at the workstation.

"Shall we check for a reply?" Jason asked.

Rosalind shot a glance at the nearest guard. He was leaning against the wall, gazing aimlessly at the ceiling. "Okay. Let's do it."

"Don't forget to connect to the network first."

Rosalind let out a sigh of irritation. A moment later, she muttered, "I've connected. I'm just reopening the website."

Time seemed to slow down for Jason. His heart thumped in his chest. It took all his self-control not to ask his mother what was happening.

Several seconds passed before she spoke again. "Right, I'm in. So, I need to look at the second article. More pictures of boats. I'm scrolling to the bottom of the page. Yes, there's a comment."

"What does it say?"

"The next fishing trip starts—"

"So, should we start another simulation?" Jason asked, raising his voice.

Rosalind turned, frowning at the unexpected interruption.

A cheerful-looking Professor Halfon stepped up behind them. "I hear we are preparing a new compound for test. Have you seen Doctor Kubar?"

Both Jason and Rosalind shook their heads.

"Never mind," Halfon said. "I am sure he will be back soon." He reached across and picked up the thick manual in which Rosalind had hidden the note. "I did not know you planned to use the mass spectrometer. What do you want to analyse?"

"Oh, it was nothing," Jason replied. "There's a machine like this at the university. I was just curious to see if it was the same model." He had to consciously force himself to breathe until Halfon replaced the manual without opening it. *That was close.*

"Very good. We will talk again when the compound is ready."

Rosalind scowled at the director. "You aren't going to test it on a human subject ahead of the cell culture trials, are you?"

Halfon's eyes narrowed as he met Rosalind's gaze. He remained silent for a moment before replying. "Doctor Kubar has persuaded me we should follow the scientific method more closely. But remember, we will still place a pregnant woman in the same room as your grandson in a few days. If the treatment is not ready, he will die."

"I'm well aware of that," Rosalind snapped.

"I am glad you understand. Now, when the doctor returns, please tell him I wish to speak to him."

"We'll do that," Jason said, keen to defuse the situation.

Halfon turned and headed towards the exit.

"Do you always have to wind him up?" Jason asked when the professor was out of earshot.

"He's a pompous idiot," Rosalind replied. "He wouldn't recognise scientific method if it bit him on the arse."

"I still don't think you should antagonise him. I was sure he'd find the note."

Rosalind rolled her eyes. "You really thought I'd be stupid enough to leave it in the manual, did you? What sort of moron do you take me for? I flushed it down the toilet when I went a few hours ago. It's just as well one of us is on the ball."

Jason bit back on his retort. "So, what does the message say?"

"The next fishing trip starts at ten o'clock on the sixth of August."

"That means they're going ahead with the plan. Did you reply?"

"I was about to when we were interrupted. What shall I write?"

"How about *we'll be ready*? Actually, I nearly forgot. We've got to include the phrase *fishing boat*."

"Okay, so *we'll be ready for the fishing boat*? Just a sec… Right, that's done."

"Don't forget to disconnect."

Rosalind's jaw muscles clenched. "Everything's sorted. How does the general propose to overpower the guards?"

"He hasn't mentioned that yet. I'll try to discuss it with him tonight. The only other question is, who else do we tell?"

"Good point. We should only inform people we trust."

"Does that include Doctor Kubar?"

"I think so," Rosalind replied. "He's the only one of us who has free run of the place. We might need his help. If he was going to turn us in, he would've done so already."

"We have a few days to come up with the plan. I'll talk to the general tonight and discuss it with the doctor tomorrow. But there is another thing we need to sort out."

"What's that?"

"Assuming we escape from here, we still have to get home. Shaladi said he could take us as far as the border, but everything after that is down to us. We can hardly call a taxi and tell it to drive us back to England. Maybe we could contact somebody in the government."

Rosalind folded her arms. "The Prime Minister and I aren't on the best of terms. They had the chance to rescue us on the ship, but they backed off. Why would they help us now? And another thing—after what we saw on the news, I must be top of the most hated people in the world list at the moment. Apart from anything else, my picture is all over the media."

"Yeah, that could be a problem. You might need to disguise yourself. But surely you still have some contacts."

"I can't think of anyone," Rosalind said. "I've been somewhat cut off since… well, since the sale of the company. Pretty much everyone I knew was related in some way to the business."

"But I remember you being friends with some important people."

"Yes, but none of them would lift a finger to help me now."

"So, it'll have to be somebody I know, then. If we emailed the Lessings, I'm sure they'd pass it on."

Rosalind scowled at Jason. "*Her* parents?" She stared at him for a moment. "I suppose beggars can't be choosers. I'll connect to my webmail and send them a message." Once again, her features took on a distant look. "That's strange."

"What?"

"There's what looks like an error box. It's in Arabic."

"I've got a CommsHub mail account. Why don't you try that?"

"Give me a second… No, I'm getting the same thing."

"I haven't given you their email address yet."

"No," Rosalind said. "You don't understand. I can't access the site at all. It seems to be blocked for some reason. What do we do now?"

"I'll see if the general has any ideas when I talk to him later. Actually, there is something else you could do; leave a message on the fishing website and ask them to pass the information to the British government. It has to be worth trying. Remember to include the words *fishing boat*."

Rosalind's face froze in concentration. A minute passed in silence. Eventually, she said, "At least that site works. I've left another comment on the second article. Their previous one has disappeared, so they definitely got my acknowledgement."

~

Professor Halfon was working in his office when the screen signalled an incoming call from his head of security.

"Yes, what is it?" he asked.

"Sorry to disturb you, sir, but I have received a report that somebody has tried to access the CommsHub webmail site."

"Who was it?"

"Unfortunately, I do not have that information, sir. A device logged into the wireless network, then disappeared after a few minutes."

"I bet one of those damned scientists still has a phone. You better hope Mullah Awad doesn't get to hear about this. I told you to confiscate all their devices."

"We did that, sir, but whoever it is must have hidden it from my men."

Halfon glared at his subordinate. "This is not acceptable. I want the culprit found. Turn off the Wi-Fi immediately. You have my permission to perform a strip search of every member of the science team."

"I'll get on it right away, sir."

"Let me know when you have identified the person."

Monday 4th August 2036

Tripoli Infectious Diseases Hospital, Republic of North Africa
3 days until the deadline

"How are Antimone and Paul?" Jason asked with a yawn as he trailed behind Dr Kubar. It had been a strange night, sleeping beside two empty beds. Three days to go. The looming deadline had occupied centre stage in his mind as he tossed and turned throughout the hours of darkness.

"I have not seen them," Kubar replied, "but I heard they are both fine."

"That bastard, Halfon, wouldn't let me visit them."

"This does not surprise me. They do not want to risk you trying to join them."

A series of sulky scowls followed the pair through the dining area. The science team's positive attitude of the previous days seemed to have evaporated.

"What's going on?" he asked the doctor as they arrived at the workstation. "Why does everybody look so angry?"

"The security people have searched for a mobile phone. The scientists are not happy because they were forced to remove their clothes."

"You mean a strip search?"

"Yes."

Jason's heart sank with a premonition of bad news, but he had to ask. "What triggered that?"

"Professor Halfon told me they detected an unauthorised device on the network. I take it Mrs Baxter has tried to log in to a CommsHub account."

"Oh, shit! Do they know it was her?"

"Not yet, but they will keep searching. In this country, they block access to most Western websites. In any case, now they have turned off the wireless link."

Jason's head spun as he considered the implications. It seemed their actions in trying to contact the outside world had triggered a security alert. Had Shaladi's people received their request to send a message to the British government? Would the North African authorities be able to read the comments from the fishing website?

"What will they do next?" he asked.

"I do not know," Kubar replied. "Why is she sending messages?"

Jason performed a surreptitious inspection of their watchers. They seemed more alert than on the previous few days, but none of them was paying particular attention. "If everything goes to plan, there'll be a power cut at ten o'clock on Wednesday night."

"So, the doors will unlock. What will happen after that?"

"The general intends to overpower the guards. He has people on the outside who will help us escape."

"But he is only one man, and he has no weapons. There are many armed men here."

"He didn't tell me any more than that. He said he'd provide more details closer to the time."

"It is important that Professor Halfon does not call for support. Although the computers will not be available, he still has a mobile phone."

"How do we stop him using it?"

Kubar hesitated before replying. "There is only one solution. I will ask him for a meeting. When the lights go out, I must prevent him from contacting anybody."

"What does that mean?"

Kubar's jaw set in a tight line. "Whatever is necessary."

"It sounds like it could be dangerous."

"There is no other option. Will your government send help to you?"

"We can't be sure. That's why we were trying to access the CommsHub website."

"So, you failed."

"Yes, but we left a message with Shaladi's people to contact the British authorities. Unfortunately, we can't tell whether they received our request."

Kubar took a deep breath. "There are many things that could go wrong. We must hope they do not. Now, if you wait here, I will fetch Mrs Baxter."

Jason stared sightlessly at the screen while he waited for the doctor to return. It was clear whatever Shaladi proposed would be dangerous. Somehow, he had to release Antimone and Paul from the isolation unit. Would the scientists stand with or against them? There was no way of knowing without asking, and that was a risk he couldn't afford to take before the power cut.

He heard Rosalind before he saw her. Her voice resounded through the laboratory. "How the hell am I supposed to do a day's work after being kept in those conditions? I barely slept a wink, and there's nowhere to wash properly." She limped forwards, flopping into the adjacent office chair. The sharp tang of body odour assaulted Jason's nostrils.

Kubar glanced nervously at the guards. "Please keep your voice down. I will talk to the professor again, but do not give them an opportunity to punish you further."

"Bloody barbaric savages," Rosalind muttered.

"Is there any news on the drug trials?" Jason asked, trying to change the subject.

Kubar dragged up another seat and sat beside them. "We applied the compound to the cell cultures yesterday. So far there is no adverse reaction. We have not yet tested whether it has any effect on the new strain of virus."

"When are they going to do that?"

"The test is due to start tomorrow."

Rosalind drummed her fingers on the surface of the desk. "Don't expect me to get excited. I plan on being out of here before we finish testing it."

"About that," Jason said. "Doctor Kubar was just telling me they noticed an unauthorised device on the network yesterday. They detected us trying to access the CommsHub site."

Rosalind leant forwards, biting her lip. "What are they doing about it?"

"They are hunting for a hidden mobile phone," Kubar replied. "They have searched all the scientists, a—how do you say?"

"Strip search," Jason reminded him. "Apparently, they've also turned off the Wi-Fi network."

"So, there's no way to tell whether our last message got through?" Rosalind asked.

"No," Jason said. "Unfortunately, not."

"Damn. I take it they don't know about the interface in my eye?"

"No, I do not think so," Kubar replied. "We must hope that they do not find out."

Monday 4th August 2036

Tripoli Infectious Diseases Hospital, Republic of North Africa
3 days until the deadline

Jason stood beside Rosalind. She had tried to freshen up in the small toilet adjoining the laboratory, but the acrid scent of body odour signalled she had only been partially successful. They waited alongside the other scientists for Halfon to arrive. Seven or eight armed guards studied the group from the periphery of the room. Jason wiped his palms on his trousers. This had to be something to do with the unauthorised access to the website.

The professor had called a stand-up meeting of the scientific staff just five minutes earlier. As they awaited his arrival, ripples of nervous conversation rose and fell. One topic dominated: the most recent indignity inflicted by the guards. If there were doubts beforehand, the scientists now understood their situation. For most, what had started out as an opportunity to benefit from lucrative, tax-free contracts had transformed into a prison sentence with little hope of release.

The low murmur of conversation died as Halfon made his way to the front.

"Good afternoon, everybody. I must first apologise for the searches you were forced to endure this morning. Please let me explain why this happened. The work we are performing here is vital, and we cannot afford for another organisation to gain an advantage by stealing our intellectual property. For this reason, we took the difficult decision to confiscate all personal communication devices. I realise it is hard for you to be out of contact with your friends and family, but it is only for a few weeks.

"Unfortunately, we discovered yesterday that somebody did not hand over their phone. That same person attempted to communicate with the outside world and sell our secrets. I am sure I need not remind you that this contravenes your contracts. I am pleased to tell you that today we have identified this individual."

Several whispered conversations broke out around the room. Jason shot Rosalind a sideways glance, but she continued to stare straight ahead. His gaze wandered to the armed men. They would shoot anybody who tried to escape before they covered two paces.

Halfon raised his hands. "Please let me finish. This person has betrayed us all. It is because of them that you have been forced to suffer the indignity of a strip search. Instead of working with you to complete this important work, your colleague has worked against you. I cannot tell you how disappointed this makes me.

"However, I am feeling generous this afternoon, so I will give the culprit one last opportunity to confess and apologise to their fellow scientists. If this person steps forwards now, I guarantee there will be no further repercussions. For the rest, to compensate for your efforts and the restrictions on your ability to communicate with the outside world, I will pay a bonus of six months wages when we demonstrate a successful treatment."

Rosalind leant into Jason as the buzz of voices once again rose from the gathered scientists. "What are they waiting for?" she whispered.

Moments later, Halfon beckoned a pair of armed guards forwards until one stood on either side of him. He raised a hand and pointed in Rosalind's direction. The men strode towards her. She closed her eyes, but they barged past and seized a rake-thin man standing behind her. Jason recognised him as a member of the team working with Dr Fernando on the cell cultures. They had never spoken, but he recalled Dr Kubar mentioning that he was Italian.

The guards dragged the scientist towards the exit, each holding an arm.

The man tried to twist around. "I never used it," he yelled. "It was in my bag. I forgot I had it."

"Quiet!" Halfon boomed. His eyes tracked the men as they left with their prisoner. He turned back to the shocked scientists. "An hour ago, we discovered a hidden mobile phone in Dr Rossi's room. I am sure you will agree I gave him every opportunity to confess."

"What will happen to him now?" a voice called out from the rear of the assembled group.

"We will terminate his contract with immediate effect. He will be held in a secure location, at least until our work here is done. In this country, industrial espionage is a serious offence. If any others of you have hidden communications devices, provided you hand them in today, I promise no further action will be taken.

"Now, we are making excellent progress, but I need you all to apply your best efforts to the challenge ahead. The sooner we complete this task, the sooner you may leave and spend your bonus. Let us get back to work."

~

"Shit. That was close," Jason said to Rosalind as they sat at the workstation. "I'm still shaking."

“They’re not the sharpest tools in the box,” she replied. “Let’s just hope they don’t figure it out.” She seemed calm, but the pair of dark sweat patches extending out from her armpits told a different story.

Dr Kubar’s face pinched in worry. “It is not over yet. When they examine the phone, they will see he did not connect to the network.”

“So, what do we do now?” Jason asked.

“We keep working and hope they do not discover what really happened.”

“But we don’t know whether the general’s people passed on the message. It’s no good if we get out of here and nobody is waiting at the border to help us.”

“There’s no point worrying about something you can’t control,” Rosalind said.

Jason scowled back at her. “That’s easy to say, but I really don’t want to spend the rest of my life in this prison.”

“Believe me, none of us want to stay here,” Kubar added.

Tuesday 5th August 2036

Prime Minister's Office, 10 Downing Street, London
2 days until the deadline

Andrew Jacobs settled himself behind the polished mahogany desk. Charles Moreland sat opposite. A man in his early sixties with a dome-shaped bald patch, wearing a military uniform, perched nervously on his seat alongside the head of MI6. Admiral David Trent was responsible for British naval operations in the Mediterranean.

"You asked for a meeting, Charles," Jacobs said. "And I see you've invited the Admiralty."

"Yes, Prime Minister."

"We can do without the formalities in here," the premier said with a half-smile to his former university colleague. "What's this about?"

"Well… you know we agreed to try to locate our people in The Republic of North Africa."

"Has there been any progress?"

Moreland interlaced his fingers across his stomach. "Maybe."

Jacobs sat forwards, his interest piqued. "Go on, then."

"Last night we received a message through somewhat unorthodox channels."

"What does that mean?"

"An anonymous caller phoned our embassy in Tunis from Tripoli."

"And…?"

"If we can believe this person, they belong to a faction inside the Reponan army."

Jacobs frowned. "That *is* strange. Why would somebody in their military be contacting us?"

"They claimed that General Shaladi is being held against his will. They plan to break him out in a day or two."

"Sorry, I'm not following. Is this the same Shaladi who was behind the kidnappings at the Olympics?"

"Correct," Moreland replied. "It seems they might be holding him in the same place as our people."

"Why would they be keeping their own man in captivity?"

"Good question. I've had various teams working on it through the night. The prevailing theory is that because they're denying responsibility for the attack, they can't allow him or his daughter—assuming both are still alive—to be seen in public."

Jacobs placed his elbows on the polished surface of the desk. "That sounds plausible. It wouldn't surprise me to hear those shifty bastards rewarded their man for a successful mission by imprisoning him. Are you sure this isn't a hoax?"

"No, Andrew. We can't believe a word they tell us."

"What would be in it for them? What are they expecting us to do?"

"The caller spoke to a member of the night staff. All he told her was that our people would be freed tomorrow at ten o'clock in the evening local time. That doesn't give us long to plan anything. He also said he couldn't or wouldn't escort them out of the country. When our officer called back, the number was dead."

"Why would they bother to contact us?"

"Well, as I see it, there are two possibilities. One, they're rattling our cage, trying to get us to respond. Who knows why? If we send in a team to pull our people out, they could have a welcoming committee waiting for us. Then they go bleating to the international community about us invading a sovereign country. They'd love to prove to the rest of the world that we're the bad guys, especially if they can cause some damage to our armed forces in the process."

"And the alternative?"

"It's genuine, and this group really is trying to help us. If I had to guess, I'd say it was the latter. There are several other ways they could pick a fight if they wanted to."

"So, that's why you invited Admiral Trent."

"Yes," Moreland replied. "If the intelligence is correct, the best way to evacuate the hostages would be from a ship-based helicopter launch."

Jacobs pinched the bridge of his nose between two fingers. "If we get this wrong, we might be putting our navy personnel in serious danger."

"The alternative is that we abandon our people."

"How quickly could we move a ship to the coast of North Africa?"

Trent cleared his throat. "We have a cruiser near Malta. It'll only take them three or four hours to reach Tripoli."

"That's all very well," Jacobs said, "but what happens after that?"

"Just before the appointed time, we perform low-level aerial reconnaissance to see what's happening," the admiral replied. "Whatever we send in will have to be small, or the Reponans will spot it. They may not have the latest gear, but their air defence systems are quite advanced. The problem with using miniature drones is the reduced range compared to the larger ones: four or five miles at most, depending upon the conditions.

"International waters extend to twelve miles. We could bring the ship in to fifteen miles—so it doesn't look like we're deliberately issuing a challenge—then use the marines and an inflatable to go the rest of the way. They'll see our cruiser, but they shouldn't be able to detect a small landing craft. Once ashore, the team would launch the drones and provide backup if required. We'd pull out both the prisoners and our men by helicopter."

Moreland rubbed his chin. "If this goes wrong, we might end up embarrassing ourselves again."

Jacobs offered a wry smile. "Things can't get much worse than they already are, can they? On the plus side, if we can get our people out, it'll show the rest of the world that the Reponans are the lying bastards we know them to be."

"Good point."

"If you're in agreement, Prime Minister," Trent said, "I'll give orders to move that cruiser. We don't want to tip off their military, so I suggest we proceed slowly and make it look like a routine patrol. Then at the last minute, we set a different course and divert towards Tripoli. Our inflatables can do about fifty knots in calm conditions, so once they launch, it won't take long for them to get to shore."

Jacobs narrowed his eyes in thought. After a few seconds, he nodded. "Let's do it. What happens when they land?"

"It'll be dark, but the landing area could be populated. If that's the case, they may need to put ashore elsewhere. According to the intel, the hospital where they're being held is just over a mile from the coast. The team will launch the drones from the beach and travel by foot to the extraction point."

"No meeting place has been arranged," Moreland said. "As I mentioned earlier, we haven't been able to contact our source to agree that level of detail."

The admiral folded his arms. "I'm well aware of that, but we do know roughly where they're holding our people, so my men will set out in that direction."

"That's if the information is correct," the head of MI6 replied. "Why don't you wait until you get confirmation the escape has been successful before launching?"

"It may be too late by then. What if the inflatable approaches to within two or three hundred metres of the shore and holds station there?"

Moreland studied the admiral for a moment. "All right, that sounds like a sensible compromise. There is one other thing we need to consider; we don't know who is infected with this new strain of the virus. If the hostages or any of the locals are carrying the infection, we can't afford for them to pass it on to anybody else."

Trent scratched his head. "That complicates things a bit."

"He's right though," Jacobs said. "We're trying to keep it from the press, but there've already been some nasty incidents over the past few days where pregnant women have been abused, and in one case, even attacked. There's a lot of fear among the general public. The last thing we need is to pass this disease on to your crew."

"I'll ensure the marines are equipped with protective gear," the admiral replied. "We also need to instigate full quarantine measures for everybody we bring back on board the ship until we can test them."

"So, are we all agreed on the plan?" Jacobs asked.

Both men on the other side of the desk responded in the affirmative.

"Good work, gentlemen. Let's keep the circle on this small, just to make sure there aren't any leaks. And please apprise me of any progress."

Wednesday 6th August 2036

Tripoli Infectious Diseases Hospital, Republic of North Africa
1 day until the deadline

Jason leant forwards to study the computer screen beside Dr Kubar and his mother. A cough came from behind them. Jason twisted around to see the tall, white-coated figure of Dr Fernando. The doctor remained impassive as he shifted from one foot to the other.

"I must apologise once again for my colleague," he said. "I had no idea he had hidden a phone."

"It is not your fault," Kubar replied.

"Still, he worked on my team, and I feel partially responsible for the discomfort we have all suffered."

"Don't worry about it," Jason said. He didn't want to explain that they had been spared from the strip search.

A slow smile rose on the Spanish doctor's face. "Thank you. Now, I have some good news. These are only preliminary results, but it seems the compound you created has prevented the activation of the virus, at least in the cell cultures."

A stunned silence greeted the scientist's announcement. Then Kubar pushed back his chair and jumped to his feet. "Are you sure?"

Fernando nodded. "We must perform more tests, but yes, from the work we have done so far, there is no evidence of a transition to the lytic stage."

"Have you told the professor yet?" Kubar asked.

"No, I thought you should be the first to know. After all, you were the one to design it."

Kubar beamed as he placed a hand on Jason's and Rosalind's shoulders. "It was not just me. I had a lot of help from my colleagues here."

"Do you want to see the analysis?"

"Of course."

Fernando led the threesome towards the glass-walled room. He pointed to a two-metre high beige cabinet standing on the other side of the window. "That is the machine where we performed the tests."

"Not particularly exciting," Rosalind muttered.

"Let me show you the results," Fernando said, his enthusiasm undimmed. He crossed to a nearby desk and lowered himself into the chair. He waved a hand in front of the computer screen as the others gathered behind him. The display lit up, showing an array of slightly distorted circles.

"These are untreated human lung cells from a juvenile," he explained. "They are infected with the virus, but it is in its dormant phase. Watch what happens when we introduce the activation agent."

He poked a finger at the image. A time-lapse video played. For the first few seconds, nothing happened. Then one circle collapsed in on itself, followed moments later by another. The rest rapidly did the same until not a single intact cell remained.

"What you saw there took place over a period of approximately four minutes. There is no point in showing you what happens when we bathe the cells in your new compound and repeat the experiment because there is no apparent change. Let me show you instead some numerical data."

He waved his hand sideways in front of the screen. A three-dimensional graph appeared.

"This is the control," he said. "You can see this drop in the cell count for the lytic stage here. This is what you observed on the display just now." He pointed at a part of the single red line where the gradient decreased rapidly.

"Let me show you what happens with the compound you designed." He reached out a finger and flicked it to the left. A second plot appeared, containing six differently coloured lines.

"What are we looking at here?" Rosalind asked, leaning forwards.

"Each line is a different concentration."

Two of the lines showed a slight decrease halfway along the horizontal axis, but the rest remained level.

"And if I superimpose the control on the same axes…" Fernando flicked his finger to introduce a third graph. In this one, the red line fell steeply as before, but the others merged into a single flat trace. The doctor extended his hand and twisted his wrist in front of the screen. The image rotated, showing six horizontal lines running across the top of the display alongside each other.

"Even at the lowest concentration, there is almost no decrease in the healthy cell count. Congratulations. I think we have found a treatment that will protect against the virus."

Kubar and Jason grinned as they accepted Fernando's handshake. Rosalind continued to stare at the screen. After a few moments, she raised her eyes and met the Spanish doctor's puzzled gaze. "Halfon will want to test this on a live subject. You better be absolutely sure it'll work before you inform him."

"Of course. I will run more tests before I tell him, but I don't expect the results to change. From what I understand, the molecular structure is very similar to the one we trialled on the child a few days ago—"

"And look how that ended up," Rosalind interrupted.

Fernando flushed. She gestured towards Jason. "Tomorrow, the test subject will be his son."

"I think we would all prefer to delay any more human trials until we have more information," Kubar said. "I will discuss this with Professor Halfon tonight. Please do what you can to confirm the results. Thank you for telling us first."

"You're welcome," Fernando replied.

Kubar led Jason and Rosalind back towards their workstations. In silence, he sat in the chair and waved his hand in front of the screen to wake up the computer. Then he navigated several menus.

"What are you doing?" Jason asked.

A low whirring sound came from a few feet away. Kubar rose, strolled to a nearby printer and picked up the sheets of paper that emerged.

"It is my insurance policy," he replied as he folded them and placed them in the back pocket of his trousers.

Part Four: Evacuation

Wednesday 6th August 2036

Tripoli Infectious Diseases Hospital, Republic of North Africa
5 minutes before the planned power cut

Jason glanced at his watch band: 21:55. Only five minutes to go. A guard had collected Perrin half an hour earlier, leaving Jason and the Shaladis as the only prisoners in the room. At the end of that day's shift, Dr Kubar had informed him that Professor Halfon planned to conduct the test on Paul at eleven o'clock the following morning. If this escape attempt failed, his son would be sedated and strapped to a trolley, then placed in close proximity to a pregnant woman. Despite the success of the cell culture trials, he had no intention of risking his son's life on a compound yet to be proven in human subjects. Now he straddled the wooden bench, his legs jiggling up and down with nervous tension.

The general flicked a glance in Jason's direction from the opposite side of the table where he sat alongside his daughter, Aya. "It would not be possible for you to look more tense," he whispered without turning his head.

"Oh, right," Jason replied. "Sorry." He studied the digits on his watch band again. No change.

"And stop checking the time," Shaladi hissed. "You will alert the guards."

He muttered a few words in Arabic to Aya. She stood, then strolled towards the guard station. The two men inside watched her approach through a haze of grey cigarette smoke. One rose and ambled through the doorway to question her. She pointed at the door to the bathroom. He shrugged and returned to his colleague. He let out a brief bark of laughter, then raised his hand to his mouth and took a long drag of his cigarette, causing the tip to turn a bright cherry-red.

"Two minutes," Shaladi whispered. "Move to the end of the table, but do not look at them."

Jason followed the command, sitting with his legs astride the bench. Despite the general's earlier instructions, he checked his watch again: 21:58. His pulse rate soared as he tried to remember the tasks he had been assigned. He ran over the first part of the plan in his head. *Do not move until the lights go out.* It was about ten metres to the office. How long would it take him to cover the distance?

Shaladi's voice intruded on his thoughts. "Any moment now. Be ready."

Jason twisted around and risked a glance at the guards. The two men seemed relaxed as they chatted and smoked. Another quick check of the time: 22:01. Was anything going to happen? "They're late," he whispered.

Shaladi lifted one leg and placed it on the other side of the bench, matching Jason's stance. Despite the general's calm outward appearance, a bead of sweat ran down the man's temple. He raised his hand and brushed it away.

Jason drummed his fingers on the wooden surface of the table. He could barely breathe. Another surreptitious glance at the watch band: 22:02. His gaze drifted across to the general. Their eyes locked onto each other. Shaladi's lips moved in silence. *Wait.*

A burst of laughter came from the office. Both prisoners turned their heads towards the noise. How much longer? Jason focused his attention on the glowing digits, making no attempt to disguise his actions. 22:03. They weren't coming. "Nothing is—"

A dull thud. The lights flickered, then died. Shaladi's urgent command: "Run!"

Jason shoved himself off the bench and ran in a low crouch with his hands out in front of him towards the office. The red tips of the two cigarettes provided the only guidance. The clamour of somebody hammering on a door rose above the harsh sound of his breathing. A series of shrill screams followed moments later.

Jason bumped into the wall and immediately dropped flat. He inched his way to the right until he came to the corner. A figure brushed past him in the darkness. Suddenly, the room brightened a little. *Shit! Emergency lighting.*

A quick glance confirmed Shaladi squatting beside him. The general raised a finger to his lips in a shushing gesture. The banging sounds continued unabated. A guard emerged through the office doorway. He held a pistol in his hand. The man crept towards the source of the noise. He yelled some words in Arabic.

The guard's focus remained on the door to the female bathroom. With a yell of fury, Shaladi rose from his crouch and charged. He barrelled into his target, slamming him against the wall. The pistol dropped to the floor and skittered away from the struggling pair. Jason flung himself forwards. Two shots rang out, throwing up splinters where the bullets smashed into the tiles, inches from his head. He scooped up the weapon and spun around just as another shot punched into the stained plaster behind him.

Jason extended his arm without thinking and squeezed the trigger. The bullet struck the guard in the shoulder, spinning him sideways.

"Give it to me," Shaladi barked. His opponent lay dazed, blood streaming from a cut to his forehead. Jason handed him the weapon. The general raised the barrel. Jason flinched at the impossibly loud bang. He turned away in horror at the sight of the gore and brain matter splattered against the wall.

A groan came from inside the office. Shaladi took a pace forwards, extended his arm and fired another two shots. Moments later, he emerged with a cigarette dangling from his mouth and a pistol in each hand. He handed one weapon to Jason and placed the other in the waistband of his trousers. "Well done. Now hold this. We have more work to do."

"You didn't have to kill them."

The general took a deep drag, then dropped the butt and ground it beneath his heel. He blew out the smoke he had been holding in his lungs. "We do not have time to take prisoners. They would have killed you without a second thought. Just be thankful they are dead and you are not. Let me fetch my daughter, then we can get out of here."

Jason stared at the pistol. "I don't think I can use this."

Shaladi shook his head in disgust. "The man you wounded would have died in a few minutes anyway. It is too late for regrets." He strode towards the bathroom and called out in Arabic. The door inched open, and a terrified Aya Shaladi peered out. A short conversation followed.

Jason stared at the dead body. He had shot somebody. The smooth black shape of the gun suddenly felt heavy in his hand. His stomach heaved. Thin bile splattered on the dirty tiles. He spat to remove the acidic taste from his mouth.

Shaladi jogged to the exit. "Quick, we must hurry. Let us hope the doctor's information was correct, and the doors are unlocked."

The general pulled the handle towards him and grinned as the door swung open. "Good, he was right."

"We need to get my mother from the cells," Jason said as he hurried to catch up.

Shaladi's face darkened. "Why do you want to rescue this woman? Did she not kill your biological mother and millions of other women? We should leave her here to suffer."

"I made a promise."

"We have a saying; promises are like eggs: fragile and easily broken."

"Look, if you aren't going to help, I'll do it by myself."

The general's eyes narrowed. "I will never understand you Westerners. Fine, let us go and free the most hated person in the world."

Wednesday 6th August 2036

Tripoli Infectious Diseases Hospital, Republic of North Africa
3 minutes before the planned power cut

Dr Kubar stood outside Halfon's office. He glanced at his watch for the third time in the last two minutes: 21:57. He was a little early, but he needed to be with the director when the power failed. His fingers closed around the object in the pocket of his white medical coat. He wondered whether he could summon the courage to use it.

Initially, the professor had been reluctant to meet him at this late hour. What had finally convinced him was Kubar's promise of important news. The scientist had persuaded his colleague, Dr Fernando, to hold off on revealing the promising results of the trials. Despite his treasonous intentions and more to keep his mind from what lay ahead, he had spent the last three hours poring through the test data looking for holes. Everything seemed to indicate the conclusions were correct.

Kubar knocked on the professor's door. He turned the handle upon hearing the muffled call to enter.

Halfon glanced up from the screen he was studying. "Sit, sit," he said, waving the doctor to a seat. "This must be important if you want to see me this late in the day."

"It is," Kubar replied. "There is some good news. We have developed a new compound, and it is effective in preventing the virus from activating in cell cultures."

Halfon's brows knitted together in a frown. "Why has nobody told me about this before now?"

"I wanted to check the results myself."

"And let me guess; you wished to delay testing on a live subject until you had done so?"

Kubar met the professor's piercing gaze. "That is correct."

Halfon rested his elbows on the desk and steepled his fingers. "I see. It is indeed good news, but I am disappointed you did not tell me sooner."

"I did not want to give you false hope."

A venomous look flitted across Halfon's face. "Or perhaps you have allowed the attitudes of the Westerners to rub off on you. Actually, Dr Brandt showed me the results a few hours ago."

Kubar flushed. "If this treatment works on a human subject, will you allow me to talk to my daughter?"

"Yes, I have already told you this."

"And you are sure she is well? May I view the records? You could access the database now."

Halfon's eyes narrowed. "You do not believe me?"

"I would like to see the information for myself."

Halfon leant back in his chair, studying the doctor. "I am beginning to think you know more than you are telling me."

"What do you mean?"

"The security people have been checking Dr Rossi's phone. There is no evidence it ever connected to the Wi-Fi. In addition, the network logs confirm the unauthorised device accessed one of our government sites: the same site you are asking me to show you now."

"I just want to know whether my daughter is alive."

"Whoever the person is, they would need the wireless password. Unless I am mistaken, you are among the people with this knowledge."

Kubar remained silent. He glanced at his watch: 21:59.

Halfon continued. "We may not be able to see from our logs what information was requested from the database, but the system maintains full records of all queries. We have the exact time the request took place, so we can use the timestamp to identify the query at their end. I have passed this along to our government's internal security agency, and I am expecting a reply shortly, although I suspect the answer will not surprise me. I do not believe in coincidences. So, I ask again; do you know something about this?"

Kubar closed his fingers around the object in his pocket. Still, he said nothing.

"How did you get the login credentials?" Halfon asked. "Did you steal mine?" He opened the top drawer and reached inside. His hand emerged holding a black cylinder. He placed it on the desk in front of him.

Kubar's eyes locked onto the shape of the stun baton. He tore his gaze away to check the time: 22:01. *Is this power cut going to happen?*

The professor glared at his subordinate. "I must say, I am disappointed in you. As one of our most talented scientists and the inventor of a cure for this virus, you could have been a national or perhaps even an international celebrity. But instead, you have betrayed your country. I will summon the security guards here in a few seconds to arrest you."

"I found out my daughter died years ago. You lied to me."

Halfon stared at his subordinate. "I did what was necessary. Get over it. Did you really think she was still alive after so long?"

Kubar pushed back his chair.

"You cannot escape," the professor said. He grasped the baton and stood.

Suddenly, the lights flickered. A moment later, the room plunged into darkness. Kubar grabbed the syringe gun from his pocket. He launched himself towards the spot where Halfon had been standing. The two men collided and crashed to the floor. Kubar was the first to react. He pressed the nozzle against the professor's body and pulled the trigger. A short hiss signalled the device had delivered its payload. He rolled away before Halfon could recover sufficiently to use his own weapon. He pushed himself upright, using the edge of the desk for support.

A second later, the dim glow of the emergency lighting clicked on to reveal the prostrate form of the director. "What did you—?"

"It is a muscle relaxant," Kubar said. "You will soon find yourself unable to move at all. Before you ask, there is not enough to kill you."

"They will torture you for this. You will die a painful death."

"They have to catch me first."

"You are a traitor. I hope your daughter died in agony." The stun baton dropped from Halfon's grasp and rolled a short distance along the carpet. Despite his situation, his features twisted into a sneer. "You lack the courage to do what needs to be done. You are too afraid to sacrifice a life for the greater good." His eyes followed the doctor as he leant forwards and scooped up the weapon.

Kubar depressed the circular button. A blue spark crackled across the tip. Wordlessly, he knelt over Halfon's incapacitated body. Kubar reached inside the professor's jacket, removed his mobile phone and key card, then slipped them into his own pocket.

Kubar moved his mouth close to the director's ear. "Oh, I am prepared to do what must be done—just not to sacrifice the lives of innocent children."

Then he placed the end of the device on the man's chest above his heart and pushed down with his thumb. Halfon's body spasmed. He pressed the button again. After three further jolts of high voltage electricity, the professor's eyes remained open, staring sightlessly at the ceiling.

Wednesday 6th August 2036

Tripoli Infectious Diseases Hospital, Republic of North Africa
2 minutes after the power cut

Jason followed the general and his daughter through the doorway. The dim emergency lighting cast a ghostly glow over the cracked walls. Their footsteps echoed as they jogged towards the staircase. Jason stopped and listened when they reached the door. A stillness seemed to have settled over the building. For a moment, he wondered whether he was imagining things, but then he identified the cause—the ever-present background hum of machinery had ceased.

"Are you coming?" Shaladi hissed.

Jason stepped into the stairwell. A dank, musty smell assaulted his nostrils. Here, the emergency lights were more widely spaced, throwing long shadows as they descended the concrete steps. Two flights down, they arrived at the ground floor and another door.

Shaladi held up a hand. "There is sure to be a guard. He will be armed. He may have heard us already, so we need to be ready. Aya, you have no weapon. You must wait here. I will go first. Do not make any sound." He pushed the handle and slid sideways through the gap, then beckoned Jason forward.

"Be careful," Aya whispered as the door closed behind them.

A narrow corridor stretched ahead. Dim strip lights extended along the ceiling. The black, circular lens of a camera pointed towards them, but it showed no signs of being active. Dark patches stained the concrete floor and walls. The musty odour was worse here. They crept forwards. A flash of movement.

Jason swung the pistol, then removed his finger from the trigger. "Only a mouse," he murmured, his heart racing.

"Or a rat," Shaladi added with a low chuckle.

"Shit. I hate rats."

"They are more scared of you than you are of them."

"I wouldn't be so sure."

Shaladi stopped. "Shh! Listen."

Jason tilted his head, his ears straining to pick up what the general had heard. The muted sound of a female voice came from the other side of the rusty metal door ahead. "My mother is trying to distract the guard," he whispered. "What's the plan?"

"There is only one route forward. We must surprise him before he has time to react." He studied the hinges. "It opens this way, but I think he will hear us before we can enter."

"So, what do we do?"

Shaladi scratched his cheek. "I will pull the door towards us. You go in and shoot him."

"What? I just step inside and—"

"No. You stay low. It gives him less of a target."

"Why can't you do the shooting?"

Shaladi stared hard at his co-conspirator. "You are the one who wants to free her. We can leave her here if you wish."

Jason met the general's gaze. "All right. I'll do it."

"Remember. Aim for the centre of the body and squeeze the trigger."

Jason drew in a deep breath. A whooshing sound rushed in his ears.

"Are you ready?" Shaladi asked. "I will count up, and on three, I will open it."

"Okay." Jason crouched and nodded at the general. "Let's go."

"One… Two… Three!"

The hinges squealed in protest as Shaladi heaved the heavy metal door towards him. Jason scuttled forwards, his arm outstretched. A concrete corridor extended away to his left. Five equally-spaced rusty doors lined the right wall. A guard was peering through the hatch at the far end. The man turned his head in surprise at the sudden interruption.

In the dim light, Jason raised the pistol and sighted along the barrel. His finger started to squeeze the trigger. The breath caught in his throat. A wave of dizziness swept over him. He swallowed hard. The guard reached towards his holster. The weapon wavered in Jason's hand. He couldn't do it. He closed his eyes, waiting for the bullets to rip through his body.

An incredibly loud bang boomed inches from his head. His own gun leapt as he inadvertently pulled the trigger. When he dared to look along the corridor, the guard lay on his side, moaning in pain. Two more thunderous bangs followed. The man jerked twice and stopped moving.

Jason dropped the weapon. He twisted around to see Shaladi's angry stare.

"Why did you not shoot?" the general yelled.

"I…"

"Do you want to die?"

"I'm sorry. I just couldn't…"

Shaladi spat on the floor and muttered a curse. He stepped forwards, scooped up Jason's pistol and hurried along the corridor. When he reached the pool of blood, he stretched out a leg and prodded the guard's body with his foot. Satisfied with the lack of response, he bent down, unfastened the man's holster and removed his gun. After placing the weapon in the waistband of his trousers, he peered through the hatch, then hauled down on the lever and pulled the heavy door towards him.

Jason crept up behind him, taking care to avoid stepping in the expanding crimson puddle. Rosalind Baxter cowered against the back wall.

"Are you coming," Shaladi said, his voice laced with disdain, "or do you like it here?"

"Is the guard dead?" she asked, unable to hide a quiver in her words.

The general rolled his eyes. "You are the doctor, no? I am not an expert, but I think so."

"Did the plan work?"

"So far, yes—no thanks to your son—but we still have much to do."

"What do you mean?"

"He could not shoot the gun."

Jason lowered his head in shame.

Rosalind grabbed his hand. "Well, I'm grateful you came for me. What now?"

"We return to my daughter and disarm the other guards," Shaladi replied. "After that, we fetch the girl and their child and get out of here."

"Okay, lead on."

The general turned and jogged back the way they had come. Both Jason and Rosalind cast nervous glances at the dead body before following. Shaladi called out in Arabic before opening the door into the stairwell. Aya's anxious face greeted them. They exchanged a few more words, then the general removed a pistol from his waistband and handed it to her.

He fixed Jason with a stare. "Unlike you, I trust my daughter to follow instructions," he said. He turned to Rosalind. "Can you use one of these?"

She nodded.

"But will you fire it if necessary?"

She flashed a sympathetic glance at Jason. "Yes."

Shaladi handed Rosalind the second spare weapon. "Good. Let us go and get the others. My men will be waiting outside."

Wednesday 6th August 2036

Tripoli Infectious Diseases Hospital, Republic of North Africa
4 minutes after the power cut

The general led them up the staircase, trailed by his daughter. Rosalind came next, with Jason bringing up the rear. His ears still burned with humiliation at his inability to use the weapon when required. As he plodded up the stairs, his brain whirled in an internal conflict. He was reluctant to take a life, but the people holding them prisoner would show no such mercy. His inaction could easily have led not only to his own demise but also the deaths of those depending upon him to escape. Next time, if there was one, he would do whatever needed to be done.

Jason was so lost in thought he nearly bumped into his mother when she stopped behind the others, two floors up from the basement.

"I will go first," Shaladi whispered. "If you see any guards, you must shoot them." He stared pointedly at Jason, then focused his attention back on the women. "When they are down, take their guns. It is possible some of the scientists remain loyal to the professor. None of them can be allowed to have weapons. Is everybody ready?"

The general didn't wait for a response. He pushed the door open, hesitated a second, then slipped through the gap. The three others followed his lead. He led them along the dimly lit corridor as far as the entrance to the dining area. The sound of angry voices penetrated from the other side.

Shaladi raised a hand and crouched down. "Keep low and do not fire until I do." He reached for the handle and twisted it slowly. The noise level rose as a crack opened. He eased his way in. Aya followed him. Rosalind turned back before entering. "Good luck," she murmured.

Jason opened his mouth to reply, but she was already moving, the gun stretched out ahead of her. He trailed her into the room. Several scientists milled about under the gloomy lighting. A guard shuffled nervously from foot to foot in the far corner, his weapon drawn. Another man stood to one side, talking into a radio as his eyes anxiously scanned the small crowd.

Jason's gaze followed the three other members of his group as they crept along the wall, their movement hidden from the guards by the intervening bodies.

A voice called out in a thick Arabic accent. "Return to your rooms."

"Why are the lights out?" came a shout from the gathering.

"You must go back to your rooms," the man repeated. Now, the second guard also drew his pistol.

"We're not moving until you tell us what's happening," somebody yelled. A murmur of approval accompanied the challenge.

A shot rang out as the nearest guard fired above the heads of the crowd. Instinctively, they flinched and dropped down, providing the opportunity for which the general had been waiting.

Another gunshot boomed from Jason's left, followed swiftly by two more. The pair of armed guards jerked backwards, then lay unmoving. The scientists scattered in panic. Jason ignored the commotion and scuttled towards the closest fallen man. He scanned the floor, searching for the dropped pistol. A glint of light on metal reflected from beneath the dead body's legs. He reached out a hand and snatched up the weapon. His gaze rose inadvertently to the blooming patch of red in the centre of the man's chest, then to the blank stare of the wide-open eyes.

Swallowing hard, he turned his attention towards the second corpse, but Aya was already crouching beside it.

Shaladi strode to the middle of the room and stood with his gun pointing downwards. "Please stay calm," he yelled. Frightened stares greeted his statement. "We mean you no harm. We are leaving this place tonight. You are free to go too."

"Why are you doing this?" a man asked. "They told us we could leave when they developed a cure, and we have done that." Jason recognised him as the Spanish doctor, Fernando.

The general barked out a laugh. "You think they will honour this agreement? You do not know these people like I do."

"What happens when we get out of here?" a different voice called. "Can you help with transport?"

"I am sorry, but no. You must arrange your own travel."

"We'll never make it across the border," another man replied. "I don't know about you, but I'm staying here. Apart from anything else, I want to get paid before I leave."

"That is your decision."

Jason tuned out the conversation. He had more important things to attend to. Before he could think about leaving, he needed to free Antimone and his son, Paul.

Wednesday 6th August 2036

Tripoli Infectious Diseases Hospital, Republic of North Africa
6 minutes after the power cut

Jason jogged across the dining area and along the corridor to the laboratory entrance. He eased the door open. The gun he had recovered from the dead guard pointed ahead of him. He exhaled the breath he had been holding; the room was deserted. The space looked different in the dim emergency lighting. Hulking machines stood like monoliths, creating patches of shadow that didn't exist when the mains power was on. The unfamiliar silence added to the threatening atmosphere of the place.

He buried his anxiety and crept towards the entry to the isolation area in which Antimone and Paul were being held. As he passed by the glass-walled observation chamber, he spotted a bright light penetrating through the frosted window in the door. It seemed Dr Kubar was right; the electricity supply continued to function here.

He pushed through the unlocked swing doors and found himself in a room, approximately five metres square, with white walls. Straight ahead, several yellow hazmat suits hung on hangers. To his left, a solitary green button occupied a position between two sets of sliding partitions. Mounted above it was a sign in Arabic script. An empty wheelchair sat in the corner.

Jason flashed a glance at his watch. Already, seven minutes had passed since the start of the escape attempt. How much time did he have before they restored power? It couldn't be long. Putting on the protective suit would waste valuable seconds. If he got Antimone and Paul out and they were infected, they would pass on the virus, anyway. *Damn it!* He'd have to take the risk. He shoved the pistol into the waistband of his trousers and slammed his palm against the button.

The left partition opened, revealing a chamber one metre wide by two long. Jason stepped forwards. The panel closed behind him, sealing him inside. The dim sound of machinery penetrated the walls. His ears popped. For a horrible moment, he wondered whether the pumps would suck out all the air and suffocate him, but after a few seconds, the door in front slid back.

Jason emerged into a foyer area. He blinked as his eyes acclimatised to the sudden increase in brightness from the overhead lighting. Antimone and Paul were in here somewhere. A passageway extended thirty or forty metres ahead. A series of rooms occupied the right side. Solid partitions separated each room from the next. Full-height windows bordered the corridor, allowing those outside to look in. Conventional white plastic doors lined the opposite wall. Halfway down, one door contained a frosted-glass panel. He identified it as the entrance to the observation chamber.

Jason crept forwards. He couldn't be sure whether anybody was still working, and he had no wish to use the pistol unless absolutely necessary. The first room was empty apart from two unoccupied beds. In the next, a bed lay against the back wall. The outline beneath the sheets belonged to an adult. The sleeping figure moved, revealing the face of the pregnant woman he had last seen in the observation area.

Jason continued along the corridor. His breath caught in his throat when he peered through the window of the third room. Antimone sat in a wheelchair, her eyes closed and her chin resting on her chest. He tapped on the glass. She jerked her head upright, and her mouth opened in shock. She gestured towards the panel mounted beside the door.

The only control was a single green button. Jason pressed it with his finger. A metallic click signalled the opening of the lock.

Antimone wheeled herself forwards, wearing a huge grin on her face. Then, just as quickly, it faded. "What are you doing? Don't you know I'm infected?"

Jason placed a foot against the door to prevent it from closing. "We're getting out of here," he whispered. "Shaladi arranged a power cut. He shot the guards. I haven't got time to explain it all. We need to find Paul."

"You don't understand. Both of us have the new strain. You'll be infecting everybody we come into contact with."

Jason glanced at his watch. "Dr Kubar and my mother came up with a cure—at least we think it is."

"What does that mean?"

"They haven't run any human trials yet, but it works in a cell culture."

Antimone's features clouded in doubt.

Jason leant forwards, placed a hand behind her head to draw her nearer and kissed her. "Look, I love you and our son. We may not be doing the right thing, but unless you want to spend the rest of your life in here, we need to leave now."

"I'm not—"

"There's no time. Do you honestly think these people will share any drug they develop with other countries? We both know the answer to that. If we get out of here, we can publish the formula and make sure everybody gets it. But that won't happen unless we go immediately."

"All right. Paul's in the next room."

Jason stood back for Antimone. She wheeled herself out and turned right. When she reached the adjacent door, she pressed the green button on the panel. "You wait here. I'll get him."

Jason's heart fluttered at the sight of the tiny figure in the single cot. "Paul," he murmured. He watched as Antimone leant forwards, scooped up the sleeping child, still wrapped in the bedsheet, and held him against her chest.

She spun the wheelchair around and headed back. "Let's go," she whispered.

Jason hesitated. "Actually, I promised Dr Kubar I'd get the other kids out as well."

"They're in the next room."

"How many are there?"

"Just two, I think."

Jason jogged further along the corridor and peered through the window. Four cots lay against the right wall, separated from each other by a gap of half a metre. The two furthermost beds held the sleeping forms of children. Antimone moved up behind him.

"I'll fetch them," Jason said. He pushed the button, crossed the small room and crouched beside the nearest occupied bed. He reached out a hand and shook the shoulder of the unconscious child.

"We haven't got time for this," Antimone hissed. "Just grab them."

Jason pulled back the thin sheet. The boy was maybe four-years-old. He wore a brightly coloured T-shirt and shorts. A mewl of protest escaped his lips when Jason picked him up. Moments later, Jason bent down and lifted the second child. The boy's eyelids fluttered open for a moment, then closed once again.

With a child resting against each shoulder, Jason hurried back towards Antimone. "Let's get out of here," he said. He took one step into the corridor, then stopped. Antimone twisted her head and gasped.

Fifteen metres away, between the escapees and the airlock, stood the pregnant woman. A figure in a white hazmat suit stayed behind her. The reflection of a scalpel blade held to the woman's throat glinted in the bright overhead lighting. She resisted, but the person pushed her forwards.

Wednesday 6th August 2036

Tripoli Infectious Diseases Hospital, Republic of North Africa
8 minutes after the power cut

Jason retreated a pace. "Is there another way out of here?" he asked.

"I don't think so," Antimone replied. "I've only ever seen them come in through that entrance."

"We might be able to get out from the observation room. I can use my gun to break the glass."

"Can't you just shoot him?"

"Not without hitting her."

The man in the hazmat suit pushed the pregnant woman forwards again. He called out something in Arabic.

Jason twisted his head and glanced behind him. The door with the frosted window was five metres away. "Come on. We have to go."

Antimone spun her wheelchair around and covered the short distance in two shoves. Jason followed, casting another backward glance. The North African pair continued to shuffle closer.

Jason shoved the swing doors open with his foot and edged through the gap. He stepped to one side to allow Antimone to pass. "I'll have to put these two down," he said. Compared to the bright illumination of the corridor, the gloomy lighting gave the observation area an oppressive feel. Jason strode to the far end and gently lowered the pair of children to the floor. Antimone manoeuvred the wheelchair alongside them.

Jason removed the pistol from his waistband. "This is going to be loud." He moved back towards the door and pointed the weapon at the window. "Are you ready?"

Antimone nodded, clutching Paul more tightly.

Jason squeezed the trigger. A deafening boom rang out in the enclosed space. The glass remained intact apart from a splinter pattern extending from the point of impact. Immediately, the three children woke and started to cry.

"Shit, it's reinforced," he said.

"Try again," Antimone replied, glancing anxiously at the door.

Jason aimed at the same spot and fired a second time. Despite the incredibly loud bang, there was still no discernible difference to the window. On the far side of the room, one of the terrified African boys screamed in fright. He leapt up and ran towards the only way out. He reached the swing doors at the same moment as the man in the hazmat suit shoved his hostage through in the opposite direction. The impact knocked the boy off his feet. He landed on his back, staring up in terror at the equally petrified woman standing over him. His arms and legs scrambled in panic as he tried to move backwards.

Jason stood rooted to the spot. Suddenly, he remembered he was holding the gun. He swung his arm towards the doors. The woman cowered as the weapon pointed in her direction. There was no sign of the man. The sound of running footsteps echoed from the corridor.

"Get back," Jason yelled, taking a forward step.

The woman backed away with hands extended, a jumbled stream of words spilling from her mouth.

"Go," he shouted, gesturing with the pistol. She needed no second invitation. She whirled around and barged through the swing doors. Jason stuck his head through the gap and checked both ways along the corridor. Other than the retreating figure of the woman, nobody was there.

A wet cough drew Jason's attention back to the room. The closest African boy sprawled on the floor, blood streaming from his nose and mouth. He twisted onto his side and coughed again, spraying bloody droplets over the white tiles. Seconds later, his whole body convulsed. Jason shoved the pistol into the waistband of his trousers and knelt beside him. The boy shuddered once more, then his eyes rolled up, and he lay still.

"Is he—?" Antimone's voice quivered as she asked the question.

A bang on the window from behind Jason saved him from having to answer. He whirled around. Rosalind Baxter stood on the other side of the glass. She gesticulated at the table and mouthed something. Jason turned, trying to identify the object of her attention.

"Oh, no, no, no." Antimone's panicked words cut through Jason like a knife. A thin trickle of blood ran from the second African boy's nose down his chin. When he opened his mouth to cry, crimson streaks stained his tiny white teeth.

The hammering on the window grew more frantic. "What?" Jason mouthed.

He studied his mother's lips as she enunciated the words more slowly. What was she trying to tell him? She jabbed a finger. "This?" Jason asked, pointing to a stack of papers. She shook her head in frustration. He pointed to another item. Rosalind gave an exaggerated nod. Jason picked up the object: a syringe gun.

Finally, he understood: the drug. He grabbed the tray of clear vials. This time, he got the single word she mouthed: *yes*. With fumbling fingers, he snatched up a sealed capsule. Rosalind gestured again. He turned the cylinder upside down: a thumbs up. *How did the damned thing fit?* He pushed a lever on the medical instrument, and a slot opened. He shoved the glass tube home. Rosalind nodded in encouragement.

Jason grabbed a couple more vials from the tray and sprinted to the end of the room. He hesitated. Who should he give it to first? The African boy coughed. Specks of blood landed on the floor. Paul wiped a hand over his nose. A thin trail of red smeared his cheek.

"Just do it," Antimone screamed.

Jason placed the syringe gun against the foreign child's upper arm and pressed the trigger. The boy stopped crying for a second, then restarted with renewed vigour before falling silent. Jason flipped out the empty vial. It bounced across the floor in a series of clinks. He slotted home a full one and held the device to his son's shoulder. A short hiss signalled the entry of the drug into Paul's body. He slid the medical instrument into his belt alongside the pistol.

Antimone cradled her son. "Is it going to work?" she asked, her voice barely a whisper.

Jason studied Paul for a moment. "We can't stay here."

"You didn't answer my question."

"I don't know."

Antimone locked eyes on Jason. Unable to meet the ferocity of her glare, he looked away. "Come on," he said. He bent down and picked up the now unconscious African boy, then headed towards the swing doors. As he passed the table, he scooped up a handful of the vials and put them in his pocket.

Holding the weapon out ahead of him, Jason stepped around the dead child and stuck his head into the corridor. Empty. He jogged, retracing his footsteps to the exit. Antimone followed, grasping Paul in a tight, one-armed embrace as she powered the wheelchair with her free arm. Jason's gaze strayed to the left as they came to the pregnant woman's room. She sat on the bed, her face buried in her hands. She didn't even look up as they rushed past.

They arrived at the airlock without further incident. Jason studied the boy in his arms. His eyes were closed, but his breathing was deep and regular. Jason glanced back towards Antimone. Paul's head rested on her shoulder.

"How is he?" Jason asked.

"The bleeding seems to have stopped," she replied. "I think he's asleep."

"Thank God for that," Jason murmured. He pushed the solitary green button. The door opened immediately.

“I can’t fit through in this thing,” Antimone said. “You’ll have to lift me out.”

“There’s no way I can carry all three of you.”

“Put the kids in first, then come back for me.”

Jason backed inside the chamber with the African boy and gently placed him on the floor. “Block the gap with your chair.”

Antimone rolled forwards until one wheel rested against the door. She handed Paul to Jason, who positioned his son beside the other unconscious child. Finally, Jason lifted Antimone and kicked the wheelchair away. The panel slid shut almost immediately. A moment later, a foul-smelling chemical mist filled the small compartment.

The ordeal lasted only a few seconds, but both adults emerged coughing. The two children remained unaware throughout.

General Shaladi awaited them.

“Can you get the kids?” Jason asked, blocking the door with his foot.

The general stepped inside the chamber and came out moments later with a child under each arm.

“At least my wheelchair’s still here,” Antimone said, pointing to the device in the corner.

Jason hurried over and lowered her into the seat. He took Paul from the general and placed him on Antimone’s lap, then returned for the African boy. “I’d prefer you to be the one holding the gun,” he said to Shaladi with a wry grin.

They followed the general through the doors into the laboratory area. To the left, a blood-soaked figure in a hazmat suit lay crumpled on the ground. Seeing the focus of Jason’s attention, Shaladi growled, “He deserved to die.” His expression softened. “How is your son?”

Jason shot a glance at Antimone. “I think he’s going to be okay.”

“And the other child?”

Jason transferred his gaze to the boy in his arms. “It looks like he’ll be all right as well.”

“Excellent. Now, it is already too long. We must leave. Follow me.”

Rosalind fell in alongside as they passed through the dimly lit laboratory. “It seems the drug works.”

Jason flashed a tense smile at her. “Yeah. Thanks for your help.”

“One good turn deserves another. I’m just glad my grandson survived.”

As the group approached the exit leading into the dining area, an armed figure stepped out from the shadows. “Where do you think you’re going? Stop right there.”

Wednesday 6th August 2036

Tripoli Infectious Diseases Hospital, Republic of North Africa
11 minutes after the power cut

A gunshot punctured the silence. The four adults flinched as a chunk of plaster exploded from the wall inches above their heads. Both the children remained unconscious.

"That was to demonstrate I'm armed, and I know how to use this. Now, place your weapons on the ground and push them towards me with your feet... and no sudden movements."

The general and Rosalind both did as instructed.

Jason still held the African boy. "I can't—"

"Put him down."

Jason laid the sleeping child on the floor, then straightened up slowly.

"Now, remove the gun from your waistband. That's it. Toss it away." Jason followed the order. The pistol landed with a metallic clatter. "And the other thing too." Something inside shattered as the syringe hit the ground and skittered over the white tiles. "Good. Now, all of you put your hands behind your head and interlock your fingers."

Max's eyes glittered in the dim illumination cast by the emergency lighting as he watched the escapees comply. All the while, the dark circle of a gun barrel pointed at Jason's stomach.

"Well, well. My four least favourite people, all together in one place. And in such a hurry to leave."

"Please let us go," Antimone said, still clutching Paul to her chest.

"Oh, I don't think that'll happen."

"You could come with us."

"It's kind of you to invite me, but you've left the invitation a little late. I wondered what you were cooking up. I must have asked you quite a few times, but you wouldn't tell me."

"Because you were working with Halfon, weren't you?"

"I might have been."

"Which just goes to prove we were right not to trust you," Antimone replied.

Jason cleared his throat. "So, what are you going to do?"

Max's lips twitched in a smirk. "I could wait for more guards to arrive. I'm sure somebody will be here any minute. With a bit of luck, they'll pay my fee. They might even give me a bonus for stopping you from escaping. But I've got a better idea. I think I might just shoot you all. I'll say you tried to jump me. There won't be any witnesses to contradict me. The only question is who goes first."

He swung the barrel to point at Shaladi. "Maybe I'll start with you. We had a deal. I delivered exactly what we agreed upon, but instead of receiving the money, my reward was to be beaten up and treated as a prisoner just like the others."

The general muttered a curse.

"Yeah, whatever." The gun pivoted towards Antimone. "And what about you, Trike Queen? If you hadn't tripped me, none of this would have happened, the police would never have been brought in, and my father would still be alive."

Antimone let out a gasp of outrage. "How many times have I got to tell you, the thing at the track was a bloody accident? Even if it wasn't, how can you justify raping me? And that's not to mention—"

"Enough!" Max bellowed. "Do you want me to shoot you now?" He glowered at her for a moment then transferred his aim to Jason. "And what about the boy scout? You're as bad as her. Do you fancy trying to beat me up again, tough guy?"

"Put the gun down," Jason growled, "and I'll gladly take you on."

Max's face darkened. "Tempting though it is, I think I'll keep hold of this." He aimed the pistol at Rosalind. "That brings me to you. You killed my father in front of me. And that's on top of the millions of other deaths you caused. I'd be doing the world a favour by pulling the trigger."

Rosalind met his angry gaze. "If he hadn't caved in and tried to confess, I wouldn't have been forced to take such drastic action. I can see you have your father's genes. You're a pussy just like him."

Max stepped forwards, his face knotted in fury. He swung his fist in a vicious arc, catching Rosalind across the cheek. She let out a cry of pain as she staggered backwards, clutching the point of impact. When she lifted her fingers, they came away smeared with blood. She glowered back at him with a look of pure hatred.

Max retreated to his original position before anybody could react. His breathing was harsh and ragged, and his pupils had reduced to pinpricks. "The next person to talk will receive a bullet for their trouble. So I need to decide. Get down on your knees."

Antimone glared at Max from her wheelchair and gestured towards her legs. "I think you're forgetting something."

"Just stay there and don't move," he snarled.

Rosalind and Shaladi slowly lowered themselves one knee at a time.

Jason was about to follow suit when he detected motion behind Max in the shadows. "No," he said. "If you want to shoot me, you can do it while I'm standing."

The movement resolved into a person creeping forwards. As the figure moved into a patch of light, Jason recognised the outline of Dr Kubar. But he was still ten metres away and seemed to be unarmed.

Max stepped up to Jason and jabbed the pistol into his chest. "I won't tell you again. Down on your knees."

Jason went down on one knee. Five metres to go. Now he could see the approaching doctor held something in his hand.

Max took a step back. His gaze landed on Rosalind. Jason studied his captor's features. A decision formed in Max's eyes. His gun arm swung to the right. His finger tightened as he exerted pressure on the trigger.

Jason lunged. The pistol boomed. Kubar closed the final few paces. A sharp crack of electricity filled the air. Max Perrin dropped to the floor, his body convulsing. Silence fell on the room. Time seemed to stand still.

Then Antimone's voice shattered the calm with a piercing scream.

Wednesday 6th August 2036

Prime Minister's Office, 10 Downing Street, London
12 minutes after the power cut

Andrew Jacobs glanced out of the window at the night sky. He removed a handkerchief from his pocket and mopped at his brow. The underlying cause of his perspiration was the tension of waiting to hear from the forces stationed just off the Tripoli coastline rather than the temperature in the air-conditioned room. Admiral Trent and Charles Moreland sat beside him, staring at the blank screen. Both looked equally uncomfortable.

Trent's phone rang. He snatched it off the desk and held it to his ear.

"Where are they?" the Prime Minister asked.

"I'm patching the pictures through now," the admiral replied. Moments later, a jerky image consisting mostly of greys and blacks appeared on the monitor. The sound of splashing water mingled with the low murmur of male voices. "The team is still holding at a distance of three-hundred metres offshore. There's no sign the North Africans have any idea they're there. The beach looks deserted. You're seeing the view through a bodycam."

The video brightened as somebody turned on an infrared light, then settled to show six figures crouching in an inflatable. One of the occupants twisted towards the camera. Dark material shrouded the man's head and body. A mask containing two large lenses covered his face, giving him the appearance of a huge insect. He muttered a few words, then resumed his original position.

The minutes stretched out as the three men in the Prime Minister's office waited for something to happen. Finally, the admiral sat forwards, the phone still held to his ear. "Yes, I understand," he said.

"What's going on?" Jacobs asked.

"We're getting reports of a power failure near the Tripoli Infectious Diseases Hospital. There's nothing yet about any shots being fired."

"That must be them."

"I agree," the admiral replied. "Do we have permission to launch?"

The head of MI6 glanced towards the Prime Minister. "You have my agreement. What do you think, Andrew?"

Jacobs paused in thought for a second, then nodded. "Let's go for it. But for heaven's sake, keep it quiet. We don't want to start a shooting match with the Reponan military if we can help it."

Trent barked a few words into the phone. Almost immediately, the figures on the screen hunched down. A low buzz replaced the sound of lapping water as the bow of the inflatable lifted. Moments later, a scraping noise signalled that the craft had reached the shore. All the occupants bar one jumped out. The man operating the camera and three of his colleagues grabbed the rope running along the gunwale of the boat and spun it around. When it faced back the way they had come, the group gave it a coordinated shove towards deeper water. The note of the engine rose and a white wake followed the vessel as it raced out of sight.

"What's happening?" Jacobs asked.

"It's returning to the ship," the admiral replied. "We don't want to leave it where somebody will spot it and call in their military."

The three marines in front of the camera feed launched themselves forwards, splashing through the last few metres of the Mediterranean Sea to join the pair on the beach. Ahead of the camera, a man crouched down, raised his weapon and stared down the sights. The hiss of two suppressed shots followed one another in quick succession. The tinkle of broken glass carried faintly to the microphone.

"What are they doing now?" Jacobs asked, his voice a whisper.

"Taking out the nearby streetlights," Trent replied without diverting his attention from the screen.

The grainy pictures showed a marine removing his backpack. He withdrew a sphere the size of a tennis ball, pressed a button on its side and tossed it into the air. He repeated the process with a further two of the devices.

"Those are the drones," the admiral explained. "They'll be directed to the target."

The image bounced up and down as the men broke into a jog. Soon, they cleared the beach and ran across a deserted road.

"Won't somebody see them?" the Prime Minister asked.

Trent pointed to the display. "May I?"

Jacobs leant back from the screen.

The admiral moved his hands in front of the monitor, reduced the video to a small window and brought up a map.

"This is the hospital," he said, pointing to a red circle in the bottom right containing a white letter H. "That's where the drones are heading as we speak. At the moment, the team is here. They'll be following this route." He drew a line with his finger from the shore across a green shaded area. "It takes them through the National Park and the Al Nasr Forest. The Reponans have established a night time curfew, and both these areas are relatively unpopulated, so there's less chance of them being spotted."

"What about the last section?" Jacobs asked, pointing to the streets between the forested region and the H symbol.

Trent turned to the Prime Minister. "There's a lot of construction work going on in the vicinity, but you're right; they will stick out if they have to cross that area. Let's just hope our mysterious benefactors come through and give the local forces something else to keep them occupied. Once we set eyes on the hostages, we'll send in a chopper and lift them out along with the marines."

"If there are two different groups out there, how will we know who's on our side and who isn't?"

"I think I can answer that," Moreland replied, his mouth set in a grim line. "If they shoot at our people, they're probably the bad guys."

Wednesday 6th August 2036

Tripoli Infectious Diseases Hospital, Republic of North Africa
13 minutes after the power cut

Antimone's scream echoed through the darkened laboratory until her lungs ran out of air. Suddenly, she seemed to notice the unconscious child clasped in her arms. A series of choking sobs wracked her body. She couldn't drag her eyes away from the figure lying still on the floor. Blood dripped from the head wound. The slowly expanding pool appeared almost black in the dim lighting.

She forced her lips to move. "Is he…?" She barely recognised her own voice. The words emerged as if somebody else was operating her vocal cords. Her breathing hastened. A wave of dizziness swept over her as she hyperventilated.

General Shaladi made a gesture towards his daughter. It took Aya a moment to catch on, but then she stepped forwards and lifted Paul from Antimone's chest.

Antimone rolled her wheelchair alongside Jason's body. Awkwardly, she leant over and gently touched his cheek. *He can't be dead.* Any second now, he would stand up and dust himself down. "Come on. Get up," she whispered.

She flinched at the hand on her shoulder. "There's nothing we can do for him," Dr Kubar murmured.

Antimone whirled around. "Why didn't you stop him sooner?" she screamed. "Couldn't you tell he was about to shoot?"

The doctor stared at her, then turned away, unable to meet the expression of pain and anger in her eyes. "I tried to get there as soon as I could. I thought I would reach him in time."

Antimone's gaze flicked down to Jason's lifeless body. "Why did he have to sacrifice himself for her? Why couldn't he just let her die? That psycho was happy to kill both of us when we were stopping her from getting what she wanted."

"I am sorry," Kubar said. "I do not have an answer. Perhaps he still thinks of her as his mother."

“Not thinks,” Antimone corrected. “Thought. He’s dead because of her.” She closed her eyes and breathed through clenched teeth.

Shaladi crouched in front of her. “Please, we have to go. If we do not leave now, his sacrifice will be for nothing. I know you are in pain, but you must continue for your son.”

The tears dripped from Antimone’s chin onto her lap. Then she looked up. She wiped her cheeks with the palms of her hands. She checked to her right, then to her left. “Where is that bastard? And where’s that bloody woman? They were both here a minute ago.”

A gunshot boomed from the other side of the laboratory. Shaladi immediately darted towards the corner where he had kicked his gun. Antimone didn’t hesitate. She propelled herself in the direction of the gunfire.

“Wait!” the general called from behind her.

Antimone ignored his call. She raced past a towering machine, then clamped her hands down against the shiny hand rings, relishing the sharp sting as it burned her palms. She skidded to a halt. At first, the dim lighting made it hard to interpret what her eyes were telling her. Max Perrin lay on a workbench. One strap ran over his neck, another across his feet. His arms were bound together in front of him by a length of electrical cable. There was no evidence of any wounds. He seemed to be unconscious. His chest rose and fell in slow, regular movements.

Rosalind stood at an adjacent table, her back to Antimone. To her right, the door of one of the metal cabinets was open. The handle dangled at an oblique angle. That explained the gunshot, but what was she doing?

Antimone scanned the contents. Labelled bottles and jars filled the shelves. A circular stain identified where something had been removed. Behind her, the sound of Shaladi’s footsteps drew nearer. “What’s going on?” she asked.

Rosalind spun around, her face an unreadable mask. “I’m ending this once and for all.”

“Ending what?”

“His miserable life.”

Rosalind turned away and picked up an object from the table. Antimone moved closer. Rosalind held a brown bottle. Its size matched the empty space on the shelf. She twisted the top and placed the stopper down. An acrid smell accompanied the thin cloud of vapour that curled upwards.

Antimone squinted at the label. The writing was mostly in Arabic, but she recognised several letters: H_2SO_4. She wracked her brains, trying to identify the compound. It sounded familiar somehow. Then, in a flash, it came to her: sulphuric acid.

Rosalind reached out a hand and grabbed a glass syringe with a long metal needle. She inserted the tip inside the open neck of the bottle and withdrew the plunger. Careful not to spill any of the corrosive substance on herself, she crossed to where Max Perrin lay restrained on the workbench.

"Hold this," she said, handing the loaded instrument to Antimone. "I want him to be awake for this. And don't drop any on yourself. It might sting a bit."

Rosalind leant forwards and slapped Max hard on the cheek. "Come on, wake up."

Her captive opened a bleary eye and stared around in confusion for a moment. Finally, his gaze settled on Rosalind. As it did so, he bucked, trying to break free from his bonds.

"Don't bother," she said. "You aren't getting out of those knots any time soon."

Max tried again with the same results. His body relaxed. "So, you're still alive. That's a shame. I thought I'd done the world a favour."

"No," Rosalind replied. "You killed my son instead. And now you're about to pay for that."

Max's eyes flicked towards the end of the laboratory leading to the rest of the hospital. "As I recall, you were only too keen to kill him yourself a year or two back."

A harsh coldness settled on Rosalind's face. "You won't be quite so talkative when I've finished with you. What is it the Bible says? An eye for an eye? This will hurt—a lot."

She held out a hand towards Antimone. Max's gaze followed the movement and landed on the syringe. His eyes widened as they locked onto the point of the needle. He blinked rapidly in the first real sign of fear. He looked up at Antimone's scowling features. "You don't have to do this," he said, his voice trembling. "Please. You're not really going to stand there and watch her stab me, are you? You'll be no better than she is."

"Oh, stabbing you in the eye is only the beginning," Rosalind said. "The concentrated acid I inject might be more of an issue."

Max's mouth opened in shock. Once more, he struggled against the knots in a vain attempt to free himself.

"You killed him," Antimone muttered.

Max dragged his attention from the syringe to her face. "I didn't mean to. I was trying to shoot her."

Antimone's tone rose as she spat the words out. Her pulse thundered in her ears. "You raped me. You forced Jason to rape me. I would have died but for a fluke of genetics."

"But you lived. Look, I'm sorry. I may have overreacted. But it was all years ago. We were still kids." Desperation edged Max's voice.

“Then you sold us out to this bunch of savages.”

“I needed the money. If they ever pay me, you can have it.”

“I don’t want your money. Finally, you murdered Jason. Together with my son, he was one of the few good things to come out of all this.”

“I told you. It was an accident.” Panic laced every word.

Antimone spoke through gritted teeth. “Now he’s lying back there, dead on the floor. And all because I accidentally collided with you in a stupid, meaningless race.”

Tears rolled down Max’s cheeks. “Please. I’m begging you. I’ll do whatever you want.”

“Come on, give it to me,” Rosalind said, impatiently.

Antimone stared at Jason’s mother for a moment, then lowered her gaze to Max. As she stretched out the hand holding the syringe, the whir of machinery started up, and bright light flooded the room.

Wednesday 6th August 2036

Tripoli Infectious Diseases Hospital, Republic of North Africa
16 minutes after the power cut

Antimone blinked in the sudden brightness. Without thinking, she withdrew the hand still holding the charged syringe.

"Let me have it," Rosalind insisted. Antimone hesitated.

Shaladi glanced towards the far end of the laboratory with a worried expression. "If the power is back on, they know it is no accident. They will be here soon. We must leave now."

As if to emphasise his warning, the creak of an opening door reached their ears, followed seconds later by a man's voice, calling out in Arabic. The general raised one finger in a shushing gesture and jabbed his gun barrel towards the exit.

Antimone started to move, then stopped. She turned her wheelchair around. A look of relief had replaced Max Perrin's abject terror. Their eyes met. "By the way, Princess," he whispered, "I'm glad I killed your boyfriend." His mouth curved in a smirk. "Over here!" he called out aloud.

A flash of molten fury surged through Antimone's veins. Her mind filled with pent up rage, obscuring all conscious thought. She lunged forwards, jabbed the needle into Max's upper arm and rammed the plunger down as far as it would go.

His lips drew back in a howl of agony. The tendons in his neck contracted like cords. He stared down in horror as the skin blackened and shrivelled in a slowly expanding circle. Wisps of smoke rose from the site of the injection. His whole body rocked and bucked against the straps holding him down. Another inhuman shriek escaped his throat.

Antimone dropped the syringe. The glass shattered on impact. Vapour rose from the floor, twisting upwards in coils. She held a hand to her mouth as she studied the effects of her handiwork in horrified fascination. A pair of rapid gunshots boomed nearby, jolting her attention from the writhing form strapped to the workbench. Two men in dark uniforms sprawled on the ground twenty metres away, their limbs twisted in death. Somebody grabbed her wheelchair from behind, spun it around and shoved her towards the exit.

Another shot rang out. Antimone accelerated under her own power. Up ahead, Paul and the African boy lay side-by-side on the floor. Aya knelt over Jason's body. *What the hell is she doing?* As Antimone drew nearer, his left foot twitched. Her mouth fell open in shock. *Is he still alive? How is that possible?* She had seen the head wound with her own eyes.

"Jason?" she murmured, her voice barely above a whisper.

Aya twisted around, revealing Jason's face. Dried blood streaked his forehead and right ear. She dabbed a white handkerchief against his scalp. His gaze rose, and he blinked at Antimone.

"But... you were..." The words stumbled out of Antimone's mouth as she struggled to form a coherent sentence. Tears of relief flooded down her cheeks. She darted forwards. "My God, you're alive."

Jason raised a shaky arm. Antimone stretched down. His skin felt cold as their fingers intertwined. "But how?" she asked.

"The bullet shaved his skull," Aya replied. "It knocked him out. Doctor Kubar said the scalp bleeds very much. He has gone to fetch—"

A gunshot cracked from nearby. Both Antimone and Aya instinctively ducked. Rosalind and the general sprinted around the corner. Shaladi crouched and turned. The gun in his hand jumped, accompanied by another deafening boom. He cursed in Arabic, then switched to English. "The power is on, so the doors are locked," he growled. "I told you before, we must leave. Now we will die here."

Before anybody could respond, the lock clunked, and Dr Kubar emerged through the swing door, pushing an empty wheelchair. "Quick," he said, "help me lift him."

"How did you—?"

The doctor held up a rectangle of plastic. "I have the professor's key card," he interrupted. "It opens all the doors in this place."

"That may buy us some time," Shaladi grunted, "but we must go immediately." He pointed the pistol around the corner and loosed off another two shots towards their unseen attackers.

Rosalind helped Kubar load Jason into the newly arrived chair. "I'll push him."

Jason's body slumped to the side as he gazed listlessly at his surroundings. Aya scooped up Paul from the floor and deposited him in Antimone's arms. "I may need to shoot," she said.

Aya handed a gun to Rosalind and offered another one to Antimone, who declined with a raised palm. The general's daughter shrugged and passed the spare to her father. Kubar crouched beside the African boy and gently lifted him.

Shaladi twisted around. "I will fire some covering shots. Move when I start shooting." Two loud bangs followed in quick succession.

The doctor held the card up to the reader and barged through the swing door, trailed closely by the others. He rushed through the dining area, clutching the unconscious child in his arms. A group of ten scientists huddled in a corner, glancing fearfully towards the escapees.

"What's happening?" one called out.

The general slowed. "The guards are coming. You should come with us or go to your rooms."

Several separate conversations broke out. A crash erupted from the other side of the door through which they had just passed.

"You must decide now," Shaladi yelled over the babble of voices. The small crowd scattered.

A solitary man remained: Dr Fernando. He flashed a nervous glance towards the general's gun. "Do you mind if I join you?"

"Can you shoot?" Shaladi asked.

The scientist swallowed hard. "Well, I have never tried."

The general handed him the spare pistol. "We do not have time for lessons. This is the safety. Point and pull the trigger."

"Okay," Fernando replied. "That sounds easy."

Shaladi turned away. "Come. We must go."

They passed into the reception area where Kubar waited for them by the same doors through which they had entered the facility three weeks earlier.

"Move to the side," Shaladi said, pointing to the walls. He took the card from Kubar and held it to the reader. The lock clicked. He crouched down and inched the door open. When no shots were fired, he edged through the gap with his gun raised, surveying the area for hostile forces. Satisfied they were alone, he beckoned the others forwards.

"Where are your people?" Rosalind asked as she pushed Jason's wheelchair onto the rough concrete. The sudden heat and humidity enveloped them like a damp rag.

Shaladi filled his lungs with the warm air before replying. "I do not know, but they will find us."

Rosalind rolled her eyes. "This is a really great plan."

The general ignored the sarcastic remark. "Aya, I want you to protect our rear. Mrs Baxter, you and I will lead." He pointed at the Spanish scientist. "You, push the boy's wheelchair. If you see somebody with a gun, do not ask; shoot. If anybody fires at us, you must take cover. Is everything clear?"

Shaladi didn't wait for a reply. He turned away and hurried along the centre of the road in a low crouch. They had covered approximately fifty metres when the sound of a revving engine and the screech of tyres echoed from the walls.

The general scuttled to the side and pointed to a concrete pillar on the other. Kubar was slow to react, weighed down by the child he was carrying.

Before he could reach cover, a pair of blazing headlights from a rapidly approaching car picked him out. The vehicle screeched to a halt and four men in dark uniforms emerged, one from each door. Moments later, the sound of automatic weapons immersed the underground tunnel in a cacophony of noise.

The escapees returned fire, but the disparity in firepower put them at a significant disadvantage. The attackers used their superiority to advance in a pincer movement. Antimone clutched Paul to her chest as the bullets dug holes into the walls around her and showered her with sharp fragments of concrete.

Fernando crouched to her left. A pillar provided cover for both the scientist and Jason's wheelchair. He held the gun in trembling hands but hadn't yet fired a shot. Suddenly, he dropped the weapon on the floor and sprinted back towards the hospital. He had covered less than ten metres when a group of three rounds found their mark and slammed him forwards into the concrete.

Just when it seemed there was no hope, the sound of a second approaching vehicle rose above the cascade of gunfire. The intensity of shots increased. Antimone dared not look out from behind the cover of the pillar, but after another thirty seconds, silence fell over the battle scene.

Shaladi stood from his crouching position on the opposite side of the roadway. He strode forwards and embraced a man wielding an automatic rifle. The newcomer wore camouflaged army trousers and a green T-shirt that accented his bulging bicep. A beard and moustache covered the lower parts of his face. The pair separated, clapped each other on the back and continued a rapid-fire conversation in Arabic.

"Come," Shaladi shouted. "This is my friend, Major Halim. We must leave now. More of our enemies will be here soon."

Wednesday 6th August 2036

Prime Minister's Office, 10 Downing Street, London
17 minutes after the power cut

"What's happening?" Andrew Jacobs asked.

Admiral Trent was holding the mobile phone to his ear. He lowered it before speaking. "We still don't have eyes on the hostages. We're picking up reports of a gun battle near the hospital, but the drones have spotted nothing so far."

"So, we can't even be sure it's anything to do with our people," the Prime Minister said.

"Where are the marines now?" Moreland asked.

"They're waiting at the edge of the forest, about half a mile from the hospital." The images from the camera showed the dark outlines of a few straggly trees growing between the shattered stumps of their predecessors, destroyed during the long years of civil war. The men crouched at the rim of a shell crater. "There's no point in breaking cover until they know their destination."

"So, all we can do is wait and hope for the best."

"Yes," Trent agreed. "I'm afraid that's right."

Silence settled on the room as the three pairs of eyes watched the screen intently, waiting for something to happen. The sudden ringing of the phone on the Prime Minister's desk made them all jump.

Jacobs snatched up the handset. "Yes," he barked.

A female voice came down the line. "We've just received a call from the British embassy in Tunis. There has been contact with somebody from The Republic of North Africa. I'll patch you through now."

A click followed. Jacobs pressed a button and replaced the receiver. "Hello, this is the Prime Minister speaking," he said. "I've put you on speaker phone. With me are Admiral Trent and Charles Moreland of MI6. What's going on?"

"Good evening, sir," a man replied. "I'm John Doyle, the duty officer on call tonight. Someone called a minute ago, claiming to be in Tripoli. He told me he had met up with our people and wanted to know the rendezvous point. He's still on the line if you want to talk to him."

"Put him through."

The muted sound of a revving engine emerged from the speaker.

Jacobs exchanged a sideways glance with his two colleagues, then leant forwards. "Hello, you're speaking to the British Prime Minister. I believe you have contacted some of my countrymen who were being held hostage."

"Yes, this is Major Halim. I—"

In the background, a man's voice yelled in Arabic. A series of bangs and a muffled scream accompanied the words. The man spoke again. "Sorry, but somebody is shooting at us. I have your people. Where shall we take them?"

"We have a team at the edge of the Al Nasr Forest," Trent replied, "where it meets the Second Ring Road. Do you know where I mean?"

"I am familiar with the location. We will be there in a few minutes." Halim paused for a second before speaking again. "If I do this for you, I will require something in exchange, however."

"What do you want?" Jacobs asked.

The major explained his request.

Trent was already on his feet, speaking urgently into his mobile phone. "I don't care. Make it happen," he yelled into the handset. He turned and nodded to the Prime Minister.

"Yes, we can do that," Jacobs said.

"Excellent," Halim replied.

The line went quiet.

"Hello. Are you still there?" Doyle asked. He repeated the question. "Sorry, sir. He just hung up."

"Thanks," Jacobs said. "If anything else comes through, please call us back."

"Right away, sir."

Trent continued to talk into his handset.

"Well?" Jacobs asked with a questioning look.

The admiral lowered the phone from his ear for a second. "The helicopter is already in the air and will be there in five minutes. They'll land close to the ring road. The marines will provide covering fire from the ground if necessary."

The images on the computer screen shifted as the armed men directed their weapons from the rim of the crater towards the potholed strip of concrete.

"Just make sure you get them out safely," Jacobs muttered.

Wednesday 6th August 2036

Outside Tripoli Infectious Diseases Hospital, Republic of North Africa

18 minutes after the power cut

The bearded major directed a reassuring grin at the group of frightened Westerners. "More of them will be here soon," he said, his baritone voice a mixture of Mediterranean and American accents. "We must hurry."

"Where are you taking us?" Rosalind asked.

"I will call now. Please get in." He pointed at the black van, straddling the road fifty metres nearer the exit. Three other armed men in military fatigues approached and shook General Shaladi by the hand. One took the child from Dr Kubar and jogged to the waiting transport. Another crouched beside Fernando's body, holding a finger to his neck. The man rose with a shake of the head, then jogged towards Jason, who lay barely conscious in his wheelchair. The third member of the rescue team slid back a door on the side of the vehicle and, with the help of the others, lifted Antimone's and Jason's wheelchairs inside.

Halim was still talking into his phone. Shaladi and the driver joined him as he climbed into the front seats. The van moved off with a squeal of tyres. The major's voice rose above the roar of the engine as they raced along the narrow roadway. A minute later, they arrived at the exit from the underground garage. The barrier was down, and a handful of men stood waiting with weapons raised.

"Everybody down!" Shaladi yelled. The driver jammed his foot down on the accelerator and ducked. One of Halim's team put an arm around Jason's shoulders, pushing him forwards so his body folded in two. Only the man's strong grip prevented Jason from toppling out of the wheelchair. The van surged towards the blockade. Immediately, all hell broke loose as the armed guards outside opened fire. Bullets ripped through the windscreen and punched holes in the roof's lining. Aya screamed as the side window shattered and showered the occupants on that side of the vehicle with fragments of glass.

Within seconds, the van smashed through the barricade and hurtled down the road. The major continued to talk on his phone. He directed the driver with a point of his finger.

"Is everyone all right?" the general called, looking behind at the pale-faced passengers. A series of nods greeted his question.

Antimone straightened up from the position she had held, shielding Paul with her own body. She brushed a strand of hair from her son's forehead. To her relief, his breathing was calm and regular. Next, she checked on Jason. Halim's man helped him to sit upright, but it was clear from the glazed look in his eyes that he was still largely oblivious to his surroundings. Antimone's gaze rose to the view ahead as she fought down the fear that threatened to overwhelm her.

Several bullets had punctured the windscreen, leaving small circular holes surrounded by a spiderweb of cracks. The van navigated a slip road and emerged onto a two-lane carriageway. Ruts and potholes peppered the uneven surface. Antimone glanced towards the speedometer: a fraction over forty miles an hour. The driver tried to steer around the obstacles, causing the occupants to sway from side to side. Only a handful of cars kept them company as they jolted along the neglected roadway.

Halim lowered the phone and twisted in his seat, his cheerful expression undiminished by the recent conflict. "It will take two or three minutes to reach the rendezvous point. Your people are waiting there."

Shaladi spoke in a low voice to the major. A rapid-fire conversation in Arabic followed. It was clear from the tone that they were having a vigorous argument. Brake lights in the road ahead brought an end to the debate. The general muttered a curse as the van slowed. A pair of black cars, parked sideways on, blocked both lanes. As they drew nearer, nine armed men in total emerged from the doors and took up position behind the barricade.

~

"Shit," a marine said, lowering his binoculars. "They're setting up a roadblock. Range is two hundred and fifty metres."

"What's the ETA on the bird?" the leader of the group asked, speaking urgently into his radio.

"Still a few minutes out," a man's voice replied.

"Permission to engage?"

"Please hold."

"Look, I don't mean to hurry you, but unless we do something quickly, the only hostages we'll be taking out of here will be in body bags."

The seconds ticked by in silence as all eyes studied the slowing traffic on the carriageway below. Finally, the radio crackled into life. "Engage at your discretion."

The sergeant breathed a sigh of relief. "Okay, guys, wait for my command. Make sure you don't hit any civilians." He peered down the sights of his automatic rifle. Below them, the men in dark uniforms crouched behind the pair of vehicles, unaware of the threat to their rear.

"Fire!"

The hiss of suppressed weapons filled the air. Five of the enemy dropped in the first volley. Three more followed in quick succession. The final soldier had identified the direction of the incoming rounds before his colleagues and flung himself over the bonnet.

"One still in play," the sergeant said.

The man to his left picked up the binoculars again. He watched through the lenses as the panicked drivers at the front of the short queue of traffic turned their cars around and tried to head back against the flow, drawing a cacophony of beeps from those behind.

The doors of the black van opened, and the three members of Major Halim's team surged out. Their bullets quickly found the sole survivor from the roadblock, but not before he had gabbled a desperate plea for help into his radio.

With no ability to manoeuvre out of the jam and facing a group of heavily armed men, the civilian occupants of the trapped vehicles jumped out and fled, leaving the carriageway completely blocked.

~

"It is impossible to get past these cars quickly," Shaladi said to the major, stepping down onto the cracked concrete. "We must go on foot."

"More troops will be here any minute," Halim replied. "I hope the helicopter arrives soon. They told me it has enough seats for all of us."

"We already discussed this," Shaladi said, referring to their earlier heated discussion. "Why could you not find our own transport?"

"I am sorry. It was not possible to organise an aircraft in such a short time. They would stop us quickly if we stayed on the road."

"I cannot go with you. Look after my daughter. Explain to the British that they would have executed both of us if we had not followed orders."

The major stared at his former commanding officer. "But what you say is true. You should tell them yourself."

"I am the man who organised the attack at the Olympics. They will never allow me to be free. I do not want to spend the rest of my life in prison, no matter that British prisons are far more comfortable than any in this country."

"So, this was all for nothing?"

"No, my friend. You have helped to save my beautiful Aya. I am trusting you to make sure she survives. You must let them know she had no part in this. I forced her to help me."

"I will do my best, General. It has been an honour serving with you."

Shaladi clapped his colleague on the shoulder. "We still have much to do—and I am not dead yet."

Two men lifted Antimone's wheelchair, then Jason's down from the van. When everybody was on the concrete, Halim led them towards the barricade. Rosalind pushed Jason. Kubar clutched the unconscious African boy to his chest. Drivers on the other side of the road slowed to rubberneck the carnage. Several took pictures or spoke into mobile phones.

"Come on," the major said. "We must hurry."

Antimone stared at the dead bodies as they skirted around the two military vehicles. The sight no longer scared her. Three weeks of random cruelty and a disdain for human life had dulled her senses to the point where death seemed commonplace. She cast an anxious downward glance to the unconscious child on her lap. To her relief, Paul continued to sleep, ignorant of the horror surrounding him.

"Over there," she called as a flashlight from a raised embankment on the right signalled the position of the marines. Every weapon in the group pointed in the direction she had indicated until a man stood up and waved back at them. The hostages picked up the pace as they raced to close the distance to the support team.

A low buzzing sound rose above the rumble of vehicle engines. Antimone raised her eyes. A dark shape blotted out a patch of stars overhead: the helicopter at last. It banked sharply and settled into a hover.

A cry drew her attention back to the ground. Three sets of headlights approached on the wrong side of the carriageway.

"Get to cover," Shaladi yelled, gesticulating towards the shrubs adjoining the cracked concrete. Moments later, gunfire erupted from the nearest vehicle, catching one of Halim's men in the open and throwing him backwards. At almost the same time, the second and third armoured cars opened up. Bullets tore up the concrete to Antimone's left. She shoved down hard on the metal ring, accelerating out of the incoming fire with milliseconds to spare. She skidded to a halt alongside Rosalind, who crouched beside Jason's wheelchair, protected from the enemy troops by a large boulder at the side of the road. Their eyes locked in fear.

Shots from the marines silenced one gunner, but the two remaining vehicles targeted another of Halim's team who was too slow in reaching cover. The rounds spun him around as they found their mark.

The battle would have been over in seconds if the helicopter hadn't joined the fray. It pivoted in mid-air and directed a hail of thirty-millimetre shells towards the three armoured vehicles. The first two disintegrated in balls of flame. The occupants of the third flung themselves out of the doors moments before it too exploded. Shots from the marines targeted the survivors, keeping them pinned down behind the burning wreckage.

The electric motors driving the huge blades of the flying weapons platform reduced in pitch. The sleek black shape flared six feet above the road surface, then settled down in the centre of the carriageway, fifty metres from the terrified escapees. A panel on the side hinged open, and a man dressed in a plastic-coated uniform with full facemask leant out, beckoning the group towards him.

Dr Kubar was the first to break cover, still carrying the African boy. Shots erupted from behind the destroyed vehicles, but the marines returned fire, silencing the source of the gunfire within moments. Strong hands reached down and hauled the child up. Rosalind rose from her hiding place, pushing Jason. Between the two of them, the doctor and Rosalind struggled to lift Jason's barely conscious body onto the lip of the aircraft's entryway.

Antimone followed Rosalind's lead and raced to the open door. A moan of protest escaped Paul's mouth as she raised him up to the helicopter's hold.

The man grabbed the three-year-old and returned almost immediately. "I'm afraid you'll have to leave that here, Miss," he said, his voice muffled by the mask as he pointed to the wheelchair.

By now, the major's only surviving team member had arrived, leading Aya by the hand. He lifted Antimone out of the chair and placed her in the waiting arms of the crewman. Seconds later, she found herself unceremoniously dumped into a cushioned seat beside the two children and Jason.

"Let's move it, people," the man shouted. "We're vulnerable on the ground."

The general's daughter was next to embark, then came Rosalind, followed by Dr Kubar.

"Another group of hostiles," a voice yelled from outside. Antimone spotted the approach of more headlights through the curved windscreen above the array of flashing dials. The haste to board the aircraft intensified as two marines trailed Halim's man through the open hatch. The noise from the electric motors rose in pitch.

Bullets pinged harmlessly against the armoured glass of the cockpit. The remaining members of the British team sprinted across the concrete. The one at the back staggered and let out a yell of pain. His colleagues grabbed him by the arms and hauled him aboard, leaving a streak of blood on the floor of the cabin. Halim was the last to arrive.

"Come on," the crewman shouted, holding out a hand to haul him in. The aircraft lifted off the ground before the major was fully inside. He scrambled aboard as the floor tilted.

"Wait!" Aya screamed. "Where is my father?"

Muzzle flash from the side of the road answered her question.

"No," she yelled, hurling herself forwards as the panel slid shut.

The thirty-millimetre cannons opened up again, shaking the whole interior as they spat out a stream of shells towards the approaching vehicles.

Halim put an arm around her shoulder and whispered into her ear.

"He didn't have to stay," she cried, pushing him away.

"Your father is a brave man," he replied. "His last command to me was to protect you. I will look after you like my own daughter."

Tears streamed down Aya's cheeks as she stared at the ground out of the window.

The helicopter banked in a tight curve and raced across the night sky towards the waiting cruiser.

~

The three men in the Prime Minister's office embraced at the news that the aircraft had landed safely on the deck of the warship.

Admiral Trent broke away to continue a hushed conversation. "All the hostages who made it out of the hospital are onboard," he announced, lowering the handset. "That includes Rosalind Baxter and the three British people abducted at the Olympics: the Lessing girl, her partner and their child. We also picked up five Reponan nationals, including their missing athlete and a four-year-old boy."

"How are they?"

"The two young children are receiving medical attention, as is Jason Floyd who was shot. But all are expected to survive."

"Any news on Perrin?"

"No," Trent said. "He wasn't among the evacuees, but I have no information on what happened to him."

"What about the marines?" Jacobs asked.

"One relatively minor bullet wound, but otherwise all fine."

"Good. Has there been any response from the Reponan military?"

"Not so far, but we're keeping a close eye on things. The Reponans don't have much of a navy. As we speak, the ship is making full speed towards Malta. They should be there in just over four hours."

"Congratulations on a job well done, gentlemen," Jacobs said.

Wednesday 27th August 2036

Tripoli Infectious Diseases Hospital, Republic of North Africa
Three weeks later

The first thing to register on his senses was the rhythmic beeping sound. The piercing electronic tone wormed its way inside his skull. He groaned. The use of his vocal cords triggered a gag reflex as he registered the object jammed down his throat. His right hand rose instinctively and grasped the flexible tubing. He tugged, but something held it in place. In mounting panic, he pulled harder. The adhesive strips surrendered their grip, and the plastic tube slid out of his mouth, provoking a coughing fit.

The rate of the beeps increased in time with his thrashing heart. A female voice spoke in a foreign language. He tried to open his eyes, but they seemed to be gummed shut.

The woman switched to strongly accented English. "Please be calm. Somebody is coming."

He raised his head, but a gentle hand pressed him back onto the pillow.

"Where…?" The attempt to speak sent a sharp pain shooting down his trachea. More coughs followed.

The sound of rapidly approaching footsteps mingled with the shrill bleeps. A rapid-fire conversation took place between the new arrival and the woman, although he still couldn't understand any of the words exchanged between the pair. Moments later, the electronic beeping stopped.

Fingers touched his face and removed the tape from his eyelids. He blinked his eyes open and immediately screwed them shut again in the bright glare from the overhead lights.

"Welcome back, Mr Perrin," the man said. "My name is Doctor Ahmed." He didn't bother to introduce the woman.

Max squinted at the medic through lowered lids. "Where am I?" he rasped.

"You are in a hospital in Tripoli. What do you remember?"

Max wracked his brain. His head seemed to be full of sawdust. "Not much."

"After a traumatic episode like the one you have recently suffered, it is natural that you will be a little disorientated."

"Can you tell me what happened?"

Ahmed hesitated before replying. "You have been in a medically induced coma for the last three weeks. There is no easy way to say this to you. Unfortunately, we could not save your left arm."

For the first time, Max opened his eyes fully and glanced down at where the limb should have been. His shoulder ended in a short stump covered by white bandages. Now the memories returned: the acid, the expanding circle of blackening skin, the unbearable pain. A scream erupted from his throat.

"Please," the doctor said. "You must conserve your energy for your recovery." He turned and spoke rapidly in Arabic to the nurse. She returned moments later with a syringe.

Max shrank back in terror. "No, no, no," he yelled. "Not again."

Ahmed quickly realised his mistake. "Do not worry. It is only a sedative."

Max twisted away and tumbled off the mattress onto the floor, toppling the drip stand, which was still attached by plastic tubing to his right hand. He scrabbled backwards to evade his carers. With only one arm to support him, he unbalanced and collapsed on his side.

The doctor rushed forwards and shoved the needle into his patient's thigh, then depressed the plunger with his thumb.

Max's panicked movements gradually subsided. Over the next few seconds, a fuzziness filled his head, sending him back to the welcoming darkness.

~

Somebody tapped him gently on the cheek. His second return to consciousness was less confusing than the first. Perhaps it had all been a bad dream. Before trying to identify who had woken him, he glanced down at his left arm. But no, the limb was still missing.

He raised his eyes. Four other people occupied the small hospital room. Among them was the doctor who had tended him earlier. Two wore dark uniforms and carried automatic weapons. The last had a thick beard and wore black robes. He looked vaguely familiar, but Max couldn't place him. Judging by their submissive body language, the others deferred to him. The man's lips moved behind his wiry facial hair. He spoke in Arabic.

"Mullah Awad is glad you are awake," Ahmed translated. "Do you know who did this to you?"

Max blinked as his sluggish brain stirred into action. Awad—of course, he was the leader of this country. Now it made sense. "It was the girl," he rasped.

Another brief exchange took place between the mullah and his translator.

"Which girl?" the doctor asked.

"That cripple, Antimone Lessing," Max replied. He detected surprise on the faces of his interrogators.

"So, it was not Mrs Baxter?" the mullah said in accented English, raising a hand to wave off Ahmed before he could translate.

"No, she was going to inject acid in my eye, but the cripple refused to give her the syringe. Your men arrived, and I called out to warn them because some of the prisoners had guns. She injected me in the arm just before they left."

"I do not understand. Why did she do this to you?"

"I shot her precious boyfriend dead. He tried to jump me. Then somebody got me from behind with that damned stun baton."

The mullah and the doctor exchanged more words in Arabic.

"You did not kill Mr Floyd," Awad said. "He survived and escaped to the UK."

"What? He's alive? So, that bitch did this to me for no good reason."

"You were lucky it happened in a hospital," the doctor added.

The words tugged at something in Max's memory. Then it came to him. "Wait. What about the virus? Weren't they all carrying it? Have I got it?"

"Yes. You, me, almost everybody in this country now. When the woman and her child escaped from isolation, they allowed this new form of the disease to escape with them."

The mullah took over. "They infected too many other people to limit the spread. But we will manufacture drugs to protect the children."

"Did the rest of them get away?" Max asked.

"Unfortunately, most did. They had outside help from the rebels and the British military. They killed at least thirty of my countrymen, including Professor Halfon. All are now in Britain. They are being held in quarantine apart from the Baxter woman, who is in prison. They keep her location secret. We requested her extradition, but I do not think they will give her to us." He let out a short, humourless laugh. "Many others also want to try her for her crimes."

"What about that bastard, Shaladi, and his daughter?"

The mullah's tongue protruded from his mouth, moistening his lips before he spoke. "That coward is dead. He shot himself as our armed forces closed in to capture him. Aya Shaladi is now in England with the other traitors. We demanded their return to face judgement, but again, it is unlikely the British authorities will comply."

"Did Dr Kubar escape with them?"

"Yes, another person who betrayed his country and this establishment. He has provided their scientists with the formula he stole from us."

"I tried to warn Professor Halfon they were planning something, but he wouldn't take me seriously."

"I see." The mullah turned to the rest of his entourage and barked a series of curt instructions in Arabic. The three other men filed out of the room. "You realise we spent much money to keep you alive?" he asked when he and Max were alone.

"Yeah, thanks."

"Now there is something you can do for me."

Max's voice took on a wary tone. "Okay. What's that?"

"We cannot allow these traitors to go unpunished. They murdered many citizens of this country and caused you serious harm."

"So, what do you need from me?"

"We have few operatives in Britain. If we send more, they do not know your customs. They... ah... stick out. You, however, are a native. You fit in. I want you to work with my men to eliminate those who have betrayed us. You will be well paid for your efforts."

"You still owe me for the last job."

The mullah stared at Max, his eyes unblinking. After a few seconds, he gave a single, slow nod. "I will ensure you receive everything you are owed, and we will transfer the money for this assignment in advance."

"I have one other condition."

Awad glared back at him. "You are in no position to make demands. Nobody outside this facility knows you are alive."

"You're right, but I think you'll like my proposal. I want payback. I want those who've hurt me to suffer. If you help me with this, I'll do whatever you ask."

"You are referring to the prisoners who escaped from here?"

"Yes." Max stared into the dark pits of the bearded man's eyes. "Do we have a deal?"

"Perhaps," the mullah replied. "As long as our objectives align, I will provide you with all the support you need to have your revenge."

"Good," Max growled. "I'm going to make them pay for what they've done."

To be continued.

The story concludes in Annihilation: Origins and Endings

Author's Notes

Dear Reader,

This is the bit where I thank people and also ask for your help. I hope you enjoyed reading this book. If you did, I would be extremely grateful if you tell your friends and leave a review on Amazon, Goodreads or preferably both. Reviews are an important factor in helping to sell books and are especially important for independent authors. I pay particular attention to all comments and use them to try to make my books better.

If you would like to keep up to date with future book releases, please sign up to the mailing list at www.rjne.uk.

I would like to express my gratitude to my advance reviewers, including Marika, Fergus, Mark, Brian, Jeanette and fellow authors Ross Greenwood, Shaun Griffiths and Terry Marchion. Between them they spotted several issues and helped to improve this book. As ever, I am eternally grateful for their support. This novel has undergone thorough review, but those typos are pesky beggars and sometimes sneak through undetected. Please let me know if you find one so that other readers can benefit from your sharp-eyed attention. The best way is to leave a comment on my website.

Thanks also to Hampton Lamoureux whose cover designs frequently win awards from those who are experts in such matters. I wouldn't count myself in that category, but to my untrained eye, he has done an excellent job on the series.

Special mention must go to my wife, Judith, and daughter, Emily, who put up with me during the writing process. In some ways I think they know the characters better than I do. Finally, I receive a lot of help and support from members of the Facebook author community through various writing groups. The Book Club and Fifteen Minutes with a Fiction Editor groups deserve special mention for their help on this book.

If you enjoyed this novel, you may be interested in the third book, Annihilation: Origins and Endings, which concludes the series. The final part of the saga links the past and the present and will answer questions about the origins of the virus, as well as tying up several loose ends.

You may wonder why there is no mention of COVID-19 in these books. The answer is simple; I wrote Decimation in 2017 and started work on Termination in 2019 before the outbreak. Think of the Decimation universe as an alternative history that diverges around that period. That said, much of the current world situation carries a chilling resemblance to the events described in this series.

To some extent I have downplayed future technologies in this book. The majority of the story takes place in a country where technological advancements have largely passed it by. However, miniature camera drones, container ships that use sail power and the advent of quantum computing are all developments that I expect to become widespread over the coming years.

If you enjoyed this book you might also like to try some of my other standalone novels including, The Rage, The Colour of the Soul and Assassin's Web.

To find out more about Annihilation: Origins and Endings, keep an eye on my website at www.rjne.uk. I would be delighted to hear from you through the comments section.

Thanks for reading.

Richard T. Burke
April 2021

To read the author's blog and to see news of upcoming books, please visit www.rjne.uk or follow him on Twitter (@RTBurkeAuthor) or Facebook (https://www.facebook.com/RichardTBurkeAuthor).